ORCHIDS
OF WAR

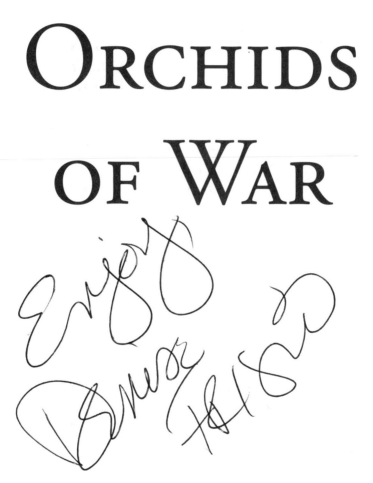

DENISE FRISINO

BOOK PUBLISHERS NETWORK
Changing the World One Book at a Time

Book Publishers Network
P.O. Box 2256
Bothell • WA • 98041
Ph • 425-483-3040
www.bookpublishersnetwork.com

First edition, first printing, April 2016
Second edition, first printing, October 2018

10 9 8 7 6 5 4 3 2

Printed in the United States of America

LCCN   2015956707
ISBN   978-1-940598-88-8

Editors: Elizabeth B., Vicki M.
Cover Designer: Laura Zugzda
Book Designer: Melissa Vail Coffman

*To my late mother, Harriette Marie Frisino, whose sense of humor
kept us afloat and whose love reached beyond our door.
To her memories of growing up in Seattle and the Second World War.*

Acknowledgements

WHILE RESEARCHING MY BOOK, *Whiskey Cove*, a gentleman I interviewed in the San Juan Islands, Mr. Thompson, told me of a young Caucasian woman studying Japanese language at the University of Washington in 1941. The FBI discovered her expertise and took her to San Francisco. Dressing her as a hooker, they established her in bars where Japanese men frequented. She would then report back to the FBI the intelligence she had gathered.

I am ever grateful for the concept and named her for my mother's best friend and partner in crime, Billie McCloud.

I wish to thank those who shared their time and stories over the years, some of whom are no long among us: Captain Richard McNees, US Navy; Captain Winslow Buxton, USCG Retired; Ruth and Ray Pennock; Dr. Donald Raleigh; Glenn Buffum; Al and Joan Beers; Al Skaret; Billee Escott; John and Ginny Beyer; Lois the Coast Guard Lady; Ray Welander and Edna Klein; Grandma B; Moya Gray and her remarkable mother Violet (Alita) Salve; and Ken Nicoles.

Also those who guided me along my way with their knowledge and research: ETCS(SS) Chris Gamblin and Sara Gamblin; CMDCM(SS) James G. Miller; Captain Gene Davis, USCG Retired; Head Curator of the Coast Guard Museum Northwest; Dan Tish and Darrell Van Ness, Curators, Coast Guard Museum Northwest; Lieutenant Commander Phil Johnson USCG, Retired; Dr. David Rosen, USCG Pacific Area Historian; Robert Fisher, Collections Manager, Wing Luke Museum; Daniel Hartwig, Stanford University Archivist, Special Collections and University Archives; Ned and Katie Borgstrom; Aliena Pawlak, Manager at The Sir Francis Drake Hotel; Mrs. Choy at the Chinese Historical Society of America, San Francisco; Thelma Kehaulani Kam, Historian for Royal Hawaiian Hotel; Cecelia Derramas and Cori Hara; the Moiliili Senior Center, Hawaii; Elias and Lisa Kauhane; Roberta Hirahara; Densho; Peter Anderson of Galvin Flight School; Dan Hagedorn, Curator and Director of Museum of Flight Boeing Field; Chris Kelley; Jon Hahn; Patrick Noonan; Barb White; and John Dayton.

And my father Joe for his service in the US Army Signal Corps in the Pacific.

And to those who unwittingly led me to my next clue—you have no idea how grateful I am.

I am certain I have probably missed someone along my years of research. Please forgive me.

My husband deserves a round of applause for his support, as does Sheryn Hara, my publisher; Melissa Coffman, for her impeccable detail; Sean McVeigh, my media rock; Laura Zugzda, for her incredible artwork; Elizabeth B. and Vicki M., my editors, and my dialect coach, Alyssa Keene.

While this book deals with a very real topic and incorporates accurate details, the story is fiction, with no intent to harm those who suffered during this horrific clash of nations, the Second World War.

ONE

THE ORCAS HAD ARRIVED. They were a bit early this June of 1941, but then the salmon were running early too.

Billi O'Shaughnessy sat on her father's lawn in Dyes Inlet that sloped to the water, watching the giant mammals force the salmon down the inlet, straight toward her. Their huffing sounds as they breeched set the rhythm of her own breath, fast and intense. The salmon flickered in the golden light of the sunset as they sprang from the water in an attempt to outswim their killers.

Her small rowboat sat in their path on the still water, which now rippled with the fierce movement in the battle for life. The black head of a seal pup appeared on the land side of her rowboat, seeking shelter from the onslaught. She held her breath for the creature and marveled at his cunning trick. As the salmon neared the bar of land, they split in two directions and the mighty orcas made easy prey of the moment as the water took on the red hue of death.

Long before Billi stood to leave, the tall shadows of the trees from up the hill had spread across the water, darkening the scene of destruction. A sense of loss, mixed with her calm understanding of the forces of nature, had distracted her enough. An immense decision loomed ahead and her father had been of no help. He had only looked at her, picked up his coffee laced with booze, and muttered about the damn Japanese.

Mr. O'Shaughnessy had never appreciated her relationship with Eileen Nakamura and her family, but had scoffed at her interest and involvement with their culture. While he had been born in Ireland, traveled to America as a young man, he seemed to find it difficult to tolerate others whose language sounded so foreign.

"Why the hell do you want to talk that Japanese, Bright Eyes?" his brogue thickening in his distaste for the idea.

Maybe jealousy sparked some of his venom. After all, when Billi's dad divorced her mother, an unheard of event for the times and the Catholic Church, Mr. Nakamura had tended to Billi as he did his garden, with thoughtfulness and care. He even went so far as to include her in his family teaching of the Japanese way, an innocent extension that could become her biggest challenge and lead to unforeseen danger.

She stopped at the door to her father's cabin, rough-planked and slightly at odds with any plumb line as it listed to one side. She could smell the fire and hear her father singing, whiskey-warmed and joyful, with his slight brogue. How she loved him for all his follies. She had to make him comprehend this was not about leaving him, but about the adventure of a lifetime. An opportunity to visit the faraway islands of her dreams: Japan.

Mr. Nakamura's eyes had lit up like a new morning at the news of the possibility of Billi stepping on the very land of his birth. But her father's reaction had been a storm as violent as the orcas kill.

Billi took a deep breath and let the memories of what had brought her to this decision play out in her mind as reassurance. At age seven, her mother had taken a job as secretary to the governor at the state capitol in Olympia, Washington. Billi, angered by the recent divorce of her parents, rebelled. Constantly, the guard escorted her to her mother's office, told her to sit in a chair, read a book, and behave. But within minutes, the irascible child would sneak off, demonstrating her emotions by raining chaos on the capitol building, sliding down the marble banisters, her school uniform flying, a guard quick on her heels. Once, the guard had placed a spittoon at the base of the low, wide railing that created the perfect long slide. When she landed in the offensive container, head first, soaking herself, she merely learned how to slide feet first and kick the spittoon at the last second.

One especially warm spring day, Billi sailed down her favorite banister, flicked the squat receptacle aside, leaving the dark ooze spreading across the floor, and raced out the door with the capitol guard in determined pursuit. She ducked into a large rhododendron bush where Mr. Nakamura intently picked the dead heads off old blooms.

"Which way did that kid go?" the guard demanded of the Japanese man, hunched over the bush.

Mr. Nakamura barely raised his shoulders as he kept his gaze on the shrub and the large blue eyes of the child who hid in its dense branches.

"Damn brat." The guard shuffled off to continue his search.

As soon as the guard strolled out of sight, Billi slipped from behind the bush. She started for the door when she was stopped by the soft voice of Mr. Nakamura.

"I will not tell of your indiscretion if you promise a favor in return."

"What's that?" Indignant at being waylaid, her small hand met with her hip, and she looked up at him with an untrusting stare.

"Meet my daughter Eileen here tomorrow at this time."

"No. What's an indiscretion? And why would I want to play with her?" Billi folded her arms with a defiant look.

"I will have the answer to both questions tomorrow, here, at four o'clock." Without another word, Mr. Nakamura picked up the can he had been putting his trimmings in and left.

As life would have it, the moment Billi met Eileen, their bond became unbreakable. They spent nights at each other's homes, carefully learning as much from one as from the other. Billi showed a deft hand with the elegant fan at the Bon Odori dances she attend with Eileen; she studied the glass-encased geisha girls that adorned the Nakamura home and began what was to become her lifelong passion for the Japanese language.

When her mother moved Billi and her older brother Eddy back to Seattle, the Nakamuras were right behind them. They opened a Nakamura Grocery store in Seattle's Japantown, with an apartment above, allowing Eileen and Billi to graduate together from Garfield High School.

And now, an incredible opportunity had been presented to her by her professor of Japanese at the University of Washington. Professor Fujihara had convinced her she would win the Japanese language competition and the prize trip to Japan.

Somehow, without the support of her father, winning would mean nothing. For pleasing James Edward O'Shaughnessy she perceived as the only way of mending his broken heart. Her mother remained the only woman he had ever loved, a love that had regrettably become slurred when he lost yet another fortune and turned to drink. Their divorce still tore at his heart.

Knowing time was running out as her father's bottle of whiskey emptied, Billi took one more deep breath, gathered her strength, and pushed open the door to try again.

"Dad, did you see the orcas?"

"Killing machines. Thank heaven today you were not a salmon." He eyed her suspiciously and waited.

"Right. Better to be the seal pup who uses our row boat as shelter."

"Clever black fiends, they are."

"Dad, I have to leave soon. I have to get back to Professor Fujihara and tell him what I have decided about the competition." She straightened and waited for his response.

"You always did like a challenge. But it's not a time to be travelin' over there."

"You've been hanging out at the naval base far too much. Any work there?"

"As a matter a fact, I've been asked to swing a hammer over at the shipyard startin' very soon." He raised his cup in her direction.

The job at the Bremerton Naval Shipyard was always on the horizon, but never a reality. She smiled at him encouragingly.

"That's great, Dad." She took time gathering her things in the hopes the conversation would turn again to her decision. But her father kept his eyes on the fire, seemingly mesmerized by the tranquility of the leaping flames.

She reached the door and stopped. "Okay. I'll let you know what I decide."

"Be careful, darlin'. I know somethin' terrible is about to happen. I just feel it comin'."

A chill ran down her body, for her father and his predictions were something of a legend. Often brushed aside as drunken prattle, his insights were the talk of the town when they came to be. If he had only had that ability with his own dealings. She shook her head at the list of the calamities they could have avoided.

But for now, Billi's only concern centered on entering the competition at the University of Washington for the chance of an adventure to Japan. If something terrible was about to take place, it certainly would not impact her.

TWO

BILLI COAXED HER MOTHER'S OLD BUICK down 30th Avenue South, just off Jackson Street, where the O'Shaughnessy house stood out in all of its Victorian splendor, badly in need of paint. As she rattled to a stop at number 304, she heard the voice of the man she loved, Raymond Wilcox Richardson. The voice she had listened to since he came home with Eddy so many years ago.

"Hey, beautiful."

Ray's words were magic to her troubled soul as she stepped from the car. Her journey back to Seattle on the Black Ball Ferry had left her feeling anything but beautiful. It had been a long two hours of turmoil as she mulled over her next steps, and how to break the news to Ray had been a big part of her dilemma.

"I've been waiting for you. Boy, do I have good news." Ray took her arm, swung her around in a happy dance, and then pulled her to him. He kissed her under the new leaves of the oak tree.

"Watch it now," Eddy, her brother, teased as he appeared on the porch. "She's not yours yet."

"We'll see about that." Ray guided Billi up the concrete steps, his broad smile a treasure to behold. "Come on, darlin'. I'll announce it to everyone at once."

Billi, used to Ray's wild ways and extravagant behavior, let him lead her into the parlor. Between Eddy and Ray, the O'Shaughnessy home vibrated with exuberance. The two boys had grown side by side into head-turning young men, dark and handsome, full of life and adventure. Like a third leg, Billi had always trailed behind them. Now, everywhere the trio went, doors opened wide to the excitement that followed in their wake.

"Go get your mom," Ray instructed Eddy. "I need a moment alone with my gal."

Eddy gave Ray a warning smack on the back before disappearing into the dining room, shouting, "Mom, you better hurry. Ray's alone with Billi."

"Billi, I have to know right now. Will you marry me or not?"

The question lingered again between them. Billi had just turned twenty-one and wanted to travel, to learn, to win the competition and visit Japan. Ray whirled through life, his fast actions not always in keeping with her stride. Just like his love of flying, his need for speed drizzled into all his endeavors.

"Ray…"

"Make it yes. Just a simple yes. Then when I get back we can—"

"Back? Where are you going?" Billi's stomach fell at the sudden thought of saying good-bye, even for a short time. Funny, her head went light, it didn't seem to matter that she planned on telling him she hoped to leave, to go on an adventure to the unknown world of the Far East. But to have Ray go off twisted her insides with a gripping sensation.

Ray put his arms around her, drawing her to him. "That's what I came to tell you. But you have to say yes first."

The kitchen door swung wide as Mrs. O'Shaughnessy stormed in, followed by a whistling Eddy. Mrs. O, her preferred name amongst loved ones, presented no slight figure. Her German stature, round and full-figured, commanded attention. To be accepted in high society became her goal, at any price. Having run the office of the governor all those years ago had spilled into every activity she undertook—and with it, a sense of entitlement. If it weren't for her one slight bad habit of pinching other people's small, shiny objects—a practice that had developed during the Depression—she would be allowed into more of society's glamorous parlors.

"Why, Raymond, you unhand my only beautiful daughter." Mrs. O's voice filled the room, her diction perfect.

"Not until she says yes, Mrs. O. I'm not leaving here without it."

Mrs. O'Shaughnessy lowered into her one good high-backed rocking chair, her seat of honor, and watched the young couple. Ray stood, eyes locked on Billi, holding her in a death grip.

"What is she saying yes to?" Mrs. O spoke to anyone who would answer.

Eddy stood behind his mother. "Just wait until she answers, Mom." The next words he spoke were whispered to her in German.

Billi shot him a dirty look. It had been so aggravating that she could not learn her mother's first language as her only sibling had. She had spent years trying, listening to the easy flow between mother and brother. At Garfield High School, Eddy had excelled in German, with Mrs. Pelton advancing him to level sixteen and an independent course. But Billi had fallen in love with Japanese. Even though several Japanese students attended Garfield, Billi had no opportunity to formally study their language until she began studies at the university, where Professor Fujihara had quickly taken her under his wing and pushed her toward the competition.

Eddy smiled back at her. She speculated how much he wanted this marriage as well. He loved Ray like a brother and would be so happy to welcome him officially into the family, and she knew he regarded her as too stubborn, his little sis who would rather be up a tree, in a boat fishing, out dancing, or learning more about the Japanese culture than saying yes to Ray and settling down.

The air thickened, suddenly stifling, and sweat began to roll down between Billi's breasts. She loved Ray beyond words and there could be no question as to their getting married. But if she promised now, before the competition, would he let her go?

"Okay." Ray collected himself and began again. "I want to make this official before I head off."

"Where?" Billi asked, tears beginning to form.

"I've signed up with the Army Air Corps. Since I have so much training as a pilot already, they asked me to join. They came to Galvin's flight training school and spoke with Jim. He said I am their best and the Air Corps wants me now. Isn't that wonderful?"

"Yes." Billi shook with fear mingled with the thrill of his announcement.

"Did you hear that Mrs. O?" Ray shouted. "She said yes!"

Mrs. O leaped out of her chair and engulfed the young couple in her arms. "Wonderful! A big wedding for you two."

Billi struggled to be free. "No. I mean, yes, it's wonderful. It's your dream."

"Our dream," Ray corrected her. "I'll become a commercial pilot and we can travel anywhere you want to go."

"Time to celebrate!" Eddy clapped his hands and hurried toward the kitchen as he continued. "I've had the champagne chilling since Ray first asked you months ago."

"We'll invite the world." Mrs. O dramatically flung her arms into the air at the opportunity to organize a grand function. "It's the moment I've been waiting for since the day you were born." She waddled off toward the kitchen, babbling as she began to create her to-do lists.

Billi stood and watched the joy spread around the room. A joy she did not fully share, as her dream of winning the competition slid further from her.

"You have to ask my father for his permission first." She crossed her arms defiantly.

The announcement brought her mother to a screeching halt midsentence. Mention of James Edward O'Shaughnessy Sr. broke an unspoken rule that hung over the house like a dark shadow.

Eddy entered, tray in hand, with the chilled bottle and four elegant champagne glasses. He sang as he made his way through the silence. "'Here comes the bride, all dressed in'—what color will you wear, sis?"

"Oh, stop that, Eddy," Billi snapped. "I think our celebration is a little premature. Ray needs to ask Dad first."

Ray took the offered full glass and handed it to Billi. "I already have." He took a second one and handed it to his mother-in-law-to-be. "And you'll be happy to know he gave us his blessing and wishes of good luck. He can't wait 'to stroll his little darlin' down the aisle.'"

"Thank heaven." Mrs. O'Shaughnessy downed her drink in one gulp. She extended the empty glass toward her son who, with a knowing smile, poured her another. "A bit more for the moment, rare and beautiful, when two lovers make the biggest decision of their lives."

"To my little sis and my new brother." Eddy held his glass high. "So cheers, to us and to our future."

Billi the last to raise her glass to toast a future that surprisingly felt binding and restrictive, forced a smile. It had also been her dream to become Mrs. Raymond Richardson. Yet, at that moment, when her champagne glass tapped that of her future husband, she swore she would go through with the competition but keep it a secret. Her first deception to her fiancé. And it felt very strange.

DANNY GUNNER TAPPED AT THE DOOR of 304 30th South, as he usually did several times a week. Elated he had concluded the final exams of his junior year at Garfield High School making him officially a senior, he let himself in. After all, Mrs. O had claimed him as family and this summer, selling candy at her concession stand at Mount Baker Beach, held so many promises.

"Dahlia says hi, Eddy." He spoke offhandedly to his idol as he stepped past him into the living room. Secretly Danny felt great pride at the fact that his older sister, with her picture-perfect blonde hair, had caught Eddy's eye. Or at least *she* was smitten—no, head over heels in love with Eddy. Danny felt his sister's attraction gave him better standing with the O'Shaughnessys, a family he spent every spare minute with.

"When do you need my help setting up your concession stands, Mrs. O?"

Danny's freckled face, red hair, and slight build gave him an even younger look than his sixteen years. But his willingness to help made him a favorite of Mrs. O'Shaughnessy's.

"Ah, sweetie, we have big news." She rocked back in her chair. "Billi and Raymond are engaged."

"Does Dahlia know? Are we…" Danny blushed; his red cheeks amplified his red curls.

"Yes." Billi helped him with his embarrassment. "Of course you and Dahlia will be there. Aren't we the gang of five?"

"Boy, will she be excited." Danny looked over at Eddy.

"Yes, I bet," Billi teased. "Better watch out. Eddy. Love is in the air."

"You should think about it." Ray slapped Eddy's back for encouragement and then checked his wristwatch. "Well, I've got to run. Have to be there for new recruits first thing in the morning." He kissed Billi's cheek and dashed out the door, flying high on love and dreams.

THREE

Billi hurried down South Jackson Street toward Chinatown and turned on 7th, entering Nihonmachi, or Japantown. Their worlds were but blocks away, yet so distinctively different. Like a knife's edge, the unseen boundary lines were sharp and cutting.

Even within the context of Seattle's Chinatown, there were divisions. The Asian district had been created after the big Seattle Fire in 1889 that destroyed most of the buildings along the waterfront. And, as in any predominantly white city, Asians were grouped together based on their skin color and the shape of their eyes, not their contributions to the city. Thus, inside Chinatown, areas were carefully created with invisible lines, the teeter-totter of life, where Japanese, Chinese, and Filipino, had their barely distinguishable boundaries throughout those few blocks.

She began up the steep hill where Mr. Nakamura had planted cherry trees, his gift to his new home, America. The young cherry saplings were the essence of this Issei, brought from his home village of Yoshino in the mountain province of Nara. He had prayed to the great deity, Zao Gorgin, whose image resided in the Kinpusen Temple, for the blessings of peace in his new home. And few could deny that, when the morning light caught the pink blossoms and softened the brash starkness of the streets in springtime, his gift indeed created a sense of serenity and beauty.

Billi passed shops on the ground floor of the brick buildings until she reached the fresh vegetables and fruits adorning the front window of Nakamura Grocery. Just beyond his store she stepped inside. The glass door to the upper apartments rattled slightly as Billi closed it behind her and started up the stairs. The aroma of cooking oils, garlic, onion, and spices escaped from each apartment, announcing the welcome approach of mealtime.

As she walked down the narrow hallway, Billi realized that in her anticipation of telling Eileen of her engagement, she had not eaten. She brushed her hunger aside and tried to envision Mr. Nakamura's reaction to her decision to enter the competition. He had been so patient with her, working as her guide and tutor as she endeavored to learn not only the language but the nuances of their culture.

Below the *2D* that marked their door in raised bronze script rested the Japanese symbol of peace, the elegant strokes of heiwa. As Billi bent over to remove her shoes, the door opened and she recognized the neatly clipped toenails of Kenny, Eileen's younger brother.

"Eileeeenn." His sing-song tone echoed into the small living room. He stood back to let Billi through the door, his loud manner so unlike the rest of the family. After the death of their youngest brother, Kenny had emerged the comedian to lighten his mother's heart and draw her out of her dark despair. But Mrs. Nakamura had never been the same, and now the destructive disease of cancer controlled her body.

"Eileeeenn." His voice grew louder, taking on a twang. "Yer girlfriend is here."

Eileen pushed her younger brother away and he faked a tumble, landing at the feet of his father. Mr. Nakamura gave his young son a stern look of disapproval, stepped over him, and approached the two young women.

"Excellent. We shall have tea." He nodded to them. "Go and prepare."

Eileen beamed with delight as she turned down the hall, waving Billi on. Remembering she still had her shoes in her hands, Billi turned back to add them to the neat row of shoes that formed a line next to the entrance. As she started in Eileen's direction, she heard muffled voices in angry discussion. Tak, the eldest son who had recently returned from studying in Japan, and Mr. Nakamura were arguing again. She hadn't meant to look up as she passed the open archway to the kitchen, but at the sound of her name, she glanced in at the two men.

Tak caught sight of her over the head of his father, disgust and rage tumbling from his body and spilling in her direction. When his eyes met hers, they were filled with hatred. His back stiffened as he glared at her. The instant fear that gripped her propelled Billi farther down the hall and into the warm sanctuary of her friend's small room.

Eileen appeared in her soft pink kimono. Umbrellas adorned with flowers were expertly positioned around the hem and across the back.

"What do you think of the kimono Auntie picked out for you?"

Billi spied a royal blue kimono lying on the single bed as if in repose, elegant stems of white iris trailing down the long sleeves. "It's beautiful."

"We don't have time to bind your breasts. Dad is in a mood. It is good you have come today. Well, hurry."

Billi's strain unraveled at the feel of the soft silk against her skin. Carefully, she wrapped the folds of the gown the traditional way, left over right across her chest, before Eileen helped secure her obi. In the turmoil brewing in the kitchen between father and son, Billi had forgotten her news.

"I guess I won't be able to wear this for much longer." Her hand moved down the long sleeves meant for unmarried women.

Eileen observed her friend as she wound her hair into a knot in anticipation of the forthcoming wig. "Don't be silly. Auntie wants you to wear it. Says it matches your blue eyes."

"I'm engaged." The weight of her announcement pulled her back onto the bed where she sat, tears welling, as she grasped one long sleeve.

Eileen's mouth opened, then quickly snapped shut at the implication of the news.

"When?"

"When Ray returns from Army Air Corps training. Or maybe sooner."

"Good." Eileen smiled. "Then we won't have to cut the sleeves shorter until after Bon Odori." Eileen always saw through a difficult situation to the practical solution for that moment. Her father's gift to her.

"But what about the competition?"

"Of course you'll win and go to the homeland of my parents. Just think, you will visit it before I do. Tak says Japan is the most beautiful place on earth. I only wish father had been able to send me to study with Tak."

"I'll put you in my suitcase." Billi stood and wrapped her arms around Eileen's dainty frame.

"Here." Eileen detached herself. "Let's see how Auntie Katsuko's wig looks on you. Isn't it great that she is letting us borrow her costumes?"

The wig fit snuggly on Billi's head and smelled of powder and old perfume.

"Your mother must be very pleased about the engagement." Eileen adjusted the ornament that dangled from Billi's wig, an imitation of white cherry blossoms.

"She's started her lists and they are spreading. Do you think your mother would make some flower arrangements for me?" Certainly this concept would not appear on any of her mother's lists, but Billi would insist.

The two young women sat pressed together looking in the mirror as they applied their makeup and discussed Billi's future. Slowly the transformation took hold. Billi had garnered a steady hand at applying the black eyeliner in a long, exaggerated stroke in an attempt to soften her round eyes. But the deep blue of the kimono only enhanced their intense color. While her figure and costume spoke of the land of the Rising Sun, her eyes were the color of a different country. She practiced lowering her lids to observe the effect.

"There." Eileen encouraged her friend, "Now you look like one of us. Try it with the sensu."

Billi took the offered fan, snapped it open in one fluid motion, and two golden cranes, wings spread, flashed before her face. She slowly lowered the fan, eyes downcast as she had practiced so many times.

"Oh, Auntie is going to be impressed with your progress!" Eileen paused, studying her friend. "Your life will always be an adventure." She snapped her own fan open and struck a pose.

The mirror reflected two beautiful Asian women. One small and delicate, Asian eyes wide and inviting. The other's eyes barely open, peering over the fan with uncertainty. In a monochrome photo there would be no way to detect the blueness of the eyes and the trouble that lay ahead in the adventure her friend had so aptly predicted.

FOUR

The apartment door slammed shut, jarring the serenity of the two friends. They shuffled out of Eileen's room and down the hall. At the lineup of shoes by the front entrance, the bare wood floor stood empty where Tak's shoes had been neatly placed. One of Billi's shoes had been kicked to the side.

Eileen bent down and replaced her friend's shoe into the order expected by the Nakamura household. Then she led the way to where her father sat alone on the grass mat with a short-legged table before him. His expression remained emotionless, devoid of the turmoil that had just swept out the door, taking with it the fury that belied the small plaque claiming peace within. He exhaled deeply as the girls watched and waited.

An angry storm had arrived with the return of Tak and his traveling trunk, which he guarded with an evil threat to anyone who came near the battered traveling case. No one could go near the battered black object for fear of sparking Tak's explosive aggression. He had changed so in his five years of study in Tokyo. He no longer appeared the self-composed, loving oldest son but wore his wrath and hatred behind a new terrifying mask.

Mr. Nakamura nodded slightly, and the young women kneeled across from him on the special mats where the kama—the kettle—sat warming in the old Raku furo, the brazier Mrs. Nakamura had brought with her from Japan.

"Your laughter and beauty are welcome." Mr. Nakamura spoke softly in his mother tongue. "It is your turn, I believe."

Billi pulled out a clean cloth, which had been neatly folded in her obi, and wiped Mr. Nakamura's favorite teacup with the hand-painted dragons circling the outside. Briefly, she held the cup to the light, and the image of the head of a geisha appeared in the bottom, the lithopone image embedded in the fine translucent china. She held her long sleeve back and reached for the black-lacquer container holding the green powdered tea.

"There is some joy you have not told me of?" Mr. Nakamura broke his usual silence as he observed every move of Billi's hands while she prepared the way of the tea.

"Yes." Eileen adjusted the small plates of artfully arranged sweets, the intricate wagashi, and answered for her friend. "Next winter, after she has won the competition and returned from Japan, our little flower will marry the honorable Raymond Richardson."

Billi looked into the warm eyes of her mentor. His cheeks wrinkled with his smile, and the last of Billi's fears flowed into the motion of preparing the tea.

Mr. Nakamura shifted, leaning toward them. "Today, let your spirit be filled with the beauty of my ancestors so that tomorrow you will flourish in the exam."

Billi blushed as she lifted the bamboo water ladle to pour the steaming water over the green mixture before whisking the brew to perfection. The three sat in silence, enjoying the warm tea and the confectionary, their private thoughts filling the room. Tomorrow would be a new beginning of a wonderful experience for Billi, one that had become their common goal.

The moment slipped away with Kenny's entrance as he bounced into the room dressed in his yukata and sporting his white hachimaki headband adorned with the Nakamura Mon or emblem. The geometrical dark-blue design centered on his forehead, while tufts of his thick black hair protruded in disarray in his unmistakably American style. He smiled at them. Holding his taiko drum sticks high, the young athlete mimed beating his drum while he imitated its sound as he danced around the small room.

"Please take my son before he disturbs the neighborhood or knocks over my geisha dolls or breaks my beautiful tea set." Mrs. Nakamura, frail and thin, the few strands of her thinning hair plastered to her head, spoke softly as she leaned against the doorjamb.

Kenny stopped his wild drumming as his father guided his mother's bent frame to the old couch. She lowered slowly onto the worn cushions and stared across the room at her two prized glass-encased geisha dolls. The dolls stood in a place of honor on a side table, flanking Buddha, with the delicate bloom of white orchids arching gracefully over his golden figure.

Kenny swiftly turned on the lamp for his mother, illuminating the two dolls. Their glass cases, framed in black lacquer, were dusted daily. Inside, the figurines posed with their fans, their white porcelain faces and hands smooth and perfect above their kimonos, one of rich gold and the other vibrant red. The dangling hair ornament of white cherry blossoms that adorned one of them appeared identical to the one in Billi's wig. Unconsciously, she fingered the small fake flowers that swayed with her slightest motion.

Her movement drew Mrs. Nakamura's attention. "You are more beautiful than my imposters." A rare compliment, as the dolls had become her world. "Go. Practice. You must be the best at Bon Odori." She laid her hand on her husband's shoulder.

At a brief nod from the father of the house, the three young adults scurried out the door.

The hall of Jodo Shinshu Temple on South Main Street vibrated with chatter and anticipation. In the cool half-light, girls swept by like colorful butterflies, giggling and waving. In one corner of the hall, Kenny joined the drummers while they waited for their turn at the rehearsal.

Billi kept her head down as she carefully stepped behind Eileen. While the two had been donning different kimonos since childhood and practicing various dances, this marked the first time Billi had been allowed to join in the community rehearsal for the festival that weekend.

She remembered how frightened she and Eileen had been just a few weeks earlier when, practicing in the temple hall and intent on the precision of the dance, they had discovered Auntie Katsuko stood in the doorway. They did not know how long she had been watching, for when the song ended, Auntie had simply turned and disappeared down the hallway.

The next day when Billi arrived, she did not even have the chance to remove her shoes before Auntie grabbed her arm and dragged her down the empty hall, shoved two fans into her hands, and left her alone. Auntie swept to the side of the stage to the record player in its tall wooden case and carefully lowered the needle onto the 78 record. The screechy sound that emitted was not the result of a scratch on the record, but the high-pitched voice of the female singer considered the ultimate vocal talent in Japanese culture.

Auntie clapped her hands and then waved them in the air. "Begin."

Billi jumped, startled.

"Dance, dance," the older woman demanded.

Slowly and uncomfortably, Billi began to move through the routine she and Eileen had practiced so many times. When the song ended, Auntie made her way back to the record player and started the song over before joining Billi on the stage.

"Again," Auntie insisted in her own language. "Snap the sensu, then hold it still, then softly, like delicate wings, feel the music." She took Billi's fans, demonstrated the moves, and then handed them back to her.

They ran the routine five times, with several interruptions, before Eileen shyly entered the room, her presence halting the older woman's driving force. Auntie turned off the music and whisked past Eileen.

"I had to help Mother," she spoke in a hush manner to her aunt.

"Hai. Tomorrow you dance too." Auntie straightened and disappeared down the hall.

In this very hall Katsuko Ito, who had danced in theaters all over Japan, had taken in the round-eyed young woman and taught her even deeper secrets of the culture that Billi already loved and admired.

Now she felt a small tremor as Auntie motioned her onto the stage opposite Eileen for their rehearsal. Word had spread that Auntie had a surprise, but none had expected a round-eye would be selected for the intricate sensu dance, the folding fan dance. While some of the others smiled politely with acceptance, others looked on with the resentment Billi had seen in Tak's eyes earlier that day. She knew she had to shake aside her mounting anxiety and calm her trembling hands, if for no other reason than to avoid the wake of Auntie's wrath if one movement did not match the intense training.

"Breathe," Eileen whispered from behind her fan.

Billi looked across the room at the many faces, only to find Kenny smiling at her. He mimed playing his drums and winked at her.

She nodded, snapped her fans open, and waited for the music to soothe her.

"Today, let your spirit be filled with the beauty of my ancestors so that tomorrow you will flourish in the exam."

Mr. Nakamura's voice broke through her fear. And with his memory, she stepped into the dance with sheer determination and concentration.

BILLI STILL HAD WHITE GREASEPAINT under her fingernails as she ran down the concrete steps of 304 to where Ray held the door of his light-green 1940 Plymouth coupe open for her.

"Come on, sweetheart. We're late, and Mother gets a head start on the drinks if left too long."

"Sorry." Billi kissed his cheek and slid onto the leather seat. "But I'm certain you'll catch up," she added as he eased behind the wheel and turned the key.

He smiled over at her. "Thank you for saying yes, Bil. You've made me the happiest man alive."

She held her smile in place as he pulled away from the curb. At the end of the block, Ray turned and headed back down South Jackson. She straightened her skirt. "Where are we going?"

"A surprise." He joined in with Frank Sinatra and sang backup to "Yours Is My Heart Alone" as he steered toward Japantown.

A sense of unease wiggled up her spine. They had passed the block for Nakamura Grocery and the temple where hours before she had been entwined in the art of the traditional dance. With a sharp twinge, her thoughts turned to her future mother-in-law.

Mrs. Gladys Cousins Richardson had been transported from San Francisco to Seattle by her wealthy husband and had resented the move. She took every opportunity presented to announce—generally without provocation—that Seattle had no culture. Aside from her family and small circle of friends, she looked with disdain on everything and everyone in the Northwest, and that included Billi. Hopefully until now.

Ray eased the car to the curb. "Mother thought you might enjoy 'a bit of Japanese culture,' as she put it."

Billi tried to brush aside the feeling that Mrs. Richardson's choice blatantly mocked her as the car stopped in front of Tokyo Restaurant. Her stomach rippled with tension as Ray guided her into the door and then wove a path through the tables to the far side where his mother, martini in one hand, waved. So like Mrs. Richardson not to want a tatami room and the privacy it offered. From her position in the main room, she could see and be seen.

"Hello, darlings." Gladys waved and adjusted her impeccably coiffed hair. She slid a cigarette from the silver case, and held the unlit cigarette, waiting.

"Here they are," Ray's father, Isaac Richardson, snapped the lighter to life and held the small flame toward his wife, and then stood as the young lovers reached the table. Isaac shook his son's hand and lightly touched Billi's arm waving toward two empty seats.

"Hey, you, boy," he shouted over Billi's head. "Let's have a bottle of your finest champagne. We're celebrating here."

Lowering into the chair that Ray held for her, Billi attempted to ignore Mr. Richardson's brash announcement.

"Come on, snap to it," the elder Richardson added, and then took his seat, apparently satisfied his last command had been heard. "I don't think half of these guys understand a word I'm saying."

"Dad, thanks for inviting us."

"Well." Mrs. Richardson leaned toward her son. "Have you given it to her yet?"

Billi froze. She had just picked up her red cloth napkin and now it draped midair, like a flag.

"I was going to wait until we were alone."

"Nonsense." Mrs. Richardson tapped her cigarette against the ashtray with impatience. "Don't be a bore. Give it to her now."

Ray looked at Billi, and she could see a slight blush emerge. She had never known him to be shy, but it seemed that since yesterday, just those few hours ago, their world had changed. It felt odd not having her brother with them, gluing them together, and for the first time Billi had a glimpse into her new world. A sense of peace settled around her. Life with Ray would be a welcome new beginning.

She smiled at him and he smiled back, once again the bold Ray of their youth. Her hands and napkin found her lap, and she too blushed at the attention.

"Well?" insisted his father.

Ray dug into his jacket pocket and as his hand hit the table it held a small cream-colored box with an intricate gold design scrawled across its acrylic top.

"I know we haven't really talked about this, but here." He nudged the ornate object in her direction.

Billi stopped breathing. Her hand floated toward the small box, and she caught sight of the white greasepaint still wedged beneath her fingernails. She quickly pulled her hand back to the safety of the napkin, hoping no one else had seen the filth.

"It won't bite, dear." Over the rim of her martini glass Mrs. Richardson glanced at Billi with what appeared to be disgust.

The white sleeves of the waiter intruded into the scene as he held a bottle of champagne in front of Isaac.

"It's about time," the older man protested. "We're celebrating here."

Billi furiously worked her napkin under her nails, glad for the distraction.

"My son's getting married." Mr. Richardson's voice grew even louder with his enthusiasm.

The waiter reached over Billi's shoulder. "May you grow fat with many children who hate you," his Japanese words barely audible as he filled her glass.

Billi's gaze followed the white sleeve of the waiter's jacket to the black, glaring eyes of Tak.

"Oh, what did he say?" Gladys perked up.

Defiantly, Billi picked up her champagne glass. "He wished us a lifetime of happiness."

"I'll drink to that." Ray lifted his glass and sipped, then turned his attention back to the small box. "Now open it."

From inside the box, the three diamonds glistened in the light, large and overstated. Ray took the gold band with the opulent gems and slipped it onto her ring finger.

The heaviness of the diamonds created a profound sensation on her hand and her heart. While the depth of their beauty and quality of cut were grander than Billi's wildest imaginings, the glitter did not appeal to her. The ring reminded her of her mother, who would wear the glitz with great pride, flashing it to all who came within a one-block distance. But to Billi, the diamonds imposed a weight.

Ray snuggled up beside her. "Do you like it?"

"Of course she does," Mrs. Richardson answered for her. "It was my Aunt Elizabeth Dragie's favorite ring. Her family being one of the founding families of my beautiful city, San Francisco. Oh, how I miss home. We'll have to take a trip down there so I can introduce the new Mrs. Richardson properly."

Ray's soft voice broke through his mother's prattling. "Do you like it, Bil? If not we can get you—"

"It's fine." She sat transfixed by the sparkle on her finger and the slight residue of makeup grease that made her nails shine.

"You order, Billi. After all, we might as well put your studies to some use." Mrs. Richardson's voice clearly held her distaste for her soon-to-be daughter-in-law's choice of paths.

Tak stood stiffly waiting next to her, his brusque nods unfriendly, as she pointed to various dishes, barely mumbling the words. After she had completed the order Tak stormed from the table.

Ray took Billi's shaking hand. "You okay?"

"Yes. Just so much going on and tomorrow is my big exam." The words slipped out before she could stop them.

He looked at her intently. "So, you are going through with the competition?"

Gladys filled the silence as she lifted her empty martini glass toward any waiter who would notice.

"Don't be absurd. Billi isn't going anywhere except to San Francisco with me. To meet the family and shop. Aren't you, dear? She'll forget all this little Japanese hogwash and settle into being the perfect Mrs. Raymond Richardson as soon as we set the date for the big event."

The waiter who relieved Gladys of her empty martini glass glared across at Billi; Tak's condescending smile not lost on her. Unexpectedly, she felt the pressure of the ring burned into her skin.

FIVE

RAY TURNED HIS HEADLIGHTS OFF as he rolled to a stop in front of the O'Shaughnessy house. A soft glow shone through the tall Victorian windows of the living room. Billi knew her mother would be in bed. Mrs. O would not want Ray to see her disappointment at not being asked to join her only daughter as the Richardson's celebrated their engagement. Mrs. Richardson set the tone, establishing boundaries of class, which Billi knew her mother would, of course, ignore.

"Are you happy, Bil?" Ray pulled her close.

"I just wish you weren't leaving."

"I know, honey. But you know Jim Galvin's flight school was one of the first chosen by the government to receive money for the Civilian Pilot Training Program, and I'm damn proud to be a part of it. The CPTP has done me well, and now another door is opening. Look, it's just a step to the kind of life we want."

"I know. I just wish you hadn't learned to fly. I hate that darn Swallow that takes you away from me."

"I'm well beyond the Hisso Swallow, powered by the old—"

"—OX-5 engine," she finished for him, barely hiding her boredom, being well versed on the aircraft he flew since he constantly relived his success and near misses.

"Billi, you know that since I saw my first airplane I've wanted to fly. And how lucky for me that Jim skippered our yacht through the San Juan Islands the summer I was fifteen. By the time we reached Roche Harbor, Dad had signed me up for lessons and written Jim the check for my birthday. I know you don't think much of my parents, but the best gift they ever gave me came in the form of flying lessons from the man himself."

"Your parents are never here. You spend more time in our house than with them."

"That's because of you. I didn't want any other fella to step in." He watched her twist the ring. "If you don't like the ring, we can get another."

She laughed. "And what would your mother, or my mother, have to say about that? It's just so…"

"Ostentatious? I know. But I want the world to know how lucky I am. And if any other guy starts in your direction, I want this beacon to set him straight. You're all mine."

He kissed her, and his hand moved down her neck toward her chest.

"Not yet I'm not," she leaned back in her seat.

The front bedroom light on the second floor blinked on, and the silhouette of Eddy filled the window frame.

"My watchdog is up." She hesitated, not really wanting the moment to end.

Ray eased out his side of the coupe, waved up at Eddy, and exaggerated his movements as he held her door open.

As Billi slid from the car, Ray pulled her to him and kissed her slowly and she felt his desire build again.

From above, Eddy rattled the window open. "Hey, unhand my sister."

"Never. Come down here and make me."

Billi crossed her arms and waited; the two best friends had been exchanging the same dare since childhood.

As the couple reached the top step, Eddy swung the door open. Ray pushed him back inside and closed it.

"Billi, the only thing in the world right now that scares me is tomorrow. This competition. I want you to win, but I'd have to be on the same boat with you if you did go to Japan. I'm not letting you out of my sight."

"What about your leaving me?"

"Only for pilot training. And since I have flown for years, it shouldn't take long. Then we'll get married and live wherever they send us."

The door snapped open again. "Are you two done yet?"

Ray kissed Billi's cheek and ushered her toward her brother. "Sweet dreams till tomorrow. And best of luck." He winked at her and closed the door softly.

"What in blue blazes is that?" Eddy raised his hand, pretending to shield his eyes from the nonexistent shine of the three large diamonds.

She swatted at him and started up the steps. "Shhh," she warned as he fell in behind her. She leaned on the railing and pulled herself up past the fifth step, the one that creaked.

Eddy mimicked his sister's move and then landed full force on the fifth step. The moan of the old stair echoed up to the second-floor landing.

"Come in, Billi," their mother's voice commanded from behind her closed bedroom door. As the siblings hit the landing, Mrs. O'Shaughnessy added, as if she could see through walls, "Eddy, go to bed."

Billi wrinkled her nose in her brother's direction and then headed off to her mother's room at the end of the long hallway.

Mrs. O sat propped up in the middle of her double bed. Her bedside lamp illuminated the aged and dull-green vines with the faded white flowers that spiraled across the wallpaper, a testimony to its former glory.

"How did the evening go?" She patted her bed for Billi to sit and then held out her large, soft hand.

The bed gave off a slight squeak as Billi's weight settled on the old mattress. She placed her left hand in her mother's palm. Mrs. O twisted the ring from side to side, letting the diamonds catch the light of her bedside lamp.

"That will do," she finally announced. "Now, tell me everything she said."

Billi raced across the campus. Her mother had kept her talking far too long into the night, subtle sabotage, for today's competition. She wondered if her mother and Ray had contrived the events of the last night to be certain her brain became dull and tired. But her eagerness propelled her up the stone steps of Suzzallo Library on the University of

Washington campus. She paused long enough outside the tall, wooden exterior doors of the Gothic-style building to take off her engagement ring and slip it in her purse. Not certain whether the rules precluded an engaged woman, she decided not to take any chances.

She scurried up the grand stairway, attempting to soften the reverberating sound of her shoes on the stone. As she reached the third floor, her instructor, Professor Fujihara, approached her just outside the reading room.

"For you. Special power for winner. And for heat this summer in my beloved Japan. Use it wisely."

He handed her a long, thin object encased in purple silk. She worked the loop over the small netsuke, hand-carved in the image of a dragon emerging from an egg. The black lacquer base of the fan slid out, and she regarded the sea-blue edges of the stiff, folded paper. Surprised and delighted, she snapped the fan open. Three dragons danced across the paper, the largest creature, angry and gray, rose above blue swirls of the ocean. She waved it through the air as Auntie Katsuko had taught her.

Professor Fujihara smiled. "Go. You will do well. And after you have won and are heading to my homeland, I will have you visit my family and bring them gifts from America."

As she tucked the fan back inside the silk shield, her eye caught the movement of a door closing across the hall. When she turned back to thank her professor, she saw only the top of his bent head as he hurried down the long stone steps.

The proctor showed her to her seat toward the back of the spacious reading room. Billi looked up at the high, arched ceiling, where ornate chandeliers of black wrought iron and golden glass hung suspended from long chains. She bowed her head in silent prayer below the glow of the tranquil stained glass windows, then placed her fan on the wooden table next to her purse. Determined, she picked up the pencil that waited for her to decide her fate. Her eyes focused on the two objects before her: the purple silk casing that symbolized all of her hopes of visiting Japan and her brown leather purse concealing the family ring steeped in old society.

The competition had begun before the test was placed before her.

Jack Huntington crossed the hall to the test room with his assistant, David, following. They slipped silently into the shadows at the rear of the long room and stood observing the backs and bent heads of the anxious competitors.

Jack had arranged with the professor that the test be administered to these twelve hand-selected students. He had thought the competitors were ten men and two women. The professor had proclaimed Billi as head of the class, but Jack had mistaken her name for that of a man's. A delightful surprise. From his first impression of her confident attitude, he breathed easier, pleased to have Billi among the other competitors.

Jack ticked off their names in his head as he sensed the students' nervousness, like a hum reverberating and swirling through the air. He had insisted on the placement of the twelve long tables, with each participant sitting facing front. The two other women, Phyllis and Ruth, sat strategically below the long-hanging lights, easy to observe. However, Billi sat in the back, dimly lit.

Stealthily, he started down a side aisle, keeping his bad eye, his right one, in as much shadow as possible. In their earlier conversations about the selection of the competitors, David had tended toward Ruth, who sat in the front row, her heavy chest barely concealed by the low cut of her blouse. Jack smirked. Ruth, with her revealing attire, was certainly more to David's personal liking. Phyllis, who occupied the seat in the third row, had a twitch and, upon closer examination, her caked-on makeup barely concealed the scars from her acne.

The nine men who rounded out the other contestants were of no interest to him. He headed to the back of the room, where he remained in the dark, observing Billi. Her short-sleeved summer blouse exposed long arms: her hand steady as she quickly worked through the answers. She appeared lithe and athletic, which only added to her qualifications. She looked to be a bit taller than he would have liked, but her legs were long and muscular with good ankles. A plus.

Jack circled one more time, like a shark, just off in the perimeter. He had to be certain. So much depended on his choice. When he stepped into the light, he stood above Billi's table. He reached for the purple silk object. Before he had it off the table, Billi's deep blue eyes snapped in his direction, unfaltering, daring. She did not flinch at the black patch shielding his right eye or the slight scar that christened his skin above and below the patch. He watched her intently, and she returned his stare. The hand she held out to retrieve her object had no ring that bound her to another. He let the fan fall, and she caught it before it hit the hard wood. He turned and headed for the door, with the irritating David at his heels.

Elated, Jack pushed through the ornate door into the hallway. The girl with the sea-blue eyes emerged his choice—pretty, smart, and fearless. He smiled. She seemed outstanding in all aspects, and by nightfall he would know everything about Miss Billi O'Shaughnessy. The purple object had made the choice for him. Unfortunately, she would not win the competition and the professed trip to Japan. He would see to that.

BILLI STOPPED AT THE BASE OF THE LIBRARY STEPS, letting the sun's warmth relax her shoulders. She craved the taste of saltwater and the fine mist it left on the body after a long swim in the chilling water. But, her father's home on Dyes Inlet beckoned from far away. For now, Lake Washington would just have to do. She hurried across campus, past Frosh Pond, as it had been dubbed due to the fact so many freshmen landed in its waters. The Olmstead Brothers had designed the fountain as the original centerpiece of the Alaskan-Yukon-Pacific Exhibition of 1909, only to have the students find another use for its glory. Heading down the road that ran beneath a bridge, she emerged by the stadium where Ray would be waiting. At the thought of his smile, Billi felt her heart lighten, and her step quickened.

JACK STOOD AT THE WINDOW and watched the fleeting figure of Billi, her skirt flowing with her sure, quick movements. He remembered how she had elegantly maneuvered the fan in the hallway before the test. She was part gazelle, part butterfly—and sheer perfection for his plan.

He turned and motioned for Professor Fujihara to sit, watching the older Asian's face set in distrust and anger. He contemplated why the professor had not previously presented Billi as a young, beautiful woman. Fujihara had wanted to protect her. Jack would have to lie to the professor, assure him his star pupil would be safe. He had to gain the older man's trust, break through his reserve, if he were to glean all that he could about Billi. Immense responsibility rode on this scheme he had concocted.

RAY LEANED AGAINST HIS PARKED CAR and caught Billi as she leaped into his arms.

"Oh, thank heaven that is over and thank heaven you are here." She squeezed him tight and kissed him. "How about a swim?"

"I thought that would be your choice. I swung by and picked up your suit, and your mother sent a lunch, with a 'don't worry about work today.' Danny is helping set up the concession stand."

"Wonderful." She hadn't thought much about her seasonal job for her mother. With summer officially starting that week and the beaches filling with children, her mother's concession stands needed readying. Thankfully, this would be her last year of selling candies and ice cream from inside the small, two-room structure that her mother erected, painted, and filled with goods each summer at two different beaches along Lake Washington. She smiled at the thought of how her mother had finagled the permits to sell her wares. Mrs. O's sly ways of getting what she desired, at times, were awe inspiring. She tossed her purse on the car seat and climbed inside.

As Ray slipped into the driver's side, he frowned at her. "Billi, why aren't you wearing your engagement ring?"

She drew in a sharp breath as she snatched up her purse.

"Oh, Ray," she purred, "it is just so beautiful and distracting. I needed to focus."

"And I need it to distract other men from heading your way."

She fished the ring from her bag and slid it on, holding it out for him to see. "There. Satisfied?"

"Only if you never take it off again."

"I promise." She kissed him briefly before they pulled away from the curb.

SIX

THE BURNING STUB OF JACK'S CIGAR glowed in the half darkness of the room he now occupied in the brick apartments on Boylston Street. He kept the shades drawn not only for security but to rest his good eye. His constant companion, his black eye patch, sat on the mahogany table next to his chair as he massaged the scar that ran across his brow and dipped slightly onto his cheek. Professor Fujihara had not divulged much during their interview; if anything at all, he had merely confirmed Miss O'Shaughnessy an excellent student with some prior training. Jack closed his eyes to further review their conversation. The professor had lied to him as well when he claimed he did not know the source of her knowledge. Jack hated the Japanese and their damn secrets. His vehement loathing of their culture had opened the door with J. Edgar Hoover, his superior. The head of the FBI in Washington, D.C., had not only listened, he had encouraged Jack's secret plan.

The three low knocks at the door announced David. Jack rose, stretched to his full six-foot-two, and crossed to the door.

David Buchanan entered and, as he passed by, Jack caught the slight whiff of whiskey. Damn the man. Why had David been assigned to him? The insolent drunk moved through life unsteady in his habits and that made him a danger to their mission.

"Why didn't you choose the one with the big tits?" David blurted before he noticed the stern look on his supervisor's face.

Jack knew his bad eye bothered David when not concealed behind the black material—for a slight gray film lingered over his retina, the fine line of the scar many found grotesque and unsettling. David squirmed a bit before turning away and sat in the chair closest to the shaded window.

Distance did not soothe Jack's disgust for David. His drinking, vulgar language, and need for fast women only heightened Jack's mistrust.

"What did you learn?"

"She's got a guy. They went swimming. She's not that bad in a swimsuit, nice long legs. The Japs will like that." He seemed to salivate at the thought.

Jack detected David's perverse longing for Billi as he described her, and his dislike for David turned to hate.

"Who's the guy?"

"She called him Ray. She's a stronger swimmer than he is, but his hands were all over her. He's heading off to train with the Air Corps flight school in three weeks. She had on a big rock. He must have money be—"

"Call the major at Randolph Field where he'll train and move up his entry date. What else?"

David's report reflected the man giving it, worthless. But the issue of a fiancé could create problems.

"You said her mother once worked for the government? Dig around there and see if you can find out more. I need her to cooperate. Focus on Ray and who Miss O'Shaughnessy learned Japanese from."

BILLI LAY ACROSS HER BED staring at the pattern that repeated across her walls of golden birdcages looped together by vines and flowers. She had loved this print as a child. Now the irony of the images echoed back at her. A bird in a gilded cage—is that what she would become when she married Ray? Their afternoon alone at the beach had been a welcome reprieve. It not only helped shake loose her disquieting tension from the test, but the vision of that obnoxious man who smelled of cigars. How dare he pick up her fan and interrupt her during the competition! She did not find his patch disturbing, but his glare unnerved her. Yet, for fear he claimed the title of judge, she had kept silent.

She recognized the knock at her door as her mother's, their private rat-a-tat-tat.

"Are you up yet?" The door opened with her words. Mrs. O carried her pen and paper. The list-maker had arrived. She sank down on the edge of the bed. "Did you set a date?'

"And a good morning to you." Billi pulled the pillow over her head.

"Billi dear, we have parties to organize, you need a dress. How many bridesmaids do you want? Do you know who you want to ask?"

Billi lowered her pillow to look at her mother. "Mom," she pleaded softly, "can we make it a small wedding?"

She watched her mother's back straighten. Billi knew no money remained for the grand manner in which they used to entertain in their flush days of old. Her father had a knack for making money, but in the flip of a dime, he lost it. Of the many businesses Edward O'Shaughnessy had owned, his last grand idea, a lumber company, had been the end of everything. The O'Shaughnessy Lumber Company he had built from scratch in Bremerton, successfully shipping large logs across the ocean to Hawaii to build docks at a place called Pearl Harbor. Then, one horrible night, the OLC burned to the ground.

That night of the fire had broken more than their bank account; it had broken their spirits. Billi remembered how frightened she had been that cold, early morning her father came home reeking of smoky embers, hands scorched, his face a mask of hate, blackened with soot and streaked with ghostly white flesh where tears had left their path. He had shuffled past them straight for the sideboard and the whiskey. That time, his drinking did not stop, even when his wife packed their bags and moved herself and their children to an apartment in Olympia.

"Mom." Billi sat up, seeing the worry cross her mother's timeworn face. "Ray leaves in less than one month. Let's invite a few people over right before he leaves. He'll be gone until Thanksgiving. That is plenty of time to plan."

Her mother's shoulders rose and fell, her signal of hurt and defeat.

Billi took her mother's soft, plump hand in hers. "Let's go to St. Mary's and talk with Father Peretti tomorrow. Shall we?"

"Wonderful." Mrs. O smiled at her daughter. "'I'm so proud of you. I'll contact Father today." She patted her daughter's cheek and left the room, mumbling her revised list for the event.

Alone, Billi sank back on her bed. Tomorrow she would talk with the priest, but today she would find out if she had won the competition.

Billi strode across campus with a sturdy gait. She had selected her best skirt and blouse, reserved for special occasions, and had rubbed color into her legs and carefully drawn a line up the back, giving the impression of the rare nylons. This added effort made her feel elegant, secure, for today she needed every ounce of strength. Certain she had answered every question correctly Billi anticipated hearing the judges call her name as the winning contestant chosen for the journey to the land of the Rising Sun. She clutched her purse tighter. Inside the protective brown leather held her two dreams: the fan encased in purple silk and her engagement ring. She skipped up the stone stairs of Suzzallo Library, through the wooden doors, and up the curved staircase to where she had sat yesterday, each step bringing sheer confidence.

Inside the large room, twelve chairs were set facing the podium. She sat near the end so that crossing to the small elevated stage would be easier when her name rang out as the winner.

The proctor stepped to the center of the riser, adjusted his bow tie, and took a paper from his pocket.

"We appreciate all of your hard work and interest in our competition." His high voice droned on, "Our months of preparation have provided us the opportunity to send the most qualified among you across the sea to the wonders of Japan." He glanced at the unfolded paper, took a second look, and then continued. "Would Irwin Thomas please step up to the podium to receive his prize?"

Irwin Thomas? Billi didn't move as the others clapped their hands in mock approval. Irwin Thomas? She kept her rage below the surface as she followed suit, bringing her hands together in the clap of hollow defeat. Irwin had barely passed the course, and only due to the additional help from the professor. There must be some mistake.

She looked around the room. Why wasn't the professor in the library? Suddenly, she saw the tall, one-eyed stranger. He returned her glare from across the room. She quickly turned her attention back to the podium where the mousy Irwin gripped his prize piece of paper in his trembling hand, his broad grin exposing his crooked teeth. She forced a smile, stood, and approached the stage, her hand extended. Irwin's weak handshake only solidified her suspicion. The test had been rigged.

FROM THE SHADOWS, JACK WATCHED Billi exit, head held high. She had shown no emotion. Her response surpassed his expectations. A twinge of remorse shot through him. The professor had been correct when he had claimed Billi the best student in the group. But that had been the extent of their conversation before Fujihara became silent. Silent. The Japanese way. Jack replaced his unease with the confidence that Billi could stand up to the task, she would survive. He only hoped the ordeal would not destroy her.

THE TEARS BEGAN ONCE BILLI SAT safely inside her bedroom with the wallpaper of vines entwined with birdcages. She wanted to scream at the lifeless print, which seemed to mock her failure. How could this have happened? She threw her purse on her bed and kneeled over it. She shook the contents onto her white cotton bedspread. Her lipstick, handkerchief, comb, ring, and fan bounced into view. She snatched the ring and thrust it on her finger. It would never leave her hand again, she vowed, as she tasted the salty tears of defeat. She pulled the blue fan from its purple case and studied the design of the dragons. Why had Professor Fujihara given her this fan? He had been so confident she would win, always encouraging. He had taken the time to show her pictures of his village, just outside of Tokyo, and ask if she would deliver a package to his family. They were expecting her.

She did not know how, but certainly the one-eyed man had something to do with her losing. The one-eyed bandit. The cheat.

Billi threw the fan onto her bed in disgust, as if it had somehow caused this tragedy. It landed first on the top and then the hilt of black lacquer, the impact cracking the frame. She didn't care. She hated the fan and what it represented. As she lifted it, a small piece of wood remained on the bed. She picked up the wood and observed it would snap perfectly back into place. She began to work the pieces together when she noticed a small rolled piece of paper in the frame. Carefully, she pulled it from its hiding place.

Spare her were the only two words written in Japanese on the delicate oil paper.

She heard Eddy's voice calling as he came up the spiral stairs. He had just passed the fifth step with its telltale creak as she carefully put the paper back inside the fan and snapped the wood in place. She hurried to secure the loop of material around the netsuke as Eddy swung the door wide.

"Oh." He stood in the doorway, hesitant to enter, comprehending the trail of tears on her face. "Well." He leaned against the doorjamb. "That settles that. Onward and upward. Ray will be relieved. And, I have to admit, I am too." He crossed the room and flopped onto the bed next to her. "Go on and have your good cry, and we'll take you out dancing tonight. The Coon Chicken it is. You need a little live music to stir the soul."

Billi examined her brother. He would make a great attorney if their mother had her way, and a wonderful father if Dahlia had hers. He seemed unflappable and content with the direction in which these two women steered his life. His eventual course established. She put the fan in her bedside drawer, away from view but not from her mind. Going dancing with the gang would indeed cleanse the soul.

SEVEN

DAVID BUCHANAN SAT MOTIONLESS in the darkened room of his superior.

"Are you certain?" Jack demanded again. "Raymond Richardson, father Isaac, mother Gladys Cousins?"

David nodded, fearful of the vile mood which had settled on Jack at the mention of the family names.

Jack paced as his words grew louder. "Holy Christ. Did you contact the major at Randolph Field?"

Again, David bobbled his head, afraid to speak.

"All right, send him to Texas." Jack stopped behind David and growled. "Do it now."

"Randolph Field." David hunched forward then slid from his chair and scurried to the door.

As the door shut behind the useless man, Jack smashed his glass against the wall. He watched as the liquid dripped down the stucco onto the broken shards. He hoped Randolph Air Base, the West Point of the Army, would satisfy Mrs. Richardson. More importantly, he hoped Ray's training would keep him away until Jack finished with the young pilots fiancée.

His mind drifted to Billi. She did not appear to be a gold digger, but there were obviously more complexities to that long-legged gazelle than he had anticipated. Maybe he should have chosen the woman with the big tits, as David had insisted.

RAY PARKED HIS PLYMOUTH in front of the Coon Chicken Inn on a suburban street in Lake City. The twelve-foot-high "coon head" caricature of a black porter that served as the door offered a controversial welcome to the white crowd that flocked there to dance and dine on coon-fried steak or the baby-coon special.

The gang of five spilled out of Ray's car, anxious to celebrate. Eddy took Dahlia's arm and led the way. Dahlia looked up at him and smiled, her soft blonde hair swaying gently with her stride. Danny, hot on their heels, almost bumped into Ray when he stopped for a moment to adjust the bottle of bourbon he had slid down his pants.

"Remember to stay close," Ray pushed the bottle of bourbon further under his jacket, hiding it.

Ray swung Billi in front of him before following the others inside the broadly smiling mouth of the winking black-face entrance. The sound of the live band lured them forward to a booth just off the dance floor. Ray took the center seat as a waiter made his way over with menus adorned with the same caricature of the coon head, which also could be found on the water glasses, placemats, and walls.

When their soft drinks arrived, Eddy kept watch while Ray liquored up all drinks except Danny's, his youth precluding him from this particular entertainment. A sense of morality existed among the old friends, even in their illegal endeavors.

Having finished their meals, and most of the bottle of booze, Ray grabbed Billi and led her to the dance floor. Today they would mark as a day to remember.

"Bil, I have wonderful news." His voice sounded low, urgent. "The Air Corps recruiter called me today and I'm off to Texas."

"You are?"

"Isn't it wonderful?"

"When?" She held her breath.

"Day after tomorrow."

She stopped moving and stared at him. What just happened? First her hopes of travel were smashed and now Ray announced his imminent departure.

"Day after tomorrow?" she repeated as if in a stupor.

"Six a.m. my train pulls out."

"But…" Her mind could not piece it together.

He kissed her long and tenderly. "It's what we wanted. I can be back earlier and we can get married. I'd marry you right this minute if I could," he pressed her close. He attempted to sing along as they swayed to the beat of the band's soulful rendition of "Body and Soul." They held each other long past the last chord reverberated in the room.

The band roared to life blaring the top hit "Boogie Woogie Bugle Boy," and the dance floor filled with jive-happy, high-steppin' swingers. Billi twisted and kicked at the air, a pure physical reaction to Ray's announcement. Weeks had shortened to days and hours. In less than forty-eight hours, Ray's train would carry him into his new future, where talk of war overshadowed all else as the main subject.

Eddy broke through the crowd, grabbed his sister, swinging her around and then holding her tight to him. "How are you doing, Bright Eyes?"

"I've never been so scared."

"Me either, Bil. Me either."

Ray cut in, the liquor moving his feet a bit slower than the rhythm. Sweat poured from his forehead, and Billi saw it in his eyes too: fear. The unknown settled upon them. She led him outside. He staggered against a tree and sank down the trunk, plopping on the pine-needle-covered earth.

"Sit," he commanded.

"Don't think I'll always be taking orders from you," she quipped as she lowered beside him.

Ray half-tackled, half-bear-hugged her as he pawed at her breasts. "Damn, I want to rip your clothes off and—"

"Raymond Richardson." She straightened up. "Stop that at once."

"I like virgins," he slurred. "They make good wives. And you, my dear, will be the best."

His hand sailed through the air with his last word, propelling him backward as he passed into unconsciousness.

Billi sat beside him and ran her fingers though his black hair. "I want to rip your clothes off too, Ray. But not until I'm your wife." She kissed his cheek and sat back against the tree, gathering her legs up to her chest.

The evening stars twinkled in the clear sky above the neon light of the Coon Chicken. The heavens that held so many bright stars had become her competition. Ray's love of flying now took hold of him as his mistress. Since childhood he had always watched the heavens, and at night he would fill the blackness above with his dreams of flying faster, farther. Then he had taken his solo flight with the help of his father's fortune, and set his course. Being a pilot would be his life, their life. Billi set her hope on the stars above and prayed to the night sky for Ray's safe and swift return; then she closed her eyes and envisioned an October wedding.

"How are the lovebirds?" Eddy lit a cigarette and leaned against the tree.

She didn't open her eyes to answer. "Just like an old married couple. He's sleeping and I'm dreaming."

"Correction." Eddy put on his legal voice. "He's passed out."

"But I'm still dreaming."

Danny appeared behind them and hovered over Ray. "I want to go with Ray. I want to join up and fly."

"Nonsense." Billi pushed herself up. "You're still in high school. Besides, you're already in the ROTC. That's enough joining for this group for quite some time. Now, let's get my fiancé on his feet."

BILLI MOUNTED THE STEPS to her home, dazed. The forty-eight hours had come and gone in the blink of an eye. And now Raymond had departed. As she reached the top step, she shivered. The train station had been cold and bustling in the early morning light. No warmth could exist in such a place that took your loved one away from you. Only she and Mr. Richardson had stood there waving away her heart. And while Ray's father had been all bravado and encouragement for the adventure his son embarked upon, his eyes had moistened as the engine pulled the cars into the distance.

Her mother and Eddy stood at the door in deathly silence, for which Billi felt thankful. She could not speak her mind and heart, for they smashed against each other as a jumble of uncontrollable contradictions. She had cried, laughed, and cried again as Ray confidently told her of their future. Bright and bold, his words had painted the empty canvas of their years to come.

"Eddy, quick, get your sister some coffee."

"Looks to me like she needs something stronger."

They each took one of Billi's arms and sat her in her mother's special chair in front of the fireplace where an unseasonal and expensive fire flickered with warmth and comfort.

"Should I be this scared?" she asked no one in particular.

"No." They insisted in unison as Eddy headed for the kitchen.

"There will be no war, and Raymond will come home safe." Her mother gently lifted a strand of loose hair that hung over Billi's eyes. "And Raymond's departure expedites his return and the wedding."

"Well put, Mother." Eddy picked up Billi's hand and put the cup of coffee between her fingers.

"Was Mrs. Richardson there?" her mother asked softly.

"Too early for her," Billi half spat. The more she learned of her future mother-in-law's habits, the more she speculated why Raymond had spent so much time in their home.

"Oh." Mrs. O brightened, obviously pleased she had not missed a social opportunity after all. "I'll fix you some breakfast, dear." She hummed her way into the kitchen.

"Cheer up, Bil." Eddy patted his sister's shoulder. "Ray is the best. Only the best for my sister. Oh." He stood and crossed to the table reclaiming an envelope he had placed there earlier. "Eileen stopped by." He extended the note toward her. When she did not move to take it, he placed it on her lap, the exacting script of Eileen's pen, face up, reaching out into the room.

He hovered a moment then spoke. "Well, I'm off to work, but we'll do something together later. So, be my gal and smile."

Billi stood, handed him back the coffee and bolted from the room. She sailed past her mother at the stove, and out the back door.

Eddy followed her to the kitchen and stood beside his mother, shaking his head.

"Oh dear. Take off your nylons first," Mrs. O called after her. She shrugged her shoulders and returned her focus to her griddle and potato pancakes. "I wanted her to wear her good pair this morning. I did not want Ray's last vision of her to be bare-legged."

He crossed to the window and watched as his sister streaked through the yard to a tall cedar tree with its graceful branches swooping down and then skyward. The morning dew still shimmered on the green branches, draping the tree in sparkling finery.

"Well, did she?" Mrs. O demanded.

Eddy watched as Billi ducked under the foliage, hesitated at the base, half hidden, her lean legs still in view. He saw her kick off her heels, carefully roll down her precious stockings, and then place them inside her shoes before being swallowed up the tree.

"Yes." He turned back to his mother and took a sip from the cup he held. "She'll be okay. Leave her up there for a while." He snatched a German potato pancake off the griddle, flipped it into the air to cool it, and hurried through the kitchen door.

BILLI SAT IN HER SPOT, back up against the reddish bark, breathing the unmistakable fragrance of the cedar. Their tree. The three of them had raced to the top of this glorious hiding place on every sort of occasion. From this perch, the world became theirs and all else fell away. The tree had grown along with them, through sorrow and joy, its strength and comfort shielding them from the outside world.

The sun rose higher over the snowcapped Cascade Mountains, with Lake Washington as smooth as shimmering blue glass below. She looked at the branch off to the right that Ray had claimed; Eddy's arched to her left. Their carved initials declaring their branches had expanded with time and were somewhat illegible. She liked it that way, private, secret. She breathed deeply and felt the stress of the past few hectic days drip down the long greenery. Nothing could harm her here.

EIGHT

Jack sat in his car across the street from the tall, white Victorian house at 304 30th South. Earlier, he had watched Billi stumble up the stairs to the front door and her brother leave as he listened to David snore beside him, emitting the rotten stench of last night's booze. He would have to replace the worthless Buchanan. But not yet.

He checked his watch. Eight-twenty, still far too early for a social call. In forty minutes, the striking young woman's life would drastically alter. He brushed aside his nagging voice of remorse. He had taken everything from her. He knew she had far surpassed everyone on the exam and by rights should be packing her luggage to sail to the land that edged closer to declaring war on America. And now Raymond. He hoped she would be more vulnerable, more malleable, now that her boyfriend had been whisked safely away. Reviewing the past few days, he remembered her icy glare when he had picked up the silk-encased gift from her professor that day of the testing that still made him shift uncomfortably.

David shifted too and lifted his hat, wincing into the sun that streamed in through the windshield. "House needs paint," he remarked in an attempt to cover for his nap.

"Your snoring and breath did most of the damage," Jack snarled, rolling down the window. But he had noticed the condition of the stately home upon arrival. While the grass and garden were impeccable, the tall structure with its scalloped siding could indeed use the artistic touch of a good paintbrush. He fixed his gaze on the side yard where a trellis adorned with climbing baby yellow roses arched over a statue. The image, placed mid-yard sat upon large boulders. Her hands were pressed together in prayer; her light-blue shawl covered most of her brown hair and flowed into the white folds of her gown as she overlooked the passerby. Adorned in newly applied paint, she gazed back at him, all-knowing, at peace. He inadvertently nodded back at the Blessed Virgin Mary in her tranquil setting, protected by the trellis and a tall cedar tree in the distance.

Forgive me for what I am about to do, Jack silently prayed to the holy image. *And keep her safe.*

At 9:02, Jack watched Mrs. O'Shaughnessy open her front door and react to their appearance. Their long trench coats and hats were the kind that people associated with trouble.

"How may I help you?" She closed the door slightly.

"Mrs. O'Shaughnessy?" David took the lead in his slick, salesman voice as Jack listened to him twist the truth. "We're here from National Defense. May we come in?"

"My son will be home around ten. Can you come back then?"

Jack noted how calmly and swiftly she had formed the lie. He had made certain the law office of Bowen and Cohen, where Eddy interned, would keep the aspiring attorney at bay far beyond the average workday.

"We are calling on all of your neighbors and really would prefer not to have to come back."

"Well..." She hesitated.

"Thank you." Jack tipped his hat and eased past the door, leaving David apologizing as he entered behind him.

"Unhöflich," she sputtered, closing the door behind them.

"Nein, Frau O'Shaughnessy, we are not impolite, we are here on behalf of America. I'm Jack. Sorry for the disruption."

She blanched, breathless, focusing on the black patch that covered the larger man's right eye.

"May we sit?" he asked in a friendly manner.

She nodded.

Jack chose what he thought to be Mrs. O's favorite overstuffed rocking chair with the intricately carved base boasting of old-country craftsmanship. Three white, crocheted antimacassars covered the back and arms of the well-worn plush upholstery. He placed his hat on his lap as he sat, taking in his surroundings. The room appeared as neat and orderly as he had expected.

David waved their hostess into a chair as she tossed an insolent sneer in Jack's direction. Her response only confirmed Jack's suspicion—he sat in her prized spot.

Jack cracked a rare smile at the woman who lowered herself into a seat across from him. He admired her bearing, which showed nothing of her hardships he had unearthed when snooping into the O'Shaughnessys' private lives, searching for a key to bind his plotting. Life with her ex-husband had been a roller-coaster ride of highs and lows. Unfortunately, she had banked on the highs and still held the airs of that society. Point taken.

"Like I said..." She broke the awkward silence watching David's every move as he slowly circled her living room. "My son will be home around—"

"We are not here for your son." David adopted an authoritarian tone.

"He's in law school and exempt from service at this time," she continued, undaunted.

"We are not here regarding your son," David repeated.

"I am block captain." Her voice deepened as she sat taller, not budging. "And I have not had any neighbor report a visit from you, I might add. So how can I help you?"

Such bullish strength, Jack mused. He knew her secrets. It had taken time to discover that this pious woman who adorned her yard with the Virgin Mary had the bad habit of collecting small cut-glass objects. It seems she cherished fine cut crystal salt and pepper shakers, the kind found in elegant homes and restaurants. The same ones that now lined her china cabinet.

David stopped his exploring and stood above her. "We would like to talk to your daughter."

"Who?"

"Billi." Jack's announcement echoed with his bluntness.

"Billi?" The older woman laughed, half nervous, half amused. "Billi is not here at the moment." When the men did not speak, she hurried to fill the void. "What has she done? Billi is a good girl. What do you want with her?" Her voice rose with every question.

"It's nothing really." David attempted to be charming. "Just a few questions about the competition she entered."

"I knew that competition would lead to no good." Mrs. O spoke before she could stop herself. "She is not in the house."

Jack looked directly at her, rocking back in her chair. "She came in."

"You've—you've been following her? Why?" She rose. "I'm calling Eddy."

David intercepted her. "Please go and get her." His words were spoken evenly, the veiled threat apparent.

"I can't." Her chin rose as she spoke.

"Why?"

"She's up a tree." Her voice bellowed like a storm through branches.

The two men exchanged looks of uncertainty.

"We'll wait." Jack placed his hat on the table next to him, settling back farther into the sway of the rocker.

Mrs. O'Shaughnessy swept toward the kitchen. "Coffee?"

David fell in behind her.

BILLI STIRRED. SHE HAD DOZED in the secure arms of the branches. A motorboat sputtered across the lake, the white froth of its wake glimmering in the sun. All would be well, she convinced herself. The need for a strong cup of her mother's brew lured her into action. That would help settle her nerves and fortify her determination as she counted the days until Ray returned.

With a light heart and the inspiration to write her first letter to him, something she had promised to do daily, she scampered down the limbs, brushed an ant off her shoe, and headed for the back door.

The smell of strong coffee greeted her as she followed the aroma and pushed through the swinging door that separated the kitchen from the dining room and hesitated. The large wood pocket doors leading from dining room to living room usually stood wide open. This closed position signaled her mother would be entertaining, which meant cookies. Billi hurried through the dining room, but then abruptly halted in the archway. She should have noticed the wooden doors were not pulled tight. She should have read her mother's subtle signals. But she stood now in full view of the man she held responsible for destroying one of her deepest dreams.

She saw her mother wince and comprehended the shortcomings of her appearance—barefoot, twigs in her hair, and sap on her skirt.

"Come in, Billi." Jack stood offering her the overstuffed rocker.

She stomped into the room, brushing past the one-eyed monster. Spotting the note from Eileen on the coffee table, she snatched it up and stuffed it in her jacket pocket before sitting next to her mother.

"Did I mention Billi is engaged?" Mrs. O blurted out, patting her daughter's knee. "Show them the ring, dear."

Billi lifted her finger in an unladylike fashion toward Jack.

TWO HOURS LATER, JACK AND DAVID left the house with nothing except the shock of seeing the ring. Jack had recognized the dinner ring on Billi's slim finger instantly. But the reappearance of the three diamonds he shelved as a private matter. He turned his thoughts back to the two stubborn women. The mother and daughter had only grown more suspicious as David had repeatedly changed his approach, telling them nothing of the plan but imploring Billi's help. He had insisted every able-bodied person needed to volunteer in anticipation of a war that soon would spill across the great ocean and penetrate American shores.

While Billi sat slumped in speechless defiance, her mother had rattled on, parrying every avenue David broached. Jack had half a mind to put this stout debater in charge of interrogation. She had exhausted him.

They would have to wait. A bit of time remained before drastic measures were needed to procure Billi's services and he would use that small window to his advantage. The one thing that stuck out in his mind was how swiftly Billi had deliberately hidden that cream-colored envelope with the Japanese characters swirling across it. He hadn't even seen her take it, distracted at that point by the mother. What a team. He unconsciously spun the black ring he wore on the little finger of his left hand, a nervous habit, and made his decision. He would have them both followed.

NINE

THE BUS STOPPED AT 30TH SOUTH at the crest of the hill leading up Jackson. Eddy stepped down in pure exhaustion before trudging toward home. The day had disappeared; the summer sun arched toward the Olympic Mountains. Every attorney in the firm had needed his help today. He would welcome being back at the University of Washington in the fall. Hopefully, with the money he made this summer, he would not have to work during the always intense school year. Possibly he should join the navy, which would pay for his schooling, if he lived.

The likelihood of the United States joining a war seemed to be inching closer. Eddy had always been a great observer of man, and from his perspective, even though President Roosevelt swore he had no intention of dragging the country into the growing conflict overseas, no one listened to the commander in chief. Man was on the march, blinders on and guns ready.

Eddy worried about the crumbling world. In these unsettling times, he could feel it in his bones that as tired as Hitler's army might appear, the Fuhrer would not stop in Europe. Hitler remained stubborn in his broad-reaching desire. "German to the bone," as his mother would say.

His mother had often told why she had left behind her mother and six sisters, to escape the temper of her "German to the bone" father, the best butcher in Jamestown, New York. She loved to tell the story of the day she made her decision to leave. The entire family had been riding home in the wagon after visiting some relatives' farm for a wedding, when an injured doe staggered into the clearing before them. An arrow dangled from her long neck, and her large eyes seemed to be pleading. Her father had quickly remedied the situation with his rifle. The beautiful creature fell before them. Grabbing his knives, her father began his butchering right then and there, instructing the girls to help. Their special pinafores became splattered with blood, as they had lifted the sides of meat into the wagon. Dusk had fallen around them and the scent of the blood brought the wolves. As the carnivorous creatures circled the wagon, her older sister took the reins while her father and mother steeled themselves to kill and protect. With one well-placed bullet, the lead wolf fell, and the others backed off.

But it had been the beauty of the doe's big brown eyes contrasted with the frenzied eyes of her father as he sliced open her belly, pulled out her intestines, and tugged at the beautiful creature's limbs that so alarmed Mrs. O as a child. At that instant she vowed to get as far away from her father as possible. It had been easy, his mother claimed, to distract the young James E. O'Shaughnessy, the ambitious clerk in the mercantile store, and point him, with ring on her finger, from the Northeast to the promises of the Northwest.

Eddy sluggishly continued around the corner toward home. His mother could take care of herself, if she could stay out of trouble. And the same held true of Billi, if she could stay on track. His darling Dahlia, his delicate sweetheart, with her contagious laugh rounded out his list of ladies. He would hate to see her laughter stop, the joy drained from those lovely brown eyes. But now he didn't just think about Mom and Sis and Dahlia. Raymond had joined his lineup of worries.

"God help us, Ray, keep your head down and wings level," he muttered to himself as he started down the block. "And come home fast."

The nagging thought presented itself again. If he did enlist and he could be sent away, who would be left to care for his women? He looked down the block toward his white-shingled home and spied Danny, easily recognized with his curly red hair, sitting on the steps. Danny, his shadow, would be left. While Danny practiced in the ROTC, he seemed far too young to tackle the cruel aspects of war. He came to his conclusion as he watched the skinny kid. Eddy would enlist to save his women and the Dannys of the world.

"Hey, Eddy," Danny yelled, running toward him. "Goddamnit, Eddy, there's—"

"Don't swear, Danny."

"But damn, Eddy, these guys were at your house today."

The sun set, drawing the shadow of the tall homes across the street over them. He pulled Danny into the darkened path between two rhododendrons. "Slow down. Facts first."

"I came by about nine this morning, after my paper route, with some flowers for Billi. You know, because Ray had left. Jeez, Ray is really gone. I really want to learn how to fly."

"Ray will be back. Now, what were you saying?"

"Well, I promised him I'd look after Billi. Oh, not that you aren't too. He just figured Billi needs two men to watch over her."

"I agree. Good plan. Go on."

"Well, as I came up the hill, I saw this big black sedan. And just then, these two guys get out of it and head right up your steps."

"What did they look like?"

"One tall, one medium. I couldn't see their faces because they had on hats and long coats."

Eddy knew the type. They swarmed the courthouse. Cops. Had his mother pinched something again? He had been able to persuade others not to prosecute a few embarrassing times. And when his mother ascertained his gift for debate, she had steered him into law school.

"What did they want?"

"I hung around for an hour." Danny kicked a rock, head down in his obvious disgrace at not knowing the answer. "But I had to go. I just got back, but no one's answering the door."

Eddy broke through the bushes at a dead run. In a flash Danny's wiry frame scooted in front of him, hell-bent on helping. The two burst into the dark house as one.

"Mom?" Eddy shouted.

"Billi?" Danny chimed in.

"Billi's not here." Mrs. O's voice sounded unperturbed, devoid of emotion.

Eddy went into the dark living room to find his mother sitting in the chair opposite her rocker.

"Where's Billi?" He stood over her as he turned on the brass lamp with the marble base.

She winced as the light shot across her face. "In Japantown with Eileen rehearsing for heaven knows what. That cute Kenny came by for her and promised to bring her home safe. Such a nice boy. Always makes me smile. Eddy," she continued in a faraway tone "build me a fire and push my rocker up close."

"I'll get it." Danny ran to fetch the wood and kindling off the back porch.

In silence Danny struggled his load of cut wood back into the room. He dropped to his knees, pushed back the chain-linked screen, and began to assemble the makings of a fire.

Eddy hadn't budged. He stood watching his mother then moved to help Danny lift the rocker closer to the burgeoning flames. As he touched the damp velvet upholstery, he caught a whiff of baking soda.

"Mom, what happened to your rocker?"

She answered him in German. "Übel"

"What'd she say?" Danny whispered.

"Evil." She repeated for him in the common language of all Americans. For every household attempted to put their pasts in their native countries behind them and assimilate into the grand melting pot.

Danny looked up at Eddy, who saw the fear in the youth's eyes.

Eddy suppressed his concern. He surmised one of the men had sat in her beloved chair. When the huffy dowager Mrs. Goodman had lowered her oversized posterior onto the gold crushed velvet and demanded the newly divorced Mrs. O'Shaughnessy send her children to boarding school, his mother had escorted her out through the tall parlor doors. The minute Mrs. Goodman's large behind had sashayed out of their home, Mrs. O tossed baking soda and salt on the chair, then wiped it down to get rid of the "evil" that had taken up residence, ever so briefly, on her throne.

He signaled to Danny and they inched the rocker closer to the growing warmth of the flames.

"Who was here, Mom? Who were they?"

Mrs. O shot her son a look. She informed him that some of the neighbors had noticed the two men, but no one else had these intruders enter their homes or sit in living rooms. Claiming her status as block captain, she had questioned each resident up and down both sides of her block and alerted them to be on the watch and report visits from strangers or unfamiliar cars. Especially to report any sightings of the tall man with the patch over one eye.

Know thy enemy and where he travels.

She pointed at Danny. "You keep an eye out too." Then her big brown eyes shifted back to Eddy. "They want Billi." The shrillness of her voice echoed off the walls and hung in the air like a dark cloud.

"That's ridiculous." Eddy tried to sound unshaken. "What for? What are they claiming she has done?"

"Nothing." His mother regained her senses. "They want her on behalf of National Defense supposedly. But they were lying, Eddy. They were bad men."

"They can't have her." Danny stepped from the half shadows. "They can't have her." His slight form shook with rage. "I'm in ROTC. We don't knock on doors to take…to take girls. I'm going down to headquarters right now and—"

"It's okay, Danny." Eddy put his arm on Danny's shoulder. "I'll have the judge look into this." He felt the tension of his younger friend ease. "But Mom is right. Keep an eye on Billi."

"I will, I promise."

"She should be home shortly," Mrs. O interjected.

"I'll go and wait for her at the bus stop. That little squirt Kenny couldn't do much against those two guys."

Danny dashed out the door before either of them could say another word.

Eddy moved to the tall window and watched him run back through the dark toward Jackson, the direction they had come from. He had to admit he did feel a bit more at ease with both Kenny and Danny as Billi's escorts. Kenny the star quarterback and Danny the running back were an untouchable team that had led Garfield High School to the football championship. And it was their teamwork that Eddy now banked on.

Eddy returned to his mother's side as the rocker sat empty and drying in front of the fireplace. He only hoped that his mother's scrubbing had indeed, once and for all, removed the evil that had entered their lives.

He controlled his voice and spoke softly, "Start at the beginning."

TEN

S LEEP HAD NOT BEEN HER COMPANION. The birds in their gilded cages stared down at Billi defiantly in the moon's light. She could no longer rest with their eyes trained on her. She hated the wallpaper she had once prized and promised herself she would paint over it in the morning.

Billi twisted in her covers and her thoughts moved to the afternoon spent in final dress rehearsal with Eileen. The physical activity had been much needed, as she had let the music and movements be her escape. But now in the shadows of her room, the only connection she could make of all that had happened this week surfaced as her upcoming performance at Bon Odori. The traditional celebration for family members who had passed away brought ghosts of its own to her home. This would be her last dance with the fans, she silently promised the birds in the cages.

Wisely, Eileen comprehended how deeply Billi's sense of failure burned, and feared her friend would no longer seek to embrace the Japanese culture. So she had sent the note of encouragement this morning scrolled in her precise language. But Eileen had a vain spot as well. She needed Billi for the fan dance they had so ardently practiced. Besides, she bubbled with eagerness to show off to the community the exquisite talent of the round-eye.

The visit from the two men had shaken her. She picked up the letter she had started to Ray and kissed it.

"Ray, come home and make this all go away."

Her fists hit her bedspread as the coolness of her tears soaked into her pillow. Finally, drained, her eyes closed in slumber.

BILLI EXAMINED HER WHITE MAKEUP and the black charcoal lines she had extended into graceful curves in an attempt to appear Asian. Unfortunately, the rich blue of her kimono only heightened the coloring she had inherited from Irish father. She pondered her reflection long and hard. This would be the last time she would appear as the imitation of a geisha doll. She slowly dipped her fingers into the thick cold cream and then rhythmically, with great purpose, applied the cream that would wipe away her ambitions.

The dance had drawn quite the crowd as the two young women had synchronized to perfection, fans fluttering, across the stage. Even Auntie Katsuko had pronounced it so.

Billi watched as the black and white of her makeup mixed as she pulled the rag across her face, exposing a pink streak of flesh in its wake.

The color of the skin of those sitting in the audience had been mostly golden. Her mother, Eddy, and Danny had occupied the same row as the Nakamuras, her mother's ample bosom so hardy next to the diminutive, ghostly appearance of Mrs. Nakamura. Billi had glimpsed her professor walking past the table of intricate bonsai plants on display, their delicate limbs sculpted to perfection. But the professor had disappeared, melted into the crowd. She suspected his behavior reflected his shame of her failure that would not allow him to acknowledge the success of her performance.

Eileen giggled as she entered the small, offstage room. "If I didn't know any better, I'd say your brother was flirting with me."

"Don't let Dahlia know. She might act delicate, but I tried to take a piece of chocolate from her once. I almost lost my hand."

"Eddy said they will be waiting by the food tables." She sat next to Billi.

"Figures. Danny is a growing kid, and if someone puts a plate of food in front of him, it's gone. Even seaweed and wasabi won't stop him."

"His red curls looked so strange amongst all the black straight hair," Eileen remarked, picking up the cream.

"I guess God has a plan for all of us."

"Whose god?" Eileen kidded.

"Mine. The one who made so many shapes and sizes and then forgot to teach tolerance."

"Don't be upset, Billi. Everything will be all right. Besides, we will always be friends. Even after we are married. The kind that can talk about anything. Even their gods." Eileen took Billi's hand and gave it a squeeze of reassurance.

JACK PULLED HIS CAR OFF SUTTER STREET into the underground parking of the Sir Francis Drake Hotel. It felt good to be back in San Francisco, to know the streets and embrace the city's life again. He had chosen this hotel for his operation, familiar with the special intricacies of the building. It would afford him complete privacy, put him close to his contacts, and provide a means of escape, if necessary. He stepped past the shining doors into the far right elevator, pulled out his special key and inserted it into the elevator lock, then pressed the button for the mezzanine floor. When the elevator stopped, the doors opened to a hidden room. He pushed back the heavy curtain then opened the glass door to the small concrete-walled room that would be his headquarters. He used his special key again to release the elevator.

He looked around and smiled as he placed his briefcase next to the phone on the wooden table, the only piece of furniture besides two chairs he wanted in the secret room. Then he dropped to his knees and looked through the peephole in the floor which provided a view of the lobby below, just outside the elevators on the main floor, and waited.

It didn't take long before the blockish figure of Niles Duckworth sauntered in to view. Jack watched as he removed his hat, exposing his receding hairline, and waited for the far right elevator to arrive.

Once Duckworth entered the elevator, Jack stood and pressed the special button twice, signaling the elevator to stop on this hidden floor. He had grown to like and trust the odd man who he came to appreciate as a genius with puzzles and possessing unflappable patience. He wished he had a million Duckworths. Then possibly he could figure out a way to halt this damn war that steamrolled toward them.

The two men shook hands, then Duckworth watched his boss shut the curtain and the door behind him.

"How did you know about this place?" Duckworth contemplated the empty shelves.

"My father loaned the money to have this hotel built. They architect designed this structure just before Prohibition and, cleverly, this room is not even on the drawings."

"Convenient."

"Made for a very popular hotel in its time." Jack motioned toward one of the wooden chairs and continued as they both sat. "They stored the illegal booze in here then had a bellboy deliver the requested bottle to the rooms. So, what is happening at the Presidio?"

"Talk of a further embargo and freezing all Japanese assets." Duckworth laid it out as he had heard it.

"Well, that should make us even more popular. But then again, the amount of Nippon War Bonds being purchased has been skyrocketing here on our very own soil. Our Japanese neighbors are sending millions back to their home country to buy guns that will be used against us." Jack pushed his hand through his hair as he digested the news. "Christ. The president is all but asking for war."

Duckworth nodded as they were both fully aware of the American money flowing back to Japan from the various Japanese organizations across the country.

When the silence became too much, Duckworth posed the looming question. "How is the Seattle project going?"

"Slow. Resistant. It's been two weeks and we can't find anything to entice her to help." Jack sat now in his own defeat and spewed out the emptiness of his research. "She mesmerized the audience at Bon Odori. The damn professor showed up there too, but he made no attempt to contact her. Her brother is steadfast at work at the law firm. Mrs. O'Shaughnessy has opened concession stands at Mount Baker Beach and Madison Park Beach for the summer. Billi and this skinny kid, Danny, run Mount Baker. Her mother and Danny's sister, Dahlia, work the Madison Park stand. Or, as noted, Dahlia works while Mrs. O'Shaughnessy fraternizes with the wealthy patrons."

Duckworth cleared his throat. "Evidently, the rich built summer cottages along Madison Beach, where an electric train ran down the hills and emptied at the site used for the 1909 World's Fair."

Jack nodded, regarding the man across from him. He admired Duckworth's research and sturdy approach to any problem.

"There is nothing there. Damn it." Jack tossed his pen disgustedly onto the desk. "My plan will crumble and we will know nothing of Akio or his movements."

"Hoover won't mind. He doesn't think it's our job anyway. He says it's the navy's problem."

"It will be all of our problem when the damn Japs attack us. Any news on that front?"

Duckworth leaned forward. "General DeWitt is expecting you tomorrow morning at his office in the Presidio. It appears Magic has cracked more Japanese Purple codes."

"Yes. God bless our Army Signal Intelligence Service for creating that machine."

"Well, SIS is convinced things are heating up, needless to say. Tokyo is requesting the consulate's report on your old friends, the Heimusha Kai. Japan wants to be certain each group is making the expected donation to their coffers."

"Then maybe my report from last year did have an impact. Almost $17,000 was donated to the Japanese war trunks just from one group, the Heieki Gimusha Kai. Or Isshin Kai, as they call themselves now."

Duckworth, evidently caught in Jack's fervor, repeated what he had read. "Currently, there are eleven, but more likely twelve, differently named groups with members spread throughout the Twelfth Naval District alone. Right here on Sutter Street, under our very noses, the biggest Japanese organization continues mobilizing, collecting information and funds."

"Yes." Jack stretched. "Their consulates are very busy these days."

"Many of their priests, teachers, and business owners, especially those who travel, have been seen coming and going. And the latest report indicates they have expanded their search for more help in the event they attack us. They are paying for information regarding the Jewish, Negro, and anti-American activities."

Jack's head went back in frustration. "I hope our boys are thoroughly reading every damn word Magic is decrypting from Purple, because it's obvious our enemies have spread their spy nets beyond military to the unsuspecting everyday man willing to support their homeland. Do you have a list of names?"

"Just a few new ones." Duckworth retrieved the papers from inside his coat and slid them across to Jack.

Jack examined the papers intently, mumbling as he recognized the mounting situation.

"Any updates from ULTRA? Have they intercepted any new messages?"

"Nothing of interest yet." Duckworth frowned.

"Besides the Presidio and Station S on Bainbridge Island, have they been able to install any other secure teletype intercept sites?"

When his assistant shook his head no, Jack ran his hand through his hair. "What the hell are they waiting for?"

"A question, sir." Duckworth stood. "Do you believe what the kitchen worker in the South American Embassy relayed he had overheard last January? What our ambassador in Japan immediately reported to Washington?"

"About the attack on Pearl Harbor?"

Duckworth nodded.

"Just a matter of time. And if the president does tighten up the embargos, it could be Christmas Day. And they will be ruthless. Remember, the Japanese like surprises. They strike on a holiday or a day of rest and send the declaration of war minutes before they attack. It is their way."

"China 1894, Russia 1904."

Jack smiled at his associate's knowledge of details. "Their culture is steeped in ancient tradition, and how they declare war is one of them."

"So, you are heading back up to Seattle soon?"

"We both are. We need this plan to succeed at any cost."

BILLI TOOK A DEEP BREATH of the salt air that drifted over the water. She had sought her father's beach, the warm stones beneath her, as a means to think and piece together her situation. An eagle soared overhead, followed by chattering black crows and, of all things, bringing up the rear trailed a squawking duck. An odd pecking order. The crows must have found the duck's nest only to have the eagle raid it first. The eagle swooped toward the water, dodging the persistent assaults of the crows.

She envisioned Ray as the eagle, swift, strong, confident. But her heart went out to the duck, the innocent bird, the one who had lost her eggs. She folded the letter she had been composing to Ray as her father swayed down the hill to join her.

"Best you to the big rock, Bright Eyes," he challenged her, dropping his pants to reveal the rest of his one-piece swim suit.

She snickered as she watched him pick his way across the barnacles and mud, where an occasional clam spit a gusher up at him, before reaching the shallow waves of the outgoing tide. She loved him dearly: his white, bare arms flailing in the sunlight, his thick brown hands looking like gloves, and the once muscular legs now bowed with age and hard labor.

"Holy Mother of God, 'tis nippy," he announced as he waded out past his waist before diving in. He surfaced, spitting a mouthful of saltwater into the air like a breeching whale, then floated on his back. He was irresistible and she eagerly joined him in the refreshing saltwater. They swam down the beach a ways and floated in the heat of the sun. Peace reigned in these gentle waves that softly pushed them to the shore with the now-changing tide. A time to cherish settled over them as silence held them together.

"Are you worried about Raymond now, Bil?"

"No."

"Good. No point." His wet hair lay flat against his head as he bobbed on the surface. "Anything else you want to talk about with your dear old father?"

She weighed his questions, not certain of their origin, fixed a smile on her face and splashed in his direction. "Only how handsome you are going to look on my wedding day."

"Sure. I'll be the bee's knees for you, darlin'."

She paced herself as she swam along the shoreline, and then abruptly disappeared below the surface. Her arm shot up above the water, the butt end of a Dungeness crab firmly in her grip. With a splash, her smiling face broke the surface.

"Dinner," she announced. "No crab pots needed today."

Boiled in saltwater from the inlet, the crabmeat tasted sweet and the meat firm. Billi sat back and savored the meal, for tonight life simply existed, satisfying and serene. She cleaned the dishes as Mr. O walked back and forth, the length of the small cabin, his gait agitated, in contrast with his smile.

"Shall I get wood for a fire?" She started for the door.

"Oh, no darlin'. I'll go." He beat her to the door and scampered through it.

Billi opened the cupboard door to stack the clean dishes and paused. A chill ran through her and she inadvertently made the sign of the cross. A bottle of expensive Jameson whiskey faced her. She noticed the bottle remained unopened, an unlikely occurrence in this household, and wondered who had brought such a gift. The cabin's door rattled, and she shut the cupboard as she heard her father's labored breathing. He entered, face buried behind his armload of dry wood.

Billi put aside her question about the whiskey as the high pitched yipping of a small dog echoed into the cabin.

Mr. O dropped the wood on the hearth. "Finally." He brushed the dirt and chips of wood from his hands and turned excitedly back toward the door. "Bright Eyes, I have a bit of a surprise for you." He flung the door open, and a small brown dachshund puppy pranced in.

"A puppy?" Billi instantly lowered onto the floor beside the dog. His tail wagged uncontrollably and he piddled a bit in excitement.

"Yes, a puppy." Frowning with disgust he grabbed newspaper from the stack by the fireplace to cover the dog's indiscretion. "Karl," he shouted at the old man shuffling down the path toward the cabin, "I thought you said he was housebroken."

"He is, in my house." Karl Rebstock struggled his words out between breaths. "Hello, Billi. Like him?"

The wiener dog jumped on her, pulling at her hair, and licking her face.

"He's wonderful, Mr. Rebstock. Does he come with a name?"

"Up to you. Your dad thought you could use the companionship."

"Pepper," she announced. "Pepper." She picked him up looking directly into his shining brown eyes. "Now, you behave, young man."

He snapped at her nose.

"He's grand." She held him to her.

"He's a bit trained." Karl sat at the kitchen table. "The pick of the litter. You should have seen your father examining and reexamining the pups for days."

Billi stood, still clutching her new best friend, and placed a kiss on her father's cheek. "Thanks, Daddy."

"And he'll bark if there's anyone around." Her father blushed as he spoke. "Your mother won't mind. She always wanted one."

She kissed his cheek again, aware the gift was threefold. Something to keep her busy, a nod of continued love for her mother, and a bodyguard, of sorts. The thought of this small creature being her rescuer made her laugh. "Are you my new bodyguard?"

Pepper barked back at her, his confirmation of the pact.

Mrs. O rocked forward in her chair. "What kind of guard dog is this? Your father is more the fool than I remembered."

Pepper lay silently on the rug between the rocker and where Billi stood. As if he sensed the tension, his eyes, like the swinging hand of a metronome, moved back and forth between the two women as they argued.

"I've always wanted a dog and I can afford one now," Billi shot back.

"A dachshund? That man will be the death of me. And why 'Pepper'?"

At the sound of his name, the puppy jumped up into Mrs. O's lap. She giggled as he circled and then settled on her plump thigh.

"Pepper." Billi's voice became stern and her hand moved in the command. "Get down."

The brown-eyed puppy tilted his head at her, then jumped back to the floor.

"Impressive." Her mother smiled down at the tiny addition to the household. "How about some iced tea?"

Billi started toward the open kitchen door with Pepper on her heels and heard her mother giggle again as she watched the retreating wiggle of the small dog's tail. Four-legged joy had joined the family.

ELEVEN

For a brief moment, Jack had been allowed some respite. But his meeting with General DeWitt and personnel from the Office of Naval Intelligence that morning had only confirmed what Duckworth had already said. Fear thickened around the globe. Fear the United States new restrictions sanctioned against Japan, preventing war materials and oil from being shipped to their desperate islands, and, now, squeezing off the money for those supplies, would provoke vehement retaliation.

He drove out of the cool morning mist of San Francisco to the place of his youth, Hillsborough, where the sun shone on sprawling, opulent mansions of the once rich. He turned into the large circular driveway off San Raymundo toward the overstated brick Tudor of the Huntington family home. As he parked near the tennis court, he observed the fallen leaves still covered the surface, hiding the precise lines that defined the game, and felt his temper begin its familiar slow boil. Couldn't Lilly pick up a broom? His spoiled-to-the-core sister, whom he referred to as Frilly, obviously preferred to still live in the past. He stormed toward the kitchen door overlooking the small patch of garden. All but the red rose had been removed to make way for vegetables, yet another sign of the hardships his family had faced when the stock market had crashed twelve years ago. His family had scraped by until the year when everything changed. That year Jack had been a senior at Stanford, the year of his accident, the year his father committed suicide.

The kitchen smelled of hot biscuits and bacon. Bella swayed over the stove in time to the tune she hummed in the all-white kitchen, the choice of paint amplifying the dark-roast shade of her skin. Jack noticed immediately how much grayer she had become and put it down to the stress of trying to keep this household together.

"How about a kiss?"

Bella jumped at the sound of his voice, somehow landing facing him, spatula gripped in her right hand, ready to defend her kitchen and those she served.

"Why, who does you thinks you is, sneakin' inta mah kitchen like dat?" She started toward him, spatula still ominously raised. "An' here I am plum sure I done trained you up raht."

"You tried."

"Hmmph. Don't be tellin' me I needs ta do dat again." She stopped scolding long enough to offer her cheek.

Jack took her bulk into his arms and held her. Over the years she developed into the mother he wished his own had been. He had felt the spatula on his backside before, the force of her firm hand, and the warmth of her loving bosom. Now, Bella remained his true friend, confidante, and whom he sought when he needed strong willed advice, backed by common sense.

"Sit, baby, and takes dat ol' patch off. Dat eye needs fresh air."

She had sat watch over him after the accident and tended to his eye, working it back beyond the doctor's expectations. While his own mother had turned away from the thin scar that the blade had cut into his right eye, injuring it, Bella had instead insisted it gave him a distinguished look.

He had taken that look and made it all his own, cloaking it not only with the patch but with hatred and the need for revenge. His darkness fostered panic in the eyes of those who looked upon him. All but Billi. She had simply glared back. But she would come to look upon him differently soon.

"I asks where's you been?" Bella had her hands on her hips, not to be ignored.

"Work."

"Um-hum." She scrutinized him closely as he removed the patch and set it on the table. She put her hand, which smelled of bacon, over his good eye then held up three fingers before the misty covered orb.

"How manys?"

"Three."

"Hmmph. You doin' your exercises?"

Jack smiled slyly.

She gently slapped his cheek, turned, and headed back to her stove. She shoved two fresh biscuits onto a plate with three strips of bacon and set them before him with a jar of honey. Next came the coffee, strong and black. By the time she finally finished her bustling about, Jack had dipped the last of the honey-filled treats into his cup.

"How's Mom?"

"Huh eyes is gettin' her." She lowered into the chair across from him. "Theys worse. But the resta her is still, 'Bella come here, Bella do dis, Bella do dat.'"

They both laughed at her imitation of Mrs. Huntington, for while his mother held the title, Bella ran the house.

"How's Frilly?"

"Dat mirror's still her bestest friend." Her tone told of her displeasure.

"No beaux?"

"Hmmph. You'd believes she be da only filly ina stable. Days parades 'round here likes bucks in heat. I spends most uh mah times chasin' dem outta dis corral."

He smiled at her, knowing he would not want to be one of the bucks taken on by Bella.

"And Howard?"

Her big black eyes softened with her voice. "I's proud as can be. Why, dat boy is lahk you. Always up ta sumpin'. He done got his-self into school at night. He was spit shinin' one of his regular's new shoes and dat man done up an' give mah boy a hunred whole dollars an' tol' him ta gets hisself ta school. An' shore 'nuf, my boy done jus' dat. Da good Lord done sent dat man. Howard's doin' fine. Jus' fine."

They smiled at each other, her one son's success brightening the sorrow of the other son's disappearance.

Bella saw the question on Jack's lips and shook her head. "Nuthen' from Tommy. He gone."

Jack stood and kissed her forehead. "I guess it's time to wake up the ladies?"

"Hmm, hmm, hmm. Yous one brave man, yous goin' in your sistuhz room afore noon."

He left the patch on the kitchen table and mounted the back stairs to the second floor. Much had changed since his youth. The rooms were sparser now, not filled with guests or as much furniture. A drastic measure in drastic times. But they still had a roof over their heads. And with his salary and some of the investments his father had made beginning to pay off, life improved. But not before the furniture and much of his mother's jewelry had left the house. His father had given up too easily and had left in his wake of his selfish actions his son Jack to shoulder the outcome.

He remembered the last time he had seen his father. Bella had softly closed the door to his bedroom, leaving his father standing over him, looking down at the large white patch the doctor had placed over his eye. His father's hand had felt cool on his sweating forehead. Mr. Huntington, the stern banker, then did the unexpected. He had lowered onto the bed next to his only son and cried, his shoulders heaving, rising and lowering with the weight of his losses.

"I'm so sorry, son." His father wiped his tears. "I love her. I love you all. I hope you'll understand and forgive me."

In confusion and horror, Jack had watched the unrecognizable, broken man in his father's suit shuffle toward the door, then unexpectedly return to stand beside Jack. He removed the square black onyx ring with the diamond in its center from his hand and placed it on Jack's bedside table.

"Guard this for me," his father instructed him.

Jack shook off the memory that followed him down the hall and headed straight for the library on the second floor. Where Bella had the sanctuary of her kitchen, Jack sought refuge in the sturdy oak walls of the library. It had been his father's, like the ring. And like the ring, he now took it as his own.

Stretching before he sat at the desk, he snapped on the light and pulled pen and paper toward him. Once again, he tried to write what his mind knew to be the truth. The scribbling of Akio's "invention" that Jack had seen glimpses of, threatened to bring unmanageable horror and destruction. Jack knew Akio's creation would soon be at the American shores, sleek and dark and deadly. He stood, and twisted the ring in determination as he paced.

Exhausted, he sank into the green leather chair, finding its broad structure a cool comfort. Resting his head against the high back, he let some of his frustration dissipate into the calm of the room. His mind drifted to Seattle and that woman. How could he get Billi to grasp how vital a role she played in his scheme without exposing secrets? Even if he had to trick her, he would convince her and use her for the good of the country. His mind settled with his new conviction.

THE SOFT CHIMING OF THE CLOCK on the mantel broke into his sleep. He must have dozed off, relaxed for once, letting the familiar seduce his nerves into rest. His long night in foggy San Francisco's Chinatown had worn him thin. He had established the front he hoped would bring him the man he hated most on earth, Akio, the man who had betrayed him and become a constant threat.

He moved to the desk, pulled out his pocket-knife and flipped it open. The blade was sharp as always. He reached for a pencil to work the lead to a fine point, when his eye rested on a new object on the corner of the desk. Someone had framed a more recent photo from the newspaper of a gathering of military elite at a defense bonds fundraiser, with Jack standing among the group. He looked at the image of the very man who had approved his wild idea for this mission, and a ripple of tension snaked down his back.

War knocked at their door. And the blind were running the country. How could America continue to listen to the lullaby of pacifism?

He put down the pencil and flipped the blade closed. Curious he crossed the room to the fireplace. His father had been brilliant in many ways. Like a good banker he had made certain there were places to secure valuables and always had a backup plan. Jack slid open the small wooden drawer neatly concealed in the paneling to the left of the hearth. He lifted the Browning handgun, its weight comforting, and removed it from its tan tooled-leathered holster. An unopened box of shells remained in the drawer. He flipped open the gun's chamber, exposing six bullets, waiting to find their mark. After securing the weapon back in its hiding place, he moved to the large wood panel to the right of the fireplace and pressed his weight against it. The panel moved ever so slightly on its hidden hinges. More importantly, it had not made the slightest sound. Excellent. He closed the panel tight. Why his father had built these hidden stairs that led down to the large living room would go unanswered, another secret he had taken to the grave.

Restless, Jack wandered down the hall to his mother's room and softly knocked before stepping inside. She rested with her back against the massive wood headboard. Her breakfast and coffee sat untouched on a tray on the empty side of the bed that had belonged to her husband. She waved him close and he bent to kiss her soft cheek.

"Good morning, Mother."

"You need a shave and a shower," she informed him as her thin hand sailed through the air and caught his sleeve. For all her frailness, strength remained in her grip. "Sit."

He did. They chatted about nothing as she asked all the usual questions. Did he have a girl? How was his law practice going? He lied through them all. Her shining star shone so brilliantly, she couldn't see the real person behind the glare.

JACK SAT IN HIS SEATTLE APARTMENT and attempted to control his anger. He had spent his first week back on Boylston looking out the bay windows at the trees, and pacing relentlessly waiting for Billi to decide. Today had not brought him any different information. He looked down at his father's ring on his left hand as it rested on his makeshift desk.

"Guard this for me." He heard his father's voice and twisted the onyx stone surrounding the small diamond from view. He could not be the failure his father had been. Faced once again with the reality of his dilemma, he picked up the phone and dialed.

"David, anything?" He listened, then growled into the receiver, "I've read the reports. It's panther piss. Get me something. Make something up." He paused for a moment. "What did you just say? Yes, bring me those. Now."

Jack shuffled photographs into a file before looking out at the large oak trees that lined Boylston. His trip to San Francisco had been successful. Everything was in place in the Bay Area's Chinatown. Not unlike Seattle, the Asian community in San Francisco had its own set of boundaries and rules. Billi remained the illusive piece to his plotting. Risky as the plan appeared, she had to be willing to see its importance. Once he convinced her, he knew his mission would be successful. It had to be. So much rested on her decision.

It hadn't taken long before he heard the knock at the door and signed with relief.

"Open." He rubbed his bad eye and put the patch back on, partially concealing the scar.

David entered with three letters. Raymond Richardson had been busy. His dull letters to Billi and Eddy had been of no use, but now they presented a twist. Jack opened the top letter addressed to Danny and smiled. In his hand he held—he hoped—the answer to his prayers. He would set a trap. Old habits die hard, and that was precisely what he was counting on.

TWELVE

Two of Ray's letters had arrived at once. When Billi flipped them over to open them, she detected the seal had been broken on each envelope. Someone had read them before her. Angry, she stuffed them in her pocket, called Pepper, and headed out back. She ducked below the branch of their cedar tree.

"Stay." She held out her hand in the signal toward her new shadow. "And give a big bark if anyone is coming."

The small dog circled, then plopped down in the cool shade, his accustomed routine, and watched Billi disappear up the cedar. Perched on her branch, she read every word carefully in the event a clue as to who would tamper with her mail presented itself. Ray claimed excitement at meeting Pepper. His training swiftly with more and more responsibilities. He had read and believed every word of *Winged Defense* by General William Mitchell, the outspoken proponent for creating an air force. Ray became convinced, as this great man had preached to the other factions of the service, that the next war would be fought and won by those who controlled the air. And to prove his point, and convince Billi of his motivation, Ray copied some of Mitchell's words.

Those interested in the future of the country, not only from a national defense standpoint but from a civil, commercial and economic one as well, should study this matter carefully, because air power has not only come to stay but is, and will be, a dominating factor in the world's development.

Ray went on to report General Mitchell had spent time in Asia and Hawaii and had returned to predict the Japanese would attack Pearl Harbor.

"Nonsense," she muttered into the branches, then reexamined both letters. Finally, she held them over her heart and looked across Lake Washington at the mountains and blue above. Ray was changing. His mistress, the sky, wrapped him in mist and fog as his image disappeared into the heavens. While he spoke of love, his letters were more of his duty, not just to her, but to all of the blank faces that made up this great country. The themes of his letters were consistent; war stealthy approached and he belonged in the air protecting those he loved. He was being swallowed by the sea of young men caught in the movement to battle a yet unseen enemy. While some young men sought jobs in factories or wherever else they could find them as their country struggled from under the dark days of the Depression, others saw the service as their ticket to success.

But Raymond did not need the money. He needed the challenge, and that was proving to be greater than his love for Billi. His last letter had brought that conclusion to the forefront. They were giving him a crew on this new P-39. A fifteen-year-old, Stuart Huckelbee, who had gotten permission from his Midwest farmer father to enlist, had been assigned as Ray's new aircraft mechanic. Stuart sent his paycheck back home to help his parents and younger sisters. Ray described him as small and wiry like Danny, but serious. Especially when it came to the engine and all parts airplane. Ray bragged of this child-man who could squeeze into the tightest part of the plane with his wrench and fix anything.

Ray's ramblings twisted Billi's heart. His metal concubine had permeated his mind and soul as she daily carried him skyward.

A soft growl emitted from below. Billi shifted on her branch to look toward the street. A stranger stood looking down her driveway. She watched him study the house, tip his hat at the statue of the Virgin Mary, and then move on. At the last moment she recognized his gait, the way he walked heavier on his left foot, giving him the appearance of listing. She had seen the same man on the Black Ball Ferry a few weeks back when returning from her father's home. His appearance could not be considered a coincidence.

She made certain he had moved on before she lowered herself to the ground and scooped up Pepper.

"Good boy," she whispered, fishing into her pocket for a well-deserved treat, then ran into the house with her guard dog tucked safely in her arm.

BILLI INSPECTED HER IMAGE in the mirror. Working for her mother in the concession stand at Mount Baker Beach had some perks. Now, her tanned legs didn't need her precious nylons. She adjusted her new light-blue chiffon dress and started down the stairs. For tonight promised to be special, especially since dear Raymond had concocted this evening from afar.

Sensing the celebration, Pepper had gone wild when Danny had arrived last Tuesday with a wad of cash and the announcement. For Mrs. O's birthday, the ladies were to each buy a new dress, and then Danny would drive them and their other escort, Eddy, to a celebration dinner. When Mrs. O clapped her hands with delight at the prospect of the evening, Pepper had run in circles, then dove up on her spacious lap.

The anticipation of this evening had brushed aside all of Billi's worries for days. The strange men who occasionally walked their block received smiles instead of glares. Everything would be just fine. Ray had not forgotten her. He still loved her, and his mistress remained in her place, overhead, not occupying his heart.

Her mother stood in the living room, radiant and beautiful. She had chosen a cocoa-brown silk with darker lace over the upper bodice. Perfect with her brown hair and eyes.

Eddy, the last one down the circular stairs that hugged the turret wall of their entry, stopped at every window to view the front street. Something they had all unconsciously started doing since the one-eyed man had arrived.

"Well, look at my dates. I'll be the envy of every man there. Available or otherwise." He kissed his mother's rouged cheek.

At preciously six o'clock, Danny bounded up the front steps with a box in his hand. As the front door opened, Pepper ran out, stopped at the top step, then growled and barked into the evening. The fearless pup waited a moment to be certain his warning had been heard, then followed Danny back through the door.

Mrs. O'Shaughnessy held the orchid Danny had given her to her chest. Although the hint of pink blossom did not match her brown gown, she smiled radiantly waiting for Eddy to pin the stunning flower on her.

"Nothing will be grander than this evening." She kissed Danny's cheek. He extended his arm and led her ceremoniously toward the door, where her old Kolinsky fur waited on its wooden hanger next to her small beaded purse.

"It's too warm out, Mom," Billi protested.

"Nonsense." She waved toward the wrap and Eddy placed the warn fur over her shoulders. "Onward," she commanded the small parade.

Pepper whined as the door shut, leaving him alone.

"Guard the house," Billi instructed back through the door and heard him bark once in response.

Mrs. O'Shaughnessy gasped as they pulled up in front of Maison Blanc at 360 Marion Street. The elegant white building, with its second floor of tall, thin windows, curved roofline, carved rosettes and arches, was known to be one of the city's finest restaurants. The establishment had even made the 1937 list of Northwest Novelties, which claimed the menu offers "fatal lures."

Danny had barely opened the door when Mrs. O, delighted, charged the stairs. Billi tucked her long handbag under her elbow and gracefully took her brother's arm to mount the steps.

The first level of Maison housed The Rathskeller, "Where True Bohemianism Prevails," as claimed by the innovative Charles J. E. Blanc, owner of both distinctly French and unique eating establishments situated beneath one roof.

Mrs. O swiftly passed the arched opening to the bohemian paradise and began up the massive stairs with the hand-carved women's figurine newel post Monsieur Blanc had imported from Europe, the grandeur of another world.

"Isn't my future son-in-law out of this world?" Mrs. O straightened her shoulders and slowly proceeded to the maître d's small desk on the second-floor landing.

"Bonsoir." Monsieur Blanc watched the foursome approach. "Do you have ze reservation?"

"Mrs. O'Shaughnessy," she announced herself royally.

As the distinguished older gentleman checked his list, Eddy stepped forward. "The birthday arranged by Mr. Raymond Richardson."

"Ah, mais oui, but of course, Monsieur Richardson."

"He is my daughter's fiancé." Mrs. O'Shaughnessy waved her hand toward Billi.

"And an exquisite choice." The Frenchman bowed in Billi's direction. "Zis way please."

He led them to a table surrounded by seven-foot-tall, hand-painted partitions. These half walls created a private and inviting room.

"May I take madame's cloak?" he asked with unmistakable graciousness.

A bottle of champagne arrived, compliments of Ray, followed within minutes by a beautiful young woman. Her smartly bobbed black hair and stylish European dress announced her heritage. Eddy hurried to his feet as he locked eyes with the diminutive beauty.

She beamed up at him. "This is for your mother's wrap." She handed Eddy a small ticket.

"Have we met before?"

"Not formally. I'm Zinny, Zinny Blanc. And I understand it is your birthday, Madame. Joyeux anniversaire!" With that, and a swish of her yellow satin dress, she disappeared.

"Sit down, Eddy before the champagne hits you and you do something stupid," his mother hissed.

Billi did not appear astonished that Zinny Blanc's beauty had Eddy's full attention.

"Now I remember Zinny from a party at a home on Capitol Hill." His smile brightened as he continued. "She attended the French Convent around the corner, The Sacred Heart. And, as of this very moment, I vowed to renew my Catholic faith."

Billi's light-hearted mood quickly soured when she noticed her mother balancing the Gorham silver spoon on her finger. Mrs. O checked the spoon for weight placement, a sign of craftsmanship. Billi shot Eddy a look of warning and, without saying a word, passed him the cut-crystal salt and pepper shakers. He placed the finely cut glass next to him on the far side of the table.

Attempting to distract her mother, she picked up the menu that claimed sans rival and giggled at her options. "I think I'll start with green turtle steaks, frog legs, escargot, and eels, then I'll try reindeer meat, all prepared for this restaurant where epicureans meet.'" Her gaze challenged the others at the table. "Anyone else ready to order?"

THE HIGH-SPIRITED SINGING of well-wishers echoed past the partitions, the crowning glory to Mrs. O's birthday celebration. She looked around the table. Billi had turned toward Danny, cake in hand.

"Tell me how Raymond arranged all of this?" Billi took a bite of cake and waited.

Danny smiled and began to slowly, with great embellishment, recite his mission of the last few days.

Eddy had disappeared at the arrival of the coffee, perhaps hoping to catch another glimpse of the beautiful French girl.

Mrs. O eyed her daughter's back. Opportunity had presented itself. She lowered Billi's long evening bag into her lap, reached for the salt and pepper shakers, and neatly tucked the beautiful Gorham silver dessert spoon in for good measure. A special gift on a special day. Then she casually set her daughter's purse back on the table and sipped her strong roasted demitasse. Life was good.

BILLI AND HER MOTHER HUDDLED at the top of the stairs outside of the beautiful restaurant and continued to remark on the exquisite French flavors. As Danny went to get the car, Billi looked back through the etched glass door where Eddy and Zinny stood tete-a-tete in bubbling conversation. Poor Dahlia, she mused. Her striking brother could be a bit of a rogue. She tapped the glass, caught his eye, and waved him on. She watched in amazement as the petite yellow flower stood on tiptoe to kiss Eddy's cheek. Vive la France! She smiled to herself at the thought of Ray.

Eddy swung through the door on a cloud not totally consisting of champagne. He took his two best gals by the arms and, whistling, ushered them down the steps to Danny and their waiting car.

Within minutes Danny stopped the car in front of the old Victorian home in need of paint. Billi felt an odd chill as she stepped into the night and paused to look at the stars. Eddy sang lightheartedly as he helped his mother up the stairs. As Danny pulled away from the curb, Billi turned to wave adieu and noticed a black Ford sedan sitting in the shadows across the street. Billi heard Pepper's furious bark and looked back up the steps in time to see a figure slip in front of the door.

Eddy stepped between the stranger and his mother, and Billi heard the car door open across the street. She turned back to see the one-eyed monster ease from the black sedan.

Jack eyed Billi as he strode directly toward her. She just stood there in the half shadow of the streetlight, bold and strong.

"Please leave the premises." Eddy's voice rose into the cool night air. "Unless you have documents that prove—"

"Shut up, kid, and open the door," David hissed.

"How dare you," Mrs. O'Shaughnessy sputtered. "How dare you talk to my son in such a fashion?"

Jack stood looking down at the brazen glare of Billi. "Unless you want the entire neighborhood to know, I'd suggest we move inside," he voice barely a whisper.

"Know what?" she demanded, not budging.

The sound of Pepper whimpering broke the silence.

"If you'll excuse me, my dog needs out."

The simple statement defused the situation, and Eddy moved forward and opened the door to the frantic pup.

Pepper shot down the stairs to the lawn and just missed Jack's shoes in his hurry to relieve himself. He then growled as he took up his position next to his owner and walked with her up the remaining stairs, then checked the street before marching inside.

Mrs. O'Shaughnessy had secured her rocker before the vile one claimed it. Eddy and David were squaring off when Pepper ran to

Eddy's side and growled up at the stranger. Billi kept her eyes leveled on the man with the patch as she positioned herself on the couch, tucking her handbag beside her.

Jack tried not to show his disappointment when he noticed the small beaded bag dangling from the older woman's wrist. Christ, he'd had the table set with Waterford crystal salt and pepper shakers and four settings of Gorham silver, all out on loan. Trinkets to attract a thief. His man had confirmed a dessert spoon and the shakers were missing after the birthday party had left. The size of Mrs. O'Shaughnessy's small, beaded handbag could not contain the items. He would have to have someone check the car.

"Let me see your bag." The obnoxious smaller one started for Mrs. O.

Eddy jumped in front of his mother. "Let me see your warrant."

David ignored the demand.

But Mrs. O'Shaughnessy snapped into motion. "Here." She insisted, pulling the small bag from her wrist and holding it up high. She smiled sweetly as Jack stepped forward.

"Thank you." He could tell instantly that her bag did not have the weight of the heavy crystal. He went through the motions of looking, extracting a kerchief, lipstick, and small gold compact that held powder, puff, and mirror.

Damn it. He had not thought to bring a female officer to search her.

Eddy proceeded in his best lawyer tone. "What is this all about?"

"We had a call from the owner of Maison Blanc," David sneered. "Some crystal is missing from your table."

Eddy's face fell in apparent horror, and he looked at his mother. Her shoulders rose and fell in answer. Her shoulders had spoken.

While Eddy took up the argument of innocence, Jack studied Billi's face as she worked the problem. And then he saw the lump in her purse. He moved to her and extended his hand.

He watched Billi's expression shift as she lifted her purse toward him and recognized the weight of the objects. Jack extracted the crystal and salt spilt onto Billi's new blue dress. Perfect, he thought. Like mother, like daughter. They were a team. And the situation could not be more to his liking.

Eddy stopped in midsentence and stared from the two sparkling objects, to his sister, then to his mother.

All eyes now fell on the matron of the household. Mrs. O'Shaughnessy's shoulders rose and fell again, as if the mere action would push aside the crime. Pepper abandoned his position next to Eddy and jumped up into her lap. She snuggled the dog close for comfort.

"Well." David leered like a wolf herding sheep. "Someone is going to jail."

Jack unceremoniously dumped the rest of the contents from Billi's purse onto the couch. Powder, lipstick, handkerchief, comb and, with a deadening thud, the silver dessert spoon hit the cushion. The last object floated to the floor, a letter from Ray.

"Was he in on this too?" Jack inquired.

Billi snatched the letter from the carpet. "No." She looked down at his letter, which she held in her left hand, where his engagement ring shone brightly.

Eddy spoke again. This time his tone sounded conciliatory, ready to deal. "Surely, there must be some way—"

"Can it, kid." David's nastiness turned from Eddy to Billi. "Let's go."

Eddy shifted in front of his sister, and the faithful Pepper came to his aide.

David kicked the puppy, and the little creature rode the wind across the room.

Instantly, Billi got on her feet. Her hand hit David's face as Eddy's fist found the ruthless agent's gut. Mrs. O screamed. Pepper regained his four small legs, shook his long ears, and ran back into the mêlée, pulling on the trousers of the very leg that kicked him.

"Enough." Jack's deep voice filled the room and the commotion subsided.

David straightened.

Jack decided he would deal with his assistant later, when he saw a look of revenge flash in David's eyes. He knew, if given the chance, David would kill the dog.

"You're coming with us." Jack placed his hand on Billi's arm.

"Not without me." Eddy's voice hung in the air, a subtle threat.

Billi freed her arm, picked up Pepper, and placed him in her mother's lap. The older woman's shoulders briefly shifted as a single tear worked its way down her plump cheek. Billi kissed her mother's forehead and bravely smiled at her. Then with the rustle of her chiffon dress, she turned to lead all three men out the door.

Jack briefly looked at Mrs. O'Shaughnessy. She sat alone in her rocker, Pepper silent in her arms, tears streamed freely down her cheeks. There was nothing he could say to assure he all would be well, for this was just part of his plan. He turned and followed the others out the door.

THIRTEEN

Billi let Eddy hold her close as they mounted the stairs to the Federal Office Building, which sat between Marion and Madison Streets on 1st Avenue. She knew how he had loved the modern art-deco design of this structure. But on this early morning, he would find no joy in the beauty of the building. Her mind clouded with the memory of the last few hours they had spent directly up the hill at Maison Blanc and perceived he could never face Zinny again.

She patted his arm. "It will be okay."

The solemn group proceeded through the dark halls with the tall one leading and the sleazy one following on their heels. They passed an empty desk with a phone and continued into a large conference room. Jack switched on the light, and the empty mahogany table gleamed with polish.

"Can I use your phone?" Eddy asked.

Jack indicated a chair for Billi, facing the windows, then nodded Eddy toward the outer office.

"Don't say anything, Bil, until I return."

David followed Eddy out.

Billi heard Jack close the door, then watched him as he took his time rounding the large table to sit across from her.

She broke the silence. "What is it you want?"

"You."

"Well, you have me. Now what?"

Jack folded his hands on the desk. "What I am about to tell you must never be repeated or your mother will go to jail for theft and your brother for assault."

"Won't stick." She shifted.

"Don't push it." He sat back as if to give her room to make the decision that would change her life beyond all imaginings.

"Proceed." She watched his one eye. "But first, remove the patch."

The one eye twitched.

"I want to look in both eyes of the monster I'm dealing with."

His reaction gave her satisfaction, as his eye hardened and his back straightened, then his hands moved to the patch.

Billi did not blink as she now met his stare straight on. The right eye looked hazy, discolored, with the thin scar that ran from eyebrow to cheek. Surprisingly, she did not fear him now. Something vulnerable overcame him without his patch, and she liked it.

Jack kept his hand over the patch as it lay on the table, as if merely touching it would give him back some of his strength. "As I mentioned before, we need your help."

"We?"

"The United States, National Defense."

"Fascinating." She sat back, discerning there had been a shift in power. They needed her.

"We need you to obtain some information for us. There is little risk, and what you could do for your country would far surpass many a man out there."

"You have my attention." She hoped she sounded smug, but her heart began to race.

"It's simple. We place you where we know Japanese espionage is being discussed, you listen, and bring us back what has been said."

At the mention of Japanese, Billi's stomach twisted. "That's ridiculous. What have the Japanese to do with all of this?"

"Plenty. More than I am at liberty to say."

"But I'm known in the community. For heaven's sake I just danced at—"

"Bon Odori. I know. That's why we're taking you elsewhere. Another city."

She swallowed, speechless. The stakes were escalating beyond measure.

"And if I don't?"

"Oh, the scandal. The betrothed of high-society Raymond Richardson—shining star of the Army Air Corps—who on the night of her mother's birthday party, which had been paid for by the influential Richardson, stole from—"

"Bastard," she spit. "You've been reading my mail."

"Among other things. Is it true your mother's family arrived from Germany and that she…should I continue?"

Billi started shaking. "When?"

A sly smile eased across his face as he reached for his patch. She could see he had gotten what he wanted. His orchestrated dirty trick could not have gone better and she hated him for it. By the time Eddy returned to the conference room the deal had been struck.

BILLI JOINED HER MOTHER in the early sunlight that rose above the statue and handed her a purple and blue pansy from the garden. Fresh flowers sat in the small vase built into the top boulder that supported the Blessed Virgin. Billi knew her mother's routine. Mrs. O'Shaughnessy had faithfully replaced the pansies each morning as she prayed for her sin. And, obviously her prayers had worked. Her children had returned home early that morning and all charges had been dropped. Her prayers had been answered with a miracle.

The pansy represented Billi's offering for the promise she had made to Jack the night before. The secret lay heavy on her heart. How to tell her mother? She couldn't. She had to meet that awful man again today after work. And between now and five thirty she had to figure out a way to say no, she could not take part in his games. It might sound unpatriotic but she held no interest in making the Japanese, especially those she loved, become the target of unwarranted suspicion and hatred.

"I'll be a little late this evening, Mom." She rearranged her flower in the mix, centering it.

"Fine, dear. I have a meeting tomorrow with the board at the Home of the Good Shepherd."

Mrs. O's involvement with her numerous charities and women's organizations throughout the city made Billi proud. Her mother helped Mother Cabrini secure land for the building of the new hospital, worked to help support the unwed mothers at the Home of the Good Shepherd, and attended events at the Women's Century Club. Thankfully, all of the bustling about kept her mother out of trouble.

They walked in silence together, toward the front of the house. Billi realized the street remained empty of those who had been sent to watch her every move. The word "spy" rolled around her mind like an unwanted headache. She put it down to exhaustion and fear that had made her agree so quickly to such a wild task. What did she know of the world of espionage? She would fail miserably. But, most importantly, she must protect her Japanese-American friends.

THE FEDERAL BUILDING LOOKED DIFFERENT in the daylight. The light-colored, art-deco trim that scalloped the top of the structure loomed grand and inviting. A black sedan pulled up to the corner of the building on the Madison Street side and the door opened. Billi slipped inside to find David at the wheel. His gaze settled on her legs, and she adjusted the smock she had worn over her bathing suit. What a startling contrast to the peaceful time she had had at the beach with Danny, working and swimming on this bright July day.

"Like your bathing suit."

She smelled booze from his breath and tried not to show her fear. No part of the suit showed through the brown floral dress. He had to have been watching her swim. A frightful and disgusting thought. She ignored him and concentrated on the path he drove. Up Madison, left on Broadway, left on Olive, right on Boylston. They stopped in front of a brick building set back from the street, its Tudor architecture in keeping with Capitol Hill, yet distinctive. But why take her to an apartment building?

"Why here?"

"Off the beaten path, so to speak."

"Hardly," she blurted. They had just passed the Women's Century Club, a place her mother frequented in her fervent attempts to be accepted in society's well-heeled groups. Billi prayed no one had seen her.

"Who are we meeting?" Billi did not reach for the door handle and weighed whether she could outrun David to the sanctuary of the Women's Century Club. She would not enter into this building alone with the man in the seat beside her.

Her car door snapped open and Billi recognized the dark-blue suit of Jack as he stood waiting. She followed him into the lobby, up two flights of stairs, and down a stucco hallway. They passed several wooden doors with small stained-glass windows, each with its own unique design above the brass numbers, elegant and stylish. Toward the end of the hall, where a skylight let the sun's rays filter down on a set of back stairs, Jack stopped at the last door, the one with the stained-glass displaying the helmet of a knight in silver and greens. A knight. How ironic. She contemplated the absurdity of the suggestion as she passed into the room. On one wall a cream fireplace stood beneath a dark mantel, accentuating okra-colored walls. In front of intricate bay windows, a long table of the sort usually found in ornate hallways stretched the entire length of the small area that hung out over the garden below. The evening sun filtered onto the pile of papers that were stacked on top of his makeshift desk.

Jack moved a chair in front of the bay windows and motioned toward it. Billi sat straight, upright, waiting. He landed in the smaller chair next to her, reached into a pile on his desk, and handed her a stack of photos.

"Tell me who you recognize." He leaned in.

The top photo showed the outside of the Golden Donut Café, which she had walked past several times. Three Japanese men stood for the camera.

"I have seen all of these men before. What have they done?"

He jabbed his finger at the first man in the picture. "Suspected of being in the Communist Party, President of the Association of Japanese Cannery Workers." His finger moved to the next man. "Legal adviser, special member of the Seattle Consulate who is assigned to propaganda. And this one is a Kibei. You understand that one? He returned to Japan for schooling and his required service for their Imperial Japanese Navy and is back here in Seattle. He has worked his way up to chancellor in the local Japanese intelligence system."

She ignored him and shifted to the next picture, afraid to discover Mr. Nakamura among the images. The Star Pool Room on Jackson rested on top of the pile and she examined it closely. According to Eileen, Tak had been spending much of his time in this establishment.

A black and white shot of the New Central Café followed, then one of the Nippon Pool Hall, four different hotels, and, lastly, the Stacy Street Tavern. Relieved that she personally did not know anyone pictured, she tried to hand back the stack.

Jack drummed his fingers. "Well?"

"I do not know these people. I recognize a few. Some are very prominent in the community and very generous." She could feel the sweat run down her back.

He showed her a picture of the headquarters of the local Japanese newspaper, just off Main Street.

She said nothing, realizing the depth of the illusion. So many of the Japanese who were arriving were not attempting to learn English, but were comfortable within their Japantown community. They spoke their language at all times, read their own newspapers, and joined the established churches and social groups, which could be misconstrued as being anti-American. They supported each other in a cloak of secrets and did not let outsiders in. Except for the young. Many attended American schools, developed friendships among other cultures, and expanded their lives during the day, only to return to the few blocks of confined existence at night under the watchful eye of their elders.

Jack continued with his scrutiny. "All of these men belong in some fashion to organizations or clubs like the Seattle Tokyo Club, ranked number two for membership behind the Tokyo Club in Los Angeles. They operate up and down the West Coast and have recently intensified their espionage activities. They deliver the information through what they call the 'post office.' Some of these men are still active officers in the Imperial Japanese Navy, here in America, as agents. They have fixed the police, gotten jobs in fishing colonies or as teachers. Some of the information is even coming from their priests. Their allegiance is to the homeland, where they are sending not only information regarding American supplies and war materials, but piles of money to support their war effort. And that war is growing ever closer to our shores."

Billi's mouth became dry, and she focused out the window at the rich, green leaves of the trees. He was lying. And this had gone too far.

Jack restacked the photos and pulled three more from a different pile on his desk. He handed her the three pictures of a young Japanese man.

In one photo the man stood on a college campus with a lone tree beside him, holding books. She flipped to the second image of what appeared a more recent image of the same man, smiling, sporting a stylish hat and coat, riding a trolley car. In the third, he did not smile, but seemed to smirk at the camera in his Imperial Japanese Navy uniform.

Billi held the pictures into the light provided by the bay windows and scrutinized the face before handing the pictures back toward Jack.

"Look again." His voice had become cross, stern.

"Who is he?" She met his gaze, unflinching.

"Have you ever seen him?"

"No." She spoke honestly and self-composed.

"Keep them and memorize every inch of his face." The way he spoke the words made Billi think he already knew every inch of the Japanese man's face.

"Is he a friend of yours?"

The look on Jack's face became so covered in hate that Billi lowered her gaze to the photos. Whoever this man was, he had a strong and personal impact on Jack's life. But that was none of her business. She repeated her speech in her mind once more and opened her mouth to begin when David entered with some groceries.

He disappeared into the small kitchen behind the built-in cabinets. Billi watched him set the bag on the counter before stepping to the dumb waiter in the wall. He worked the ropes, and bottles of milk, mixed with a few containers of soda water, set in a wooden box, rattled into view.

"Something to drink?" Jack asked.

"No." She spoke quickly and looked back at Jack.

He smiled. "Bring in the soda water and two glasses."

"I can't stay," she began. "In fact, I can't do what you are asking of me. I don't know this man. You need to leave me alone." Clearly not the speech she had prepared but she could not hold back the words that tumbled out.

Jack leaned closer, his breath hot against her skin. "Akio Sumiyoshi. Akio is thirty-one, grandson of the Admiral Kawamura Sumiyoshi. He comes from a long line of samurai. As part of his training, he attended school in America." He tapped the picture of the youth on the lawn with a lone, giant tree before a horizon of long buildings sporting graceful arches.

"Also, as part of his military training, he had to behead captured Chinese all day long until his arms ached. He had to master the technique of one swift blow, of not having his actions amount to more than mere practice. For him, to kill is to live honorably."

Billi swallowed hard, trying not to let her hands that held the killers images tremble as Jack tapped the military picture.

"He has been seen recently in America." Jack's finger moved to the last picture of the smiling, handsome face below the stylish Stetson hat. The man smiled boldly as he held the long pole of a cable car as it pressed up the tracks in a busy city. "We need to find him, who he is dealing with, and what they are planning."

"I can't stay," she mumbled again, tears forming, blurring her sight of the detestable pictures.

Jack accepted the two glasses from David and poured Billi a soda. He took the picture and replaced them with the fizzing drink.

Her hand shook as she took a sip, regaining her voice.

"You're lying. You're trying to make me hate the Japanese. I never will. I hate you." Without hesitation she flung the soda water and it hit its mark, Jack's face.

He had not ducked, and the water dripped into his eyes. He removed his patch and wiped his face with his handkerchief. He set the handkerchief aside but left his patch off.

David appeared angry, and she heard his footsteps as he left the room. Jack picked up her hand, but she did not pull away.

"If you could help save Raymond—"

"What has Raymond got to do with this?" She jerked her hand back, clasping both of them together so tightly her knuckles turned white.

"Nothing and everything. If we can find Akio, find him before he sets into motion whatever it is he is up to—and believe me he is up to something—we could save many innocent lives and perhaps not get pulled into the ugly war that is before us."

"But the president has repeatedly assured us there will be no war."

Jack looked past her out the windows. The beautiful summer light caught the leaves of the oak trees that ran down the block, casting them in shimmering gold and green. If life were only that simple. If only the president's words could be heeded by their enemies. It seemed too late. He could feel it. The Japanese had marched easily through China, into French Indochina, and now had their sights set on the Philippines and the vast horizon of America. Furthermore, Emperor Hirohito, though thought to be in command, in reality remained a symbol. The rising, war-hungry ministers of the current Japanese military brutally ruled their country and viewed the United States as easy prey for their expansion presented the ultimate threat. If one of the more aggressive army ministers replaced the current Prime Minister, Konoe Fumimaro, the only leader who continued to attempt negotiations with President Roosevelt, then war would be imminent.

He had learned much at his time at Stanford. By chance, Akio Sumiyoshi had been his roommate. In the years they were together, Jack had come to realize the other man's ambitious mission. Behind his handsome smile and polite exterior existed a dangerous man who practiced his kendo daily. They had been on the fencing team together, and as they sparred, hatred had grown between them. There were no words to explain Akio's behavior, for the pure bestiality of life surfaced the moment he had a sword in his grip.

She stood and put down her half empty glass. "I have to go now. My mother will become suspicious."

He rose and walked her to the door.

"I can't help you. You must appreciate my situation." She continued to speak softly. "I love Raymond, but I also love Eileen's family. They are my friends. In not betraying the Nakamuras, I betray Raymond, if half of what you are saying is true."

Beautiful but smart, the qualities she possessed that convinced him to choose her. He relied on her figure to attract Akio and her wits to keep her alive. What was he doing? His job, he told himself.

He opened the door as David came from the back room. "You'll be hearing from us."

As she passed him into the hall, he caught the slight fragrance that reminded him of sunshine and frolicking on the beach. A lifetime away. Damn, he hated his job at times.

FOURTEEN

A LETTER FROM RAY sat on her bed. Billi could not open it. But sat regarding the envelope as if it had a life of its own. How could she tell him all that has happened in his absence? A myriad of lies floated through her mind. He had been gone just over one month and there seemed no end to the trouble that brewed, not only in the world, but in her home and heart.

At the familiar scratch on her door, she opened it, and Pepper ran around her legs. The aroma of her mother's sauerkraut wafted up from the kitchen. The heat vent in the kitchen's tall ceiling not only let the conversation float up to the second-floor hallway, but also the smells from the cook. Her stomach grumbled, not ready for food as she heard her mother's call. But it would be wise, she reasoned, to put in an appearance, especially for her mother.

As she started down the spiral stairs and looked out the windows, she noted that no black car waited across the street. She sighed with a bit of relief but then noticed Eddy watching her. She hadn't heard him come home.

"They've gone. What a relief. But I still can't figure out what you told them." He would not budge from the base of the stairs, holding his ground in the foyer.

Billi gripped the ornate newel post with her left hand for strength. "Nothing. They want to hire me for a job but I told them I did not have time, with working for Mom. But I did promise them I'd think about it and get back to them in the fall." She smiled for him and brushed past, avoiding his gaze, as she headed for the kitchen.

"What did Raymond have to say?" Her mother took up the questioning as she piled the sauerkraut next to sausage and scalloped potatoes on three plates.

"I'm saving the letter for later. My treat."

"You will not mention the one-eyed man, will you?" Her mother did not look up from the pots on the stove.

"Of course not." Billi's response came too fast and too strong. "Besides, that's behind us now." She carried her plate back into the dining room with Pepper following and sat across from Eddy. She could not tell if she had been convincing.

"Well, I'm glad that we had such fun." Mrs. O joined them and sat at her usual spot. "That is what you must tell Raymond and thank him dearly for me."

The meal proceeded quieter than usual, each brooding over the events of the past few days. When the phone rang, the sound knocked them out of their stupor. Billi, the first one up, hurried to the living room, where she snatched at the receiver with a vengeance.

"Hello." When she heard the voice on the other end she turned her back and sat. "Where is she now? Yes, I'll come." She lowered the phone with tears in her eyes and approached the table.

"That was Eileen. Her mother is dying, and I'm going to their house to sit with her."

"How awful." Her mother's concern genuine. "Can we send some food?" She must have realized the irony of sending sauerkraut and sausage to a Japanese home, for her shoulders rose and fell in defense of her offer.

"Thanks anyway, Mom. I'll get my coat." Billi headed toward the front door when she heard Eddy's chair push back.

"Pepper and I will walk you to the bus."

At the sound of his name, Pepper flew from beneath the table where he had taken up his post in the hopes bits of food would find their way to him.

The three started down the block toward South Jackson, Pepper stopping to inspect every tree along the way.

"What's up, Bil?" Eddy asked in a low voice.

"Nothing."

"Come on. I know nothing when I see it, and this is not nothing. Is something the matter with Ray?"

"No."

"Then is it that son of son bitch Jack?"

"Could be. I'm just confused. Can we talk about this when I get back?"

"Promise?"

"Yes." She felt better just at the thought of talking over the situation.

"I'll have your Manhattan waiting."

The Nakamuras' small apartment felt crowded when Billi entered. The number of shoes lined up along the front entry told of the many loyal relatives there for support. Eileen grabbed at Billi and tugged her down the hall past Auntie Katsuko to her bedroom.

"Thank you for coming." She began to sob, and Billi put her arms around her friend. "I am so afraid. Losing my mother is a terrible feeling," she choked out.

"I am so sorry" were the only words Billi kept repeating.

"She liked you." Eileen took her handkerchief and patted her eyes. "She was proud that you would visit us. It made her feel more American. She loved living in America, making it her home."

"Did she miss Japan do you think?"

"Only that she never made it back to see the cherry blossoms in bloom on the side of the mountain. And now she'll never…"

"She'll see them her own way."

The door snapped open and Tak barged in his frame rigid, his voice harsh. "What are you doing here?"

Eileen stepped in front of Billi. "I asked her to come. Go away."

"She is gone." Tak slammed the door.

The two friends stood in silence. What had he meant? With great trepidation, Eileen opened the door, and the smell of the incense floated toward them with the sound of the mourning relatives. Billi took Eileen's hand and led her toward the living room where Kenny lay folded on the couch, his agile frame heaving with sorrow. The arch of the beautiful white orchid beside him appearing to be a shield to the boy's grief. Mr.

Nakamura stood in the middle of the room as a line formed outside of his bedroom, where the shadow of candles flickered against the walls.

Eileen pulled Billi with her to the bedroom door, and they went in side by side to bid the small frame of Mrs. Nakamura farewell. Someone had placed her cherished geisha dolls at the side of the bed so she could see them as she drifted into another realm. Eileen gracefully went to her bedside and dabbed water on her mother's lips, following the tradition of water at the last moment. The other ladies were preparing to wash the body as Auntie's tears spilled onto the white kimono she held in anticipation of the last time she would help her younger sister dress. The kimono would be crossed right over left in death, instead of the usual left over right.

Billi stood to the side, watching the women move gently through the customs steeped in Japanese tradition. Those gathered move as one tending to Mrs. Nakamura, so that her afterlife would be blessed.

She nodded and waved goodbye to her grieving friend then turned and headed into the cramped living room. As she continued toward the front door she noticed the Buddhist shrine had been closed and covered in white paper to keep away the impure spirits of the dead.

In the sorrow of the moment, she found herself searching the faces of those gathered to see if that handsome Akio, the killer, whose picture she had held just a few hours ago, had somehow made his way into this gathering of loved ones. It made her sick to think that she actually dwelt on this possibility when her best friend's mother lay dead a few feet away. As she grabbed her shoes and hurried down the stairs, she stopped short as one of the women entered the building. She had been in one of the photos, pictured with her husband outside their hotel. Billi stormed out the door. She needed air, she needed time to think. She knew these people, they were not murderers, they did not want war.

The light of a cigarette caught her eye. Tak stepped from behind a cherry tree and blew smoke in her direction before he turned and headed up the block. She sought the opposite direction and walked toward the bus line. As she approached Jackson Street, the black sedan pulled up beside her and stopped.

Although his hat shaded his face, Billi recognized his height and stride as Jack rounded the car and held the door open for her. Without so much as a single word, she slid into the front seat.

"I need a swim." She couldn't explain her request and thankfully Jack said nothing.

In silence he drove her to a small beach. The Ostranders' home spread from Lake Washington Boulevard to the water on the north side, while two large homes took up their posts to the south. Tucked between these mansions overlooking the lake, sat a grassy, public park with tall, old streetlights set back from the wall and steep steps that led to the quiet water.

She did not question his choice and let him take her elbow on the dark stone steps. Once below, where darkness surrounded them, she moved to the water's edge and slipped off the smock that covered her bathing suit, which she had not changed out of all day. The inky water brushed against her, cool and refreshing, as she moved forward. She stepped gingerly, feeling the sand and rocks beneath her feet. Yet, the chill did not stop her, for her mind turned circles with the finality of death. How peaceful Mrs. Nakamura had looked. How still.

She dove below the surface, and the water felt like silk against her skin—smooth, refreshing, and alive. She had never seen a dead person before, let alone someone she knew and admired. She let loose her stroke and swam into the dark, headed for nowhere. She beat the water as if her motion would bring the solution to her dilemma. Exhausted she rolled onto her back and floated, looking up at the heavens and the twinkling of the stars. A few pale yellow lights glowed down the beach a ways. Peace found her briefly before she heard the unmistakable splash of someone swimming near her.

Jack's white arms glistened in the dark. And somehow she found it funny and comforting that he swam beside her. "Cold yet?" She didn't face him but kept her gaze on the heavens.

"Not that bad," he growled.

"Didn't know you could swim."

"You'd be surprised."

With the ease of a seal, she rolled in the soothing water, then headed back toward shore with Jack keeping pace just behind her. Her wet footprints marked the sand as she snatched up her cotton smock and dried her body with it.

"Keep your eyes looking uphill," he cautioned.

She heard the splash of his feet as he emerged and she caught her breath. She realized she was a betrothed woman with a half-naked man and the situation hit her, as did her empty stomach. Her knees gave way. He caught her before she hit the ground and she felt his strong, bare arms and chest as he lowered her down gently. She shivered against the prickly grass.

"Want a cup of coffee?"

She could hear him rustling with his clothing but could not face him. "Yes."

FEW PATRONS STILL LINGERED AT EARL'S DINER, as Billi swept her last French fry across the plate that once held a deluxe burger, smothered in cheese.

"Rough night?"

They were the first words he had spoken since she had gotten her meal. He seemed to know not to interrupt her when she consumed her food.

"Usually is when someone dies." She looked at him full on.

"Sorry for the family."

"Really? They're Japanese." She sounded like a shrew, but could not help herself.

"So you have been thinking about my proposition."

"Hardly a proposition when one has no choice." She put her napkin down and folded her hands on the table.

"Since that is how you want to approach it, shall I tell you more?"

She did not answer but watched him, observing the seriousness of his one brown eye.

"You will need to leave for training." He would not let up.

"Impossible. Where to?" Came out all at once.

"First to Port Townsend, I know someone there who can help you learn the trade." He toyed with the sugar bowl and the cubes jiggled slightly with his touch.

"Trade? What trade? I thought you simply needed me to tell you if I saw your Mr.—"

He reached across the table and had her hand. "Not here." His shoulders hunched forward and his head lowered, his good eye watching her. He looked like a bull about to attack. "Not here, dear. We can have ice cream at home."

The waiter reached over Billi's shoulder and picked up her empty plate. "So, that'll be it?"

Startled, she withdrew her hand. "Yes." Then she repeated as if in a daze, "We will be having ice cream at home."

SHE DISCOVERED EDDY ASLEEP ON THE COUCH with the puppy snuggled up against him as she tiptoed into the living room. Aroused from his slumber, Pepper jumped through the air barking happily.

"There you are." Eddy sat up rubbing his hands together. "How's Eileen?"

"Mrs. Nakamura is in a better place."

"Sorry. Want that drink and talk now?"

"I'm just too tired. Rain check." She picked up Pepper and started up the spiral stairs hoping Eddy would appreciate her need for space.

Inside her room, the letter from Ray still waited for her on her bed. She slipped into her nightgown, snapped on her bedside lamp, and flopped on her white bedspread. She examined the unopened envelope while Pepper settled by her side. The birds on the wallpaper watched her. They knew more about her last few days than the man whose letter she held. They sensed her secrets.

Sleep took her fast and in the morning, the crumpled unopened letter rest on the floor. When her mother entered to check on her, Pepper shot past her down the stairs.

"Do you want to take the day off, honey?" Her mother scooped up the letter and set it on her night stand.

"No, I want to be at the beach today." The thought of Eileen not having her mother anymore struck her and she reached for her mother's hand.

"Good." Mrs. O took Billi's hand and sat on the bed beside her. Idly, she stroked her daughter's hair. "Danny will be by soon to pick you up. But if you need to leave he said he would take care of everything. Is there a problem with Ray? You haven't opened his letter."

"No, just with Mrs. Nakamura and all."

Pepper returned announcing his urgent need.

Mrs. O'Shaughnessy sprang up and hollered down the stairs, "Eddy, let the dog out."

The moment was broken and the day had begun.

FIFTEEN

THE WEEK HAD PASSED QUICKLY with Mrs. Nakamura's funeral and work. There had been no sign of the black sedan or its sullen occupant. But that was to change.

Mrs. O'Shaughnessy rushed into the kitchen, breathless with her enthusiasm. "Come quick and see." She motioned to Billi who had rolled out the ginger and molasses cookie dough, a special treat to send Ray. "Hurry," her mother threw back over her shoulder and disappeared.

Billi pulled the string of her apron and set it on the counter next to the uncut dough.

Her mother held the front door open while the dog ran in and out, yelping. "Just look."

Billi stopped short at the door. On the street stood a newer Pontiac, a rich, deep blue and shiny.

"Where did that come from?" She stood stunned.

"The police chief gave it to me today at their Ladies Auxiliary luncheon for all of my hard work and charity sponsorships. Isn't it grand?"

"The police chief?" Billi followed her mother down the stairs and stood beside her, watching their reflections in the high polish of the car's paint.

Mrs. O dangled the keys in her hand. "Want to go for a ride?" She opened the driver's door and Pepper jumped in. "Get out. No. No. No." Her mother batted at the dog, who simply jumped into the backseat and looked at her from the side window.

Billi laughed and opened the back door, scooping up her puppy. "That is not for you."

"It certainly is," her mother retorted.

"I was talking to Pepper."

"I just can't believe it," Mrs. O kept saying as she waltzed around the car.

"Neither can I," Billi mumbled into the soft fur of her puppy. "Does Eddy know?"

"I telephoned him at work and told him I had a surprise." She worked her hand across the smooth fender. "This will knock his socks off."

"I bet it will." Billi turned to head back toward the house, her frustration mounting with each step. That bastard was now playing with her mother's emotions.

Returning to her baking, she smashed the cookie cutter onto the cutting board. How dare he? She would tell him to take it back. Did he think he could simply trade a car for her?

By the time Eddy rounded the corner down 30th South, Mrs. O sat in anticipation on the porch ready to take him for a spin. He wore an expression of mixed joy and fear as he watched his ample mother crawl behind the wheel.

"Wait, Mom." He put his hat on the concrete steps.

"Well, come on," she commanded.

He walked around the car, entranced by its gleaming dark blue. "Where's Billi?"

"She's not interested right now." Mrs. O turned the key and the car purred to life.

Eddy barely had time to get situated before they launched away from the curb.

Billi had been watching from the upstairs window and went to the phone the minute they were around the corner. She held the card with Jack's number on it and dialed. There were several rings before a man answered.

"Duckworth," the unfamiliar voice answered.

Her anger dissipated into confusion. "Jack Huntington please?" She had never spoken his full name, and she stumbled a bit getting it out.

"He's not in. Who's calling?" the indifferent man asked.

"When do you expect him back?"

"Can I take a message?"

"Tell him the blue Pontiac called. And not to call back." She slammed the phone down.

JACK ADJUSTED HIS HAT as he stood on the corner of Water Street and Tyler, checking for any traffic before heading down the dark alley to the back door of the old brick building. He hoped he did not run into anyone who had decided to take up residence in the basement that night. The old Palace Hotel in Port Townsend had had a varied history since its inception in the late 1800s, and guidance from the ladies of the oldest trade known to man became his mission. The once-elegant, Romanesque hotel had taken in unspeakable tenants who continued to service those in need. The basement held testimony to that false love, for the bodies of the babies, born dead, were quietly buried there in the damp and dark, some with the blessing of Father Patrick. Rumors swirl around this wayward priest, who had even fallen in love with one of the girls who worked the second floor and fathered a child that died at birth. He had administered the blessing to his stillbirth offspring, evidence of his sinful actions, before giving up the cloth.

Most of the unspoken business had seen its heyday within the four inner rooms on the second floor that did not have the tall windows overlooking the bay. These small inner quarters were lit by the massive green-and-white leaded glass from above the stairwell. This unique lighting provided a mellow glow to the activities frowned upon by society.

Jack crept up the back stairs and down the hall to Marie's private residence, madame of what became nicknamed the Palace of Sweets. He knocked gently before entering. The fireplace glowed, illuminating the deep, green woodwork and lush, red wallpaper. The tall windows of her corner suite provided a mystifying view of the moon shimmering on the water.

"Right on time." Marie moved to a sideboard. "Drink?"

"Not right yet."

She pointed him into a chair facing her. "So, you need my help?"

Her matter-of-fact approach appealed to Jack in his constricted time frame. "I understand you can keep your lips sealed." He rested his hat on his knee.

She laughed loudly. "Besides kissing, those are the only lips I have around here. Closed." She drew out the last word, using almost an entire breath to finish it.

"Comes in handy for business."

"Yes, a business I would like to keep open." She raised her glass and swirled the brown whiskey she had poured. "So, how can I help you?"

Jack sat back and gave her a conspiratorial smile. "I'll take that drink now."

DAVID RETURNED TO THE CAR from down the block where he had been exploring the waterfront of Port Townsend. He had sneaked off to find a drink, but nothing remained open in this wretched little port town except one dive down at the end of the few blocks they called Main Street. He hurried back to the car, relieved that his need for a nip had not interfered with his boss's obvious corporeal desires. Why did Jack get all the good perks? Damn, he just wanted ten minutes in that whorehouse. What the hell was taking him so long? He drew his coat closer to his body and leaned his head back as his eyes instantly shut.

Jack crossed the street toward the car, satisfied with his meeting with Marie. He walked the length of the Ford, somewhat alarmed not to see anyone inside but the front windows covered with condensation. He felt for his pocket knife before reaching for his holster and pulled his gun, the weight reassuring. As he flung open the driver's door, David's head fell from its resting place and dangled in the cool night air. The smell of booze floated past Jack.

"Get the hell up." Jack seethed through clenched teeth.

David gathered his legs and sat up, bumping against the steering wheel. "Shit."

"Yes, that is what I think of your ability to be on guard." He slammed the door, nearly hitting David, and rounded to the passenger side.

David shook his head. The whore must not have been any good or Jack would not be that grumpy.

SIXTEEN

Mrs. O'Shaughnessy swung her car off North 50th Street and down Sunnyside Avenue North to the large circular entrance of the Home of the Good Shepherd. She slowed before the steps that led to the foyer, lingering as long as possible before parking her gleaming new car close to the entrance, hoping someone would be there to notice. She could not stay by her new prize for long or the summer rain would damage her hat. She adjusted her Kolinskey fur so that the long tail trailed down her arm, then she mounted the steps.

Today was her day to be recognized for her years of support and fundraising for this invaluable Catholic organization. A few years back she had helped Mother Cabrini find the property in the Laurelhurst neighborhood where the church constructed the Sacred Heart Villa for the orphans that once resided in this building. And now, the Sisters of the Order of the Good Shepherd and the new board of trustees were honoring Mrs. O for her continued hard work and devotion. Her fundraising efforts had helped maintain this large compound erected on over eleven acres, complete with garden and cows. The enormous building was now split into two sections, one for girls brought for training by their families and the other for those appointed by the court. And being Mrs. O, she placed her attention on the girls the court had sent, the side for girls living in poverty or in conditions declared immoral. It was in support of this side that she had found the proper picture to represent its inhabitants. And today the billboard was to be unveiled.

She walked across the wide hall, her heels clicking on the hardwood floor with its boarder of delicate dark-wood inlay, past the many pictures of Catholic visions and saints, to the appointed room with the large balcony overlooking the gardens. Fresh flowers, bright and beautiful, sat in large urns on either side of the small stage where the podium stood, matching the red, blue, and yellow of the smaller arrangements that adorned each table. The noise level was increasing as voices rose and fell against the tall walls and windows and bounced back as if for review of their words.

Mrs. Foss, the head of the board, found her in the crowd and led her to the front table. The billboard was propped up on the stage, draped in white sheets, waiting to be presented at the correct moment during the program. How symbolic, Mrs. O surmised, for it was the washing of sheets and other laundry that the wayward, rougher girls toiled over daily as part of their training.

As the lunch ended, Mrs. Foss called Mrs. O'Shaughnessy to the stage. Once again, she adjusted her fur and rose, giving a slight bow to the room before heading to the small stage at the front of the room. As the crowd clapped, Mrs. Foss instructed her to remove the sheets. With a flourish, she pulled away the cotton cloth, and the larger-than-life image of a younger Billi's head and shoulders emerged to yet louder applause.

Mrs. O staggered. Good heavens, it was enormous. She had thought they were only going to use the picture in a small corner of the advertisement, not splayed across the entire board. Or, as originally planned, Billi's photo printed on small, heart-shaped, pink felt pins to sell for one dollar each as a fundraiser. Mrs. O's idea for the heart-shaped pins had been met with nothing but praise. However, she did not know the members of the board had changed their minds, instead utilizing this huge photo of the unsuspecting Billi as the street billboard as advertisement for this home of unwed mothers.

"Isn't that remarkable?" Mrs. Foss was leading the crowd into further acknowledgment of their new poster child.

The crowd responded with resounding applause and a titter of approval.

Billi's blue eyes looked back at her mother, serene, sensitive, and definitely distinguishable as her child's. But the photo was over five years old and not in color. Someone had touched it up with paint, only making the image more recognizable from far away.

Mrs. O backed into the podium and held onto it for support. What had she done? She would have to race home and somehow tell Billi of her unwanted new fame before others had the chance. She made the sign of the cross in a silent prayer and looked out at the ladies in attendance. Unexpectedly, they were copying her movement.

"In the name of the Father…" Sister Mary Kathleen mounted the stage and led the group in prayer. The chairs shuffled as the ladies stood to join in.

Mrs. O'Shaughnessy bowed her head and prayed for her own skin once her daughter and son had seen her handiwork.

Billi sat in the living room with Pepper curled up at her side, trying to knit. She was not very good at it, but had reasoned that she had better learn if she was going to be a mother someday. The phone had not rung yet. Ray had promised to call by three o'clock and it was just a little after that hour. She dropped yet another stitch and held the lopsided project up to review her progress. Hopefully, they would have enough money so that she could buy clothes instead of depending on her ability to create them.

It was quiet in the house, being the Sunday her mother was attending the luncheon in her honor across town. She sighed at the situation with the new car. Jack had not responded in any way to her call. And now her mother was so proud of that damn vehicle, she devised any excuse to roam the streets with her shiny new possession.

The patter of soft summer rain lightly hitting the large windows made her think of Eddy, minding the concession stand as the drizzle bounced off the lake. Summers in Seattle were never without their rainy days.

Glad to be alone, she unfolded her last letter from Ray, the one she had picked from the top of the box she had decorated to hold his promises of return and their future, and reread it for the one hundredth time.

"Call you at 3 p.m. sharp, sweetheart. Guard the phone and I'll be talking with you soon."

She checked the clock over the mantle—3:15. How unusual for him to be late. She would not let her mind be occupied by fear of any kind. He was just busy. She turned her attention back to her knitting as her mother burst through the door.

"Where's Eddy?" Mrs. O shouted. The commotion woke Pepper, who dutifully ran to greet her. She brushed him away from her dress and stormed into the room. "Is he back yet? Why is he still there in the rain?"

It had not occurred to Billi that the reason he might still be there was the swooning Dahlia. "I'm certain he'll be home soon."

"I'm going after him." She was gone with the rattle of the door.

Billi knew there was no accounting for her mother's ways, so she simply continued her heartfelt work on her patchwork knitting. The phone finally rang at 3:35. She jumped to answer it, sending Pepper flying across the room. Landing on his short legs, he huffed over to another chair and jumped up to establish his territory.

"Hello." She attempted to sound nonchalant. It had been weeks since she had heard his voice.

"Hi, darling. You staying out of trouble?" Ray's excited voice boomed into the receiver from faraway Texas.

Her first comment to her future husband was a lie. "Yes. It's boring around here."

She had not noticed how long they had talked about nothing of importance until her mother, with Eddy in tow, stormed through the front door.

"It's Raymond." She offered the phone to Eddy who snatched it up. He immediately began drilling Ray with question after question.

Her mother sat in her rocker, twisting her gloves in both hands. When Billi shot her a smile, her mother raised and lowered her shoulders in the manner that spoke of trouble. Trouble could wait. She wrestled the phone back from her brother and blew Ray a kiss and promises.

When the line went dead she returned to her spot on the couch and felt the uncomfortable stare from her brother and mother.

Eddy broke the tension by heading for the small sideboard that housed their booze. "How about a Manhattan?"

"Something must be very wrong." Billi picked up her knitting and attempted to ignore them.

"Well," her mother began. "I didn't think that—"

"With a twist or a cherry?" Eddy interrupted.

Billi laughed. "I don't want one."

"You will."

"Twist." She lowered her knitting and contemplated her mother's nervous wringing of her favorite gloves. Tension crept down her back.

Eddy offered her the glass of dark alcohol with a twist. "Down this before we get into the car."

Had Jack contacted them directly? Did they know what he expected of her? She looked at the drink she was expected to down as fortification. The phone rang again, and she brushed past her brother to answer it.

"It's for you." She handed the receiver to her mother and watched her put the it close to her ear.

"Yes." Her mother's voice changed up a notch. "Yes." And as if her mother knew no other word, a third yes was uttered.

She handed Billi back the phone, snatched the suspended drink from Eddy, and downed a large gulp. "Off we go." She started for the door.

Eddy was at the wheel, chauffeuring the two women through the spitting rain as he drove north along Lake Washington Boulevard, past the empty beach, and turned up Madrona Drive. At Howell Street he turned right, and then right again down 39th Ave past the large white home on the corner with the three layers of balconies facing Lake Washington. He pulled over to the curb below 1717, and Mrs. O finally broke her silence.

"That was Mrs. Foss on the phone. It appears Mr. Broderick wants to meet you, Billi." Her voice was apologetic.

"Henry Broderick?" Billi knew something was up at the mention of the real estate baron's name. A name associated with so many prominent civic leaders and supporters of the Roman Catholic faith. "Is this his house?"

"Yes." Her mother was already out of the car, adjusting the old Kolinsky, and starting up the concrete stairs that cut through a tall grassy bank to the homes perched along the west side of the street.

Eddy fell in behind Billi as if he was afraid she was going to bolt, and the trio formed a single line as they headed past luscious gardens and a stone holding the marble bust of a serene-looking man. A bronze plaque below the ancient image stated:

> Happiness and freedom begin with a clear
> understanding of one principle,
> Some things are within your control,
> And some things are not.
>
> —Epictetus

Billi wondered if Epictetus had been thinking of a creature such as her mother when he wrote those words so many centuries ago.

The wooden stairs up to the front porch creaked a bit as they mounted them. Mrs. O smiled brightly as she rang the doorbell, throwing back her shoulders in preparation. The maid, dressed in red, answered the door and led them through the unadorned interior of the Broderick home to the music room, which overlooked even more greenery.

Mr. and Mrs. Broderick rose in unison as the O'Shaughnessys approached.

"Welcome," Mrs. Broderick greeted them, gesturing them toward seats, as her husband walked straight up to Billi and extended his hand.

"Thank you so much. See?" He pointed to the heart-shaped pink felt pin that he wore on his lapel with her face printed on it in dark-gray ink. "What a fabulous idea of your mother's. So simple but so eye-catching. The Home of the Good Shepherd should make money with this fundraiser. In fact, I have ordered one hundred more for my realtors to wear and hand out. Such a good deed you are doing."

Billi wasn't certain how to take the praise as her eyes had never left her image attached to Broderick's suit. Her mind was whirling. Her mother had done it to her again. Words drifted around her as she stood stunned at the obvious appreciation from this man. The word *poster* drifted through her foggy mind, and she snapped her head toward her mother, who was sipping a cup of coffee and with Mrs. Broderick as if they were old friends.

"Yes," Eddy was saying to the man he had always admired. "My sister is a great believer in charity and helping those less fortunate."

Billi forced a smile on her face and sat.

SEVENTEEN

"CHRIST ALMIGHTY," JACK SPUTTERED as David pulled up in front of the billboard of Billi's face and unforgettable blue eyes that now adorned the busy thoroughfare of North 50th Street. The road led to Woodlawn Park, the zoo, and Green Lake, all playgrounds sculpted by the Olmsted Brothers for the citizens of their beloved city.

Jack's mind swirled as he looked into the blue eyes of Billi's image. Did she have a child before? That must be why she had been chosen for this so-called honor. But why would she allow her image to be plastered across the sign for the home for unwed mothers? How would Raymond's family have allowed such a brazen filly into their flock? It did not make any sense. His thoughts turned to the ring she wore. The very ring his mother had sold to a distant cousin to maintain their household. This new twist added elements beyond his comprehension.

Duckworth approached them from around the corner, and Jack lowered his window. He watched this plug of a man steadily make his way to the car. Without saying a word, the short, blockish fellow placed an object in Jack's hand, tipped his hat, and kept walking.

Jack twisted the pink felt heart in his hand and weighed the importance of these new circumstances. The only bright side he could conjure—her training would not take as long as he had anticipated. She was a soiled woman and already knew the needs of men. With bile forming in his stomach, he waved David into action as he stuffed the pin into his pocket.

Billi and Eileen shared a cup of tea in the quiet home of the Nakamuras. A photo of Mrs. Nakamura, young and beautiful, dressed in traditional kimono with her hair styled high, hung above the Buddha between her two geishas, with the white orchid standing guard. As the August heat increased the apartment above the grocery store felt cramped and airless.

"Father wants to send me back to Japan, as he did Tak," Eileen dabbed at the perspiration on her forehead. "But I have told him I will not go. He needs someone to look after him and Kenny."

"And me." Billi attempted to lighten the conversation. "What about me?"

The image of the man in the picture, the one who had beheaded so many, came to mind. She did not want her friend in a land governed by such brutality. And the dawning of what Eileen might face upon her return to her family's forsaken homeland made Billi shift with discomfort. That would explain why Tak had changed so. He had been born a Nisei on American soil, then traveled to Japan for education and to satisfy his required time in their service, only to return to America. Tak was a Kibei like so many others now living in the United States.

"Don't worry," Eileen smiled, and her eyes were almost lost in the movement of her cheeks. "I know how to convince my father."

"Do you think we will have war?" Billi could not stop herself and the question dangled between them.

"No." Eileen smiled, confirming her belief. "Why would you think such things? What has Raymond told you?"

"Nothing. His mind is in the sky, literally. That's all he talks about, the young men he works with, most of them just out of high school. But he should be home on leave in two months."

"You must miss him so."

"We all do. Eddy is grumpy without him. Mother doesn't have that other willing pair of hands at her beck and call, and I miss his sense of humor."

"Is that all?" Eileen teased.

"Welllll…" Billi dragged out the word and then giggled.

Eileen looked around at the empty room as if to chase away ghosts. "Look what I found among Mother's things." She rose and disappeared down the hall to her bedroom. "Father would not touch her clothing and asked me to give everything away." She continued as she returned, carrying a small, well-worn book. "But I could not part with this. My grandmother gave this to my mother as a wedding present." She handed the ornately decorated object to her friend.

Billi opened the first page and saw the old script blessing the marriage, and then she turned the page and nearly fainted.

"Do you believe it?" Eileen laughed softly as she sat next to her friend. "My mother owned such a book. But it is merely shunga, a traditional present for a young bride as guidance in the art of lovemaking. It depicts scenes from *The Tale of Genji*." Her words became almost defensive as her friend slowly turned the pages of the erotic drawings of ukiyo-e woodblock prints.

"Who is the artist?" Billi raised her eyebrows, dumbfounded by the beautiful depictions of sex.

"It is Hokusai. The Edo period."

Billi kept turning page after page, admiring the artistry, aware she knew nothing of the private behavior between men and women. "My heavens," she blurted at one point. "How do they do that?"

The sound of footsteps mounting the stairs in the outside hallway raised panic in both young women.

"You take it home." Eileen stuffed the book inside Billi's handbag. "Study it and then give it back to me when I marry."

The proposition sounded logical; and since they had not made it through the entire book, Billi willingly accepted the offer.

THE DARK SEDAN KEPT PACE with Billi as she walked home up Jackson.

"Get in the car." David did not cloak his nasty demand.

Billi ignored him, keeping her stride strong.

"Get in the car now." He tried to sound nice.

"What for?"

"We have business."

His leer as he dragged out the word *business* made her feel dirty.

"I have no business with you," she shot back.

"He wants to see you and he said now." David pulled the car to the curb, blocking her from crossing the street.

She had known Jack would try again. Reluctantly, she got into the back seat of the car, in the hopes that this would be the last meeting. Besides, she had a few things to say as well.

The brick building on Boylston felt cool in the summer heat. But as she mounted the stairs, the temperature rose as did her heart rate. Her pulse raced not only from the exertion of the climb but the anticipation of the coming confrontation.

Jack sat with his back to the bay windows, facing the door as she entered. He had rolled up the sleeves on his white shirt and the pale skin of his arms reminded her of their midnight swim the night Mrs. Nakamura passed away. She unconsciously held her purse closer, the purse that held the forbidden depictions of man and woman. Their cultures were so different.

"You shouldn't have gotten my mother that car," she blurted, not budging far into the room. She had not planned to begin the negotiations in such a manner, but his stern dark eye made her nervous today.

"Just the beginning. A fair trade, don't you think?"

David closed the door behind her, and within seconds the airless room made her sweat. She could feel the dampness trickle down her back.

"Sit." He pointed to the small wooden chair, the hard surface, she observed, perfect to keep her uncomfortable, perfect for interrogation. Things were different, something in his manner had changed. He seemed as hard and unyielding as the chair she lowered onto.

"Your training will begin in one week," he continued. "I have everything set up. I don't care what excuse you use for your friends. But since you already have some experience in the nature of your duty, things should move along much quicker. Which is good. We need to move fast."

His short, clipped speech slowly sank in. "One week? And what training?"

He snickered. "Nothing you haven't done before."

His meanness shot across the room, jolting her further and increasing her confusion. "I've made it perfectly clear, I can't help you. I have never seen this Akio Sumiyoshi gentleman before. I would tell you if I had."

"He is hardly a gentleman. He is a killer. And you seem to have more secrets than my agency."

"I don't know what you are talking about."

"I will inform your mother and brother of your departure if you don't."

"Wait, what is it exactly that you want of me?"

"We are going to put you in a surrounding where no one will suspect that you speak Japanese and then you will report to us what is being said and by whom."

"You want me to spy?"

"If you want to call it that, yes."

"And where are you going to put me?" She tried to look relaxed.

"Nowhere around here. Not with your face plastered all over the city."

Billi's breath caught in her throat. Of course he would have seen the billboard.

"Oh, that. You see—"

"I see." A muscle in his right cheek, below his scar, twitched. "This is a necessary service for your country." He sounded as if he were trying to convince himself. "If Raymond were here he would agree. In one week we will send you to Port Townsend. I've made the arrangements. With your expertise further training shouldn't take long."

"What kind of Japanese training am I going to get in Port Townsend?"

"It is not to further your love of the Japanese, but for occupational training."

"What occupation will I be learning that will attract unsuspecting Japanese men?" she scoffed.

"The oldest one around, sister."

A NEW LETTER FROM RAY waited for her on her bed. How had her life been set upside down so swiftly? And how had this evil man gotten under her skin with plans to destroy her future for a war which everyone claim would not touch their shores? At least, the devil Jack promised they could ward off such turmoil if she would help. Would Ray approve? Of course not. She simply would not go through with it. She did not care if he put her in jail for being a thief and took back her mother's prized car. How else could he hurt her? Ray. Her breath caught in her throat. He had sent Ray away. That explained why his departure had been so unexpected, so hurried. The long arm of Jack Huntington's evil reached far. Who was he? Her mind flashed to her Professor Fujihara. He must know something about this. Tomorrow after work, she would go to the university and find the professor. She needed to start asking questions.

A whore? He expected her to play a whore in the so-called war efforts? Recalling the book Eileen had given her, she pulled it from her handbag and shoved it below her bed. She attempted to shake the images from her mind. Jack had promised she would never be alone with a man. She would sit among the Japanese men only to listen, never to be touched. But how the hell could he arrange that?

She forced the thoughts from her mind and picked up Ray's words of sky and love. Oh, how she needed him now. Time was of the essence. Maybe she could go to him in Texas and get married there. The answer floated before her. She would write him immediately of her plans. She did not care where they were married, only that she became Mrs. Raymond Richardson, and the sooner the better.

THE AFTERNOON HEAT VIBRATED OFF THE GROUND as Billi walked past Frosh Pond on the university campus the next day. Enjoying the slight breeze picking up a mist that blanketed the north side of the fountain, she stood there for a moment, letting the coolness land on her face and clothing. She needed her wits about her to resolve her predicament. The night before, after she had written her new proposal to Ray, she had made a list of questions for the professor. How long had he known Jack? Did he know who Jack worked for or who sent him? She smiled at her thoroughness, and knew her professor would be impressed. He would nod in his gentle way and help. She knew he would.

Billi passed a handful of students who lounged on the library steps enjoying the suns warmth. Inside Suzzallo felt dark, cavernous, and cool. She mounted the stone steps that curved up to the reading room and stopped in front of Professor Fujihara's office. She knocked then turned the knob. The solid wood did not budge and the brass bracket that had held his name sat empty. She tried the door again in disbelief.

Her feet flew down the steps to the main library room. An older woman sat behind the desk and Billi swiftly moved toward her.

"Where is Professor Fujihara?" Her voice echoed, far too loud for the surroundings.

"I have no inkling." The older woman's words were even and controlled.

"Do you know where I might find him?" Billi lowered her voice as well and attempted a smile to hide her panic.

"He is gone."

"I can see that, but where?"

"No one knows. He simply disappeared."

Fear quickened Billi's heartbeat. Had Jack gotten rid of the professor as well?

"How long ago?"

"About one month. Everyone commented on how he left right after that competition. He left behind an enormous mess, by the way."

"What do you mean, a mess?" Obviously, this librarian enjoyed the gossip of these hallowed halls.

"Papers everywhere I heard."

"What happened to those papers?"

"Why?"

"I am one of his students and had written a long essay he had promised to return. I hope I can have it back."

The women eyed her suspiciously. "Sorry." She bent her gray head over her work again.

"Is there someone else I could ask—"

The librarian's head snapped up and her hardened look of superiority stopped Billi.

"Why does everyone want to know about this man?" She softened when she saw Billi's frame stiffen with what she must have interpreted as sadness over the loss of her paper. "Just a minute and I'll check. They were all gathered and put in a box."

She rose, as did Billi's hopes. Maybe some clue would surface from the box of papers. She held her breath and watched the soft frame of the older woman move soundlessly through the back door into further, private archives, reserved only for those who worked the desk to distribute and share.

She returned with an expression of confusion on her face that made Billi's stomach tighten.

"Gone." She frowned in Billi's direction.

"Gone?"

"The box is gone. The shelf is empty." She resumed her post at the front desk ignoring Billi. "No one tells me anything anymore."

Billi turned toward the bright sunshine flowing through the exit door, feeling colder than the flat stone she walked across.

EIGHTEEN

Darling Raymond.

She had begun the letter over and over, the strewn pieces of paper with ink scratches across them littered her white cotton bedspread and the floor; each page a different attempt at suggesting her traveling back to Texas to be married. It occurred to her she should have given in to Ray, let him take her to bed before he left. She could claim to be pregnant and then the wedding would take place immediately. She surprisingly hated her virgin status. There had to be some way around Jack's scheme.

Keep it simple, she told herself, and don't put anything through the mail that watching eyes could read.

Call me Sunday evening at 6:30. I have a surprise.
I'll wait by the phone every Sunday to hear your voice.
Love you,
Billi

Short, sweet, and to the point. She addressed two envelopes with the same message, and in the early morning light she walked down the street and dropped one letter into the neighborhood post box. She would send the other one from the post office later. Two could play this game. With a serenity not felt in days, she returned home to think about what she would pack to become Mrs. Raymond Richardson.

For now, she could tell no one her plan, not even Eileen, and that felt strange. But she could not risk involving the one person she must protect. She had not visited her friend as much of late, not only due to her summer schedule at the concession stand, but because she did not want to encourage Jack to poke his nose into the affairs of the innocent Nakamura family.

In her room, Billi opened her closet and picked through a few of her best belongings as Pepper nestled on her pillow. The new light-blue dress she had worn to dinner that fateful night would be perfect to be married in. She could buy a white hat, shoes, purse, and matching gloves. She had three outfits laid out on her bed when it occurred to her she would need a bigger suitcase. A trip down South Lander Street to Sears and Roebuck would solve that issue. But hauling a suit case home on the bus would draw too much attention. Her mind worked through several scenarios, and with a gush of longing she discovered the depth of her love for her fiancé.

SHE HEARD THE CREAK OF THE FIFTH STEP and looked at Pepper nestled against her pillow on her bed, his head had not popped up. The clock on her nightstand read—9:10. Eddy had already left for work. Danny and her mother were out buying supplies for the concession stands. Who could be coming up the stairs? Fear gripped her when abruptly Pepper shot toward her bedroom door, growling. She managed to get behind the door before it opened slightly. Pepper held his ground, furiously barking at the intruder. Through the slim crack of the door she saw the sleeve of a man's suit jacket. Looking down she recognized the unpolished, worn shoes belonging to David. When he closed her door, she could barely hear his movements over her guard dog's threats. Pepper scratched at the door in his fury, and she tried to silently hush him. If David were checking all the upstairs rooms, he would be in her mother's bedroom by now. Pepper's increased yelping sent shivers down her spine, David approached her room again. She heard a slight sound as the door opened to Eddy's room across the hall. Sweat dripped between her breasts as she leaned against the wall, shaking. Her doorknob twisted again, and instantly, her brave little protector jumped in the air at the knob.

"Don't worry, little mutt. Your day will come," David threatened through the closed door. Alerted by the sound of voices from outside, the weasel of a man ran down the stairs.

She hurried to her window in time to see her neighbors climb up their steps, laughing in the early-morning sunshine. She ducked away from the window as David walked around from the back of her house, down the side driveway, past the statue of the Virgin Mary, and out to the street.

At the sound of a whimper, Billi spun toward her exhausted Pepper, who stood embarrassed next to a small pool of piddle by the door.

"Good boy, Pepper." She scooped him up, hurried down the circular stairs, and swung the front door open wide. Pepper wiggled free and charged onto the lawn, leaving Billi by the white railing, glaring at the sedan across the street. Pepper barked as he pawed the grass where he had left his mark, then he stood guard at the base of the steps. When the car engine started and the sedan rolled down the street, Billi noticed only one person in the car.

Hurrying back inside, she went to the back door, which sat slightly ajar, and secured it. She would have Eddy double the locks. Then she picked up the phone and dialed the number on the card Jack had given her that first night in his apartment.

"Duckworth," the man on the other end of the line answered.

"Hey, Duckworth. Tell Mr. Huntington to keep his nasty little man out of my house. Breaking and entering will set me free from his plan."

"Who was there?" Jack's voice boomed.

"Don't you know? What kind of spy are you that you don't even know who you send to break into my house?"

"Who was there, Billi?" His voice direct and unemotional.

"Your goon, David. Well, I'm calling the police and telling them about your little intrusion. I'm certain they will find this interesting. Then you can try to make up stories about me. Sorry, you lose." While her accusation sounded reasonable, it remained all bluff and bravado.

"I'm sorry if he disturbed you." His voice sounded tight, as if he were trying to keep his anger in check. "I'm glad you called. We need to meet."

"No." She hung up the phone.

She snatched up an old newspaper to cover Pepper's piddle and, with her guard dog at her heels, she ran back up the stairs. She had missed the bus and would be late for work. As she pushed her bedroom door open, she saw the stack of clothing she had neatly piled across her bed. Had he seen them? Had that disgusting David's snooping through their house given him a hint as to her plans? She closed the door so that it stood barely open and peeked into her own room as if she had never seen it before. The bed and some of the stacks of clothes were in view. She pushed the newspaper over Pepper's nervous indiscretion, then piled her clothes back in her closet. She would have to hurry.

"I SWEAR I SAW HER LEAVE," David pleaded. "She must have come in when I was checking around back." He didn't dare look up. The eye appeared more than angry.

"This is a warning, and you are damn lucky you're getting even one. Don't go near the house again unless I'm with you and give you very specific instructions. Tell me again about Billi's room."

"Well, the dog was in there and I couldn't see much." He winced at his weak response. "I didn't want to let that stupid animal out," he added. "She was doing laundry."

"What do you mean?"

"Clothes were stacked in piles on the bed."

"Describe them."

Jack was silently amused that David shifted nervously in his seat before him as he attempted to recall what he had seen. When David had repeated his findings several times, Jack sat back in his chair and threw his pen on his stack of papers.

"All right, go." He waited for David to close the door behind him. He could not allow his hatred of David to get in his way. He could not trust the man, but needed him at the same time. His guts felt like a rolling ball of acid. He shoved his coffee cup aside and held his head, ticking through the scene David could barely describe.

He thought of his sister Lilly and her room, and how their maid Bella always stacked like items together. What could Billi be up to? He would definitely meet with her tonight.

"YOU OKAY?" DANNY LEANED FROM THE WINDOW of the concession stand as Billi approached. "I was about to shut down and come and find you."

The young blonde who had been starting for the concession stand spun on her heel, embarrassed, and went back to her beach blanket.

"Thanks, Danny." Billi climbed inside and shook the sand from her shoes. "I'm fine."

The blonde looked at the white stand again. Seeing Billi had stepped inside, she regained her courage and walked back toward the stand.

Billi waited in the background as Danny took the teenage girl's order. The blonde head bobbed from side to side as Danny ran through a number of items he would willing provide for the cute smile.

The several minutes of watching the two flirt, coupled with the soothing water lapping against the sand, composed Billi. Jack seemed to have no boundaries. She would send Ray a telegram and have him call soon. Raymond, her love, her escape.

By three o'clock the beach emptied out for the dinner hour. Young children, having played furiously in the sand and the blue waters, were being gathered up for their journey home. The blonde girl, who had spent much of the day flitting between her blanket and the concession stand, waved goodbye to Danny.

"Would you mind if I ran some errands?" Billi had sorted the money and put the extra cash in the bag they carried home daily.

"Sure. I'll be by later tonight because your mom said she is baking a cake. Is everything okay? Those guys haven't been around lately, have they?"

"No." She avoided looking at him, picking up the broom to sweep.

"I'll do that." He took the broom from her. "You go. I told Ray I'd help you out."

"You're a doll. Don't break that cute blonde's heart." She grabbed the money and headed out the door.

"Susie." He said her name as if it were a poem.

BILLI MADE IT TO 113 CHERRY in time to send her telegram. Abbot Van Hissel stood behind the counter in his Western Union uniform and smiled across at her. When he saw her engagement ring, his attitude spun quickly to the matter at hand. She paid for the telegram and he swiftly sent her message. She walked a few blocks to a mailbox and posted the second letter to Ray in the event Jack's reach stretched longer than she knew. And then she headed south toward Sears and Roebuck.

The clock on the large brick tower that stood prominently above the two wings of the building read—4:15. She would have to hurry.

Inside, the long aisles drew her down toward the luggage. She picked a strong bag, large, tan, rimmed in dark leather that matched the handle. One that would not draw attention but would hold the items she had chosen earlier. Ray would just have to buy his new bride more upon her arrival. She carried the empty piece of luggage out of the store and down the steps, hailing a yellow cab. With the suitcase secured in the trunk, the cabby started toward her home.

After a few blocks the driver spoke over his shoulder in his thick Greek accent. "Miss, you in some, ah, trouble?"

"No." She shifted in the back seat. "Why?"

"Someone, ah, maybe they follow us?"

Billi did not turn around but felt the perspiration prickle across her forehead. She took her powder case out of her purse and opened it. Using the small mirror, she attempted to catch a look at the car the cabby referred to. Then she saw it, like a shark, following in a very obvious manner.

"Just drop me at the house. I'll give you extra if you will then drive around the block and deliver the luggage to the back door. No, just put it behind the statue in the yard."

"Okay, miss. Is bad?"

"Yes." She found herself looking at her ring. "You see, my husband is in flight training in the army in Texas. The man following me won't leave me alone. So, I'm going to go live with my aunt for a while." The lies came so smoothly.

"I, ah, sign papers. My son, he seventeen, but he join army. My son, he eighteen, he in coast a guard. Do you want I talk with fella?"

"Thank you but no. Please just be careful he does not see my suitcase. It's very important I leave unnoticed."

"Yes, miss. An' you need ride, you call Popanoplis. Poppi—" He pointed to his chest. "—Poppi take care ah you."

"Thank you, sir. I will do that." His willingness to help gave her a slight relief.

"Poppi," he corrected her.

As he pulled up to the house, Poppi sat facing the front yard. "Is Blessed Virgin you want me to put case behind?"

"Yes. She will protect it for me." Billi almost felt badly about her fibs now.

"You take care, and remember, Poppi."

Billi handed the older man the fare along with the promised extra and stepped from the cab. The sedan waited down the street. She ran inside and watched from the window with Pepper bouncing around her feet. The cabby pulled away from the curb and the sedan fell in behind.

NINETEEN

THE PHONE RANG AT SEVEN that night. Billi had thought of every excuse to change the flowers in the vase below the Blessed Virgin Mary, but no luggage had arrived. She ran to the phone and snatched up the receiver.

"Hello."

"I have something for you." Jack's voice held intrigue.

"Pray tell, what might that be?"

"We need to talk tonight. I'm sending someone for you now. Be on the corner in twenty minutes." The phone went dead.

Billi walked into the kitchen where Danny, Eddy, and her mother were cutting into the German chocolate Kuchen, its creamy frosting topped with slivers of Bavarian chocolate. Pepper had positioned himself directly below Mrs. O'Shaughnessy in the hopes she dropped some crumbs.

"Chocolate is not good for dogs," Mrs. O sang out. "Who was on the phone, Billi?"

"I'm heading down to see Eileen. None for me." She turned and disappeared before any of them thought it odd. Grabbing a light sweater, she pulled it on as she hurried down the front stairs. She ran to the end of the block and stepped into the shadows to wait.

JACK'S UPPER ROOM DRIPPED HEAT, with the windows closed, and he wanted it that way. He had gone with David to pick Billi up, not fully trusting his underling around her. He held the door for her as she stepped into the room and, without waiting, she took the large chair.

"I'll take that water now," she demanded, her head held high.

Jack nodded toward David, who headed into the kitchen.

"You have something for me?" She folded her hands in her lap.

"How was your day?"

"Why ask if you are following me?"

He smiled at her without answering. They sat locked in a silent tug of war as David entered with two glasses of water, then continued out of the room. Jack removed the patch and sat back in the smaller wooden chair, preparing to win through her resistance.

"What happened to Professor Fujihara? What did you do with him?"

"We don't know. That's part of our problem. We think he's in Hawaii." He handed her a glass.

"Hawaii?"

Jack watched her drink her water. "Did he ever say he had family there?"

"No." She put the glass down; the coolness of the liquid had not helped.

"What family did he mention?"

"Only the ones in Japan."

"Have you ever been to Hawaii?"

"No."

"San Francisco?"

"No?"

"How many states have you been in?"

"We took the train to Oregon once."

"Do you like to travel by train or by boat?"

"Depends on where I'm going."

"Where are you going?"

She caught herself before answering. He had purposely shot the questions at her fast and now she looked confused.

"Nowhere." She took her time answering. "That is what I have been telling you. I am not going anywhere, especially for you."

"It's not for me." He leaned toward her. "It's for your country."

"I haven't seen your Akio Sumiyoshi."

"But you will." He deliberated as he ran his fingers through his hair before speaking again. "Recently, the Imperial Japanese Navy captured a British Royal Navy vessel. Unfortunately, the Brit's had some very valuable papers aboard intended for their South East Asia holdings. Both officers assigned to destroy the documents and not allow the messages to fall into enemy hands, were killed before they could carry out their orders. The papers contained a very telling situation. Britain did not have the man power or ships to defend the Pacific. It was just the motivation Yamamoto and the Japanese Empire needed to make the decision for further expansion for what they are calling the Greater East Asian Co-Prosperity Sphere. Led by the Japanese, of course, and free of all western influence. So, that leaves the wide ocean open for the Japanese to attack us with little allied help."

She felt her throat go dry and swallowed hard.

He took two newspaper articles from the pile on his desk and handed them to her. The tattered pages of the *Tokyo Nichi Nichi Shimbun* in Japanese lay on top. She shifted it to read the headline in the *Japan Advertiser*. Both dated back to 1938 with the story of a contest between two Japanese lieutenants who were racing to see who would be the first to wield their sword and behead one hundred Chinese. He handed her more articles, saw tears form in her eyes as she read the names of Emperor Hirohito and Prince Yasuhiko, of the rape of Nanking, of the countless deaths of children, women, babies, men.

She clutched the arm of the high-backed chair with a terrifying expression. She had read enough.

"This really happened," he hoped she could hear him through her shock. "I am not making this up. Members of the Imperial Japanese Navy, along with merchants, language students, priests, professors, are up and down our west coast from Mexico to Canada. They take their information to the consulates and are paid for spying on our naval bases, at Boeing Field, anywhere there might be information to help them fight against us. We need your help."

"But I—"

"We want to send you to training next week and then get you set up. I will go with you."

"Where?"

"I can't say yet. Do you want to read any more?"

She shoved the papers at him with disgust. Her hands trembling as he took them.

"We'll meet next Tuesday night and go over the plan." He picked up his patch, ending the meeting. "It's obvious that you cannot share any of this with anyone."

He rose and took her elbow to help her to her feet. David rounded the corner and she stiffened.

"I'll take her home." Jack brushed past David and led Billi out the door.

Pepper charged down the spiral stairs at the sound of his mistress's footsteps on the porch. When Billi opened the door, he flew past her and barked into the darkness. After announcing himself, he lifted his leg on the rose bush at the base of the stairs and followed her inside.

Her new suitcase stood just inside the door. So did Eddy.

He watched his sister's reaction to the luggage. "A nice man named Poppi said you left this in his cab this afternoon."

"Oh, yes." She grabbed it and started up the stairs. "How nice of him. I thought I'd be ready when Ray returns."

Through the ornate rungs of the banister, Eddy watched his sister climb the spiral stairs and disappear around the corner. He pocketed the card Poppi had handed him to give to Billi. He would have to give this cabby a call and thank him for helping his sister—and possibly to see if he knew more than Billi let on.

The phone rang at 6:30 p.m. sharp that Sunday and Billi snatched it from it from the wall before the second ring.

"You must miss me terribly." Ray's voice boomed from the receiver.

"I do."

"Love those two little words. Hope you repeat them in front of the priest soon. With me by your side, that is."

She giggled. "I promise."

"Where's the gang?"

"They'll be here soon. I wanted you all to myself for a moment." She held her breath and began her practiced speech. "Darling, I have an idea. Please say yes."

In the few minutes before her mother and brother returned from the grocery store, Billi had convinced Ray to let her travel to Texas to be married. They would talk again when he had his end of affairs arranged. He had agreed they could plan a big reception for his return. Her future husband's excited response inspired her.

The door rattled as the shoppers entered.

"For me?" Eddy steamed past his sister with the bags of food, Pepper nipping at his heels.

She held out the receiver to her mother. "It's Ray. He wants to say hello to his favorite Mrs. O."

She held her breath as her mother grasped the receiver. Ray had promised not to say a word, but her mother had a sixth sense that could ferret out the most innocent of plans.

Eddy paced, waiting for his turn to say hello to his best friend. Pepper sensed the anticipation and chased his tail for attention, but no one noticed the young pup as their focus centered on the words being exchanged long distance.

When the phone finally made the rounds back to Billi, she quietly confirmed the time for the next phone call on Monday. Then, she breathed deeply. In a matter of days she would be off to Texas.

EILEEN TIGHTENED HER HOLD on the handle of Billi's new suitcase. It wasn't overly heavy considering all that Billi had stuffed inside, but she found it a bit cumbersome as she lifted the case onto the bus down the block from the O'Shaughnessy home. The eagerness to help Billi with her scheme to elope mixed with a touch of sorrow, and also with the intrigue of a deep secret between friends. Eileen had not thought it strange for her best friend to ask such a favor. She felt honored, and knew her mother would have been proud that she helped her Caucasian friend in matters of the heart. She had helped with the packing, and they had both giggled as Billi slid Mrs. Nakamuras shunga book neatly in the folds of her new white silk nightgown with the thick lace gracing the top. As Eileen paid for her short trip down Jackson, she tried not to think of life without her mother and best friend. She had her father and younger brother to care for now. But first she must help her friend get off safely to her beloved Raymond.

She bumped the suitcase up the stairs to the Nakamura family apartment. No empty shoes met her inside the door. The stark emptiness of the rooms slid over her as she passed down the hallway and opened her bedroom door. Eileen knelt and slid the tan case beneath her single bed, and then neatly pulled down her long bedspread, hiding the evidence of the lovers' plan to elope. She had not seen her father or Kenny as she hurried by the windows of their grocery store. She hoped her luck held as she started back down the stairs for the train station. She could almost see Union Station just a few blocks away, but to be certain, she walked up the hill around the other direction so as to not pass by the store windows a second time.

The Northern Pacific train to San Antonio, Texas, would take days and a link to the Southern Pacific. Eileen became fascinated by the prospect of such a journey, as her family remained confined to the activities of just a few blocks. She gathered the information Billi needed, the time table and the costs, secured them in her handbag, then hurried toward the door. She paused when she noticed a man in a dark suit enter the cavernous, ornate interior of the station. This marked the second time she had seen him that day. Billi had said to be careful and to make certain no one discovered her destination. Instinctively, Eileen hurried back to a different ticket window.

"I sorry." She smiled at the man with the thick glasses behind the counter. Using the broken speech of those who had just arrived in the United States from Japan she continued, "Ohio? Yes?"

"Ohio?" The clerk scrutinized her suspiciously. "That's a long ways." When she did not budge, he handed her a copy of the route and costs.

She smiled and stuffed the second set of papers in her purse before hurrying out the door past the man in the dark suit who had come to stand in line behind her.

"What's up?" Danny asked Billi as he hovered over the candy in the concession shed. "I'm so mad I missed Ray's call last night. He must have had something good to say. You've been a bit distracted all day."

"Oh, Danny." Billi rearranged the stacks of candy yet again. "Everything is going to be just fine."

"Sure, but why the dizzy smiles?" Excited, he grabbed her arm. "Is Ray coming home? Is that it? Oh, shucks, I just can't wait to see him."

"No." She forced the smile from her face. "No, he is not coming home for a long time. We were just talking about the wedding is all."

"Won't that be some swell affair? I know Mrs. O has big plans."

"When doesn't she?" Billi moved to the window to watch the swimmers. "Where's Susie?" The young blonde had become a regular at the stand and with Danny.

"Babysitting her younger cousin who can't swim. So they won't let her bring him to the beach." His disgust at someone's inability to navigate the placid waters of Lake Washington apparent in his voice. A voice that also held a twinge of desire and maturing of a man.

"How long is this cousin staying?" She needed to be certain Danny would not run off on her mother as she plotted to do.

"Leaves tomorrow and then Susie is back on my beach." His hopeful smile filled Billi's heart with love for all the freckles that covered his young face.

She would miss Danny just as much as her mother and brother. She reassured herself, their separation would be for a short period of time. She just needed to leave before Jack swept her away for his so-called training.

"Danny, I know that you will always look after Mom, and Eddy, and Pepper. It is what Ray would want, and what I want as well. You will do that for us, won't you?"

"Of course. But there's nothing wrong, is there?"

She did not get a chance to answer as Susie rode her bike into view and waved.

Danny snatched a Mounds candy bar from the stack and dashed out the door. "Break time and dock this from my account."

Billi watched him race across the sand and up the hill. Observing the young lovers made her blush with lust. In a few days, she would be Mrs. Raymond Richardson.

"OHIO," DUCKWORTH REPEATED for the third time to his boss and David.

"Damn. Now what?" Jack sat back in his chair and concentrated on the dwindling light filtering through the trees outside the window.

"Maybe the Jap is just playing games. Or maybe she is the one leaving town," David suggested.

Jack turned and looked at David in disbelief. The worthless man continued to hamper his efforts to secure Billi. "When is the soonest we can get a wiretap at the house?"

"Tomorrow," David snapped to answer.

Duckworth fiddled with his hat. "Where do you want me, sir?"

"Do you think the Japanese woman noticed you?"

"I don't think so."

"Then stay with her. She knows something, but I don't want to upset Billi just yet." He rubbed his good eye in exasperation.

"Got it." Duckworth stood, paused, but then left the stuffy room.

David toyed with a pencil, nervously spinning it between his fingers. "Where do you want me?"

"Outside the O'Shaughnessy house. I want to know who goes in and out. Radio me with every movement. And get the wiretap on now."

"Yes, boss."

David shot up from his chair, tossed the pencil on the makeshift desk, and hurried for the door. Another chance. Someday that bitch would be his.

TWENTY

WHEN THE PHONE RANG, Eddy rushed to pick up the receiver. He had called Poppi and made a deal with the Greek taxi driver. If his sister called him for any reason, Poppi would let Eddy know. For Billi's sake, Eddy had assured the man. The appearance of the new suitcase had him wondering. Especially when he got home that afternoon, and discovered it had disappeared. What were his sister and his best friend up to?

"Ray. Just the man I wanted to talk to." Eddy had the question on his lips when Billi rushed through the kitchen door and nearly tackled him. Pepper barked and wagged his tail as the siblings struggled over the receiver. When Eddy would not release it, Billi kicked him in the shin. He grabbed his left leg and hopped around the room with Pepper at his side.

"Be careful, Ray," he shouted. "She just kicked me. You're in for it, pal."

Billi stood with her back to her brother and waited to hear the news.

"I'm flying high, baby," Ray spoke excitedly. "Just get down here. I couldn't sleep last night thinking about you and your great idea. I love you so much, Bil."

Billi turned coolheaded and confidently toward her injured brother. "That's nice to know, dear. Yes. Of course I love you." She put the phone to her chest and spoke to Eddy. "Can I have one second alone please?"

Eddy straightened. "Come on, Pepper, we know when we're not wanted. Say hi to my best friend for me." Man and dog stomped out of the room.

She made certain he made it through the kitchen door before she began speaking again. "He's gone. Poor Eddy. I have everything organized and will catch the train tomorrow and be there by the weekend. I love you, Ray. Everything will work out swell. I'll telegram you my arrival time."

"I'll be back by then. They're sending me cross-country. Too bad I just can't scoop you up and bring you along."

"Don't you worry. I'll be there soon enough and we'll be married. I can't wait, Ray. You have no idea how happy that will make me."

The sun burned unusually hot for a Seattle summer as Billi sat watching the swimmers at Mount Baker Beach. The concession stand baked like an oven, even with the door open, and she and Danny had to put the candy in the backroom so it would not melt. Ice cream sales were good that day; and as nap time approached, mothers were, once again, dragging exhausted children to the shade of the tall trees that skirted the sand. A tranquility surrounded her day, a quiet confidence that reflected Billi's decision to leave unnoticed. She had spent most of the night writing letters to her mother, father, and brother. She would leave a note for Danny and one for Dahlia in the backroom of the stand. He would find it tomorrow when he opened without her. Her goodbye to Eileen would be in person.

Danny returned from his break, which consisted of sitting as close as possible to his summer love, Susie. "What a day." He spoke dreamily, propping the door open further before entering the stand.

Billi looked longingly at the cool water. "I'm going to take a quick swim."

"I've got it covered." Danny smiled, eyes fixed on the tanning blonde.

"I know you do and that you will take good care of this place." She wanted to explode with her news. She leaned over and ruffled his curls, then stepped into the sunshine.

The water blanketed her with its coolness. She pushed forward into the refreshing liquid as she headed out past the floating raft to the colder, deeper portion of the lake. She flipped onto her back and faced away from the newly constructed Lake Washington floating bridge to catch her favorite view of Mount Rainier. Its regal, snowcapped mass loomed in the distance like an enticing ice cream cone, high above the foothills.

She caught the sparkle of her ring below the water's surface. She would leave before dinner, in just a few hours. Poppi had said he would pick her up down the block at 5 p.m. sharp. She trembled at the thought. She had to get away before Jack came for her tonight. He could not have her. He could not use her in his vicious plan if she were miles away and newly married. She dove under the surface toward the cooler bottom and then swiftly turned and rocketed to the top. She would miss her swims. From the map, it appeared Randolph Air Field, the West Point of the air, rested nowhere near salt or freshwater. She dove again as if her life depended on it, attempting to imprint the sensation. The memory had to last until the happily married couple could return. As she surfaced, the air tasted sweet. She took one more deep breath then decided to head in. Her smooth stroke pulled her back to the beach until her hand hit the sand.

THE RADIO CRACKLED TO LIFE in Jack's back room and he hurried to pick it up.

"Boss, Duckworth here."

"I'm all ears." Jack's nerves were tight.

"She came by cab to the Japanese home and is upstairs with them now. But the cab is still here."

"Stay with her and let me know what happens next."

A knock at the door drew Jack back down the hall. Through the small, arched stained-glass window in the wooden door, he recognized the uniform of a telegram delivery person and slowly opened the door.

"Mr. Jack Huntington?" The boy's voice fluctuated with youth and his reaction to the patch over Jack's eye.

Jack nodded, and the boy held out the telegram. Jack fished in his pocket for a tip as he accepted the small envelope, then closed the door and quickly opened the message.

"Oh my God." He fumbled into the large chair before the windows, his head dropped to his hands, and he sat breathing heavily.

The radio beckoned him again. Listlessly he stood and slumped toward the back room.

"Here," he said into the radio.

"She's come down the stairs with a suitcase. Wait a minute. Her brother just showed up. They're talking and he doesn't look happy."

"She's headed to the train station. Follow them and don't let her leave. I'm on my way. Don't let her go. I have to talk with her."

He gently folded the telegram into his pocket, wiped his eyes, and headed out the door.

"WHAT ARE YOU DOING HERE, EDDY?" Billi asked, trying not to scream at him.

"What are you up to? Is everything okay?" He stood between her and the cab door.

"Yes. Now let me go."

Eddy held his ground. "Is it that Jack fellow?"

"No. I'm going to San Antonio and marry Ray. And I'm leaving in one hour, so get out of my way."

Poppi stood by the open trunk of his cab, attempting not to get between the siblings.

Eddy took her new luggage and passed it over to Poppi. Snapping the cab door open he crawled inside. "I'm going with you."

"Oh, for heaven's sake." She scrambled in beside him.

"Look, when Mom finds out you've eloped she's going to go crazy. If she knows I had something to do with it, then she will be mad at me."

"I love you." She patted her brother's knee.

"Yeah. And you tell that devil Ray he owes me." He smiled at his sister.

"You no married?" Poppi looked confused.

"I'm going to be married as soon as I arrive." She showed him the ring again, and all three laughed.

"Is very good." Poppi started down Jackson Street with the dark car following not far behind.

JACK RACED ACROSS TOWN. Why hadn't he thought of this? That damn worthless David. He picked up the car radio.

"David, come in," he shouted into the receiver.

"Ten-four, I'm here."

"Where?"

"Outside the house. She came out about an hour ago, put some flowers in the vase of the statue, and walked the dog a bit. It's quiet."

"Get your ass down to the train station and give Duckworth back-up until I can get there."

"The train station?" David's voice trembled.

Jack swerved around a slower vehicle, almost hitting a pedestrian, as he raced south down Broadway. At Yesler he honked his way through the intersection to take a sharp right, and then a left on 4th to Jackson and the train station. He stopped before the red brick building with the clock tower. He leapt out of the car and dashed through the arched doorway of the station by the time his car door closed behind him. He ran down the grand staircase between marble pillars into the main waiting room below the hand-carved coffered ceiling and straight to the foursome that sat upright and silent on a long wooden bench. Duckworth sat next to Billi, with Eddy on her other side, and the last in the lineup, the idiot David.

One look at Billi's sharp blue eyes told the story. He braced himself for the storm.

"Not here." He took her arm and gently assisted her off the bench, then threw over his shoulder to Eddy, "I'm glad to see you. Come with us."

Eddy stood and followed close behind his sister.

"Grab her bag and put it in my car," Jack snapped at David.

Duckworth fell in behind his boss as David fumbled with the suitcase. A new pecking order had been established.

"I have told you to leave me alone." Billi's voice echoed off the walls.

"Not here," Jack repeated as calmly as possible.

Outside his car stood at the awkward angle he had left it in his rush to get to Billi before anyone else could. He opened the back door and she slid inside. Eddy hurried around to the front and sat next to Jack.

"Where are you taking us, Mr. Huntington?" Eddy's tone matched his tense frame.

"Home." He turned the key and backed up onto the street.

"Why are you here? Why can't you get this through your damn thick skull, I am not going to work for you?" Billi's fist pounded against the car seat.

"So is that what this is all about?" Eddy snapped.

"There's been a situation." These were the only words Jack could think of for now. He had no idea how he would proceed with what he had to tell her.

As the three cars pulled in front of the peeling white house, Pepper appeared at the door. Soon Mrs. O stood over him.

All the car doors seemed to open in unison.

She flung the front door open. "Oh, may the dear Lord have mercy. Now what?"

Jack nodded to David and Duckworth. "Wait outside."

They filed into the living room. Only the puppy's whine and the *thunk* of the suitcase as it hit the hardwood floor filled the room.

Jack removed his hat and coat, not certain how to begin. "How about a drink?"

"I don't want a drink." Billi plopped onto the sofa.

"Make hers a double." Jack looked at Eddy. "In fact, make one for each of us."

Mrs. O planted herself in her rocker and called the dog to her lap. "What are you doing here and whose suitcase is that?"

When no one spoke, Billi finally answered. "Mine. I was eloping before this idiot stopped me."

"Eloping? But Billi dear, we have plans. We have a guest list, we have—"

"That's why I'm here."

Jack paced, waiting as the shaker rattled the drinks to life.

"Billi, why didn't you tell me you were leaving? We could have gone down and picked out a dress together at least." Mrs. O directed her mounting anger at the intruder. "Did you have something to do with this?"

"Yes, ma'am. I made certain Raymond made it into the Army Air Corps at Randolph Field like he wanted. And now I regret my—"

He waited as Eddy approached with two drinks. Taking them both, he held one out to Billi then hesitated at the hatred in her eyes.

"You what? What did you do to Ray?" she spit out between clenched teeth.

"I'm very sorry." He took her hand and put the glass in it. "More sorry than I can explain right now."

Her hand began to tremble, and the dark brown liquid jiggled against the edges of her glass. "What's wrong?"

Jack reached in his pocket and handed the folded telegram to Eddy.

Eddy unfolded it and began to gasp for breath. Jack caught his elbow, helping him sit next to his sister.

"There has been an accident." Jack regretted every word. "No one knows for certain yet—"

"Where?" Billi snatched the telegram from her brother's hand as Jack took the glass away from her. "Oh. No. No." Tears streamed from her face. "We're going to be married this week. He can't be dead."

"Oh, no. Raymond." Mrs. O fell to her knees in prayer, making the sign of the cross. "Dear Lord, help us."

Pepper, displaced in the turmoil, put his paws against the old women's chest and attempted to lick the tears that ran freely down her cheeks.

Jack stood watching the O'Shaughnessys and spoke the only words he could formulate. "He died in duty for his country."

"You son of a bitch. This all started when you entered this house." Eddy shot to his feet and swung at Jack.

Jack grabbed Eddy's arm halting the blow. "Yes. I'm sorry. I had no way of knowing this would happen." Jack released the younger man's arm.

"You had him killed." Billi could not take her eyes off of the telegram.

"No. No, that I did not do. He was a remarkable young pilot. Their top man. That's why they sent him with others on this mission." He squatted down to look Billi in the eyes. "The minute I find out what happened, you will be the first to know. Now just take a sip." He put the drink back in her hand and waited until she had swallowed some.

"Does his family know yet?" Eddy fell back on the couch by Billi.

"Someone is probably over there right now."

Mrs. O let Jack help her back into her chair. "How did you find out so fast?"

"I've been keeping my eye on Ray for Billi's sake. I didn't want any harm to come to him until—"

Billi finished the sentence for him. "Until after you had me do your dirty work?"

"It's for your country. The country Raymond just died for." Jack spoke with soft intensity.

"What the hell are you two talking about?" Eddy grabbed his drink and downed it as Billi and Jack continued to watch each other in silence.

"I just can't believe it. You're lying." Billi's voice held a glimmer of hope.

"Not about this. I'm so sorry." He handed Mrs. O her drink and picked up the last one and held it high. "To Raymond Richardson, for his dedication and love of his fellow man. And to those he has left behind."

"To my best damn friend," Eddy added as his tears began in earnest.

"God Bless Raymond." Mrs. O's words fell around them, heavy with sorrow.

Jack waited, but Billi said nothing as the harsh sting of the liquor and reality seemed to stick in her throat.

TWENTY-ONE

Billi sat on her branch in the cedar tree. The funeral would be held tomorrow. How quickly her life had changed. One minute she made plans to marry the love of her life and the next to bury him, to never hear his laugh again or feel his touch. He had been so young, so full of dreams to share.

She did not pretend to grasp any of it. The speculation that the new plane he piloted bounced too high over the cloud cover of a storm, and Ray had lost consciousness due to lack of oxygen, became a jumble of words in her mind. Words. Words that mean nothing and everything. For Billi, the words meant the worst, that Ray's journey home lay in the heavens somewhere. As another tear marked her face Billi faced his limb on their tree that would remain empty.

Impulsively, she reached out toward his branch, the one with his initials carved into it, and her ring caught on the dropping bough. A bit of the green cedar leaf stuck between the diamonds. She drew in the intoxicating scent of the cedar as the memories of their tree played across her mind. They had hidden below these very boughs as children, kissed beneath it as teenagers, and, just a few months ago, sat on these very limbs creating dreams of a lifetime together.

She admired the ring, now useless, except it reflected the memory Raymond and their promises. She plucked the green out from the setting and wondered if his family would insist she give it back.

"Hey, you okay?"

She heard small twigs snap as Eddy worked his long frame through the branches toward her.

"I just miss him so."

"Yeah, so do I." He straddled his limb.

They sat in silence for a few moments. The setting sun painted a pink glow on the water and mountains as it reflected the last flares of light for the day.

Eddy sighed deeply. "Are you ready?"

"I guess so." She heaved a deep sigh. "Poor Danny. He's so broken up over this."

"He's riding with us tomorrow. Both he and Dahlia."

"Good. Mom's going to need all the support she can get."

"I've enlisted." His statement shot across the darkening boughs of evergreen and stabbed Billi in the heart.

"What?" She clung to the cedar for support. "You can't. I can't lose anyone else. You can't go."

"I did it for Ray, Billi. He believed he was needed. I feel that way now too."

"Edward O'Shaughnessy, you are crazy. Does Mom know?" She shifted on her branch to see him better in the dim light.

"Not until after the funeral tomorrow. You have to promise me."

"Oh, my God, I can't take this." The tears she thought had run dry rolled down her cheeks.

"Yes, you can, Bil. You are the strongest person I know. You were meant for great things. I can't explain why Ray was taken from us, but there is a reason. You have to believe that and help me not let the memory of our Raymond die."

"When do you go?"

"Two weeks."

"But there is not going to be a war, is there?"

"No, maybe not," his answer did not sound convincing. "But, the good news is, once I'm out, I'll be able to pay for law school."

Danny's voice drifted up to them. "Hey, dinner is ready. Dahlia made dessert."

Billi raised her eyebrow in questions at her brother, and he shook his head no as he whispered, "They don't know either."

THE CHURCH DOORS WERE FLUNG OPEN, and those arriving to give condolences and hear of the shortened life of Raymond Richardson bowed their heads as they entered. Billi and her mother were followed by the remaining members of the band of five, of which Ray had been an integral part. Solemnly, they walked toward the front of the church. Mr. O'Shaughnessy followed behind them, keeping his distance out of respect for the women he loved. Billi slowed as she passed one of the back pews where Mr. Nakamura, Kenny, Eileen, and Auntie Katsuko huddled in the strange surroundings.

Raymond's mother, draped in black and barely able to walk down the aisle, didn't even acknowledge Billi and her family as she sat next to her grief-stricken husband.

The funeral mass dissolved into a blur. Jim Galvin spoke. The man who had taught Ray to fly stood before them and spoke of honor and service to country and sadness. Someone in uniform also took the podium, talking again about the country and the fight for freedom. Freedom became the theme for the loss of Ray's life. Billi gripped Eddy's hand. She did not want him die for a war that did not belong on American soil.

The words to "Ave Maria" floated down across the wooden beams from the choir loft and the funeral finished. Done. Gone. And the somber mood carried them out into the sunshine. When Billi looked down the church steps, she nearly fainted. There, talking with Gladys Richardson, stood Jack. She watched in disbelief as he put his arms around her and they hugged. The man who had sent Ray to his death now shook hands with Mr. Richardson.

JACK LOOKED UP THE STEPS AT BILLI and nodded in her direction. Watching her face cloud over, he knew he should leave, but one more business matter still needed his attention. As Billi approached them, Gladys took hold of his arm.

"Oh, there you are Billi." Gladys swayed a bit as she spoke. It appeared an early martini before the service, or maybe two, had been her breakfast. "About the ring."

Jack spoke quickly. "It's yours. Raymond would want you to have it."

"Really?" Gladys sounded disgusted as she turned toward Jack. "Now who said—"

"How about a drink?" Jack smiled at Mrs. Richardson.

"About time someone made sense around here." She listed toward the reception hall of the church.

Jack shifted his grip on Mrs. Richardson's arm and assisted her inside the hall, attempting to guide her in a relatively straight line.

Stunned, Billi stared after them.

Eddy, with Dahlia attached to his arm, sidled up to her. "Mom's inside with Danny. Come in with us. You can do this."

Billi stood facing the door to the reception where the niceties would begin. The raw anger of death had not traveled inside these walls like it had in her heart. Startled, she remembered Eileen and headed back up the stairs to the church.

"I'll be there in a minute." She took the steps two at a time as she spoke.

The Nakamuras were entering the arch of the church door when she spotted them. Their smiles were a salve to her soul.

"You will join us for dinner tomorrow night as planned?" She heard the insistence in Mr. Nakamura's statement.

"Yes, thank you." Billi walked with them out into the sun's light.

"Go." Eileen nudged her. "You need to be inside there now. We'll talk tomorrow."

Billi hugged her friend and left them to enter the reception hall. The buzz of conversations met her ears as plates of food were carried to the tables. Her mother held court in the center, talking with some of the wealthy crowd that had come out to show their support for the Richardsons. In the shadows on the far side stood the man she held responsible. She watched him approach and struggled to keep her feelings in check.

"I'm leaving town. I thought you would like to know that."

Jack stood close to her and she could smell his cologne. Something she had never noticed before.

"Yes, that is good news." She looked away. "Are you coming back?"

"Only if you say you will help. Duckworth will be here."

"What about that other creep?"

"David? He'll be with me." Jack shifted. "There's something—"

"Eddy enlisted in the navy." She meant for her blunt statement to sting.

She saw the muscle around his good eye twitch, but he said nothing.

"Everyone is talking about the war that is not going to happen." She wanted him to be wrong.

"I believe otherwise and would like to stop it from happening. Or, at the very least, help protect as many innocent people as possible if we do go to war. But I need your help."

"What in blue blazes are you doin' talkin' to Billi?" Mr. O stepped between them, chest puffed up, ready for action.

Billi stifled a laugh and took her father's arm before he could throw a punch in Jack's direction. "Mr. Huntington was just leaving."

"Mr. Huntington, is it? A good riddance to you." He escorted Billi on his arm into the crowd. "You keep yer distance from that one, Bright Eyes."

"Don't worry, Daddy, I will never see him again. I promise."

TWENTY-TWO

JACK LEANED BACK INTO THE OVERSIZED COUCH in front of the fireplace, letting his mind go blank as he looked at the five coats of arms hand-carved into the wood paneling above the hearth. They represented the joining of the families from each side of his parents. He had returned to his family home in Hillsborough once again, not just for rest but to revamp his plan. Billi had had enough of a shock. Maybe he could locate someone in the Bay Area who could do the job he needed to accomplish. But the risks would be higher with a local woman. The damn isolationists had their heads in the sand. War would not pass them by, but would be on their doorstep soon.

His sister Lilly appeared on the small balcony above the living room. Like Juliette, she looked down into the large room with its massive windows, which, from floor to ceiling, reached two stories. Five panels of leaded glass with intricate designs of green, blue, and yellow hues adorned each of the fifteen windows. Two sets of French doors led to the patios. Coupled with the oversized fireplace, these attributes made their home one of the grandest on the corner of San Raymundo and La Cumbre.

Lilly's silk bathrobe swirled around her as she leaned over the ornate carved railing. "Look what the cat dragged in."

"A little early for you to be up, isn't it?" He didn't even look in her direction.

"A little early for you to be drinking, isn't it?"

"Come on down and join me." He patted the worn fabric of the couch. While the nine bedrooms were mostly emptied of all their glory, his mother had insisted the living and dining room remain intact. Appearances still mattered.

"Does Bella know her baby is home?" Lilly disappeared into the alcove that led to a small set of side stairs that spilled into the foyer.

Jack heard her slippers clapping against the bare wood as she came down. "I've had my breakfast. At eight, I might add."

"Bully for you, dear brother. So now it's on to Scotch?" she plopped down beside him. "What's up? I can tell when you're brooding." A single, thin feather from the trim on the cuff of her sleeve floated toward him.

When he didn't answer she tried again. "Jack, I'm heading into town and then to a big party later tonight. Will you be my escort?"

"Who are you entertaining these days?"

"Well, I've taken a cotton to men in uniform. There seems to be no end of them flooding into San Francisco. But I'm very careful about rank."

"I bet." His blatant sarcasm not lost on his sibling.

"Oh, pooh. Don't be a spoil sport. Come and have some fun." When again he didn't answer, she rose and started up the two stairs to the foyer. "I'll expect you to be ready at seven. You do stay up that late, don't you?"

That got a chuckle out of him as he turned to watch the lithe figure of his baby sister strut toward the kitchen. He should go with her, if for no other reason than to make certain she made it home safely.

"I thought I heard your voice." This time the figure standing at the balcony was his mother.

"I didn't want to wake you. I'll be right up." He set his drink on the end table and headed for the stairs. Gently taking his mother's arm, he helped her back down the hall to the master bedroom. The long, heavy curtains had been drawn, and the sunlight streamed in.

"No, the chair," she insisted when he steered her toward her canopied bed. "I'm not dead yet."

He settled her into the high-backed floral-print armchair and pulled another one close to her. He picked up her thin hand and held it. Her eyes were gray with the mist of glaucoma as she looked at him.

"Were you going to tell me?"

He found her question disturbing. "How much do you know?"

"The plane crash. Helen called. Poor Gladys and Isaac."

It startled him to hear his mother's kind words for the family who had bought so many of her prized possessions and at such a pittance. But the many surgeries he had required in an attempt to save his eye had stripped the family's finances even more during the Depression. The guilt ripped through him.

"I hear there was a girl?"

It amazed him at what his mother could extract from others. Possibly her deteriorating condition brought the pity of gossip to her doorstep.

"Yes." He looked out the window again, his mother's hazy gaze too much for him.

"What is she like?"

"Why?"

"I heard you were talking with her?"

"Damn, Mother. How do you do it?"

"I see." She smiled and retracted her hand, folding it sedately with her other hand on her lap. "So why are you here?"

"Work." His answer sounded so hollow, even to him.

"Work is good, I suppose. And I certainly appreciate all you do for us, Jack." She fingered her robe. "How are we doing financially?"

"Fine. Don't worry. Everything is looking up. And I'll be able to get you more funds soon for running the house."

"Lilly should get married. Then we could sell the house." Bluntness had become Mrs. Huntington's strong suit.

"Don't worry, Mother." He patted her knee. "I think she's working toward that end."

She laughed and it filled the room with warmth. "A bit too hard, I'd wager. But go with her tonight, will you?"

"What don't you hear?"

"Amazing what happens when the eyes start to go. But you should know that."

He still felt the sting of her anger over the accident that had cost him his eye and the family part of their fortune.

DANNY'S EYES WERE RED AGAIN. He had been crying. "The gang of five," he had repeated several times a day for the last week. His emotions were stuck in grief.

"Hey, Danny." Billi put her hand on his shoulder. "Go take your break and then I'll take one. Okay?" The high temperature inside the small concession melted some of the chocolate.

"Why is Eddy going too?" A single tear formed in his left eye and he wiped it away quickly.

"They believe in something I can't explain."

"As soon as I'm through at Garfield, as soon as I graduate, I'm joining too. Mom won't let me right now. She's too sick to let me go."

"Stay where you are needed and that is here with your mother and with me. You do enough with the ROTC. And what about Susie?"

"Aw, she's just a kid." He pushed some sand off the countertop.

Manhood challenged the skinny teenager beside her. Billi nudged him. "Go and have some fun while you can. Go on. Get out of here." She half pushed him through the door and watched a smile cross the face of the young blonde positioned on her beach blanket whom Danny had ignored for the last few days.

Billi worked at trying to keep things together. The impact of Ray's death had shaken the O'Shaughnessy household to the foundation. The self-composed manner with which she had moved through the past weeks surprised her. Her mother had stayed in bed for two days after the funeral and Eddy's announcement that he had enlisted. And then she had sprung back with a vengeance. If any one single person could persevere in stopping this war before it began, it would be Mrs. O. Her mother launched her attack on Washington, D.C., and composed letter upon letter to President Roosevelt. These long essays swayed between *stop the war* to *support our troops*. From *do not rip our children from our bosoms* to *protect all women and their innocent offspring*. The dinner table dissolved into a war zone in and of itself, with Eddy defending his choice and their mother trying to find a loophole to retract his enlistment. Once that failed, she placed calls to every senator and admiral she knew to make certain Eddy had a good welcome into the navy and that all were aware of his potential. The flowers offered at the base of the statue of the Virgin Mary grew even larger and more exotic, as the one act of placing the blooms at Mary's feet seemed to have a stabilizing effect on Mrs. O.

The hours, like the days, drifted by. The Nakamuras had invited Billi to join them weekly for a special dinner. Tonight she decided to walk to their apartment. Her feet shuffled with a sense of loss. Her anchor had drifted into the heavens. And she had heard nothing from that nuisance Jack. She looked over her shoulder just to confirm no one followed her and breathed deeply of the summer night. It grew darker earlier now, with schools opening their doors again in just a few days. Soon, they would close down the concession stands, leaving her with idle days to cope with. The thought grabbed at her stomach. Continuing her studies in Japanese at the university held no interest for her. No one had heard from Professor Fujihara and that bothered her. She decided to find a new course of study.

She left her shoes at the door and followed Eileen down the hall to her bedroom. She had remembered Mrs. Nakamura's book this time and pulled it from her purse, reverently placing it on her friend's bed.

"Here. I won't be needing this. Hopefully you will soon." With that simple statement, the tears that she had held at bay for the last week started again.

Eileen wrapped her arms around Billi. "You will need it someday. Keep it as a gift. I will be given my own in the traditional way."

"I wanted to try those things with Ray." She smiled through her grief.

"There will be someone else to try them with. I know this to be true." Eileen picked up the book and slid it back inside Billi's handbag.

At the soft knock on the door, both women spun in its direction. Kenny entered shyly. "I have something for you." He extended his hand in which lay two origami cranes, one gold, one red. "For good luck."

"Did you make these?" Billi gently lifted them out of his hand.

"Yes, I had some—"

A loud crash echoed down the hall followed by shouts. The three stood in uncomfortable silence. They could clearly hear the argument in the small apartment without opening the door.

"It is dangerous to have that round-eyed one in our home. She is spying on us. I have warned you about this before." Tak's rage could be felt though the walls.

"This is not your house in which to make such accusations." In contrast, Mr. Nakamura's voice was barely audible.

"Where is she?" Tak's voice became louder as he approached the small bedroom door. "I will get rid of her myself."

A sudden thud reverberated as something hit against the wall. "Do not disgrace this house. Leave now. We will discuss it later."

"You will be sorry one day, old man." A second thump followed the threat. "When the emperor's forces take over—"

The sound of a brutal slap stopped all hearts. Then footsteps rang against the floor and the front door slammed.

The clammy hot air of the cramped room clung in their throats. Kenny opened the door and braced himself for an onslaught of his brother's fury. Instead, the three gawked at the bent figure of Mr. Nakamura as the older man straightened. A trickle of blood ran from a scrape above his eye.

"Father." Eileen ran to him.

"Forgive me." He let her guide him to the couch. "He has gone war crazy since his return from studying in my homeland. You, my beautiful flower, will never return to the country that has destroyed such a brilliant young man."

Billi reluctantly slipped from the sanctuary of the bedroom. With her head down from the shame she knew this scene had caused the family, she stood behind the couch. "Maybe I should go now and let peace once again bless this beautiful home."

"Come." Mr. Nakamura pointed to a chair opposite him. "The evil spirit will not prevail. It has a strong hold of my son for now. But that will change with time. America is our home and we cannot listen to the thoughts of an empire that desires destruction. His teaching will be unwoven. Your presence here only brings us hope."

"Thank you." Billi offered him a genuine smile, the sort she had not felt since Ray's death.

"Ah, thank *you*. But now I am hungry and feeding that beast can solve many worries."

TWENTY-THREE

HIS SISTER HAD BEEN RIGHT, but then again, Lilly knew her parties. They had swept past the tall black-marble columns topped with the golden Doric design and up the stairs of the St. Francis Hotel in the heart of the San Francisco. The tall wooden clock had chimed a greeting as they hurried down the hall toward the sound of jazz from the ballroom.

Lilly, fulfilling Jack's nickname for her as Frilly, appeared a picture of coiffed and styled perfection, her blonde hair pulled back in a perfect updo and peach outfit no match for the other bland girls she had giggled with when they first arrived.

Jack sat at a table to the side just to watch her in action. Her grace and ease in the luxurious room heightened the other men's attention. She floated across the dance floor, Jack noticed, partially due to the extraordinarily handsome man she had as her dance partner. Prince Charming wore his navy whites with enough medals and ribbons on his chest to qualify him as the perfect contender for his sister's aspiration. As the music swirled to a finish and the band announced a well-deserved break, the two beautiful, beaming lovebirds danced in his direction.

Jack stood as they approached, sizing up the man who had the honor of being this night's chosen one. He extended his hand and felt a strong grip in response. So far, so good.

"Lieutenant Junior Grade, Todd Achers," he introduced himself, then nodded toward Jack's eye patch. "War?"

"No." Jack indicated a seat and watched as Achers pulled out a chair for his sister.

"Jack is a very famous attorney. Aren't you dear?" Lilly fetched a cigarette out of her evening bag.

Achers had his lighter out and bent in toward her. "Miss Huntington, may I?" The two locked gazes as the lighter flickered, the heat between them palpable.

"How do you know my sister?" Jack rattled the ice in his Scotch glass, not taking his eye off the sailor.

"A mutual friend introduced us a few days ago," Achers answered, not looking away from the pretty face.

"How mutual?" The phrase "a few days ago" struck his gut and seeped down his spine. So this was not their first meeting. His radar for worry increased.

"Jack. Be nice." Lilly bent down to light her cigarette and blew the smoke in her brother's direction.

Jack continued to drill Archers. "How long are you here for?"

"I'm just in town for a brief stay. Then I'm off back East to reunite with my ship the USS *Rueben James*. I'm here on navy affairs." He raised his glass and offered Jack a brilliant smile. "To the beauty of San Francisco."

"Why, Frilly, I do believe he means you," Jack smiled back and lifted his drink. "To a man of good taste."

"Now, boys, behave. To a wonderful night among friends, and one crusty brother." Lilly tapped her champagne glass against Todd's.

Jack settled back in his chair. He would have Duckworth do a background check on Achers in the morning, and he would be certain this lieutenant kept his distance from his sister during his short time ashore. But for now, the evening reassured him that there still were beautiful people and beautiful places to observe in his turbulent world.

"EDDY." BILLI TOOK THE DINNER PLATE from her brother, every bit of the creamy beef stroganoff scraped clean with thick bread. "Do you really think there will be a war?"

Pepper followed close behind her as she hurried into the kitchen, with Eddy trailing after. Mrs. O had gone to bed early with exhaustion. Her effort to make Eddy's presence known to those who were in command in the navy had been overwhelming.

"The news is full of horror in Europe and Asia, and it seems we are headed that way. Unless there is a miracle of some sort." He stacked the empty serving dishes to the side of the sink. "You wash, I'll dry."

"Isn't that how it always works?" She tossed the towel in his direction. "Do you think the Japanese will do anything to us?"

"No, they're too far away. Why are you worrying about this anyway?"

"Ray thought something terrible might come our way and we need to be prepared."

"So do I." He took the cleaned, dripping dish to dry. "Does this have something to do with that Huntington fellow?"

"Not really." She scrubbed an already clean plate with unmistakable determination.

"What was he after, Bil? He sure left in a hurry."

"Just looking for someone."

"What did this someone do?"

She shrugged in response.

"I'll tell you what, I wouldn't want that guy tracking me. You about done with that plate yet?"

"Sorry. Here."

The bubbles from the dish soap clung to her hand as she held it out. One drifted down toward Pepper, and he snapped at it, which brought laughter from the siblings.

"It's good to hear you laugh again, Bil. Ray would want you to move on."

"I know. It's just way too soon. Hey, let's go see Dad together before you have to leave. Can you get one day off?"

"You read my mind. Tomorrow is my last day at the law office, although they're paying me for the entire week. So we'll head over there on Wednesday."

"Great."

BILLI PULLED ON THE OARS AS EDDY SAT in the stern of the small rowboat. It felt good to be on the saltwater again. They had grown up on this water and somehow saw it as theirs. The navy would suit Eddy, Billi mused. Boats had been an integral part of their lives with their father.

Eddy had insisted they pass the navy shipyard in Bremerton on their way to their father's home on Dyes Inlet. He liked looking at the big ships, their massive hulls reigning high above the water line. And now with his reporting to duty only a few days out, he seemed at peace and more eager to be near the vessels.

"A bit harder on port side." Eddy motioned with his left hand as if his sister had never heard the terms "port" and "starboard" before.

"Aye, aye, captain," she mockingly replied, pulling harder on the one oar.

Eddy leaned over and caught the buoy in his hand. The boat drifted to a stop as the line with the weight of the crab pot acted as an anchor. With no wind broadsiding them, Billi boated the oars to help Eddy pull aboard what they hoped would be their dinner.

She sat back and watched his muscles flex as he drew the pot to the surface, the pile of rope growing at his feet. "I think we're lucky today, sis."

She shifted to the other side to counter the weight of the crab pot, the slowness of Eddy's pull consistent with the weight of a catch. With one last heave, he hoisted the dripping pot over the side of the boat and rested it on the neat circle of rope. Five large Dungeness crabs scurried, pinchers raised, from one side to the other and then back again.

"Look at all of them!" Billi squealed. "We'll have some to take back to Mom. Let's check. No ladies please." She handed her brother a large empty bucket.

Eddy caught one by the back, pulled it from the pot, and flipped it over. The long, pointed design of the underbelly made that crab a keeper.

"One for me." His teasing made her smile. He continued the process until four of the five large crabs struggled against the sides of the bucket. He tossed back the only female for good luck.

A boat sped past them at full throttle, heading for the opening of the inlet at Rocky Point that led boaters out past Point Turner and the naval shipyard. Billi quickly put the oars back in the oarlocks and turned their boat to face the incoming wake head on so they would not get swamped. As she turned to make certain she had positioned the row boat into the waves, she noticed only one occupant in the motorboat. He looked tall, showed skill with the craft, and Japanese. She quickly turned back to face her brother.

"Where did that boat come from?" Billi's impatience caught her brother's attention.

"He must have put in at Silverdale. Seems like he's in a hurry." Eddy watched the boat disappear.

"Did you see any fishing gear?" She continued to look away as the roar of the motor dimmed in the distance.

"Someone you know?"

"No." She picked up her oars again and turned the bow of the boat toward shore and home. "Just curious where he's heading on an outgoing tide. Fish aren't hitting right now."

She pulled with all her might in the confusion that unexpectedly overwhelmed her, and her stomach flipped at the thought. She had to be wrong. What would Akio Sumiyoshi, the man Jack asked about, be doing here? What lurked out in the waters that would attract him?

She looked over at her brother as he lazed back in the stern of the boat, face to the sun. He would look so handsome in his white uniform. And then it registered, if the man at the helm of the motorboat was Akio, there could be only one destination he would be racing his boat toward.

TWENTY-FOUR

JACK KICKED AT THE DOOR OF ROOM 864 in the Palace Hotel and it gave way. The scream that followed from inside the hotel suite came from his sister. And the man that hurried half-dressed from the bedroom was Lieutenant J. G. Todd Achers.

Both of Todd's hands went up in defense. "Now just a minute. It's all right."

Jack did not stop and the blow he landed on the others man's face sent the lieutenant tumbling.

"Stop. Jack, stop. We're married." Lilly wrapped her white silk robe tighter around her small frame and ran to her new husband, kneeling beside him.

Jack stood over them, fists clenching and unclenching as he attempted to comprehend his sister's words.

"Goddamn it," he uttered. "When and who by and why didn't you ask permission first?"

His interrogation fell on deaf ears as the two lovers consoled each other. Lilly helped Todd to his feet and pulled back his hand to examine the cut on his cheek.

"Ice." She pointed to the bucket on the small round marble table that held an empty bottle of champagne and floating pieces of melting ice.

Jack silently obeyed. He scooped out a few dripping cubes and handed them to his new brother-in-law. "Sorry about that."

"No. I would have done the same." Todd accepted the cool cubes and put them against the lump rising on his cheek. "Glad you're on our side with a swing like that."

"Oh, my dear brother boxed, fenced, sailed—everything to stay out of the classroom at that expensive Stanford University of his."

Todd assessed Jack before speaking. "Will you excuse me for a minute while I get some clothes on? And I would suggest you do the same, Mrs. Achers."

"Don't you just love him?" Lilly gushed as she kissed Todd's cheek and hurried from the room.

Jack staggered, still processing the situation when he noticed Todd fix him with a stern gaze before disappearing into the bedroom. The line had been drawn between the men. Just like that, his kid sister transformed into the wife of someone he had met only once.

He had left her alone only for the afternoon while he and Duckworth visited their contacts in San Francisco's Japantown and then Chinatown, trying to piece together an alternative plan now that Billi adamantly refused to help. How could this have happened? And how would he face his mother? Or, the family's beloved Bella, for that matter, the one who had actually raised both of them. He dreaded the hell he would catch from the two women back in Hillsborough. He called to have management send someone to fix the door, along with more ice and another bottle of champagne. He slumped into a chair and held his spinning head. He would call General DeWitt and Hoover and hope they would understand that his concept had failed. His scheme dissolved before him. Akio had evaded him at every turn, and Jack had lost track of him. With that stress went his ability to focus and reason clearly. He would make the call tomorrow. Right now, he intended to get drunk with his new brother-in-law.

BILLI SAT NEAR THE SHORELINE below her father's cabin, his binoculars at her side. Even as a child she had loved his binoculars. She would spend hours memorizing the way the water sent out rings of waves from the movement of fish, sea gulls, changing of the tide, or any other patterns the waters made when disturbed. She could tell which direction to row the boat by the way the fish flipped in the air to put a hook closer to the fish's path. Her father always bragged that, in his book, Billi and the water were the same creature, a balance of stormy and placidly smooth, ever-changing and something to behold reverently.

She shifted on the edge of the sun-browned grass where it fell to the beach at Dyes Inlet and waited. She had gathered a bowl of warm blackberries from the vines that grew at the base of the tall evergreens and set it by her side next to her father's old field glasses. She had polished both sides of the lenses carefully so that nothing would hamper her view when the boat carrying that tall Japanese man roared past again. At least she hoped he would return.

Eddy and her father had cleaned the crabs and were conversing over a beer in anticipation of Eddy's departure.

She could not think of that now, of Eddy leaving. She had to focus. Could Jack be correct? Could someone with the knowledge of Akio's movements alter the collision course that the United States desperately attempted to avoid? By reporting what she has seen, could she stop Eddy from leaving her too? With sheer determination and the memory of the soul she had already said goodbye to, she listened for the boat to pass Rocky Point and emerge into view.

"Come on, darlin'," her father called down the slope to her. "What in heaven's name is it you hope to see? Damn the glasses. Let's have a bite a crab."

Pink laced clouds began to fill the blue sky, the sun setting earlier now with the onset of the fall. The boat had not emerged in the two hours she had been listening for it. She ate the last of the blackberries then stood holding the empty bowl, exhausted by the anticipation. She ambled up the hill and sat below the slant of the extended roof, where her father had proudly set his feast on the outdoor table.

"I'm comin' to the train station to see you off, son. Remember, head down an' heart up. That's how you'll survive."

"I will, Dad. And I'll be back before you know it and then on to law school. Now that's something to toast."

While she did not agree with the concept of the toast, Billi raised her glass and silently prayed. And then she heard it, the slight puttering of an engine in the distance. Wiping the crab from her fingers she picked up the binoculars and raced back down the hill. The water had gotten a bit thicker, with a small chop, and the setting sun reflected off of the windshield of the boat, but she had him in her sights. Her hand moved the field glasses slowly but steadily, keeping the skipping craft in view as it crossed the Inlet. She did not catch a good enough look at the man until the boat skimmed the surface directly across from her and the reflection of the sunlight did not blind her. She worked the focus slightly and he came into view, still too far away for her to be absolutely certain. However, the nose and chin seemed similar, and the tallness fit as well.

There were several Japanese who had chosen the fertile soil of Bainbridge Island for their farms. She would have to go to the local market and ask questions. But the biggest question on her mind became whether she should tell Jack Huntington of her suspicions.

Just before the boat disappeared around the corner, Billi saw the glint of the sun reflect off of something in the boat. She spun around and dropped to the summer-dried grass. Had he been watching her? Had that brief glare been off of his binoculars? She had been careless standing in the open for so long. Angry at herself, she rose and started back up the hill where Eddy and her father were laughing as if without a care in the world.

She remembered Jack's words. "You can help change the course if you help me." She would have to let him know. If this man surfaced in this community, he brought the imminent threat of danger.

"Come on, Bil." Eddy waved down at her. "Who the hell were you spying on anyway?"

"What da hell da yous mean, *married?*" Bella roared at Jack. "My baby girl ain't dat stupid. She ain't gonna marry no man ain't got no money. We don't knows nothen' about da family. He best not bring hisself here, an' dat's dat." She hunkered down next to Mrs. Huntington with a look of disgust.

"Jack, please repeat what you know of him again," his mother demanded.

"Not much. And they are coming for dinner tonight, so you can ask him a few of these questions yourself." His hand went to his forehead where the champagne still rattled his ability to answer the inquisition he faced. "He leaves tomorrow for his ship. And then he will be gone for months. Maybe we can get the marriage annulled if you think it best. But I'm not telling Lilly that." He stood and started out of the living room.

"Well, I ain't cooken' for some cradle-robbin', uppity nobody."
Bella crossed her arms over her ample bosom.

Jack turned back and regarded the sour faces of the two women
who held his heart. "Now, ladies, let's look at this from a different
perspective." He employed his most tolerant approach. "This young
man is now part of the family. He is a lieutenant and, I think you will
find, quite charming. So, let's put on the Huntington smile and get
through this as best we can. For Lilly's sake."

He scrutinized them sternly until Bella rose and huffed off toward
the kitchen. "I'll puts fresh sheets on da twin beds," she mumbled as she
disappeared into her realm of the house.

His mother's eyebrows shot up at the thought and she finally started
to laugh. "Oh, dear Jack. What are we in for?"

The phone rang and he crossed to the table and picked up the
receiver.

"Huntington home." He smiled at his mother as he played the
servant. "What?" His tone changed quickly. "I'll call you right back."

Without a word to his mother, he ran up the stairs, entered his
father's office, and closed the door.

Lilly and Todd arrived promptly at 5:30. When Todd entered
through the massive wooden door with his bags and the new luggage he
had purchased for his bride, Jack had to intercept the charging Bella and
snatch the articles. He placed these blatant acknowledgements of their
union inside the hall closet and hurried the couple into the living room,
where their mother sat waiting. Bella had taken the time to massage
some color into Mrs. Huntington's cheeks, and the prim figure sat bolt
upright in her high-back, rose-colored chair next to the grand fireplace.

"Well, it appears some introductions are in order. I'm Lilly's mother,
Mrs. Huntington."

Jack noted the formal name their mother offered and hoped Lilly
perceived the uphill battle she and Todd now faced.

Lilly hurried to her mother's side and kissed her. "Isn't he wonderful,
Mother?"

"That remains to be seen. But you seem to have fared the ordeal
well."

"It wasn't an ordeal, Mother. We just got married." Lilly looked toward Jack with what he recognized as a plea for help.

Todd stepped forward and almost clicked his heels. "It is a pleasure and an honor to meet the mother of the one and only woman I have pledged my life to."

Bell emitted a "Hmmph" as she entered with a tray of stuffed celery and cheese and crackers. The large black woman lowered the hors d'oeuvres onto the coffee table before the fireplace, stood tall to examine Todd, then let loose another "Hmmph" and exited.

"That is Bella." Jack handed a bewildered-looking Todd a strong drink. "She's the one you need to impress."

Mrs. Huntington smiled at her daughter's new husband. "I suppose the marriage is legal?"

"Yes, ma'am. We intend to have another service with all the trimmings when I get back."

"Won't that be fantastic, Mother? We can hold it right here and then—"

"Is there a child involved?" Mrs. Huntington's bluntness stunned Lilly into silence.

Todd's chin went up. "I can assure you, Mrs. Huntington, I did not touch your daughter until after the vows. If there is a child then we will be doubly blessed."

Slowly Mrs. Huntington raised her frail hand toward him, a hand stripped of all its former glittering jewels and bobbles, where now only a small gold band remained. "Welcome."

Todd stepped forward and took the hand of his mother-in-law. "Thank you. That means a lot."

With a growing appreciation for the man his sister had chosen, Jack watched the private exchange of acceptance. However, knowing the battle that would ensue between mother and daughter, Jack motioned Todd toward the foyer to retrieve the suitcases.

"We better get your things upstairs and out of Bella's way or there will be hell to pay. Come on, Todd, I'll show you around."

Jack led Todd up the stairs to his sister's room, the one with the two single beds. Something he felt certain would not inconvenience this sailor.

In the morning, the home would be devoid of men again as both Todd and Jack would head in opposite directions of the northern hemisphere. Duty called. And for that Jack was most thankful.

TWENTY-FIVE

"YES, I HEARD YOU," Billi spoke into the phone in her mother's living room. "Listen Duckworth, I told you all I know and I promise I will not go to Bainbridge Island to talk with the Japanese families." She felt her heart tighten at Duckworth's next words. "He is? Yes, call me when he arrives."

She hurried into the kitchen, which smelled of vinegar and bacon, where her mother stood over her special platters that held the feast. It seemed all of Eddy's favorite dishes had made it onto the menu. Tonight belonged to Eddy, for the hope and the fear that settled in everyone's mind as they fortified themselves to say farewell to another of the gang of five. Billi had made it clear there were no goodbyes, just "See you soon and stay well."

"Do you think I should put out some of my homemade dill pickles as well? I rolled pickles inside my flank steak to make rouladen for Eddy." Her mother sounded confused.

"Yes. Let's put out everything. You sit for a moment." Billi took the serving dish her mother hold.

That made Mrs. O smile, heave a deep sigh, and wander over to the chair in the corner.

"I hope I didn't put the cream in the stroganoff too soon. You know how it will curdle if you do. I think I have everything." She mumbled, and her hand floated through the air as she did when mentally taking stock of the dishes she had painstakingly cooked. "Yes," she finally pronounced.

Billi placed the homemade dumplings on a platter. "Thanks, Mother, for letting Eileen join us tonight. It made her feel very special." Billi did not look at her mother but wondered at her impulsive invitation.

"She is such a nice girl, and she makes everyone calm somehow. Besides, Eddy was the one who thought of it first."

"Just like Eddy. He wants as many beautiful women around him as possible."

"I heard that." Eddy entered from the living room with Dahlia.

"So did I." Dahlia dug her elbow into his side.

The doorbell rang and Pepper scurried to the door. Danny entered with Eileen, and the pup ran circles in greeting. "Let the party begin," Danny hollered.

Eileen followed behind the wagging tail of Pepper, a basket of fresh vegetables and fruit from her father's store in her arms. "My father sent these in honor of Eddy's bravery. I picked out the pears."

"Thank you, they are beautiful." Eddy took the offering, placed the basket on the counter, and reached for the golden fruit.

His mother swatted at his hand before he could grab it.

"Out, out, everyone." Mrs. O took charge of the situation. "I can't serve a proper dinner with all you rascals in here."

"Eileen and I will serve, Mom. You go sit down." Billi guided her mother toward the door, grabbing Eileen's arm with the same sure movement. "You too, Pepper, out of here." The dachshund sat on his haunches, raised his long body, and cocked his head in an effort to stay in proximity of the food.

The dinner, crowned by apple strudel and Mrs. O's famous Black Forest cake with cherries, emerged a great success. More food remained on the platters than had been consumed.

"To Eddy's swift return from the war." Danny raised the unaccustomed drink allowed him for the occasion.

"There will be no war." At Billi's stern interjection, a silence fell over the room. Even Pepper lay down at the harsh tone of his master's voice.

Eileen unexpectedly raised her glass. "To the privilege that comes with being an American and being able to serve your country."

"Brilliant." Eddy lifted his glass in high spirits. "To America and the country I willing go to serve."

"And to coming home to your mother soon." Mrs. O's shoulders rose and fell, punctuating the tension and fear that hung over the gathering.

BILLI COULD NOT HOLD BACK HER TEARS at the train station. She walked down the grand staircase into the same high-ceilinged main hall, with the ornate sculptures and marble pillars, where she had gotten her last kiss from Ray. Where she had fled to ride the rails with all the hope of a bride-to-be. And now she stood here again in so short a time.

"It's okay, ladies." Eddy stood before his mother, sister, and Dahlia. "I'll be back before you know it. Dad." He turned to his father "You have your hands full with this lot."

"That I do." He shifted his hat from hand to hand, tears fighting their way into his eyes. "Remember now son…"

"I know, head down, heart up. Will do."

Eddy kissed each cheek and dashed onto the train as the wheels slowly began their churning toward his new destination.

JACK SAT IN HIS APARTMENT ON BOYLSTON STREET and waited for the call from Duckworth. The Seattle clouds had moved in, partially blocking the sky. They appeared to be heavy with rain. He had left the untrustworthy David at the Presidio in the San Francisco with a stack of paperwork. Mindless work for a mindless person, he had reasoned. Furthermore, he could not afford to frighten off Billi with any wrong moves. And David near Billi held an explosive component that he could not explain. He had to smile. She demonstrated excellent instincts and knew a suspicious rotten egg when she encountered one.

He poured himself a stiff drink and removed his eye patch. He had to move quickly. Waiting had never been one of his strong suits. When he emptied his glass, he entertained the idea of a second, but put it aside and began to pace. The knock at the door brought relief.

Through the small, arched, stained-glass window in the wooden door he saw the blurred image of Billi. He swung the door wide, surprised at how glad he was to see her.

"Sorry." She twisted her gloves in her hands, the diamonds against the gold band still prominent on her ring finger. "I told Duckworth I would come alone. I was afraid that…" She attempted to peer past him into the room.

"David is not here and won't be here."

"Good." She visibly relaxed and walked past him into the small apartment, directly to the wingback chair then sat, clutching her bag and gloves.

Jack contemplated that she had on her good outfit. The one she had worn to say goodbye to Raymond. And somehow that pleased him.

"Would you care for a drink?" He motioned toward the bourbon bottle next to his Scotch.

"No, thank you. I—I just wanted to tell you what I saw and then hear what it is exactly that you have in store for me."

"Do you mind if I have one?"

He watched her raise and lower her shoulders as he had seen her mother do when confused and suppressed a smile. He poured himself another drink and began to explain the approach, direct and to the point. He spoke, allowing her questions, for more than an hour.

At the end of their discussion Billi allowed herself one Manhattan for good luck and to strengthen her nerves.

"With a twist? Correct?" Jack sliced the peel from the lemon.

"I'll have to be more careful what I say around you?" she quipped.

"Do you want me to talk with your mother?" he asked as he handed her his rendition of her favorite cocktail.

"No." She almost spilt her drink with her adamant declaration. "I'll tell her I'm going to a special school for secretaries. She has always thought I would make a great president of a company, but that I should work my way up."

Surprised at her quick answer he questioned the reasoning. "Will she buy that?"

"No. But she has several engagements for her various clubs in the coming months, and those will distract her. She'll have Danny and Pepper to keep her busy as well. I think she will simply be relieved I'm not at the university studying Japanese." She laughed.

He wondered if her laugh resulted from the intoxicating drink or the irony of the situation.

"What about your friend Eileen?"

Billi appeared nonchalant as she picked up the end of his eye patch on the table next to her where he had left it. He had forgotten he had removed it, and nothing in her reaction had suggested he needed to hide his scar.

"That will be harder than leaving my mother. I feel like a traitor to her friendship and family." Her concern overlapped her fear.

"The information we need stems from the Imperial Japanese Navy. I'm certain Eileen is not a member."

"My, you have been doing your homework. Eileen is Nikkei American Jin and extremely proud to have been born here. But why the Japanese Navy? They are millions of miles away."

He did not answer. He did not tell her of the activity of the Japanese submarines along American shores in the Hawaiian Islands and the mainland.

She set down her empty glass and lifted his patch as she posed the question. "How dangerous is this exactly?"

"I will be close by at all times."

She flinched and he discerned she saw through his answer.

"How close?" Her cheeks reddened with her question and he saw her swallow hard.

He smiled as she bit her lip and concentrated on his eye patch, avoiding him.

The two quick strong knocks at the door dissipated the tension between them as Jack stood to open the door.

Duckworth stood there, hat in hand, embarrassed. "She asked me to be here promptly at eight to give her a ride home." He nodded toward Billi.

"Thank you, Duckworth." She handed Jack his patch, picked up her purse and gloves, and headed toward the door.

Jack held his patch, dumbfounded.

"What time tomorrow afternoon?" Her attitude returned to business.

"Will 4:30 meet Madame President's schedule?"

"Perfect." She almost missed her step with her headiness and the effects of the alcohol.

TWENTY-SIX

"WHAT DO YOU MEAN you are leaving for training?" Mrs. O slumped back into her rocker and held Pepper closer to her.

"Isn't it just what you always said? Know a company by starting as a secretary. That way you can learn more from the inside." Billi sat across from her mother with her suitcase, coat, hat, and gloves neatly waiting by the front door.

"But why so soon? I need you here." She whined in her apparent despair, her shoulders rising and falling in hopelessness.

"Mother, it will only be for a short time. I need a change for a while. I miss Ray so. Please?"

Ray's name had not been mentioned in their house for a long time out of respect for Billi. And at the mere mention of the loss, Mrs. O's eyes filled with tears.

"Yes, of course, dear. Will you write?" It sounded pathetic from the strongest member of the family.

"Of course. I'll write often. Eileen said she would stop by from time to time, and, of course, Danny will be here."

"And Pepper." She cradled the dog like a baby, and in response he licked her cheek.

"Our grand guard dog." Billi dare not call her puppy to her as she barely held back her emotions that threatened to surface and sabotage her decision. "I'll call you when I get there. Tell the neighbors we need to talk between ourselves, and not to listen in on our phone conversations."

The party line shared by the four homes on the block had proven useful at times but mostly it presented an opportunity for entertainment in the other homes. However, Billi knew that since her mother supervised as block captain, she did most of the listening. As her duty, Mrs. O reasoned.

She heard a car pull up in front of the house and rose to look out the window. Poppi slid from the driver's seat of his cab and waved at her. She waved back, then went to her mother and kissed her forehead.

"Don't get up, Mom. That way it will feel like I'm just going out for a short while. Pepper, you take good care of Mother. Don't let her get into any trouble. I'll be back before you know it."

"Are you going to wear the ring?"

"Until I'm ready, yes."

"That makes me feel better." Her mother smiled up at her. "Be careful. I love you."

"I love you too." She planted another kiss on her mother's ample cheek, grabbed her things, and stepped out into the day that had grown darker with every hour.

BILLI LEANED BACK IN POPPI'S CAB, watched the first drops of rain splatter against the windshield, and thought of her loved ones' reactions to her departure. Eileen had been excited by the deception Billi had presented her with. Learning a new trade held unforeseen promise. Dahlia had just mooned over missing Eddy and how her nursing courses at Seattle University were so boring. Danny had turned red and said nothing but had promised to check on Mrs. O every day after high school. Billi had promised to be back well before Christmas, in time to hear all the news of his senior year classes.

"Eddy is okay?" Poppi drew her out of her silence.

"We heard he has learned the correct way to make a bed, do push-ups, and peel a potato."

"My son's same. But now they more busy, build engines, make tanks. At least is work." He smiled into the rearview mirror, exposing his crooked teeth.

When they pulled up in front of the Boylston address, Poppi looked back at Billi. He obviously recognized the dark sedan parked beneath the tree just down the block.

"Don't worry. And don't tell Mother. I'm going to work for the government. They're training me to be an administrative secretary." She hoped the job title would appease him. "It's very specialized work."

"Okay." He shifted in his discomfort. "But call Poppi you need anything." He handed her another of his cards.

"I promise." She tucked the card into her purse.

Duckworth opened the door for her and then paid Poppi along with a hefty tip. She waved back at the older Greek man behind the steering wheel, and then walked through the arch of tall laurels toward the main door of the apartments.

As the cab pulled away, Jack slipped from behind a shrub and grabbed her arm. "Let's get going. We don't want to be late for your first day." His curtness unmistakable.

He guided her back through the tall hedge and into the waiting car.

"Where are we headed?" Billi ventured from the back seat as Duckworth started the engine.

Jack closed his door but did not offer an answer. After they turned onto Madison and rolled down the hill, she began to calculate their destination. They were not headed for the Federal Office Building where she had first been questioned, but the ferry docks she knew so well.

"I'm sorry. I missed your answer." She tried again.

Jack heaved a sigh, as if irritated. "After we arrive in Bremerton we have a bit of a drive to reach Port Townsend."

"And what is in Port Townsend?" She leaned forward.

"Highlights of your new career," Jack mumbled. He sat back and tipped his hat over his face in feigned repose.

When they finally arrived at the corner of Water and Tyler in Port Townsend, it neared 10 p.m. They had stayed in the car as the MV *Enetai* chugged across Puget Sound, which Billi found uncomfortable. She had not been allowed to walk outside to catch the distinct breeze off the water and that irritated her. They had traveled the back way up Beaver Valley Road and stopped in the farmland area of Chimacum for a quick dinner. A shroud of silence prevailed, with very little exchanged between her and Jack. Only Duckworth had engaged her in a brief conversation over the meal. Now, here they all sat in front of the Old

Palace Hotel. They waited as a man emerged from the door, pulled his hat low, and then wandered down the street toward the water.

"Well, let's get this over with." Jack threw open his door, stepped into the night, and then held the back door for Billi. He took her suitcase from the trunk and nodded for her to head down the dark alley toward the back of the old brick building.

"What is this place?" Billi stood her ground, not budging from the side of the car.

"They call it 'The Pleasure Palace' or sometimes the 'Palace of Sweets.'"

"A whore house?" she shot back, stunned.

He quickly grabbed her elbow and tugged her toward the alley and the back door.

"I've never been inside a house of ill repute," she found herself saying to no one in particular.

"I should hope not."

He caught himself from saying more as the image of the Billi's face imprinted on the pink, heart-shaped pin promoted as a fundraiser for the home for unwed mothers came to mind. How could she act so innocent? The whole situation bothered him. He held the back door for her but could not bring himself to look at her. At the top of the stairs, he put her bag down.

"Wait here." He turned and started down the hall.

"You seem to know your way around here pretty well."

He laughed before disappearing inside the tall door with a brass plaque inscribed with the name "Marie."

Billi stood in the half light, the sounds of music, laughter, and occasional groaning drifted from various parts of the upper level. Most seemed to come from the stairwell. She walked toward the noises and came to another hallway. There appeared to be rooms everywhere. The door to one opened and she slid into the darkness.

A man, buttoning his shirt over his expansive midriff, stumbled from the room, followed by a partially clad woman, whose disheveled hair and half-burnt cigarette told the story.

Suddenly Jack stood beside her, taking her arm and dragging her back toward the door he had entered. He pushed her inside.

"This is Billi." He introduced her without emotion. "Billi, this is Marie. I'll be back soon. Good luck."

Without so much as a good-bye, he clamped his hat on his head and trudged down the hallway.

"Well, you seem to have him in a snit."

Billi looked at the woman Jack had left her with. Her head rested against the velvet-backed chair, her skin pulled tight across her cheeks from the force of her upswept hairdo. While her makeup displayed artistry, not overly applied, her lipstick blazed fiery red.

A puff of smoke emitted from Marie's lips as she stared back at Billi. "I understand you have some experience."

Billi took in the green woodwork, red wallpaper, and view from the tall windows but did not answer.

"All right." Marie began again. "So what has Jack told you about us?"

"I'm here for training. For the government." Her skin began to crawl as the sounds from down the hall briefly escalated then died down.

"Some men are moaners. Goes with the territory." She leaned forward to assess Billi. "So, I have only a few days to make you a believable working girl. Well, sit down and let's get started. You can meet the others after noon tomorrow."

"Can't this wait until the morning?" Exhaustion, with a tinge of fear, pushed her words.

"Darling, we don't work mornings." Marie emitted a deep, throaty laugh and pointed to the other chair across from her.

At two-thirty the next day, Marie clapped her hands and the small gathering of boisterous women who had spent the night before providing for their customers, fell silent. The large receiving area on the upper floor of the Palace of Sweets, at the top of the long flight of stairs where the men usually waited impatiently, smelled overwhelmingly of perfume. Billi stood next to Marie, noticing the other women were regarding her with looks of distaste.

"Who's payin' us to teach her?" A thick-wasted woman snarled. Her large breasts drooping without her corset, and she drew her fuchsia Chinese-silk robe closer in defiance.

"No one, Clara." Marie glared at her. "See it as a gift to your country."

A tall blonde woman wagged her finger. "Vell, zis is not my country."

"But, Greta, this is my house." At Marie's answer, the women shifted and collected themselves.

"Besides," Clara brightened, "who'd want that skinny thing?"

All but Marie and a women sitting off to the right laughed at the mean jest directed toward Billi.

Marie pursed her lips and waited for the silence that soon followed. "Again, ladies, she won't be working this house, she isn't competition for your regulars. In fact, she won't work here at all. But it's your responsibility to make certain that she will do extremely well in her next house."

"Let's zee her valk," Greta egged Billi on. "Valk, you do know how?"

Billi started across the room, and the giggles began.

"Halt. Stop zis now." Greta moved her hips enticingly toward Billi. "Zee hips, move zee hips."

Billi nearly threw out her hip trying to imitate Greta.

"Zat's it. Zeer goot." Her laughter was infectious.

Clara's big bosoms jiggled as she walked up to Billi and grabbed her breast. "Holy shit, she's got little tits. She'll need lifts."

Billi swung at Clara but the large woman ducked.

"An' fightin' lessons." Clara laughed as she turned to walk away but abruptly stopped as Billi's foot kicked her large backside.

The audible intake of breath moved around the room as Clara straightened then rounded on Billi. But this time it became Billi's turn to duck, sending the oversized women lurching forward.

"Enough." Marie clapped her hands again then looked at the seated woman on her right. "Annie, take Billi and teach her your potions. Especially the ones to knock someone out quickly. Greta work with her on a wardrobe; take whatever you need from my closet."

"Vell, Vell, you are special," Greta purred.

"Clara, you can tell her the 'how tos' in a dangerous situation. But you are not to touch her. Is that clear?"

Clara licked her lips before answering. "Yeah. But be sure she gets some tits. She's a skinny little bitch."

"She's got great legs," Annie's soft voice interjected. "Do you exercise a lot?"

"I like to swim." Billi liked Annie immediately.

"Well, that ain't the exercise you'll be getting around here," Clara's loud laugh echoed down the hall.

"All right. And thank you for your help." Marie waved Billi toward Annie and left the room.

"Ven you are done, I vill be soaking in zee tub. Come in and ve vill begin." Greta's hips move with a rhythm of fluidity unknown to Billi as she left the room.

"Don't be soakin' too damn long. I have a four o'clock." Clara stormed behind her.

"Don't mind them." Annie rose, surprising tall. "Come to my room."

She gently took Billi's hand and began to limp toward the stairway hugging the wall that overlooked the waiting area that led up to the various rooms. She did not look at Billi as she spoke. "Before I knew the secret of the potions, I had an angry customer. They stitched me up as best they could. So I spent years developing my soothing concoctions in the hopes no one else gets mad at one of our girls. Marie took very good care of me. I would do anything to help her."

They entered Annie's domain and Billi smelled the essence of herbs and chemicals. Bottles lined the shelves. When Annie turned back toward Billi, the light from the window shone on the woman's cheek where a scar ran down the length of her face.

"Some men still find me attractive." She blushed slightly at Billi's concerned look. "Sit here. I hope you can memorize quickly."

TWENTY-SEVEN

R ESTLESS, JACK DROVE THE DISTANCE to Fort Ward, on Bainbridge Island. He parked in front of the new concrete Navy Administration Building and entered the long two story structure. Commander Purrington showed Jack the eight-hundred-foot tower intercepting Japanese diplomatic radio messages that they decoded in the new structure. Station S, as it had been recently renamed, also assisted in tracking radio signals to pin point the positions of Japan's merchant ships—a vital, quiet endeavor by the navy to help protect its many bases in the area. The meeting with Purrington established a channel of communication between the men that Jack hoped would pay off.

He dreaded his drive back to Port Townsend. Avoiding the corner of Water and Tyler, he drove straight to the expansive grounds at Fort Worden, but that did not present enough of a distraction. He had already spent the last days walking the perimeter of the Harbor Defense Command, which both the army and the navy shared as a base, past the bunkers, guns, barracks, and lighthouse.

Irritated, he headed down the hill to the beach and stood on the end of the dock watching the small white caps form and glide past him. The wind held a chill beneath gray clouds. His mind went to Billi and his ludicrous idea. If she couldn't pull this off, if the brutal Akio discovered her true identity, Jack knew only too well the swift results that would be bestowed on her.

He walked back up the hill, feeling no better for his exercise, and went inside the long white structure of the main headquarters. He climbed the wooden stairs that were mid-building, to the office they had provided him, a small room with a simple desk and a phone where Duckworth sat collecting his notes for his report. Jack stepped up to the window and looked out across at the bay, but the blue waters did not soothe him. The sound of the men marching on the field between where he stood and the massive brick structures that housed the commanders on the far side only made him edgy. The long lane of grass crawled with men in uniform who stepped and turned with their wooden guns to the shouts of their sergeants. Most of them appeared to be just kids, straight out of high school, in search of a job and adventure. Not a war.

"I'm ready, sir." Duckworth thumped his stack of papers with his pen.

"Let's have it." Jack did not turn from his view of the grounds.

"No one on Bainbridge Island claims to have seen our man. I showed his picture to several of the Japanese farmers and at the stores."

"Did you question Mr. Sato?" Jack's voice turned edgy.

"Yes, the one that is on the list from the consulate as being a spy in charge in this area. I made certain he was with a group of men when I asked. Didn't want to single him out. He wasn't convincing, but denied any knowledge."

"Good work. What about the boat?"

"The old man, Alfred Johnston, rented his boat to Akio on the dock at Silverdale. Said Akio introduced himself as Charles Kino."

"Charles Kino?" Jack snorted. "Kino is the name of the student who served as the president of the Japanese Club at Stanford when we were there."

Duckworth circled the name and then continued. "Akio used the name of one of Alfred's friends as an introduction, a Herbert Freeland. When I checked with Freeland, he said he'd never heard of 'Charles Kino.' Alfred said the Jap behaved politely, paid cash, showed identification as a merchant marine, and seemed to know his way around boats and the water. He brought the boat back when he said he would, handed Alfred a tip, and a promised to come back and rent his boat again. Alfred said he would call if he does show up."

"He won't." Jack finally turned to face Duckworth.

"Alfred said he had a duffel bag with him but no fishing gear. Thought it strange."

"A duffel bag full of cameras and maps would be my guess."

"No one at the shipyard in Bremerton reported anything out of the ordinary that day." Duckworth stiffened, "Holy crap, do you think the Japs have reached inside Bremerton Naval Base like they're claiming?"

"And Boeing Field? And all up and down this coast? I do. And even though Hoover thinks we should leave the job to the navy to unravel this information, I can't sit by and watch. I know Akio and what he is capable of. And it is that very handsome, calm face that can tell lies without blinking or kill while smiling, which is the most dangerous." Jack ran his fingers though his hair.

"The damn Japanese. They really want to rule the world. What they did in China makes my skin crawl. We are lucky the SIS got Magic up and running. At least by decrypting the Purple Code we get an inkling of what the hell they're up to. Just hope it holds. If they get wind we're reading their correspondence, they will change the code and we'll be sunk."

"Luck is fickle." Jack half smiled. "But getting scraps of our enemy's plans and their positions is more than we could hope for. So, yes, God bless Magic, and pray our luck holds."

"I'm with you on that, sir."

Jack nodded at his assistant. "All right, we've done what we can here. Let's go and see what Marie and the girls have been able to teach Billi." At the mention of her name, he felt his jaw tighten. God help them all.

JACK STEPPED FROM THE CAR into the darkness and headed toward the back of the Palace Hotel, leaving Duckworth at the wheel. He walked slowly up the stairs, in no hurry to see the transformation of Billi. He hated himself at the moment.

He knocked at Marie's door and it swung wide open. The swaying backside of a girl as she led him into the room caught his eye. She turned defiantly and stood with one hand on her hip. Her hair swirled high; the deep red of her lipstick offset the orchid print dress with frills that edged its low-cut bodice. His eye followed the strand of long pearls that hung between her breasts in the deep cleavage of soft white skin. Her chin went up as she observed him with a haughty, sexual gaze. She was magnificent.

"About time ya got here." Billi tested her new deep sensual voice. "Shouldn't keep a gal waiting. Care for a drink?"

He smiled. "No thanks. Another time. I'm looking for Miss Billi O'Shaughnessy."

"Never heard of her," Billi answered with a shrug. "I'm Ginger. And I can give ya whatever it is ya need." She smiled slow and calculating as she looked him up and down.

"Well, Ginger, why don't you grab your things and we'll get out of here."

"Not so fast." She perched on the arm of the chair, her skirt working up her long leg. "Let's talk business first. I'm expensive."

Jack couldn't help but chuckle. "I bet. And experienced."

"Ah-ha." She rose and came toward him, hips in motion. She ran her hand down his face and leaned in closer, then whispered. "So, what will it be?"

Her usually earthy scent of sunshine and fresh air had been expertly dowsed with French lilac water, and the sensation mesmerized him.

"Christ, am I glad to see you, Ginger." He grabbed her and pulled her close. He ran one hand down her side and leg. They stayed connected for a few moments before he let her go. "Well done."

Marie stepped into the room. "I thought you would be pleased."

"You'll never know how much. We had better be going." He picked up Billi's suitcase and headed for the door.

Billi turned to Marie, who held out a smaller case. "Here, the girls sent this along for you. Stay in touch as best you can."

"Thanks." Billi changed back to her normal way of speaking. "It certainly has been instructional. To say the least."

Marie kissed Billi's cheek. "Be careful. And use these wisely." She pointed to the smaller case.

Billi nodded and then followed Jack down the stairs and into the dark.

EDDY SAT ALONE AT THE TABLE in the galley at Camp Luce, the naval training center at the north end of San Diego Bay. His weeks in boot camp were sliding by since he had first arrived and entered the compound through the ornate wrought-iron arch that spanned the two stone guardhouses at the gate. The okra-stucco buildings with repeated arches below red tile roofs were imposing and housed the classrooms overlooking the spacious fields for morning exercise, daily drills, and marching. Always marching, until inbred and routine. He found the weather to be a different reality here at the Cradle of the Navy compared to the gray skies of Seattle. It had been a long day but he had one more letter to write. Having finished brief and simple notes to Dahlia and another to Danny, he started on the one to his mother and sister. This proved to be the hardest, for he had come to realize all Ray had talked about was indeed coming to pass. The air would become the principal factor in the next war, whenever the United States became involved in what appeared to be the approaching mêlée. And like Ray, Eddy insisted his position for battle would be scouring the sky for the enemy.

He had been selected for decoding and found it very interesting; however, he wanted to feel the wind lift his wings. Something Ray had always talked about, the many stories of loops and dives, bumpy landings and near misses. He had gone up a few times with Ray, but he had never had the desire to become a pilot, until now. Watching some of the short films of navy aircraft during classes and hearing the constant buzz of the pilots in training on North Island had struck him in such a fashion that the need to be airborne grew to become a living extension of his being. While he remained in the office training with Morse code and intricate information used by the armed forces, he spent his spare time reading and memorizing to further his training in the cockpit.

He looked at the blank piece of paper before him and decided this was not the time to introduce his new found goal. The scars were still too fresh. His pen poised above the paper, he began his mundane report. All is well. He misses them, loves them, and hopes they are safe.

THEY WERE JUST ENTERING CALIFORNIA when Jack joined Billi at the dining car table. As the train rattled into the dawn, she traced her finger down the path they had already taken, past Portland, Eugene, and Ashland.

"How did you sleep?" His voice still held the deep tones of morning.

"The rocking is somewhat soothing." She inspected him over the tip of the map.

"For some." He waited while the black porter filled his coffee cup and then ordered a breakfast of eggs and ham.

"Do you realize how close I will be to Eddy?" She pushed away her empty plate and put the map between them to demonstrate the distance with two fingers—one at their destination, San Francisco, and the other on yet another city she had never visited, San Diego.

Jack did not answer her but looked out the window, watching the large trees and scenery float past. Billi's nonchalance disturbed him. Either the danger surrounding her situation had not sunk in yet or she had developed into a better actress than he had gauged. They had been over the plan a dozen times, and she claimed she had no more questions—something he knew would change the minute she stepped out on her own. By this evening they would be on his turf and they would finally begin. He checked his watch for the third time, glad when his food arrived for the distraction it presented.

"I wrote a letter to Mom and one to Eileen." Billi pushed the envelopes toward him. "And yes, I was vague. My training to be a secretary is going well, and I miss them. Hi to Danny and the others. Etc."

"May I read them?" His question sounded flat and unemotional, the way he had been treating her for days.

"If you must." Billi turned and stared out the window.

He picked them up and stuffed them inside his jacket pocket. "I'll see they get posted."

TWENTY-EIGHT

B Y MIDAFTERNOON, BILLI HAD DEPARTED the train alone. She had taken a bus and then walked to the corner of Stockton and Maiden Lane. She dragged her suitcase and the smaller case up the flights of stairs to Room 401. Though small, the room had a view over Union Square, past the victory statue in honor of Admiral Dewey, with the sumptuous Alma de Bretteville seemingly floating on top. Just beyond loomed the St. Francis Hotel where she planned to meet her contact by the clock that stood watch in the main foyer.

She smiled at the festive changing screen, on which someone had hand-painted abstract, large roses in reds, yellows, and pinks against a black background. Folding back the artwork, she found a small closet where she hung up her few dresses from her visit to Port Townsend, then neatly arranged her two pairs of high heels.

She reverently placed the pillow Eileen had made for her on the single bed. The presence of the gift made her smile. The design of the pillowslip had been divided into four squares, each with delicate embroidery. One section displayed the golden chrysanthemum for good luck; another, the Japanese kengi for peace; an orchid and a fan covered the last sections. American-style lace and tucking surrounded Eileen's handiwork. But in the Japanese way, she had incorporated a hidden pocket in the folds of the tucking. An amalgamation of both worlds.

She reached inside Eileen's gift and pulled out the purple case holding the fan the professor had given her. She pinched the small pouch she had tied to the netsuke that hung from the purple case and felt Raymond's ring. It had been sheer impulse to bring the gifts and

Ray's ring, but somehow they belonged together. And they reminded her of those she loved, who had taught her so much. They represented the impact where her two worlds collided, her lost love and the very culture she now spied upon. She replaced the ring and fan, then patted the bedspread into a perfectly smooth surface. The small gesture brought her a sense of ease and structure.

Further exploring the room, she checked out the tiny stove next to a wooden table and a cupboard. She found a bottle of chlorine below the sink and began scrubbing. The motion made her think of her mother cleaning her chair. Next she would tackle the bathroom. Keeping busy became her distraction.

At 8 p.m. that evening, Billi started across the square, her heels clicking as she swayed in Marie's orchid floral dress. She had applied her makeup as boldly as the women who had trained her and then checked inside her purse for her only armor, a small vial of Anna's potion. Her first day on the job held a bit of a thrill.

"Meet at the clock at eight-ten and don't be late" were the instructions on the note she found slipped under her door. She sashayed inside the lobby of the St. Francis Hotel, past tall black-marble columns topped with ornate golden paint that rose two stories above her, and straight toward the famous wooden clock on the far side of the lobby. She posed in an obvious fashion next to the twelve-foot tall grandfather clock with its intricate detailing. She placed her hand on her hip in pure defiance as one of the managers scurried toward her.

"I am sorry," he began in a hushed tone, "but you will have to move on…ah, miss. We do not allow loitering of your kind in our hotel."

"I ain't loiterin'. I just got here. And what 'kind' is it ya mean?" Billi looked him up and down in a brazen fashion she enjoyed.

The manager took a step closer, head bent toward her. "Now look. I don't want any trouble here."

"That makes two of us. Ain't this a hotel? Don't ya let people in here?" She began to raise her voice.

"I think you'd better—"

"There you are. Sorry I'm late." Duckworth took off his hat and extended his elbow in her direction. He turned to the manager. "Thank you for keeping an eye on my little prize, Anthony."

"Of course, Mr. Rosenblum. Any time." The manager stepped back.

Arms linked, the two swept past the manager and out the front doors to the chiming of the cable cars.

"Hurry." Duckworth pulled her toward the reddish-brown cable car as it stopped across Powell Street. He helped her onto the seat facing the street and sat next to her as the trolley car clanked into action and they jerked toward the steep hillside.

"Thank you, Mr. Rosenblum," Billi giggled.

"No problem, Ginger," Duckworth smiled. "Great job, by the way, fooling Anthony back at the hotel. How are you doing?"

For the first time she let down her guard with Duckworth. "Okay. I hope this doesn't take long." She half shouted above the clanking of the cable car.

Duckworth signaled to her, and they hopped off on Clay Street and started down the hill into Chinatown. At number 965, midblock, stood a brick building designed by Julia Morgan, which represented a unique blend of Chinese and Caucasian cultures. Duckworth led Billi through the blockish-designed doors below an arch of white stone. The Chinese-style lantern shown on a brass plaque designated the building as the YWCA. The woman at the front desk nodded at them, and Duckworth led the way down the hall. Billi stepped lightly over the dragon painted on the floor, past the wall of windows that overlooked a small courtyard with a garden and fountain lit by the soft glow of candles. The peace it represented not in keeping with her racing heart.

Shirley Choy sat in an ornate chair in a small back room just off the stairway. Her elbows rested on dragon heads holding globes that formed the armrests of the finely carved wood, her dull gown drab in comparison. She motioned Duckworth forward as Jack stepped from the shadows.

"She the girl?" Shirley pointed at Billi, her long fingernail slightly curved at the tip.

Jack nodded. "Ginger, this is Shirley Choy. If you have any problems and you can't find me, come here and ask for her."

Shirley rose and moved toward her. Her bowed legs gave her walk a distinctive sway. Her graying hair formed a perfect bun at the base of her neck, her skin appeared luminescent, but her eyes were dark and hard. A shiver ran through Billi as Shirley circled her.

"She okay," Shirley proclaimed as she started back to her chair. "Akio maybe like her." She turned and faced Billi with her dagger eyes. "You make sure Akio like you."

It was a command, direct and brutal, with all the implications of attracting the enemy.

Billi remained silent. The brassy young women who had entered as Ginger now stood somewhat dazed as Shirley scribbled a note and then handed it to her.

"Take to door. First show 9:30. Go. Go." She waved her hand again and Duckworth took Billi by the arm.

Once outside Billi sighed deeply. "What was all that about?"

"Shirley Choy has developed several deep connections in Chinatown since her arrival. She's a bit scary, don't you think?"

"I wouldn't want to meet her in a dark alley, if that is what you mean."

"We're going to head down Grant Street toward Sutter. I'll go up first. Just wait by the streetlight for a few minutes, then come on up. You remember how to get in touch with Jack if you need to?"

She nodded and watched as Duckworth scooted ahead and turned right down Grant Street. Even at this hour the lively street bubbled with activity. The many buildings reflected the culture forced to stay inside these few blocks emitting the smells and sounds distinctly Chinese.

As she neared the end of the unseen boundary line and crossed Sutter, she could hear the music blaring from above Number 363. The street lamp in front of the doorway illuminated the stairs that led up to the nightclub Forbidden City. The creation of Charlie Low developed into the top draw for men and women of all races. Tonight's show boasted the crooning of Larry Ching, the club's Chinese Frank Sinatra.

She stood under the light and watched as men entered for the late show. Unintended, a short, plump man approached her.

"You headed up?" His speech thick with booze, clashed with his neat and clean appearance.

"You buyin'?" She tilted her head and smiled.

"You bet, baby. Come on." He took her elbow and led her beneath the canopy that announced "Forbidden City All-Chinese Floor Show." The round man held her elbow tightly as they climbed the stairs, then he worked his way to a group of men who sat at a back table.

The crowd shifted from those who arrived at five-thirty for dinner and dancing, to a more gregarious audience, there to hoot and holler at the late performance.

"I'm Roger. From New York," he added to impress her as he grabbed another chair for their table.

"I'm Ginger from nowhere," she threw back at him and the others in his group exploded into laughter.

"Well, Ginger from nowhere, what are you drinking?" He offered her a cigarette.

"Manhattan with a twist." She pushed the pack of Lucky Strikes away.

"A woman of taste," one of the men quipped.

"That should leave out Roger," another joined in at her host's expense.

She sat back and let the men banter as she took in her surroundings. Duckworth sat across the room at a small table, his legs crossed as he leaned back in his chair observing the crowd. There were women dressed in their finest, men of all ages, and a variety of uniforms being seated in the packed space. But she could not find a particular tall Japanese man among them.

The lights dimmed and Chinese girls wearing short-shorts and low-cut tops danced onto the stage. In true burlesque style, they hoofed a fantastic number. Larry Ching followed their act to welcome the crowd and introduce the next number of exotic dancers in Egyptian-style costumes. As the evening moved on, Roger had inched closer to Billi, his hands attempting to stroke her leg. While the men were on their third round, Billi had hardly sipped her first drink.

"Hey." Roger leaned in closer to her. "Don't you like your drink?"

"Sure, but I don't like your hand on my leg." Billi picked up his hand and dropped it onto the table with a thud.

"What kind of working girl are you?" He tried to put his hand back even farther up her thigh.

"Expensive." She rose. "Excuse me, I need ta powder my nose."

"I'll help."

Roger started to stand, but Billi steamed through the door and into the restroom. She waited for several minutes before stepping out into the hallway. She had not seen him standing behind the door, but felt the hunger in his grasp as Roger pushed her up against the wall and attempted to kiss her, pressing his body against hers. Her purse slipped from her hand and tumbled to the floor.

"Expensive, huh?" His pushed his whiskey-laden breath inches from her skin as his hand worked down her breasts. She slid her knee between his legs and snapped it up into his groin, as Clara had taught her to do in awkward situations. Roger moaned and backed off, hands over his crotch.

"Shit! You bitch."

He started for her, but she quickly scooped up her purse and dashed down the hall. She rounded the corner and bumped into the back of a tall man just entering from the stairwell. The stranger turned in her direction and stared down at her, his dark eyes taking in her disheveled appearance. Billi quickly adjusted her dress and smiled up at Akio.

A seething Roger slipped past them. "Goddamn whore." He looked back at her one last time before slouching into the chair next to his friends.

She stood in awkward silence as the others at Roger's table laughed and nodded in her direction.

"In my country, to service men is a respected business." His smooth English told of his years at Stanford.

"Oh, an' what country is that?" Billi took out her small compact.

"An older country than this one." He seemed enticed by the way she applied a new coat of lipstick.

"Ya want ta buy me a drink and tell me about it?" She snapped her purse shut.

"Maybe some other time."

"Ginger." She looked up at him again. "You can ask for me. I'm Ginger."

"Ginger, like the root. Strong and potent and healing."

"Some say that. I'm not so sure about the healing part," she laughed.

"Ah, but you heal the most basic of desires, Ginger."

"Yeah. I guess I do."

She smiled again and then moved her hips toward the bar at the back of the club. When she looked back, Akio had joined a table of three other men. She ordered a drink and sat watching them. Drifts of smoke surrounded the four men and they all seemed to hang on Akio's words. She stirred her drink, trying to figure out a way to get closer, when Akio abruptly stood, stubbed out his cigarette, and started for the door. Just before exiting, he turned and looked her way. She raised her glass at him and winked. He nodded and disappeared as the finale began and all of the half-clad girls danced back onto the stage.

TWENTY-NINE

IT WAS TWO-THIRTY IN THE MORNING and Billi sat slumped in a chair in Jack's suite at the Sir Francis Drake Hotel overlooking Powell Street.

"Tell me again exactly what happened after he left." Jack's tone hardened.

For the third time she replayed the evening. She had finished her drink at the bar of the club and waited until Roger and his drunken cohorts had exited. Her behavior had drawn the attention of Charlie Low himself. When the owner of the club introduced himself, she slipped him the note with Shirley Chow's squiggles across the paper. He had merely lifted his eyebrows in her direction and paid for her drink. Duckworth had waited outside, and she followed him at a distance to the side door of this hotel and to the elevators. She did not speak to Duckworth but got on the elevator with him when it opened and let him lead her to Jack's room on the sixth floor. And now she sat here repeating herself.

"Good." Jack finally acknowledged. "Details. You need to remember all details. Can you recognize Akio's men?"

"Not tonight." Her voice dripped with exhaustion.

"Three o'clock tomorrow. Be in the Square. Not as Ginger."

"Very funny." She pushed herself up and started for the door. She saw an exhausted Duckworth rise from the couch and follow her out into the hall.

Again he led the way out the side door on Sutter Street, around the corner to Powell and then across Union Square. Her high heels had less *click* to them at this hour. She took them off as she entered her building and climbed the stairs alone.

At her window, she looked down onto the square. It was empty. She let go of her emotions, the longing to be home with her mother and Pepper, to hear her father's singing and see Eileen's smile. Eddy was stationed a few hours away and yet not within her reach. She had never felt so lonely in her life. Tears ran through her caked-on make up as she turned from the window and fell onto the single bed.

JACK HELD OUT another picture.

"No." Billi leaned back. "There was a lot of smoke in the room and the lights were low, but I don't think any of these men were the ones at the table. Maybe I should carry a camera?"

Jack fell silent for a moment. "Not you, but I can get someone in there to take photos of tables during the breaks." Impressed with her train of thought he made a mental note to talk with Charlie Low later. She looked tired and this concerned him. "You didn't sleep much last night?"

"I tried. New place, all this going on. A bit out of the ordinary." He noticed she did not smile as she spoke.

"I heard about the man in the hallway. Sorry about that. Are you all right?"

"Yes," she snapped.

"Look." He began hopefully. "Having you speak with Akio, having made the initial connection is incredible for your first night. He will be back, and he will look for you. Be careful." He dared not say more of his knowledge of the dangerous man he had come to know.

"How long are we going to do this?" She had never asked the question before.

"Not long." He looked away as he lied again. "Why don't you explore the city this afternoon? Take a bus, cable car, go on a walk. Try to relax. If he's in town, he won't be for long. He is here to secure contacts before he heads out. He is never in one place for any length of time."

"How did you know he was here?"

He could not answer her.

Out of frustration, Billi had inadvertently taken Jack's advice. When he had dismissed her after the grueling hour of looking over pictures and even more questions, she slammed out of the side door of the hotel onto Sutter Street. Instead of heading toward Chinatown, and the Forbidden City Nightclub, she turned left and headed north. She did not even count the blocks as she worked through her anger attempting to determine the underlying connection between Jack and the man she had met last night. A tremor ran through her as she remembered the look Akio had given her when she had accidently bumped into him. It had made her go cold, his look of pure disdain transforming into lust. She had skirted that impression when talking to Jack for some reason, and now it bothered her. She should have told him.

Startled she stopped and looked around in amazement. She looked back at the street sign and noted Laguna Street, then up at the shop signs with their distinct Japanese characters. Before her were the Yamaguchi-ya Hotel, the Mizuko Skokai Dry Goods, and Uyeda Shokai Grocery. All around her, tucked into the ground floor of the San Francisco Victorian-style homes, were Japanese businesses, their owners, and patrons. She had stumbled into Nihonjin Ohi, Japanese people's town.

Her heart felt light as she wandered through the stores and listened to the dialect of the people she had come to love. She ached to tell Eileen and Mr. Nakamura of her find, of the thriving Japanese business and culture of this city. She wandered into Gosha-do Books and Stationery and paged through a book written in the beautiful Japanese kanji with great interest. The engaging book displayed of the opulent garden of the Emperor's Palace, telling of the seasonal blooms. She clutched it, reading, when she sensed someone stood next to her. She snapped the book closed and looked up at a handsome young Japanese man. In the background she overheard an older woman, probably a relative, scold him in Japanese for making the white woman wait for service.

"May I help you?" A slight accent accompanied his otherwise perfect English. "Do you read Japanese?" he asked in his native tongue.

Billi stopped herself before responding to the question. With a catch of her breath, she concluded she stood in dangerous territory. If seen here, if she ran into Akio or any of the men he had been talking to, she would destroy all of Jack's efforts.

She shook her head but saw the eyes of the young man harden.

"I don't need help," she mumbled, handing him back the book. "Just lookin'."

She stepped from the store and hurried south, back toward Union Square. She slowed, realizing she could be drawing attention, made it home, and collapsed on the bed. Billi pulled the covers over her face, hating the duplicity of her new existence.

Jack looked across at the useless David. Like a bad boomerang, he came back. If his uncle were not at the top of the pile, Jack would have cut him loose long ago. How did they expect him to utilize this incompetent bastard? Yet, David had turned up a scrap of pertinent information. And Jack intended to unearth the source.

"You will be here as back up. Duckworth will keep you informed if you don't hear from me." It pleased Jack to see David squirm at his new position under Duckworth. "Just keep your eyes open and keep me posted constantly."

"Sure, boss," David did not sound convincing. "How are things going with Billi? She'd make a fine whore."

Jack felt his muscles tighten and decided not to answer. The less David knew about Billi and their target, the better.

"You'll be staying near the Presidio again." Jack bit back his hatred.

"Should I keep an eye on the South Park area? Lots of Japs there. You want me there?" David flicked the ashes from his cigarette.

"Fine. I want to know every detail." Jack felt a sense of relief that David showed some interest. Even though most of the Japanese had vacated South Park after the big earthquake of 1906 and relocated to Japantown, some still operated thriving businesses in that area. He had one man already in that area, and Jack would have him keep an eye on David.

Jack felt like a frustrated puppeteer. He pulled one string to keep David away from Billi, another to keep Billi's spirits up, and the situation at his mother's did not improve matters. Adding to his boiling temper, too much time had passed with no sign of Akio. Stretched taut with no more to give, his nerves propelled him around the tight confinement of his hidden office. He had nowhere to go. He could not be seen on the streets, and between his suite and the walls of this room an evil emerged from within he had not known existed.

Updates from the decodings of Magic, reports from the Presidio, and Station S at Fort Ward on Bainbridge Island of increased Japanese activities all pointed to an impending attack by the nation that spread across the Pacific.

The president continued to promise America he did not want to go to war. He recently materialized from behind a closed doors meeting with Britain's Prime Minister, Churchill. The two demonstrated a consensus of the measure put into play to entice the Imperial Japanese Navy to strike the first blow against the United States. Roosevelt wanted the Americans behind him in this war, and his sanctions against Japan baited the trap that would spark the Empire of the Sun into action.

Jack rationalized he needed a break. The concrete walls of this small office were turning red with blood. He would head to his family home in the early hours—as soon as he knew Billi had safely returned to her room.

BILLI DRAGGED HERSELF UP THE STAIRS to the entrance of the Forbidden City at nine o'clock, the peak time between shows. Her character, Ginger, had been assaulted by lurid looks, attempted gropes, and disturbing comments. She could barely look at herself in the mirror for all the degrading remarks whispered at the club about her. Pretending to be a hooker turned into one of the hardest things she had ever done. She had been alone the last four nights. They could not afford to have Duckworth there every night, as his appearance could jeopardize their plan.

Billi half laughed. What plan? Nothing was happening. She wanted to go home.

The Chinese woman behind the desk called her over. "Ginger." She spoke her name with distaste. "Some man call for you."

"Yeah?" She instantly became the sassy wanton woman. "And did this guy have a name?"

"No. But as Mr. Low instruct, I tell him you here most nights." She winked.

"Thanks." Billi adjusted her long beads and gripped her purse with Anna's potions.

With more enthusiasm, she swayed toward the bar and what had become her stool. The wait seemed like a lifetime. She had batted away one man's attempt at conversation in a laughing manner, but he still eyed her from across the room. He reminded her of a bulldog, short and squat, with a wide nose barely etched into his face. Just before the music started and the girls paraded onto the stage, four men entered the room led by Charlie Low. The three short Japanese men again demurred to the tallest of their group, Akio.

She slid her skirt up a bit, exposing her left leg that dangled over her right and faced the bar. In between the bottles that lined the mirrored wall behind the bartender, she could barely make out the men's faces as they sat in the shadows.

The tap on her shoulder made her jump. The bulldog-faced man leered down at her.

"Nice gams there, doll. You sure I can't buy you a drink?"

"Sorry, I'm waitin' for someone." She looked back at the mirror, but Mr. Low stood talking with the four men and blocked her view. Finally, Low left the gentlemen and approached her.

"Come on. I got a lot of cash," the bulldog insisted.

Charlie Low appeared next to both of them. "Your table is waiting for you, Ginger. Sorry for the delay."

"Thanks." She slid from the stool and slowly made her way toward the empty seat next to Akio. Her heart thumped against her chest as she approached them.

"Hello, fellas. Nice ya could join me." She smiled at the men seated at the table.

One of the gentleman across from her laughed then spoke in his own tongue. "She makes jokes."

"This is Ginger," Akio announced in English as he stood and pulled a chair up for her.

The man who had laughed spoke again as the men resumed their conversation in Japanese. "I hope she pleases you in bed as well as makes you laugh."

"Not to worry, Ito, we know with your connections you can fill Akio's bed at any time," the youngest-looking of the group added.

"Ah, yes. But it is my other connections that will win us this city with ease. My men are organized and await your instructions." He half-bowed toward Akio.

Again, the young one, who had not taken his eyes from Billi, put in, "Do we get rewarded with whores, like in China?"

"Patience, Hatsuro. Let us enjoy the one we have among us first." Akio smiled at his men.

Billi fiddled with the twist in her drink, keeping her face devoid of emotion as they discussed her anatomy with lurid speculations. How Akio's eel would have good pleasure in her white cave. The blueness of her eyes, like the sea, would bring him strength for his voyage.

The lights dimmed abruptly, and conversation stopped as the show began. Billi spent the next half hour memorizing every detail about the men around her. The one called Ito wore a thick ring, while Hatsuro, the youngest, appeared stout and had a wide scar that ran across the top of his hand. More than likely from a blade. The third one, the one with the graying hair, said nothing but wistfully watched the young girls dance. She had not turned to study Akio. She would have time at the break, she reasoned. Besides, she already knew about him.

Dotty Sun finished her number to a roar of applause when the lights came up. Startled, Billi sat motionless. The bulldog of a man stood beside her.

"So, you like Japs, huh? Whites not good enough for you?"

Instantly, the odious man was slammed to the floor. The movement had been so swift and sure that Billi had barely seen the blow strike.

Akio got to his feet, helping the injured man up. "You must have slipped. Do you need help back to your table?"

The bulldog held his stomach and groaned out a "No" as he shuffled off.

Akio sat, and the three other men slightly nodded. Their eyes had hardened and an intensity had fallen over the table.

"Thanks." Billi smiled up at Akio.

"I did nothing. He was a clumsy fly going after sweet honey."

She could tell the exchange had aroused his lust and she looked away.

Ito leaned forward, continuing in Japanese. "I have brought you Mr. Tamura. He helped Mr. Abiko establish the *Nichi Bei Times*. It is our largest newspaper. The honorable Tamura serves on many committee boards, more than I can list. He helped establish the California Flower Market, the Japanese Tea Garden, and has expansive connections with shrines and churches. He travels to Japan frequently, and his connections will help us reach more soldiers for victory for our emperor. He has people who will contact the Negro and Jewish communities to enlist their assistance."

Billi didn't breathe as she watched Akio and the silent man with graying hair study each other, eyes unflinching. Neither spoke, nor did their expressions change. Finally, Akio nodded, abrupt, accepting.

"Since the United States has frozen all Japanese assets," Akio spoke with authority, "the monies to pay for information is being hand-delivered to all consulates. The stupid Americans have not broken the codes we use to communicate between Japan and our consulates. Please inform your spies to continue to bring information and money collected for the emperor to the consulates. They will be greatly rewarded for their efforts."

The silent Tamura nodded, sealing the arrangement.

With noticeable relief, Ito continued, "I have prepared for tomorrow as you instructed. What else will you need?"

"You have the time set for the game?" Akio asked.

"The earliest I could get. The light will be good from the hill before noon, and it is believed they monitor transmissions somewhere in one of the buildings."

"I remember the clubhouse," Akio remarked. "But that was some time ago."

"Hatsuro will be your driver and you will have to leave very early."

Billi had been observing the exchange, nibbling on her lemon twist to appear distracted. However, she had become so engrossed in the discussion she had not noticed Hatsuro studying her.

"Do you understand Japanese?" the young man asked in English, his accent thick.

"Ginger?" Akio looked at him in surprise.

She looked at him now, eyes wide, the lemon twist still between her lips, almost bitten in half, marked with her lipstick.

"Are you going to devour that?"

"Oh." She pulled it from her mouth.

"Hatsuro was talking to you."

"Me? I don't know any Hats Or O." She purposely mispronounced his name and added a giggle. "Is that you?" She looked at the strong young face. "We ain't been introduced."

The other two men looked toward the youngest.

Hatsuro reddened, his seething anger apparent, then hissed in his mother language. "This whore would be better off with a blade driven down her useless mouth."

"In due time her laugh will be extinguished." Akio smiled at her as he answered his underling.

Billi heard Ito and Hatsuro grunt in agreement of the ruthless deed, her own death. She forced the taste of bile from her throat.

"You must of said something pretty funny. Was it about me?" She batted her eyes at Akio.

"No. Just business."

"Don't ya ever have time for pleasure? Or are ya here just for business?"

"One should always enjoy both." He lifted his glass toward her.

"Ya here for long then?"

He sipped his drink. "Until the job is done."

She thought to prod for more information, but the music started up again.

Abruptly, Hatsuro rose, nodded toward Akio, and left without saying another word.

Billi crossed her legs and let her one foot sway to the music, inching her skirt up a bit higher during the dance routine onstage. Akio appeared not to notice. Nervous, she wiggled in her seat contemplating her next move and settled on a course of action. At the end of the song she leaned toward Akio then quickly straightened as all three of the remaining men at the table stood.

Akio bent toward her. "Thank you, Ginger, for your valuable time. But I must go, for now."

She looked up at him. "Business or pleasure?"

"Business first, pleasure later." With that he turned and left her sitting alone at the table.

She watched them go, then gathered her purse and hurried behind them to the top of the stairs. She stopped and caught her breath. At the bottom, facing the street, stood Bulldog Man. She ducked into the ladies room and waited, forcing herself to remember every word and movement of the Japanese men she had sat with.

After what seemed hours, she crept out the door and hesitantly ventured down the stairs and out under the canopy. She headed away from the Sir Francis Drake to the end of the block and turned right on Grant. Once on Maiden Lane, she headed down the narrow road toward her apartment. Suddenly, the unmistakable sound of footsteps echoed down the alley from behind her. They did not stop when she turned around but kept coming toward her. She could not identify the figure in the dark. She ducked into the cover of a doorway and waited. The sound of the feet on pavement grew softer. Whoever had been following must have circled back toward Grant.

She stepped into the street and saw no one. She took off her heels and hurried to her own door, unaware that the man who had retreated farther down the block still watched her.

THIRTY

Eddy drew the best hula gals he could conjure on each of the letters that sat before him, purposely putting the most curvaceous figure on the one going to Danny. Eagerness streamed through him. His new orders had arrived and the navy planned to ship them to paradise. Eddy had excelled, especially in his deciphering course, and had completed most phases of his flight training. For now, the navy wanted him in Hawaii for more training and that pleased him immensely.

He reread his letter to Billi, in which he admitted he wished he spoke some Japanese. Flummoxed to discover his kid sister's choice not as ridiculous as he had thought, he shook his head at life's many curveballs.

He put his pen down as visions of home drifted before him. His mother in her new car, bustling about town with her charities. His dad by the fire at his peaceful home on Dyes Inlet. Dahlia in nursing school, Danny finishing his senior year at Garfield High, and his little sister safely tucked away in an office. He felt he could breathe deeply.

He picked up the stack of pamphlets about the island of Oahu and browsed through them again before tossing them aside. Who was he kidding? The news caused concern regarding the escalating war efforts of the Germans and Japanese, as the two countries bond strengthened in their aggression toward Britain and the United States.

The most horrifying part of his recent studies centered on articles relating to the Zimmerman telegram. The message, sent in 1917 from Arthur Zimmerman, the foreign secretary of the German Empire, to Heinrich von Eckardt, the German ambassador in Mexico, luckily had been decoded by the British. The terrifying communication called for "unrestricted submarine warfare" against the United States. Subsequently, the following attacks by German submarines in the Atlantic, on both passenger and merchant vessels, had angered the American public.

Yet the decoding of the note and its value in reconnaissance for America had been followed in 1929 by the premise that "Gentlemen do not read other gentlemen's mail." That concept had been prescribed by Secretary of State Stimson when he cut the funds to the governmental bureau engaged in decrypting messages between various embassies and their countries. Even though 1929 seemed a long ago, he had been told the government still encouraged Stimson's policy.

It frustrated Eddy. He had to be missing something in his studies, and he hungered for more knowledge. But a secret silence prevailed. America could no longer turn its back on the warring empire that wanted to swallow up China, Indochina, and the Philippines. Once they had plundered resources from those countries, they would crave more, and America stood in their way. A blind eye trained on the enemy would not reap victory. Eddy swore he would keep both eyes open.

He gently placed each letter inside their envelope and kissed each one good night.

Billi regarded her image in the mirror. She had quickly swapped her hooker attire and makeup for her plain, midnight-blue dress. What she saw she liked. After adding a touch of lipstick, she hurried for the door, then turned back and, out of habit, straightened the covers on her bed, checking for the fan and ring hidden in the pillow. Just touching it made her feel better, thinking of Eileen and home. Excited with what she had learned that evening she hoped, somehow, it would help prevent the brewing promise of war. She couldn't wait to tell Jack, knowing he would be pleased and perhaps make him smile. With a warming sensation, she contemplated how much she liked his smile, and this quickened her step.

She walked up the street toward the hotel, knowing Duckworth watched from above. As she entered from the side door, he stepped below the large chandeliers on the upper level foyer and down the ornate stairs toward the alcove for the elevators and stood next to her. Without so much as a nod of recognition, they slipped inside and he pushed the button for the twenty-first floor, far above the usual sixth floor of their previous rendezvous in Jack's room.

The doors closed before he spoke. "You okay?"

"I sat with him tonight." The electricity of their meeting reverting through her.

"Stay well." He smiled at her as the doors slid open, revealing unexpected opulence. Duckworth remained in the elevator as Billi stepped out into a foyer, lit by a chandelier heavy with crystals that spanned the entire alcove.

As the doors closed behind her, she ventured through heavy drapes that led into one long room with expansive windows on three sides overlooking the night lights of the other hotels and the city. Plush chairs and couches sat against the only solid wall off what appeared to be a small dance floor. At a round table at the end of the room, two couples sat over drinks. An older couple leaned across the white linen tablecloth toward a beautiful blonde, small and elegant, next to Jack. Her attire spoke of money and culture. Billi watched as she put her hand on his arm and whispered in his ear. They both laughed, and she kissed his cheek. Her large wedding ring sparkled, like the room.

Billi felt dizzy. Jack was married? That must be why he never talked of his personal life. She stepped behind a large fern to breathe deeply and regain her dignity. She fumed that she had changed into her nice dress and had not appeared as Ginger, the whore.

"My sweet Lilly," she heard him say and the rest went blank. She hurried back to the elevator and pushed the button.

The bell that sounded as the door opened made her jump. She hesitated, gathered her strength, and turned back toward the curtains. Jack stood before her holding the curtain aside, his tall figure filling the opening. His dinner jacket and everything about him echoed the sophistication of the woman who sat beside him. They belonged together.

"Come." He took her arm and briskly walked her toward the table. He pulled a chair out for her to the right of his seat. "This is an associate of mine." He presented Billi to the others.

Billi nodded and sank into the chair.

"What kind of an associate, Jack?" the blonde quipped, leaning forward to peek around him.

"Behave, Lilly." The older woman, draped in jewels, reached for her cigarette and smiled in Billi's direction. "Watch her, she's vicious."

"Well, does she have a name?" Lilly's voice rose as she pressed herself into Jack.

Jack looked perplexed and the older gentleman across the way burst into laughter. "Jack, my boy, I've never seen you tongue-tied."

"I have several names," Billi answered for him. "My father calls me 'Bright Eyes.'"

"Oh." The cigarette now lit in the bejeweled hand of the older women waved through the air. "I like that one. Bright Eyes it is."

"How mysterious." Lilly went back to her drink and eyed Jack.

"And I suppose you have names as well?" Billi sat taller, ignoring Jack's low cough.

"This is Mr. and Mrs. Fisher." Lilly took the lead. "Old family friends."

"We were just discussing what you would do if you fell off a boat into the water." Mrs. Fisher looked expectantly at Billi.

Billi smiled. "It depends on the boat and the water."

"How so?" Mr. Fisher leaned forward in interest.

"Can you swim back and get into the boat? If not, is the water salt or fresh?"

Lilly leaned forward again to observe Billi.

Billi ignored the blonde and kept on speaking. "You'll float better in the saltwater."

Mr. Fisher clapped his hands. "Bravo, Bright Eyes. I certainly want you on my team. Where are you from?"

Before Jack could stop her she slipped out Seattle.

Lilly elbowed Jack. "Time for me to head to bed. I'm just so tired all the time." She leaned on Jack as she stood.

"Oh." Mrs. Fisher stood as well. "Do you have news you aren't sharing?" She grabbed her fur coat and fell in behind Lilly. "Your mother will be so thrilled." The women's voices trailed off.

Mr. Fisher rounded the table and patted Jack on the back. "Good pick. We'll talk tomorrow then. Nice to have met you, whoever you are."

His words hurt to the core. Who had she become? Billi began to stand, when Jack's hand grabbed her arm and pulled her back down.

"Don't be too late, dear." She heard Lilly call back, and then they were alone.

Billi could not look at him. She felt numb.

Jack poured coffee into two cups. He pushed one in her direction. "I heard you were very successful tonight. Go slow and tell me everything."

JACK STOOD BY THE LARGE WINDOWS watching the clouds turn pink with the morning light. He lit his last cigar and looked out over the tops of the buildings. Fear for Billi made his hand shake. They had not left the suite on the twenty-first floor all night. He turned and watched her deep blue dress move up and down as she slept on a couch below the palm plant. His eye patch still sat between their half-full coffee cups at the table. Her behavior that evening had been noticeably odd. While she had insisted he remove the patch, she had not looked at him once. And that made him feel uneasy. They had gone over the details of her time at the table with Akio several times until she had slumped onto the small couch and instantly fallen asleep. He had draped his dinner jacket over her long legs and removed her shoes. The urge to kiss her had been strong.

The smoke he exhaled twirled around him. His hunch that Akio surfaced to gather information and more spies had been correct. But there had to be more. Akio would not come just for that; he was preparing something big, and the urgency to unravel his plans meant exposing Billi to even more danger. He replayed the key words he had memorized from her description of the evening: game, earliest I can get, view good from hill before noon, transmission, clubhouse.

He would alert his men to keep a close eye on Mr. Tamura, the renowned journalist. He had already put a tail on Hatsuro. He had men looking for the young Japanese man even now. But the clubhouse remained a mystery. Jack remembered Akio's love of all sports, including baseball. Anything involving hitting with a bat, club, or sword fit his aggressive nature.

Jack's men were already spread thin. He couldn't send them out to every clubhouse, hill, or transmission site in the Bay Area. Except for the World Series, fall was not the season for baseball. So what did he want to observe and from what hill? Seals Stadium at the corner of 16th and Bryant hardly presented a view except of the surrounding Mission District. No. He was missing something simple, and he had blamed Billi for his inability to piece it together.

The light sound of the bell as the elevator arrived announced the arrival of Duckworth. Jack retrieved his patch as Duckworth swung through the curtained entrance. He shook his head as he approached his boss.

"David's in the South Park area but hasn't seen anything or heard of a Hatsuro."

Jack shook his head. "Not surprising. Give her a few more minutes to sleep, then make certain she gets back to her hotel unnoticed."

He could not face Billi right now. She had to go back to her barstool, to being the seductive hooker. She had to get closer, and guilt ripped through him because he could not figure out the meaning of a few phrases. He hated himself, and his fist slammed against the button for the elevator.

THIRTY-ONE

D AVID SHOOK UNCONTROLLABLY. The body before him did not have a head, at least not attached. The startled eyes of the severed head looked at him from a few feet away. It had been propped up against a garbage can that held several bunches of dying flowers overflowing in an arch, as if the drooping blooms were paying homage to the bodiless head. David stepped past his pile of vomit and approached the policeman at the scene, who had roped off the area waiting for back up.

What a mess. David needed to get away but knew his boss would have questions about how he had happened on the situation. He forced his mind to remember. He had strolled through the California Flower Market and asked some of the Japanese farmers selling their exquisite flora if any of them had heard of a man named Hatsuro. All had answers no, except one woman who looked away in disgust and headed for the back of the building where trucks made early morning deliveries. David had decided to try and get her alone for more questioning. He had exited out the front of the building onto Market Street, turned on 5th, and then gone down the alley, hurrying past the length of the large structure the Japanese-American community had established. The alley appeared empty. As he walked further, past the back doors to the many businesses, searching for the Asian woman, he had found the dismembered body.

He flashed his badge again at the large officer. "I have to report this to my boss." He spoke gruffly in the hopes the officer would not make him stay any longer.

"Ya sure ya don't recognize him?"

"Nope. Hard to forget a face like that." He didn't turn back to look again. The dead man's lifeless eyes set deep in his fat, bulldog face were now embedded in David's memory.

"If you're needed, I'll have me chief call ya. Must a' been some blow ta get that clean a cut."

David needed a drink and wondered where he could find one so early in the morning. When he reached the St. Francis Hotel, he stepped inside. He walked past the large black marble columns and up the few steps to a small area where they were serving breakfast. The thought of food turned his stomach. He ordered a coffee and something stronger. The waiter raised an eyebrow but delivered one whiskey coffee, and then a second.

Fortified, David pushed through the large doors of the hotel, but then quickly stepped back inside. Heading across Union Square, in a deep blue dress, strode the long-legged Billi. The sight brought a surge of desire and he licked his lips. The doorman, not comprehending David's hesitancy, continued to hold the door open, and the cool breeze swept into the lobby until one patron made a comment.

David stepped out into the day, which had begun so disastrously, with a lighter step. He tipped his hat into the wind and slunk across the street. Only when Billi disappeared down the steps on the far side of the square did he hurry across, just in time to see her enter the building on the corner of Maiden Lane—the former "street of whores"—where the most notorious cribs of San Francisco drew men of all walks of life, and where many lost their lives in the brawls that ensued. He smiled. How appropriate.

Jack sat across from Mr. Robert Fisher, his head resting against the high backed chair in exhaustion. His jacket hung off one of the wings. Robert and Mildred were the oldest friends his parents had. They were extended family and Jack knew he could tell him just about anything.

"It is nice of Mrs. Fisher to visit mother before you leave."

"They are best friends. And since we're not here as much, it's hard on them. I think she plans to convince your mother to visit us on Oahu."

"Good luck. We can't get her out of the house, let alone on a boat or airplane. But with Lilly getting married and now having in-laws on the East Coast, there may be some hope."

"Well, see what you can do. The sunshine and palm trees would do her good." Fisher poured himself more coffee and held the pot out toward Jack.

"No thanks. I was up late last night." Jack stretched his legs out in front of him.

"She's quick and charming. I would have been up late with her too." The older man smiled.

"It's not like that." Jack didn't mean to sound irritated.

"Well, whatever it is, she seemed to be drawing a line where Lilly is concerned."

"Lilly." Jack chuckled. "I sure in hell hope her husband can control her a bit."

"Jack." Fisher leaned forward. "How much longer on this project? When can you come to Hawaii? You can relax there, play golf. Remember when you used to caddy for your father? Or brought along friends from Stanford to be my caddy when I came to town? I'll be damned if that one fella wasn't great. Had an innate sense for the game. Real competitive. And I beat Admiral Nimitz that day. Now that was fantastic. Got some contacts in the Island with that game. Whenever the admiral's in Pearl Harbor, we have him up to the plantation. We still hit the links, but he has not forgotten that day. Blames that Japanese kid. Said he asked questions about submarines and that distracted him."

Jack shot up in his chair. "Where did we play that game? Mare Island?"

"Yep. The admiral's course, the oldest golf links west of the Mississippi. That's what burned him so." Fisher sat back obviously relishing the memory.

Jack grabbed his jacket and hurried toward the door. "Thanks, Mr. Fisher. Golf."

"Mildred will be mad at me if I don't get you to come for dinner again tonight up in the private room," Fisher shouted.

Back in his room, Jack snatched up the phone. Within minutes he had the highest commander he could find on the line at Mare Island Naval Base, the heart of the Twelfth Naval District.

Akio held his nine iron on the crest of the hill on Mare Island overlooking San Pablo Bay. The sloping hillsides across the strait held the same blue hue as the water in this light. The wind ruffled the waves, bringing with it a few cooling clouds. But that was not what he found beautiful. His focus centered just beyond the navy buildings below to the long, open slips, where the submarines were moored, under construction. Their sleek mammoth bodies were his to openly observe from this vantage point.

"I believe it is your ball?" The noisy American lumbered up the hill behind him.

He did not turn to look at the man whose garish plaid attire disgusted him. Typical American. He loathed the chubby-cheeked fool and the time he had to waste pretending they would become business partners.

"Ah, but one must take time to enjoy the game. Hatsuro." He called in the younger man's direction. "Come take a picture of me with my new partner."

He stepped to the side so as not to block the vital view of the submarines below.

"Oh, wonderful." The man in plaid moved in closer with a broad smile.

A navy officer appeared from over the hill. "Sorry, the course is closed. Closing early today." He planted his feet and waited for them to leave.

Hatsuro, with his back to the officer, slid the camera into the golf bag.

"Well, this is outrageous," the loud American protested. "I called personally and set this up and—"

"Sorry." The officer held his ground.

"It is no problem." Akio smiled then strode down the hill in advance of the huffing man who verbosely objected to the inconvenience.

Submarines, Jack thought. It all fit together. Akio had been a student in the engineering department at Stanford. Jack remembered his doodles. Or at least that was what he had speculated the drawings contained at the time.

How long had this betrayal been in the works? He remembered that once Akio calculated the long reach of Jack's father's influence, the Japanese student had taken a greater interest in Jack as a friend. Whenever Jack went to caddy for his father, Akio's insisted that he be allowed go along and caddy for Mr. Fisher or other influential friends at Mare Island. And Jack had unwittingly driven Akio out to Vallejo to the first established naval base on the Pacific Ocean. Since 1854 that strip of island had served as a naval shipyard, where the first submarines on the West Coast were constructed in 1927.

Jack held his head in his hands as his elbows drove into his knees. He could not blame himself. He had to think. Besides the funny pencil drawings of what he now deduced had to be submarines, there were other sketched objects. He had thought them butterflies, but he had only gotten a quick glance. Akio had entered the dorm room, slammed a book over his drawing, scooped them up and angrily slammed the door as he left. Jack had thought nothing of it. Akio's outbursts were as unpredictable as March weather, first bright and sunny, then a pounding force of stinging rain.

The navy officer sent to stop Akio had not been able to reach the golfing party quickly enough, and the Japanese man had stood overlooking the submarines for a brief time.

Jack knew that Akio would not have come just for Mare Island and the submarines. There had to be more, and Billi remained Jack's only hope in unearthing the rest of Akio's mission.

The face powder sat on her makeup table untouched, as did the shocking red lipstick. Billi ran her finger over the brightly decorated case that held the lip coloring. How she wanted to be with Eileen. To sit beside her friend and giggle as they applied the traditional Japanese white color over their skin, clean and pure, perfect in its ability to mask emotion.

She had wandered the streets a bit in the afternoon and now readied herself for yet another evening at her post on the barstool. But she had no desire to continue the charade. The realization that Jack was married had sent her spiraling. She could not explain her reaction or the emotions that startling bit of information had brought to the surface, but it wormed uneasily through her. She felt drained and exhausted. She wanted Raymond. She wanted Eddy. The realization that she had been a fool to think she could help devastated her.

She became determined, tomorrow she would go home to her mother and Pepper. She would spend time with her father and forget the last month.

She applied her foundation and powder; exaggerated her lips, making them full and alluring; put Vaseline on her eyebrows and lashes and then gently combed them. Her war paint applied, she slid into her revealing dress covered in orchids and fought back the tears.

For Eddy, she told herself and she stepped out the door. A mist had rolled up the hills from the bay. She shivered, pulling her wrap closer. Her feet moved unguided over the few blocks to where the canopy announced her destination.

"They're looking for you," the small Chinese woman spoke softly from behind the podium where she greeted customers.

"Right." Billi fell in behind the hostess, only to be led down the back hall to a door at the end.

When the door opened, Billi plastered a smile on her face and swayed inside, then bristled. Before her sat a police officer and Charlie Low.

"Have a seat, Ginger." The man in uniform drew out her name with a tinge of disgust. "I'm Officer Hennessy."

She eased down across from the tall man with the high cheek bones.

"Ya new in town?" he leaned forward.

"Not exactly." She wondered why Jack was not in the room.

"Well, I don't like workin' gals that bring trouble." His anger vividly apparent.

"What trouble?" Billi adjusted her wrap and looked him straight in the eye.

"Recognize this man?" He pushed a picture of a decapitated head across the table at her. She instantly recognized the bulldog-faced man. Her hand flew to her mouth as she looked away.

Charlie slid a glass of water in her direction. "I told Officer Hennessy that he had been bothering you last night, but that you left here alone."

"Yes, that's correct." Her voice trembled. "He kept trying to buy me a drink, but I told him no. When I went to leave I saw him at the base of the stairs. So I waited until he had gone and then went home."

Billi met Hennessy's gaze. He weighed the truth of her story. "Do ya know his name?"

"No." She heard the sound of the picture travel back across the table and let out a sigh.

"Where he lived? Who he was with?"

"Nothing." She swallowed the bile that kept wanting to surface.

"Did anythin' happen between him and the Japanese men you were sittin' with?"

She did not look at Mr. Low. "No."

"Well, someone wanted him dead."

"What happened?" she asked softly.

"Somebody chopped his head off, and from the looks of it, they did it with one blow."

She shuddered. "I see."

He pushed his card across the table. "Call me if ya see anythin' else, doll." Hennessey stood, nodded toward Charlie, and let himself out the door.

The ornate screen behind Charlie slid open and Shirley Chow ambled forward, her crooked legs tossing her torso from right to left. Charlie stood and held out a chair for her, in which she sat without uttering thank you. Obviously, she held unseen power.

"You do well." Her pidgin English speech sounded stern. "But be careful. He like you."

"Who?" Billi tried to piece this together.

"The devil." She answered then spoke to Charlie in Chinese.

Charlie listened then nodded at Shirley. As he stood he signaled for Billi to follow him. "Come on. You look like you could use a drink."

She sat at the bar with her Manhattan and let the popular songs performed by Chinese crooners take her mind elsewhere. She had finished her first and ordered a second, against the rules, but as of tonight there were no rules.

Just before Mary Mommon launched into her steaming, sensual rendition of "My Heart Belongs To Daddy," Akio, trailed by Ito and Hatsuro, followed the hostess to a table off to the side. Billi ignored them. She wasn't in the mood. Forget Akio and his secrets. She let the liquor slide down her throat, and the sweet burning felt good. She put her half-empty drink on the counter just as a hand reached for it.

"You join please," Hatsuro demanded, his look of contempt barely hidden. He turned his back to her and carried her glass toward the table.

Billi sat a moment longer, gathering her strength. Taking one long breath, she shrugged her shoulders in seeming indifference before pushing away from the bar. When she caught up to the arrogant young Hatsuro, she snatched her drink, sneering at him, then took a long deep drink.

Akio stood and held the chair for her, an honor, especially for a hooker.

She slunk into the seat he held. "Howdy."

He smiled as he sat beside her. "I like orchids." His English polished and refined. "Ginger and orchids. You are a beautiful garden."

It took her a moment to figure out his remark referred to her dress, the one Marie had given her with the orchid print. She leaned toward him and smiled back.

"I thought of you last night." He bent closer. "And your garden."

Did he think of her when he beheaded that poor man? She began to shake, and he gently put his hand, smooth and manicured, over hers. She pulled back and drew her wrap closer to her. His touch felt repulsive.

"It's a bit cool tonight." She looked over at the stage.

"Hopefully not too cool." His voice held a tinge of what Billi perceived to be a threat, his demand clear.

"How's business?" The liquor made her feisty and she didn't care.

"We had a bit of an interruption but are making progress."

The music stopped and the lights came up, indicating a small break between acts. Ito looked over at Akio and spoke in Japanese. "We are so sorry your day did not proceed as planned."

"We have one photo." Akio spoke in their language between tight lips. "But we will need to move faster. The attack is being practiced on a special island made to replicate the target. Soon these weak people will understand our power. Have you found more men willing?"

"Some do not trust us. They like their new life in America. They are soft and worthless. But there are many Kibei, trained properly to honor the emperor, who are helping in gathering more loyalists."

When Akio did not respond, Ito interjected, "We also have many who have served in the Imperial Navy here as students of language. They will be assigned as commanders when the time is appropriate. Besides, it does not make any difference if Nisei are born on this soil. They still must report for duty to our emperor when they turn eighteen. They must fight for the land of the Rising Sun. Our emperor's dynasty will last time immemorial."

Hatsuro, caught up in the partisan fever, added, "Those who have forsaken their homeland should all be killed. They no longer pay respect to the emperor. They will die along with the other fat Americans, and we will prevail."

In contrast to Hatsuro, Ito's voice remained composed as he continued his report. "We have many spies already who are telling us when ships enter and leave ports and what they are carrying and the number of American troops onboard. They will make our landing a success. The Nippon war bonds continue to be bountiful. But more funds for our quest are still needed."

Billi had understood every word of their frightening discussion and the meaning rattled her nerves. She snorted out a laugh. All eyes at the table fell on her. She scrambled to cover her blunder. "I just figured out ya were talkin' about my dress. Orchids." She laughed again.

Hatsuro did not attempt to hide his disgust as he continued in Japanese. "She is a stupid woman. Her only goodness is between her legs."

The men all snickered before Akio took over the conversation.

"You must find me men all up the coast. I have submitted my plan to Yamamoto for our new submarines. After the initial attack we will sit off the West Coast and strike the mainland. We are to destroy America's confidence and cut their faith in their leader, the cripple. They are lazy. They do not think we have the power. Once we have them running like rats in mass confusion, we will deal with those who have not joined us in spreading the glory of Emperor Hirohito."

Ito hunched forward. "When?"

"Christmas will bring these shores unimaginable presents. Have you found the drawing?"

"No. No one has seen the professor."

Billi inadvertently stopped stirring her drink at the mention of the professor. Instantly conscious of her actions she began twirling her swizzle stick swiftly and humming.

"Find him at all costs. I need that drawing." Akio picked up his glass and held it high. "To the emperor."

The three men followed suit.

Billi looked at him innocently and picked up her glass, tapping his. "What are we drinking to?"

"Success." Hatsuro sputtered in English, his eyes appeared glazed with visions of glory.

"Well, to success." Billi smiled. "What kind of business it is we are celebrating?"

Akio returned her smile and reverted to his polished English. "It is nothing we can share as yet. But you will hear of it when it happens."

"How exciting." She shifted in his direction. "Are you the boss?"

"Someday." He touched her under her chin, and she fought the urge to pull away.

THIRTY-TWO

BILLI STOOD TO EXCUSE HERSELF and felt the ground beneath her swirl. Akio caught her as she wavered. Through her daze she heard him speak to his men in their language.

"Hatsuro, the powder you put in her drink is working quicker than expected." He signaled his men. "Let's get her down the stairs."

They surrounded Billi. Akio gripped her around the waist for support and started for the exit. As they reached the archway at the top of the flight of steps, a voice stopped them.

"Oh, my," Charlie exclaimed, bustling toward them. "Give me that worthless girl."

Without hesitation, he broke Billi free of their hold and placed her in the arms of the hostess. She struggled to remain conscious.

"I am so sorry for the display." Charlie turned the stunned men back toward the exit and graciously bowed them toward the tunnel of steep steps. "Please join us again, on the house."

"We will indeed accept your hospitality." Akio gave a slight gesture, and his men filed down the stairs.

Billi watched them descend before slipping into blackness.

BILLI LIE SPRAWLED ACROSS THE COUCH at all angles. One leg dangled toward the ground while the other straddled the silk upholstery. Her slight snoring raised her chest in a deep rhythm of sleep.

Charlie opened the door and let in Duckworth.

"Holy Mother of...what the hell happened?" Duckworth stood above her.

"The bartender said one of the men picked up her drink. He must have drugged her."

"Did she have a coat or anything? I'll get her out of here." He bent down to shake her.

"We wish you a Merry Chris…" Billi slurred. She rolled her face toward the back of the couch and went under again.

"Come on, sweetheart." Duckworth struggled her up into his arms. Like a rag doll, her limbs flopped with his movements.

"Wait." Charlie helped him get her onto her feet. They wrapped a blanket around her and escorted her down the stairs. As they hit the fresh air, Billi straightened.

"Look at all the pretty lights." She began giggling. "Where am I?"

"Off we go, darling." Duckworth pulled his hat down over his eyes and adopted a drunken swagger that matched Billi's. Arm in arm, they swayed and staggered up the block, covering the short distance to the Sir Francis Drake Hotel in several long minutes.

He guided her down the small side hallway to the elevators.

"Oopsie daisy." Billi slouched in his arms as the elevator opened, and they stumbled inside. She pressed her cheek against the cool dark wood paneling as Duckworth punched the button for the top floor.

When the elevator doors opened, Billi burst into song. "We wish you a Merry Christmas…"

Within seconds Jack appeared before them. He caught her in his arms and headed her toward the couch.

"Look at the lights. Merry Christmas." Billi's arm rose above her as if she were about to pirouette. Her gaze fixed on the several building lights that shimmered in the dark outside the massive windows.

Mr. and Mrs. Fisher, sitting at the table at the end of the large room, looked at each other in surprise.

"My heavens." Mrs. Fisher shot to her feet as did her husband.

Duckworth blushed toward his boss. "Sorry, I thought you were alone."

"My heavens." Billi echoed, turning toward the Fishers. "Oh, it's you. Where's the wife?"

"Why, Bright Eyes. I believe you have had a few too many," Mr. Fisher scolded.

"Never. I'm fine perfectly." She stood taller and immediately fell back into Jack. He scooped her up and carried her to the couch. "There are going to be presents for Christmas. What will you buy me, Jack?" She burst into song again.

"Robert, dear, I believe we had better get going." Mrs. Fisher grabbed her beaded bag. "And I promise not to tell about your entanglement with this kind of woman."

"What kinda woman?" Billi tried to sit up.

"Shut up," Jack hissed at her.

Billi flopped back on the couch, hit her head on the arm, and started to cry. "But you made me do this. And now you're—"

"Yes." Mr. Fisher took his wife's elbow and steered the gawking woman toward the door. "No need to hear this dirty laundry."

Jack followed them to the alcove.

Mr. Fisher punched the elevator button. "We sail at noon. Take care of this mess and meet me in the morning for coffee."

Jack simply nodded back at his longtime family friends, offering no explanation, thankful when the elevator arrived.

"Jack, why, she's a hooker!" Mrs. Fisher straightened as she stepped into the elevator. "Shame on you."

The doors slid closed and Jack let out the breath he had been holding since Billi had descended upon them.

Duckworth had filled him in on all he knew and had left hours ago.

The most disturbing aspect of Billi's contact with Akio was the blatant use of the drug. He would have to thank Charlie for his watchful eye and warn his friend, Shirley Chow. His good fortune had held with his relationship with Shirley, for they shared the same goal: Akio. However, he knew her motive for finding Akio stemmed from her desire to fulfill a very personal vendetta. But he intended to beat her to the prize.

At 3 a.m., Billi pushed herself up and saw the silhouette of Jack slumped in a chair across from her. His eye patch rested on his knee and she watched him breathe deeply as he slept. As soundlessly as possible, she slowly rose and took one step toward the exit before his arm went up and pulled her back. She landed, unceremoniously, on his lap.

"Ouch!" she protested.

"What hurts most? Your head or your throat?"

"My throat?"

"Yes. You sang every Christmas song you knew and then some last night."

She squirmed, but he held her tight. "How was I?"

"What?"

"How was my singing?" She crossed her arms and leveled a stare at him.

"What happened?"

"I was about to ask you the same thing."

"Duckworth brought you here. You put on quite the show."

"And I sang?" Her back straightened. "My goodness, your friends were here. Or am I imagining that?"

"Good." He leaned back against his chair. "That's good news. The drug didn't knock you completely out."

"Drug!" She shot up off his lap and then collapsed onto the couch again. "But how?"

"Don't ever let any of them near your drink or food." Jack stood and went to the table and poured her cup of coffee. "What do you remember?"

"Give me a minute." She sipped the tepid black liquid.

"You told me there would be presents and asked what I would buy you. Does that ring a bell?"

Billi turned ashen as the conversation of the Japanese men spilled from her and filled the room with the dread of urgency.

Jack stood at the large windows. "Christmas," he kept repeating to the sleeping city below.

BILLI WATCHED FROM HER APARTMENT WINDOW as Duckworth disappeared across Maiden Lane, heading in the opposite direction from Jack's hotel. When she turned on the light, her stomach tightened. The small pillow she had brought, the one Eileen had made for her, had been moved, and she noticed a slight crease in the bedspread she always straightened before leaving. Someone had been in her room. She quickly checked behind the changing screen and curtain that acted as her closet, but her dresses seemed to be in order. Trembling, she reached for the pillow and exhaled a long breath as her hand wrapped around the hilt of the fan and fingered the small silk bag that held Ray's ring and her broken heart. She fell asleep cradling the pillow to her chest.

Lilly sat across from her brother. The dark hue below his one exposed eye was troubling. She looked at Robert Fisher. "What has the old boy been up to?"

"Just a bit of fun. Of the questionable kind." Mr. Fisher looked sternly at Jack as he let the ashes from his cigar fall into the cut glass ashtray.

"Not my pious brother. Mr. Fisher, I believe you are kidding me. But do go on." Lilly leaned closer to the older man, the feather on her hat almost touching his graying hair.

"Lilly," Jack interrupted, "go play somewhere else for a moment. I need to talk with Mr. Fisher." Jack did not back down from the older man's gaze.

"I don't want to…" She unexpectedly bolted out of her chair and ran for the bathroom.

"Sorry." Fisher stubbed out his cigar. "I forgot about her condition."

"I need you to forget what you saw last night. This is critical to my project. Not a word, Mr. Fisher, and I mean that. Can you control Mrs. Fisher? She must not mention the woman or let on she saw her. It is a matter of many lives."

"Jack, what are you up to?" Fisher smashed his cigar until it split, his voice hushed with worry.

"When I can, you will be the first one I tell. Thank you for offering your ships when needed."

"I'm having more built. Must be age, but Mildred likes bigger boats these days. There is one in Seattle that I just love, a Blanchard, that we are having worked on. Didn't you say you were just up that way? Is that where you met Bright Eyes?"

When Jack didn't answer he changed the subject. "When are you coming to Hawaii? Like I said, you could use a break."

"Don't know. But be careful and let me know if you hear or see anything unusual in your waters."

"Like what?"

"You'll know when you see it."

Mrs. Fisher entered the room in her dark traveling clothes. She swung her matching fur-lined cape around her and adjusted her hat. "Where's Lilly?"

"My cigar—"

"Oh, Lilly." Her voice rose in concern as she headed for the closed bathroom door and gently knocked.

The door opened and a pale figure emerged, quiet and uncomfortable. "Sorry," she murmured.

"Nonsense." The older women hushed her and patted her back. "Jack will drive you home and you need to rest, dear. You don't want anything to happen to you or the baby."

The news finally taking hold of him, Jack twisted in his seat. His sister stood with her head hanging, her hand over her stomach, her wedding ring glistening. She was no longer just his little sister, but a wife and soon to be mother.

He smiled as he stood and walked to her. "Come on, Frilly, let's get you home before Mom and Bella send out a search party."

He had postponed another visit to the family home for far too long. An afternoon away would do him good.

THIRTY-THREE

J ACK SAT IN HIS FATHER'S OFFICE in the dark. When the door opened, he saw his mother standing in the hallway. He knew she had not entered this room since that day his father had chosen the easy way out. He stood to join her and silently followed her down the hall to the small balcony that overlooked the large living room with its massive windows. He stood a minute taking in the view and the memories. As children, he and Lilly had loved to sneak down the hall in their pajamas to this vantage point and listen to the various conversations of the numerous guests their parents entertained. He remembered the arguments, political and religious, the laughter, the vibrant stories, and the singing.

At the thought of singing, another voice filled his ears, slurred and off-key, but singing Christmas carols with great gusto. He began to sweat with anxiety. He had to find out more, and soon.

Jack guided his mother down the wooden stairs, and as they reached the bottom step, a lump on the couch moved. Mrs. Huntington crossed the room and Lilly pushed herself upright.

"How are you feeling, dear?" his mother asked as she eased into a chair next to her daughter.

"Awful. I'll never make it." Lilly sobbed into the blanket that covered her.

"Oh, yes you wills, baby," Bella boomed as she carried a tray with tea and soup into the room. "I done made you the best cure I knows." She lowered the tray, only to raise it quickly as Lilly's hand covered her mouth. "Oh my, you gots it bad, honey."

Lilly sank back on the couch. "How did this happen?"

Mrs. Huntington raised her eyes at her son.

Jack shook his head and attempted a joke. "Mrs. Todd Achers, do you remember your husband had something to do with this?"

Lilly moaned. "I hate him."

"No ya don't. Dis will pass." Bella put down the tray, tucked the covers up around the thin, expectant mother, and left the room.

"Lilly, have you heard from him recently?" Mrs. Huntington smiled as she posed the question, as the subject remained tender.

"Yes. His letters come in batches from Iceland, wherever that is. I hate the ship *Reuben James*, his captain, and that stupid war in England. I need him to come home now. Why is he even there? We're not at war."

"He's an officer in the navy, dear. That is who you picked to be the father of your child." At Mrs. Huntington's unruffled reply a hush fell over the room.

"What does he think of the joyous news?" Jack finally ventured.

"He's certain it's a boy and he can't wait. Well, I can't wait to get this over with. I hate being pregnant."

"It is a minor inconvenience for the joy it will bring." The matriarch spoke softly.

Jack looked at his mother and speculated how this turn of events had changed her. She rose from bed early and dressed for the day. Part of her shadow had lifted, and the baby would be welcomed, if not by the mother, by the other women of this house. A renewed sense of responsibility and awe came over him. Had his world really become so dark and distracted that he had not thought of what a child could mean to a family?

He looked at his watch. He could afford a few more hours. Besides, he could smell the brisket of beef simmering in the kitchen.

"I'm heading up for a moment. Call me for dinner." He yawned as he mounted the stairs to retrace his steps to his father's office and the silence of its darkness.

BILLI HAD SPENT THE DAY WALKING AGAIN. She assumed that, like Seattle, those of Asian descent were mostly confined to neighborhoods of their own kind. To avoid Japantown, she headed in the opposite direction from her last walk. Finding herself on Market Street, she attempted to sweat off the effects of the drug and her agitation. Who had been in her room and why, nothing appeared to be missing? More importantly, she now questioned Jack's involvement behind this devious behavior?

She forced his image from her mind, the warm feel of his arm around her just hours ago. She reminded herself of his marital status, a man soon to be a father. She became hypnotized by her sturdy shoes, traveling down the sidewalk to nowhere. Finally, hot and sweaty, she contemplated leaving when she noticed a large tower rising high into the air with a clock that read 2:26. The stunning building beckoned her closer. She passed markets and venders and finally stood before a massive ferry building topped with the tiered beaux-arts-style spire. The smell of the salt air drew her farther toward the dock, where a mist moved low over the water as she approached. She watched, mesmerized, as the ferries, like those in Seattle, slipped in and out of the fog. She had never felt so far from home in her life.

It seemed two of Akio's comments held her in this strange city: his reference to the presents at Christmas and a professor. Could it be her Professor Fujihara? Could he be the reason Jack had brought her down here? And what drawing? She remembered the professor's office in Suzzallo, left in disarray, and that someone else had been asking for him and his papers.

She breathed deeply of the briny air. Now that she had seen Akio up close, closer than comfortable, she became certain she had observed him in the boat off the shore on Dyes Inlet, so close to the naval shipyard.

With a sickening realization, she sank onto the nearest bench and let the damp air cover her. Ray had been right. The pressure of a future battle surrounded them. She looked out at the dense fog that had hidden the harbor. The ships' horns blasted from time to time. How easy it would be to slip to shore in this thick soup, unload or go aboard, and take off again. As if she had called up a spirit, a man came out of the fog toward her. She sat rigid, realizing her vulnerability, and attempted to control her fears that crept down her spine. She felt her mist-filled hair cling to her neck as she sat tensely waiting. The stranger pulled his overcoat closer and did not even look in her direction as he passed, but the brief encounter put her in motion. Every city held an edge of danger and today San Francisco felt temperamental, with many facets of beauty and peril, and she did not like the sensation at all.

As she climbed back up the slope toward her small apartment, she stepped clear of the fog and the midday sun brightened her spirits. She would write home and lie to her mother and dear friends. The holidays were swiftly approaching, with Halloween just around the corner, and the unknown threat hung over the promise of joy.

THE DEEP DARKNESS OF FULL NIGHT settled around Billi as she stood on the far side of Union Square looking back at her room on the fourth floor of the corner building on Maiden Lane. She discovered how easily anyone could see inside her room from where she stood. She moved around the square to where she thought she had seen a cigarette burning the other night from her window. Her breath caught in her throat at the clear view inside her apartment from where she now stood. She would watch again tonight to see if the cigarette appeared.

She started across the square and saw Duckworth slip into her building. She backed up to watch and see if he could be the intruder, but her apartment light never went on, nor did the appearance of the windows change. Reluctantly, she started toward the front door of the building. Jack had insisted she take one night off and not go to the club, so why would Duckworth be here? She found herself hurrying. At the top of the stairs, she hesitated. Her door remained closed but no Duckworth in sight. He had to be inside then. She went to her door and twisted the knob, but found it locked. She unlocked it and stepped inside. Around her lay a still darkness. She let out a sigh of relief when she flipped on the light and discover her small room empty and her pillow and bed had not been touched.

She jumped at the knock at the door.

"Who is it?" she all but screamed.

"Quiet, it's me."

She opened the door and Duckworth stepped inside. "Are you okay?"

"Yes." She plopped onto her bed and watched him.

"Stay in tonight…okay?"

She could tell his nerves were stretched thin, and she became aware of the enormity of his responsibility toward her. "Yes. I'm exhausted and going straight to bed. Has anything happened?"

"No." His shoulders sank a bit. "There's nothing going on and for just one night that's okay with me."

She smiled up at him. "Me too."

"Is there anything you need?"

"No. But thanks for asking."

"Okay. Call if that changes."

"Do you have any cigarettes?" she asked coyly.

"No. I don't smoke. And when did you take up smoking?"

She didn't answer him, but stood and patted his arm. "I'll be fine. Go home and get some rest. I have everything here and am not heading out."

"Promise?"

"Cross my heart."

DAVID WATCHED DUCKWORTH EXIT Billi's building and lit another cigarette. His boss had been sending him in all directions except this one. Find out all he could about the bulldog-faced man whose head he had found in the back alley. Like hell. Somehow, those long legs of Billi's were connected to the murder, of that he was convinced. He would get her to tell him the link, one way or another. Then he would bypass that asshole of a boss, Jack, and find the man responsible. He could taste the promotion that would lead to. But for now his lips longed for something softer. He sipped from the bottle of Scotch he had tucked inside his coat, stomped his cigarette into the ground, and started across the square.

AT THE KNOCK ON HER DOOR, Billi put down her pen and crossed the room to unlock it.

"Hello, Duckwor—"

The force of the hand that slapped her face drove her to the ground. She sat a moment stunned and then looked up as her assailant closed and locked the door. She watched in disbelief as David circled her, took off his coat, and threw it across the chair. He set his bottle of booze on the small table and checked out the window before drawing the curtain tight.

"Surprised to see me, doll?" he sneered as he checked out the rest of her apartment.

She stood before answering. "You have a key. Why don't you use it?"

He hissed as he picked up the bottle and looked around for glasses. "Naw. They don't hand out keys to whore's apartments in the office. But that would make the job easier, wouldn't it? Want some?"

He took down two glasses from the small cupboard above the folding table set to one side of the porcelain sink.

"Sure." She felt her cheek for blood but found none.

He handed her a drink. "Take your time, baby. I plan to." With a sickening smile, he raised his glass in her direction.

"What brings you here?" She fought the tremor of her shaking hand.

"A head that lost a body." He sat at the table, and his tongue moved across his lips.

Billi stepped toward him, put down her drink, and gathered the letters she had been writing. "How awful. Where was this?"

He grabbed her arm and jerked her closer. "Don't fool with me."

"I'm not." She pulled free and stuffed the letters inside the table drawer, then sat across from him. She saw him eyeing the drawer as she refilled his glass. "Do you have a name for this person?" She attempted to calculate how much booze he had already consumed.

"Roger someone. He'd been to the Forbidden City Nightclub and then lost his head." She listened as he snickered at his own cruel joke.

She forced a laugh, hoping to placate him. But his fist found her other cheek with such force she hit her head against the wall.

He stood over her, panting. "Don't laugh. Don't talk unless I tell you to. Savvy?"

She didn't dare look up but nodded slightly, clenching her fists, ready to fight.

He gripped her arm and pulled her to her feet. He began to kiss her cheek, then down her neck, his free hand working down her left breast.

"Wait." She struggled, pushing him off as best she could. "Wait."

"What for?"

"I know who he was." She shoved him back.

He staggered a moment and then leered at her. "I thought so. Did you let him between your legs too?"

"Sit down." Her command and sheer determination made him step to his chair. "If that's what you want, let me put on something more... more..." She couldn't even finish her sentence, but started across the room and into the bathroom.

"Now that's more like it." She heard him gulp down his drink.

The mirror reflected a woman with two red welts, one on each cheek, and hair disheveled. She gripped the sink and breathed slowly, then splashed water on her face. Turning, she found the small case with Anna's potions. She selected one and put it inside the cabinet in the event she could figure out a way to put the mixture into his drink. He would be expecting her to try something. She slipped into a floral dress. Dousing herself with perfume, she attempted to ease her nerves. Play the part, she told herself.

"Shit. Hurry up in there."

She emerged empty-handed, trembling.

"That's better. Come here."

She started toward him, her heart pounding. She forced her mind to focus on the aspects of the room. He had removed his jacket and hung it over the chair, and partially unbuttoned his shirt in anticipation of quenching his desire.

He pulled her close and put his liquored lips over hers, almost falling in his eagerness.

"I need a drink," she tried to sound strong. "I thought you said you were going to go slowly."

"Oh yeah." He stood back. "Help yourself. I have to piss."

He disappeared into the bathroom. She bent down and pulled out a bottle of bleach from below the sink. She put a few drops in her empty glass and replaced the bottle before he returned. When she heard the door open, she began to trickle the Scotch into her glass.

"Join me?" She continued filling her glass and held his Scotch out toward him.

He grabbed the drink she poured for herself and downed it in one gulp. His eyes bulged a bit and he grabbed at her. Catching the material of her dress, he ripped it open.

"What the hell?" He coughed.

His hand found more of her dress, and the sound of tearing filled her ears. She pushed as hard as she could but got nowhere as he dragged her closer and groped the inside of her leg. As his hand touched her bare skin, her knee came up, and he went cascading backwards, grabbing his private parts.

"You bitch!" He lunged toward her, but she side-stepped him and grabbed the bottle.

David, slowed, cocked his head and watched her. Then he smiled, the smile that turned her insides. "That's right. We're taking it slow."

"Don't come any closer." She backed toward the door, the bottle hanging by her side.

His eyes glossed over as he stepped forward.

She broke the bottle against the wall and held the jagged end out toward him as the booze slithered down onto the linoleum. "Get out." She turned the knob on her door.

He leaped in her direction and the jagged bottle cut into his arm.

"Shit." He staggered back, staring at the bloody gouge on his arm. He looked at her with building rage. "I'm bleeding. I'll kill you."

Before he could carry out his threat, he began to vomit.

She opened the door and pushed his bent, heaving body out into the hall, followed by his coat. Then she closed the door, locked it, pushed the chair up against it, and sat. She heard him start down the stairs and then fall. The sound of his tumbling body was followed by doors opening.

"What's going on here?" a voice from below echoed. "Hey, buddy, you okay?"

She heard mumbling, followed by the sound of retching, and then more footsteps heading down to the exit four flights below.

Billi looked around the room. She went to the table and picked up his untouched drink, swallowing long and slowly in the hopes of sooth her shattered nerves. As she moved to the window and peeked through the blinds, she felt the strength of the drink work through her tightened frame and she burst into tears. Below David, hunched over and bleeding, staggered toward the square.

THIRTY-FOUR

JACK WOKE TO THE SOUND OF BIRDS twittering in the trees outside his father's study. He looked at his wristwatch and read 6:24. No one had called him for dinner. He opened the door and all seemed silent. As he shuffled down the back steps, he smelled the bacon in the kitchen and began to run.

As Jack burst through the door, Bella broke away from her humming to slip out her greeting. "Mornen'."

"What the hell time is it?" he demanded.

She faced him now, hands on ample hips. "I says mornen'. An what kind a greeten' is dat? You knows better than comin' inta my kitchen and acks like dat." She turned from him then, giving him the full vantage point of her rigid back and silence.

"Christ. Why the hell—"

He didn't get any further as she raised her hand with the spatula in it. He knew that taking the good Lord's name in vain brought swift repercussions.

"Sorry, but why didn't anyone wake me?" He sank into a chair and waited.

She unceremoniously shoved a plate with biscuits and bacon onto the table and jabbed her spatula at the coffee pot.

Jack realized there was no point in asking any further questions. He filled a cup of coffee and dunked a biscuit in the dark brew as he took his place at the table. He watched as she slid eggs onto his plate next to the bacon.

"Thank you," he mumbled.

"Dat's better. You comes in here all tired and sickly looken'. You needs sleep. I done got my hands full enough with yo' mama and little miss not taken' to her condition well." She lowered beside him.

He looked at her tired dark eyes. "Looks like you could use some sleep too."

"Not till dat baby come." She smiled, broad and bright, and full of hope.

"Just wake me next time, okay?" He smiled back, hoping to seal the deal.

"Maybes." She nodded and slapped his shoulder as she stood. "Oh, Lordy helps us. We's got our hands full. Hmmph, hmmph." She stepped heavily toward the stove.

Jack bit his lip, contemplating what he knew lay ahead and the further impact it would have on this household.

Duckworth sat uneasy in the chair in Jack's sixth floor suite in the Sir Francis Drake, watching his boss pace from the window to the table. "What exactly did you tell him again?"

"I instructed David, as you asked, to report to me at 10 p.m. last night. When he didn't, I went to his apartment near the Presidio this morning, but he wasn't there. No one at the desk saw him come in last night."

"Damn him. What about Billi?" Jack's hand went through his hair in a nervous manner.

"She promised to stay in last night."

"Good." He sat, head in hands. "I guess we just wait to see when he surfaces and the—"

A soft rap at the door stopped him.

Duckworth hurried to it. "There he is now." He opened the door slightly, then threw it wide. "Holy Mother of God."

Jack jumped to his feet. "What is it?"

Billi stepped inside, her large-brimmed hat shading only one of her bruises that marked both cheeks.

"Christ Almighty?" Jack helped her to the comfortable chair. "Who did this?"

"Your man, David." Her lips were drawn tight.

Jack took the hat from her head and gently lifted her chin toward him. "You okay?"

"Did he rape me like he wanted to?" She all but spat the words at him, and when he didn't answer, she continued, "He wasn't that lucky."

"Do you know where he is?" Jack's hand still lightly held her chin as he stared down at her, watching intently.

"No. When he left he was a bit worse for wear. I cut his arm." She smirked.

"That's not all I'll do to him when I find him." Jack's words came from between clenched teeth. "I am so sorry." He drew his hand back. He turned away and took a deep breath. While he had been peacefully sleeping, she had been fighting for her life.

"How bad did you cut him? Do you think he went to a doctor for stitches?"

"If he stopped vomiting. I put bleach in his drink."

Duckworth snickered. Then Jack joined in as he turned back to eye Billi. Her abilities continued to stun him. He breathed deeply and put his hand on her shoulder. Nodding toward Duckworth he issued instructions. "Get me some ice and then check the hospitals. I want him in front of me pronto."

"You bet." Duckworth rushed out the door.

"Get in the other room and lie down," Jack guided her toward his bedroom.

"Why?"

"You look like you didn't sleep at all last night. You're staying here until I find him."

"How many of your men have keys to my room?" she asked as she stepped into the bedroom.

"Only me. Why?"

As she lay down he took a blanket from the closet and put it over her.

"I don't suppose you were snooping around my room recently were you?"

He looked into her blue eyes and saw the fear. He would get to the bottom of this immediately. He could not risk losing Billi.

"Just rest."

A knock at the door drew him into the outer room. By the time he returned with ice wrapped in a towel, Billi was asleep. He hesitated, then placed the cool towel against the cheek with the deepest bruise. She jerked slightly, and her eyes flew open.

"It won't do much now," he spoke tenderly, "but it's the best I can do. I'm so sorry. Please don't give up on me."

Billi looked at his one eye, the good one, and closed hers.

EDDY WALKED DOWN THE GANGPLANK into the Hawaiian heat. The smell of the sea mixed with the essence of the hot air radiating off the wooden docks, added to the scent of diesel and wood pitch. He stood still and let the moment take hold. He would have to write to his father immediately and let him know that the large timber he had shipped from his lumber mill on Dyes Inlet, across the sea to where Eddy now stood, had been put to good use in building the expansive docks of Pearl Harbor. There were several bays for the massive ships that ringed Ford Island across the way. He took a step and swayed a bit, the movement of the boat still in his legs.

So this was paradise. He let out a deep breath as he looked up at the smattering of homes that stepped down the green hillside. He had made a note of everything he could as they steamed between the two headlands that created Pearl Harbor. If not for the presence of the navy battleships, Luke Air Field on Ford Island, Hickam Field, the large white oil drums scattered around and barracks, the place would not be half bad. He shrugged his duffel bag over his shoulder and fell in behind the others, letting his lower limbs become reacquainted with solid ground.

The barracks were nondescript and his bunk felt sturdy. He tidied up his few belongings and waited. It didn't take long before the ensign came in, giving them the onceover. They drilled until noon and then were sent to chow. But the afternoons proved the biggest surprise. They were free to swim, explore, do anything they wanted. Duty began at 7 a.m. and they were free by 1 p.m. This truly was paradise!

Eddy stood in the glare of the afternoon, his view of the green-blue sea beyond Pearl Harbor still a wonder to behold.

"You joining us?"

He turned and faced the two young men he had become fast friends with. He looked Scooter in the eye before responding to his challenge. "Depends."

They had flown together back on the mainland and had developed a quick bond. Aboard the ship, the two had adopted the youthful Sam, whose innocence they desired to both protect and destroy.

"They did tell us to explore our surroundings." The twinkle in Eddy's eye unmistakable. "You ready, Sam?"

"Yep" the skinny kid stood taller. The youth nodded, expressing his delight at the acceptance of these older and wiser men.

"Then grab your Kimmel." Eddy put on his Panama-style hat, following the request of their new Commander, Admiral Kimmel, that all his sailors wear hats in public. And the sailors had quickly adopted the nickname "Kimmel" for their new headgear.

Scooter mimicked Eddy and they waited until Sam had his Panama hat secured over his blonde hair.

The trio jumped on the bus and headed for Waikiki. They rumbled past Bishop Street and Honolulu Harbor with its massive Matson Aloha Tower, named for the Matson Line passenger boats. The clock on top and the tall steeple beckoned the new arrivals that swamped the harbor and kept the lei-makers busy.

"Ain't this somethin'?" Sam's twang spiraled out the window as he whistled at any women that passed by. "Holy mackerel" He pointed at the large advertisement for Ka-La, "The Sun Brand" fruit. Quality fruit picked and packed in Honolulu.

Eddy eyed Scooter as they watched the young boy's reaction to the billboard. It appeared not the fruit he ogled, but the half-naked Hawaiian girl, one exposed breast protruding over the platter of fruit she held, smiling down at the young virgin.

"We sure don't grow nothin' like that back home in Missouri. But I sure would like to meet that little darlin'."

"Hold on, sailor," Eddy cautioned the seventeen-year-old. "I think you need to visit the High Life." He had read every scrap of material he could find about the island as they had sailed over the Pacific Ocean, along with every manual on defense. British, Canadian, U.S., anything that might contain a fraction of information on tactics and provide an inkling of entertainment for the voyage.

"The High Life?" Sam's fixed his gaze on the aqua colored water and white sand of the beach they were passing.

"Just the place for you. In Chinatown," Scooter echoed.

"Chinktown? Why the hell would I go there?" His youth and exuberance at odds with his worldly ways.

"Girls, my young man. Girls." Eddy clapped the youngster on his thin shoulder.

"Sign me up," Sam boomed. "And a tattoo? I want a tattoo."

"The guys said you can get both in Chinatown. What will your tattoo be?"

"I ain't decided yet." Sam's lips twisted into a youthful pout as he fell silent.

Scooter whistled a tune as they bumped along, mesmerized by the softly rolling waves and the heat, which swept through the mostly empty bus.

"Next stop, the Pink Lady," the driver yelled back in their direction. "Last bus is at 10 p.m. It's a long walk. Don't miss it."

Eddy nudged Sam, who had dozed off with the rhythm of the bus as it swayed down Kalakaua Avenue. His eyes shot open, and he jumped from his seat, his joy and eagerness seemingly up for the promise of paradise. They hurried behind Scooter, who had already stepped off the bus.

"Yee-haw. Ain't this somethin'?" Sam leaped from the bus and stood still a moment, adjusting his gait to land.

The three stood in awe, admiring the massive pink structure of the Royal Hawaiian Hotel.

"Come on, sailors," Eddy commanded as he led the way through the lush vegetation and palm trees. The delicate fragrance of the yellow and pink plumeria became intoxicating as they followed the path around the building. The sound of the surf greeted them, and as they stepped from the grass, their shoes became heavy with white sand.

"Would ya look at that?" Sam had turned toward the jagged green-and-brown volcanic mound that formed Diamond Head in the distance. "Ain't that somethin'?"

"Let's go." Eddy moved down the beach toward the swimmers, removing his Kimmel and shirt. He piled his trousers over his shoes and stood in his swimming trunks watching the surfers ride their long boards to shore.

Sam ambled up beside him. "I'll stay here and guard your stuff." He dropped to the ground, his blonde hair and white skin in glaring contrast with the bronzed bodies on the beach.

Eddy did not want to embarrass Sam. He picked up his small stack of belongings and handed them to him. "Great idea. But better get up there in the shade before you end up the same color as the hotel."

"We swam in lakes back home, and I passed the tests and all, but those waves…I just don't know." Sam got to his feet and brushed himself off.

"You'll get used to it. Where's Scooter?"

They looked around and saw the smiling face of their friend engaged in conversation with two beautiful young women poised beneath a red umbrella on the grass behind them.

"You better go look out for Scooter. He might be in over his head." Eddy nudged the virgin toward the threesome.

"Ya got that right." Sam snapped into action.

Eddy had never felt anything like the warm, crystal-blue waters that greeted him. He dove under one wave only to be greeted by another. He repeated this until he reached the far side of the breakers. Floating on his back, he thought of Billi and how she would give anything to be here with him. He felt a bit of remorse that she was stuck in some office building in the cold and damp of San Francisco.

He scanned the beach for his buddies. The lanky Sam's arms animated a story that held the two young beauties in rapt attention as Scooter looked on. Eddy observed he would have to keep his eye on Sam. And that, he reasoned, would be his excuse if Dahlia ever questioned his actions. After all, their code of ethics required that they "Always have your buddy's back." Of course, he would not mention that he intended to steer the youth toward the ladies so he could be there to protect him. With that ingenious plan set in motion, Eddy let the waves carry him to shore.

THIRTY-FIVE

IT HAD BEEN ONE WEEK, and still David refused to leave his new room during the day. He had stumbled into this rancid hotel that disastrous night when that bitch Billi had cut him, and emerged only in the evening's fog for food and drink. He assumed Jack would be out hunting him by now and that the whore had filled his ear with tales. She would pay for that. But Jack seemed to be the least of his worries at the moment. Someone had followed him that night as he left Billi's building. He had gone back to his room at the Presidio briefly, but had thought it best to leave again. So he had wrapped his bleeding arm, climbed out the window, and, in the dark shadows of the buildings, worked his way back to the Embarcadero area. Without questions, he had rented a room where no one would think to look, in Hotel Bo-Chow, just down the alley from where he had found the severed head amongst the discarded foliage. He had not decided how he would fix his situation with Jack, but felt if he moved in the dark, he would find the light.

He headed through the drizzle down the alley behind the Flower Market when someone stepped in front of him. The tall man strutted forward, followed by another shorter figure, but they did not appear to have seen him. David slid up to the wall and pressed his body against the wet building. Drips of rain fell onto his hat from the overhang above. A third man joined them, and they spoke quickly and softly in Japanese. Then, with a swift and violent force, the tall man slapped one of the others, driving him to his knees. Then the tall one stormed in David's direction. He stopped a few feet away. The man from the ground recovered and ran toward his attacker, only to fall to his knees before him and offer up a knife, held high in both hands.

A car started down the alley, headlights glaring. The three men disappeared into the back of the Flower Market, but not before David caught sight of the tall one's face. Akio led his men out of the rain before the beams of light from the car found them.

David held his breath and hunched down behind some garbage cans as the police car slowly passed, then stopped. The foreboding figure of Officer Hennessy, whom he had spoken with regarding the beheading, emerged from the driver's side. He briskly walked to the door that the three Japanese men had entered and gave it a tug. The door was locked solid. Hennessy looked around. As the intensity of the rain thickened, he hurried back to his car and slowly drove away.

Standing, David tipped his hat forward, and a stream of water poured from its brim. He scurried into the downpour, down the dark alley to the main street, and into the safety of his small room. Cracking open a bottle of Scotch, he drank deeply before removing his wet coat and soaked hat. That had been close. But now he had information that would put him back in his boss's good graces. He hoped.

After finishing half the bottle and encouraged by the brown liquid, he came up with a different plan. He would bring in Akio himself. If this Jap was that valuable to Jack, he would kidnap Akio and use him as a pawn toward advancement. With that thought in mind, he finished most of the bottle before passing out.

BILLI HAD NOT RETURNED TO HER APARTMENT, but had returned to her stool at the Forbidden City. Her bruises had healed and she had bought some new dresses, the vampy kind that both excited and disgusted Jack.

There had been no more visits from Akio or any of his men, but they hoped tonight would be different. The nightclub advertised a gala masked party for Halloween. Billi had kept herself busy creating her costume, Hawaiian in spirit, adapted from the very funny letters of her brother's adventures as he explored the island of Oahu. She had asked some of the gals at the club if they would help her, and they had gladly poured their resources into the project.

She slid onto her stool and winked at the bartender. He nodded back and that gave her strength while she waited in her grass skirt, fitted red bathing suit, and white lei, with matching red and white flowers in her hair. The girls had added a small band of flowers around her ankle, which fluttered as she now bounced her foot to the music.

The place was packed, with a line of party-goers waiting for tables extending down the stairs, out under the canopy, and into the cold mist. Some of the elaborate costumes came complete with masks. Billi watched the parade, fascinated by the imagination of some and the sheer unwillingness to participate in the spectacle of others. Her eye caught a tall figure, replete with mask, in a group of others, and her heart quickened. She easily detected Akio's gait as he led his soldiers. His royal robes and Venetian-style mask were topped with a wig and headpiece in maroon and gold, the tail of which draped onto his left shoulder. The others were dressed as knights, their mock chainmail hoods covering their black hair but not the slant of their eyes.

A chill ran through her. How clever. No one would be able to describe them if they could get her out the door. She put her drink down and asked for soda water with lemon as she nervously fingered her purse.

She looked over at the mask and sombrero that Duckworth wore to conceal his identity, and he gently nodded back. She suppressed her smile. It felt reassuring having someone on the inside with her.

"Welcome." Charlie Low entered onstage and picked up the microphone." Welcome. As a special treat for tonight's Halloween event, we are offering a prize for the best costume." He paused for the applause. "Oh, I see so many choices. You are making this very hard for us. Our judge will be Dorothy Sun." He waited again as Dorothy danced onto the stage, her see-through skirt accentuating her long legs. Whistles and hoots came from the audience, and Charlie let the sound roll across the room. "And, of course—" His voice rose with gusto. "— Mary Mammon." He stretched out her name to even more catcalls as the actress arrived in a scanty outfit of Asian design.

Billi watched the table of knights as they clapped in approval of the beautiful girls who were working their way through the crowd, teasing the various men in their disguises. After a few minutes, the knights at their roundtable leaned in to huddle. Then, as hoped, one of the knights approached her.

"Join please." He grabbed her elbow and she felt his grip tighten.

Billi eased from her stool, grabbing her purse as he half-pulled her between the overflowing tables to the one they occupied.

Charlie Low brought her a chair and placed it next to Akio's flowing robes. "Well, well, knights and their lord. And now a damsel."

"I ain't no damsel." Billi wiggled her hips mockingly. "I'm a hula gal." Her hands gracefully floated through the air, a movement not unnoticed by the lord as his eyes shifted behind his mask.

"Thank you for joining us, Ginger the Hula Gal." Akio's voice sounded a bit muffled. "I hope you are feeling better."

"Yeah." She swallowed hard as she smiled at the eyes behind the mask. The waiter arrived with a drink and placed it beside her purse.

"Thanks." She shook the glass, letting the ice clank from side to side. Billi scrutinized a new member in the group. His stern Japanese face seemed familiar, and she worked the new puzzle he presented.

"Do you recognize our friend?" Akio's eyes shifted behind his mask as he nodded in the new man's direction.

"Naw, should I?" Billi's bare shoulders raised and lowered.

"He was in the movies."

"A star?" She leaned into Akio, eyes wide with wonder.

"He worked for a famous star."

Billi wanted to ask more questions when she noticed Akio's eyes focused over her head with an impatient expression.

She followed his gaze and saw a pirate picking his way through the costumes toward them. His mask did not conceal the tan hue of his skin, and his shorter frame in keeping with the younger, brazen Hatsuro. The one who had drugged her.

The pirate bowed almost imperceptible to his commander before he sank into the last empty chair at the table. He spoke breathlessly in Japanese. "We think we have found the professor. And that will lead us to the drawings."

"Is he near?" The mask did not hinder the sternness of Akio's response in their common language.

Hatsuro's guttural use of the language and the mask made it hard for Billi to follow all of his words. She struggled to stay self-composed when she caught the phrase "seen in Seattle but lost him."

The eyes behind the Venetian mask did not blink as his ruthless instructions were given with more volume. "Send word to Tokyo to slit his sister's throat and spread the word that he must come to us soon or his wife and children will meet the same fate. I must have those drawings." He took a breath. "Now that the weakling, Konoe, has been replaced and our rightful prime minister, Tojo, is in command, we cannot lose. Soon, our winged forces will be on every shore of this worthless country, and their very arrival will not be detected as they will arrive from below."

"With Razor Tojo, we will destroy their navy first as the fools sleep." Billi recognized the voice of the knight as that of Ito and waited breathlessly for him to continue. "Our contact has almost finished sketching the layout of the harbor and the ships' positions. The emperor will soon rule all." His declaration sent tremors of zealous ambition through the men.

"We have waited for that moment for some time." Hollywood's dark eyes hardened.

Billi shifted her gaze to the man who had spoken in his clipped native tongue.

Akio tapped the table. "Detailed reports are flowing into our consulates along the coast, and it is very much worth the cost. We have some shortwave radios set up, and other radio communications are set up in Mexico to continue our intelligence once war has been declared."

"Deep waters will flow with our navy and we—" Hatsuro broke off as the band had reached an ear-piercing crescendo with the last note of the song.

Billi watched as all attention shifted once again on the two talented women who began to work the crowd.

Ito finally resumed the conversation. "I visited the oil company in Los Angeles. They graciously took me around their refinery. I will have no trouble finding the exact spot from the submarine. Also, news from up north is very encouraging. There are men noting the number of aircraft being built in that factory and the movement of the navy."

"Excellent. Let us go." The grand lord gathered his robes around him. "Bring the girl after I have gone." His harsh last words in their language shot through Billi.

"Hey, you comin' back?" Billi sat back, swinging her leg with the flowers around the ankle, and her grass skirt fell away, exposing most of her thigh.

He looked down at her. "Do not worry. We will see each other soon." His English perfect to the ear.

"Promise?" Her shoulders lifted coyly.

"Promise." His response lingered like a muffled hiss.

As his robes disappeared down the stairs, Akio's men picked back up their conversation.

"Hatsuro." The man from Hollywood leaned forward and continued in Japanese. "Do you know what the drawings are of that the professor has?"

"The details for a very special airplane."

Billi observed that with Akio gone, the young man did not protect his information. She briefly wondered if she could get him to expose more.

"Can't others do the same?"

"I heard they were Akio's design and very valuable."

"So how did the professor get them?" Hollywood questioned.

Hatsuro shrugged and fell silent.

Ito nodded toward Billi and then spoke. "Why is the girl always so still when we are talking?"

"Whores are dead between the ears," Hollywood remarked.

Hatsuro did not respond as he glared at Billi.

She quickly opened her purse and then snapped it shut. "Anyone got a cigarette?" She briefly shuddered when she speculated she had provided them with an opportunity to give her more drugs.

The stocky Hatsuro chuckled. "She is dead between the ears. But it is her other region that our commander desires." He slid a cigarette from his pack and handed it to her.

"Thanks." She took the offered smoke and put it between her two fingers on her right hand. "What kind are these?" She examined the cigarette with its long white filter.

"French," Hatsuro smiled, the smile that drove waves of anxiety through her body.

She snapped the filter off and tossed it on the table. "I don't like filters. Those sissy French."

The lids on Hatsuro's eyes lowered. Obviously, he did not like her brassy ways, and he was not afraid to show it. The two knights shifted uncomfortably.

"So, who's the famous star?" She nodded in Hollywood's direction.

"No one you would remember." Ito signaled the men as he switched to Japanese. "Let us get her out of here now. He will not want to wait long."

Just then the band started a Cuban cha-cha, and Dorothy led the way through the tables with others forming a line behind her. One of the knights had slipped behind Billi and Hatsuro leaned toward her when a hand shot between them. Billi grabbed her purse as someone dragged her into the chain of dancers. She put her hands on the hips of the man wearing a sombrero as it bounced before her.

The pirate and knights exchanged heated looks and watched the dancers snake through the room, their eyes fixed on the hula girl bouncing behind the man with the large Mexican hat. Dorothy, rattling castanets, led the line behind the risers where the band stood. When the line emerged again, the three knights moved toward the sombrero. When they stepped up to the bobbing hat, they found a heavy-set woman dressed as a Greek, below the brim. Ginger the hula girl was nowhere to be found.

THIRTY-SIX

BILLI PULLED THE LONG COAT closer to her as she and the hatless Duckworth stole up Sutter Street toward the Sir Francis Drake. She hoped the flowers around her ankle did not give her away. She had not had time to remove them before donning Duckworth's dark overcoat and sneaking down the stairs through the crowd of costumed partiers.

They left the mist as they entered the hotel by the side door and waited by the intricate, glossy elevator door. Duckworth did not push the button to call the device. When the elevator door on the far side opened, Jack stood inside. They got in without so much as a nod and waited for the doors to close.

"I've been watching for you." Jack flipped open the panel of controls below the buttons and inserted a special key into the slot. He then pushed the button for the garage.

"My, aren't you full of tricks?" Billi watched him intently.

"Not me, darlin'. This building is full of surprises from Prohibition. I take it he showed up tonight?"

"And so did his merry men. Who have very loose lips. And some new man from Hollywood. I've seen him but can't put it together."

"Charlie Chaplin's driver?" Jack looked at Duckworth.

Duckworth nodded.

"You're kidding me?" Billi looked from one to the other. "Of course. The Tramp and his driver Kono. I can't believe I didn't think of it."

"You can tell me as we go."

"Where? I'm barely dressed if you haven't noticed."

He ignored her and turned to Duckworth. "I might be a day. There are complications. Stay close to the phone and keep your eyes out for…"

His sudden stop in mid-sentence made Billi take in a sharp breath. They had not located David as yet.

"Got it." Duckworth had obviously watched her expression change to fear. "Don't worry." He added a smile of encouragement.

Jack sent the elevator back up with Duckworth inside. Then he took Billi's arm and led her past the loading dock into the dark recesses of the service garage. His car sat tucked in the back of the very dark and thin alcove.

He opened the passenger door for her. As she slid in, her coat fell back, as did her hula skirt. Her lean leg with the flowers around the ankle held his attention before she snapped the coat over herself.

Jack slowly maneuvered the car out of the garage. "Get down," he commanded.

She slid down the seat and watched his hands turn the wheel right, then right again, and soon a left. They bumped along for a few minutes until she felt the car pick up speed.

"Can I sit up now?"

He did not answer, his mood reflected in the concentration of his driving. Finally he broke his silence.

"Join me. There's no one behind us."

She pushed her bottom back up onto the seat and let out a sigh. She was wet, tired, and hungry. And Jack's black mood did not come as a welcome addition to the situation.

"Where are we going?"

"Sorry." She could see him struggling for an answer. "Home."

"Home? To your house?" She sat taller, her voice rising with anxiety. She knew she could not bear seeing Jack with his pregnant blonde wife by his side. She had been able to push the image of his wife out of her mind. When he had touched her with such concern and warmth, she had let herself believe he liked her. She had hope he saw her as something more than just a tool in his crazy plot to save the world. She pulled the damp coat closer and looked out her side window at the lights in the hills. She would tell him what she had overheard and then head back to Seattle. She had had enough of this game playing.

They rode in silence, both brooding over their private demons as they headed south past a mass of water and then further inland.

Billi concluded she had nodded off when she felt the car take a sharp right and begin to climb up a steep hill. The expansive homes they passed were barely distinguishable in the darkness.

"You live in a nice neighborhood."

"This is my parents' home. My father is deceased."

Billi noted the strain in his voice when he mentioned his father.

"You live with your mother, too, then?" She laughed. The almighty Jack had dings in his armor.

"I don't live anywhere." His terse words revealing his frustration.

"What about your wi…" Billi couldn't say the word. If this arrogant man didn't care about his pregnant wife, why should she? She shot him a look of disgust.

"Look, there are complications right now. Try to be nice." He pulled the car into a long driveway and parked.

Billi sat dreamily studying the grand Tudor estate, but rocketed back to consciousness when Jack flung the door open and a blast of cool, damp air hit her.

Jack had her arm and hurried her toward a large wooden door beneath the arches of the front porch. The warmth inside spread welcomingly down her limbs as she entered the foyer. She stood alone as Jack hurried across the polished wooden floor and down the two steps into the living room.

"Where's Lilly?" he asked.

Dutiful husband in front of the others, Billi thought. The thin disguise disgusted her. He had just been blatantly ogling her bare leg.

"She's asleep," the voice of an older woman answered.

Billi walked toward Jack and looked into an enormous room with floor-to-ceiling lead-glass windows and large fireplace, the flickering flames casting shadows across the Oriental rug. As Jack stood at the coffee table in front of the large couch to pick up a silver cigarette case, Billi saw the elderly woman seated before the hearth. Her graying hair was swept back, simply styled, and she wore a thick brocade robe in a soft yellow. There could be no question, as the striking resemblance to Jack claimed her as his mother. Even without speaking, Mrs. Huntington commanded authority, a trait she had passed on to her son.

"Who have you brought with you Jack? Is that why you wanted me to stay up?" Her voice level, while she sat taller observing the newcomer.

"Oh." Jack turned and regarded Billi.

She saw his expression change and calculated her appearance must be a bit in question: her hair damp and drooping, Duckworth's long coat covering all but the flowers that circled her ankle above the straps of her high heels. She imagined it was certainly not how he would have liked her to appear for the first time before his mother's scrutiny.

He forced a smile on his face and walked up to Billi as she came down the two steps into the room. "This is a friend." He paused, and Billi waited to hear which name he would prefer she use in this palatial home.

"What kind of friend is she, Jack, that you don't know her name?" His mother's question lingered in the room, thick with sarcasm.

"I'm Ginger. We haven't known each other that long." She swayed into the room in full swing of her Ginger persona, then stopped. "Whoa, ain't this some place?" Out of the corner of her eye, she saw the older women cringe at her choice of words.

"Ya gonna offer me one of those?" She pointed to the cigarette that still dangled unlit in Jack's hand. "Or some whiskey? I bet ya got the good stuff here." She plopped on the couch and bounced a few times, letting the coat slip away, exposing her hula skirt and bare legs. "Nice."

Jack's one good eye bore down on her, and she smiled broadly up at him.

"Good Lordy." The deep, rich voice came from the top of the steps leading into the living room. "What done ya brung home?"

Billi picked a cigarette from the silver cigarette box on the tray, then crossed her leg and swung the flowered anklet a little higher. Locking eyes with the thick black women who appeared fixed in place, she cocked her head to the side. "I'll have a whiskey. Your best."

"Hmmph." The large woman raised her eyebrows at Jack, then turned her broad back to them before stomping away. "I ain't serven' no white trash in dis house."

"I'll get you that drink, Ginger." Jack leaned down and picked up the heavy, silver lighter with its Greek design. He snapped the flame to life and held it out for her. "Stay put," he hissed.

She took a deep breath of cigarette and coughed the smoke into his face. "Sorry."

Jack crossed to the side cabinet and poured two stiff drinks.

"Bright Eyes!" The thrill in Lilly's voice genuine as it floated down from above.

Billi looked up at the small balcony that overlooked the living room at the slim figure of Lilly. She waved and then disappeared into the alcove, her bare feet pattering on the wooden steps as she hurried down, then stopped under the archway. Jack rushed instantly by her side offering his hand to help her down the last two steps under the main arch.

Billi quickly put out her cigarette and began to fumble with the buttons on Duckworth's overcoat.

Lilly looked tired, the dark rings below her eyes were new since she and Billi had first met. She brushed away Jack's hand and walked directly to Billi. "What a surprise!"

Billi caught a whiff of gardenia perfume as Lilly gracefully sat beside her. The soft white feathers that adorned the cuffs of her robe floated to rest as she placed her hands in her lap. She was beautiful.

"I'll have one of those." She nodded at the glasses of whiskey Jack carried.

"No you won't." He handed the drink to Billi.

"Oh, pooh," Lilly pouted. "I hate being pregnant. Do this, don't do that."

"Lilly, is this the same girl you mentioned before? The one you met with the Fishers?" Mrs. Huntington directed her question past Billi to the woman beside her.

"Yes." Lilly reached for a cigarette from the silver container. "The Fishers found Bright Eyes to be very entertaining."

"Fascinating." Mrs. Huntington began working her gaze over Billi as if she were a new horse for the stable.

Jack took the cigarette from Lilly's hand, and she kicked him. "I want one," she snarled.

Billi watched their interchange and had to hide her surprise.

"Children," Mrs. Huntington scolded. "Well, Jack, why are you here with your…friend?"

The knock at the door startled the group, and Jack quickly went to answer it.

Left alone with the other two women, Billi looked up at the large wooden beams that arched across the ceiling and the two brass chandeliers. Her gaze scanned down past white stucco that met with a band of hand-tooled, oak-inlaid scrawling designs of leaves and acorns above solid massive panels. She contemplated the five carved family crests spaced perfectly above the large stone fireplace. Strong, stately, and rich. One could not question the wealth that resided here.

Jack shoved something into his jacket pocket as he returned. His other hand streamed through his thick hair, a trait Billi had come to associate with stress. What had he meant by "complications" when he spoke with Duckworth? And why hadn't he asked her one question about what she had overheard at the club?

He gulped down his drink then sat next to Lilly. His behavior had caught the attention of all three women. He picked up Lilly's hand, and Billi looked away, straight into the eyes of his mother. She quickly downed her drink and bumped the empty glass onto the coffee table.

"That's some good stuff." Her voice loud in the silent, tense room. "Any more? Never mind, I see the bottle." Purposely, she left the coat on the couch, snatched up her empty glass, and stood in her hula attire.

The three watched her sway across the room without a word. She turned toward Jack and defiantly smirked in his direction as she filled her glass beyond reason.

"Why, Jack," Lilly laughed. "She is quite the handful."

"Yes," his mother dryly agreed.

"Lilly." Jack patted her hand attempting to draw her attention. "Look at me. Something has happened."

Billi felt a chill at his words.

"Oh, Jack." Lilly sank back against the couch, pulling her hand from his grasp. "You are so dramatic."

Bella entered with a tray of tea and set it on the coffee table. "Some o' us likes to behaves like ladies." She poured a cup for Mrs. Huntington, handed it to her, and a second for Lilly. She straightened to her full height, ignoring Billi, then turned to leave.

"Bella, sit for a minute please." Anxious, Jack wove his hand through his hair.

Bella turned and eyed Jack, and then quietly sat in the far chair facing him, a deep look of concern covering her face.

"Lilly," Jack began again, picking up her hand again.

A lump formed in Billi's throat, and she wanted to scream. Why had he brought her here to witness his passion for his wife?

"There's been an accident. While escorting other ships from Newfoundland to Britain…" He choked, then began again. "There was a German wolf pack of submarines in the area, and one of them torpedoed and sank the *Reuben James*."

The string of his words fell into the room, bearing a vision of ripped flesh, fire, and death.

"Well, that's impossible." Lilly let her brother continue to hold her hand. "Todd is on the *Reuben James* in Iceland. And they are on neutrality patrol. That's what he called it. 'Neutrality.'"

"Yes." Jack spoke slowly and softly to her now. "The *Reuben James* was with four other destroyers protecting supplies headed for Britain."

"Where's Todd?" Lilly looked at him as the others in the room held their breath. "Where's my husband?"

Billi wasn't certain she had heard right. And she stepped a little closer to listen.

"Where's my husband?" Lilly jumped up, her fists clenched tight. "Where's Todd? Where's my husband?" she screamed.

Billi watched in tortured silence as Mrs. Huntington rose and drifted toward her daughter. Bella thundered the short distance to Lilly and held her to her breast. "Theres, now baby."

"I want my Todd. I want Todd." Lilly struggled against the larger black woman.

Bella held Lilly away from her, tears streaming down her dark cheeks. "Now, baby, the Good Lord done somethen' that ain't quite right. But yous has to think of dat child. You hear me?"

Billi realized Jack had quickly moved to stand beside her. He took the drink from her hand and downed it. Billi felt tears sting her eyes too as the image of her beloved Ray floated before her. She felt the devastating depth of Lilly's pain.

"Are you certain?" she asked Jack, stunned. She retrieved her glass to refill it, hands shaking.

He turned away from the grieving women and faced Billi, his voice a whisper. "I spoke with the naval station in Newfoundland when the report came in a few hours ago. There were 159 courageous men in that crew, they pulled only 44 from the water. Todd was not among them."

"Does this mean we are at war?" She matched his whisper.

He shrugged and turned back toward the beautiful blonde that Billi now gathered was his baby sister.

Bella had Lilly in her arms again, rocking and humming to the limp figure as the impact of her husband's death brought on uncontrollable sobbing. "Alls will be well," she half sang in a deep, soothing croon. "Alls will be well."

Mrs. Huntington stood above her daughter and Bella. As she turned to regard her son, Billi watched the silent exchange with all of the implications. Soon a fatherless child would enter the world and Jack would have to add that to his concerns. Bella was right, the safe birth of the child remained all that mattered. Mrs. Huntington turned back to her distraught daughter and laid a hand on her heaving shoulder.

Jack took his hand from his jacket pocket and withdrew a small vile of pills.

"What are those for?"

"To calm Lil and help her sleep. Her doctor assured me they would not harm the baby. The last thing we need in this house is a miscarriage." He looked down at her. "Billi, the sinking of this U.S. destroyer alters everything."

She turned back toward the silver tray that held the decanter of liquor and picked up another heavy cut glass. Her hands shook so, the Scotch missed the crystal and spilled onto the tray. Jack reached down and put his hand over hers, holding the glass steady. Together they put the empty glass down.

His head brushed the flower in her hair. "Give me a minute to get Lilly upstairs." The heat of his breath stirred other emotions as he continued in his hushed tone. "Sit down and rest. I'll be right back."

She felt his warmth leave her as she busied herself mopping up the small spill of brown liquid. His touch had made her blood race, and she felt a bit dizzy. She heard an anguished moan from behind her and recognized the agony of losing the man you love. Gathering her strength, she turned back to watch the heartbreaking scene.

"Come on, Lil." Jack coaxed her from Bella's arms. "Let's get you up to bed."

"Oh, Jack. I don't want to live without Todd. I don't want this ba—"

"Hush, Lil." Jack scooped his sister up in his arms and led the sad procession, with Bella helping his mother following close behind. Grief set the pace, slow and heavy.

Billi stood before the fireplace, facing the flames, with the slightest movement of the hula skirt, her exaggerated shadow swept across the thick Oriental rug. She heard Jack's deep sigh as he returned.

"I've called Duckworth. He's bringing you a few things."

Billi didn't register his words but continued to watch the flicker of the fire.

He stepped behind her and ran his hands down her bare arms. "How are you doing?"

"I don't know." She liked the feel of his hands, but tonight the memories of Ray were strong with the other shadow that had filled this room. The shadow of death.

"Come with me." His hand trailed down her arm and found her hand. He led her away from the warmth, across the hall, and into the kitchen.

The large white room sat empty except for the lingering aroma of onions, garlic, and coffee. He seated Billi at the kitchen table and she heard him rifle through the refrigerator. He put meat and cheese before her. Bread and butter were next. When she still didn't move, he added milk to the array of hopefuls. He waited hovering over her when the door flew open.

"What ya doen' messen' in my kitchen?" Bella stood like a raging bull in the doorway. "And what ya doen' waiten' on her?"

Billi jumped as Jack moved behind her.

"Dis house done been turned upside down tonight. Now gets out and I'll brings somethen' up." She headed toward them as she barked her command.

Jack smiled. "Thanks, Bella. We'll be in the library."

"Yous better be. I don' want ta be catchen' her in your bed or nothen' like dat." The large woman glared down at Billi. "She can has the back bedroom, next ta mine."

"How's Lilly?" Jack helped Billi stand.

"She's drunk dat medicine and is cryen' her eyes out. But your mother's sitten' by her."

Jack nodded and led Billi up the back stairs, past the muffled sounds of mourning, to the library he used as his office. Inside the solid wooden walls, Billi felt the emotions of the last hour begin to slip away. She sat in a big leather chair, and although the coolness against her exposed back was refreshing, she shivered slightly. Jack handed her a plaid blanket from the couch.

She accepted the blanket with a nod. "Take off the patch."

Unhesitating, he removed the blasted thing and flipped in onto the desk, then moved to light the already prepared fire. Bella entered a few minutes later with a tray, and taking in the fact that Billi was occupying Jack's favorite chair, she let out a "hmmph." When Bella set the tray on the desk next to Jack's patch, she emitted another "hmmph."

Jack handed Billi a sandwich as Bella stormed into the room again, an old blue, chenille robe dangling in her hand.

"Put dis on before yous catch youselfs a cold. I don' needs two skinny women ta be sickly in my house."

Billi stood and accepted the robe. "Thanks." She spoke as Ginger as she wrapped the robe around her.

Then Bella turned a warning glare toward Jack, sent a "hmmph" in his direction, and left.

"I think she's beginning to like you," Jack laughed.

"How can you tell?" Billi, suddenly hungry, plopped back in the chair and took a bite of sandwich.

He didn't answer but sat across from her on the couch and grabbed the other half of the sandwich. They ate in silence before Jack ventured into the topic that had been sidelined.

"You were saying Akio's merry men had loose lips?"

THIRTY-SEVEN

AT 7:30 THE NEXT MORNING, a soft rat-a-tat-tat sounded at the back door. Jack opened it, and Billi, seeing Duckworth, flew into his arms, giving him a big hug and thank you.

The joy she felt was not due to the small bag of clothes that he held, but the pillow Eileen had made tucked under his arm. She snatched it from her unsuspecting co-conspirator and dashed back inside. Bella stood at the stove, and as she turned from her cooking, a look of uncertainty furrowed her brow. Billi smiled at her, realizing Bella would not decipher the embroidered kanji on her pillow claiming peace. The large woman's world revolved solely around the occupants of this house. The two men remained outside, deep in hushed discussion for some time. When Jack reentered the kitchen, Billi sat waiting, along with two hot plates of pancakes and sausage.

Shortly after nine Billi started down the back stairs again. She had taken a bath and put on her blue dress. Seeing her pillow had brought her a sense of relief and comfort. In the privacy of the small back room that Bella had assigned her, she had slipped her hand into the secret compartment and withdrawn the fan and Raymond's ring. She had slipped the large, three-diamond band onto her finger, and it felt solid, not heavy as it had before. The diamonds twinkled up at her and, for the first time, they felt as if they belonged on her hand.

She stood alone in the foyer, uncertain of where to go, when she heard a sharp knock at the front door. Bella entered from the kitchen, wiping her hands on her spotless apron. She ignored Billi as she opened the door to find three men in dress-white navy uniforms standing in the morning mist.

The one closest removed his hat. "We are here on official business to see Mrs. Todd Achers. Please." They waited in uncomfortable silence.

"She ain't up yet." Bella's formidable frame filled the doorway.

"I'm sorry, ma'am, but we must speak directly to her."

"It's all right, Bella." Billi slipped in front of the housekeeper. "I'm Mrs. Todd Achers. How may I help you?"

"May we come in?" The spokesman nodded and stood taller.

"Of course, this way please." Billi did not even pause in her stride. "Bella, some coffee for the gentlemen please."

Bella, hands on hips, stood back as Billi elegantly led the three men into the living room. At the landing, Billi turned back to the shocked older woman, whose hair seemed to have gone whiter over the last twenty-four hours.

"Cream or sugar, gentlemen?" Billi asked.

In unison they mumbled, "No, thank you, no time, not necessary," but that was enough to put Bella in motion and the kitchen door slammed.

The three men sat rigid on the couch while Billi took the chair Mrs. Huntington had occupied the night before.

The spokesman cleared his throat. "We came in person, ma'am, at this terrible time to bring you rather difficult news."

Billi folded her hands on her lap, the ring catching the sun's light, and waited. She knew their words of grief and sorrow would fall around her. She also knew Lilly could not hear them again. She waited.

As they spoke, Bella entered with the tray of coffee and four delicate cups. The speaker had not reached the announcement as yet, and they all tensed at the interruption. Bella served the steaming black liquid, then stood regarding Billi.

"Thank you, Bella. Would you stay for a moment please?" Billi needed the housekeeper's strength, as a strange bond had formed between them.

"Yes, miss," Bella mumbled.

The three men exchanged looks, and then the lead began again with his unfamiliar speech. As the words fell from his mouth, Billi remembered only a few. "Died a hero. No body found. Wolf packs dangerous because they travel in groups." Those were the ones that registered the most, the ones that reflected Ray, and the tears for her own love and hero began again.

"He didn't die in vain," she found herself saying. "He was right all along."

"Absolutely not, ma'am," the spokesman agreed. "Their ship saved several lives. They were an escort…"

She lost his remarks again when she saw movement up in the small balcony. Jack stood beside his mother as she leaned on her cane.

Billi looked straight at Jack as she spoke. "Are we at war then?"

The question lingered, not addressed to anyone in particular, and she turned back to the three men who looked at each other before the lead responded.

"As of this moment there has been no declaration from either side." He coughed in obvious embarrassment, contemplating the implication of her question and his response.

Grief took hold and tears spilled freely from her.

"Mrs. Achers," Billi heard him say again.

Bella approached and stood by her side offering her a napkin, which she readily accepted and dabbed at the stream of bitter tears. "Oh, yes. I'm sorry. It's all so shocking."

"We're sorry, ma'am, but where did you want us to send his effects?"

"Here…of course." Her words were slow and lifeless. She slumped forward. Pulled down by the wrenching memory of Ray's funeral. Poor Lilly, she had to keep the child safe.

The man held an envelope in Billi's direction. She looked at it and shook her head. He placed the unopened envelope, embossed with the Seal of the Department of the Navy, on the coffee table—useless words that could not resurrect the man.

They stood in uneasy unison. "We're sorry for your loss."

"We all lose at times like this." Her voice grew stronger. "We lose loved ones, and still we fight. We fight in a war that is yet to arrive, as we fight to hold the memories of those who have been taken from us." Once again, her eyes locked on Jack. "But if that is to be our fate, then God help us fight against those who harm our men."

"Yes, ma'am." The three stood taller and turned as Bella led them toward the front door and closed it behind them.

Billi rose as Jack escorted his mother into the living room. Her cane pointed at the couch, and Jack walked her toward it instead of her own chair. Once Mrs. Huntington sat, she picked up one of the untouched cups of coffee and studied Billi, who stood nervously twisting the napkin.

"Sit." Mrs. Huntington spoke into the silent room. "Who is she, Jack?"

"Mother, meet Billi O'Shaughnessy. She is helping me with a project." Jack walked over to stand next to Billi.

"Quite the actress, aren't you?"

She sighed at the intensity of the older woman's glare. "I—I didn't think Lilly was up to the—"

"Show me your hand," Mrs. Huntington demanded.

"What? Oh, that." Billi held out her shaking hand with the ring. "A bit ostentatious, I know, but it was—"

"Really?" Mrs. Huntington's eyes crinkled into a brief smile.

Bella entered. At the sight of the ring, her eyes grew to the size of quarters, accompanied by three long "Hmmph"s.

Billi withdrew her hand and began twisting the napkin again. She looked quickly at Jack, but his lips were sealed tight as he held his breath.

"I didn't mean any harm." She looked back at the matriarch. "I know what it is like when they show up on your door. The pain. And Lilly is so delicate right now."

"Yes." Jack's mother watched the movement of the ring on Billi's hand. "Who did you say gave you that ring?"

"I hadn't yet." Billi's shoulders went back, and she swallowed hard. She had not said his name out loud for such a long time. "Raymond, my fiancé. We were to be married—"

"Oh, my heavens. Raymond Richardson?" The coffee splashed in the delicate cup Mrs. Huntington held.

"Yes." Billi could not control her breathing. None of this made sense. And then she remembered that Gladys Richardson had wanted her to come to San Francisco to meet some of her relatives. She quickly turned to Jack. "That's right. You knew Ray. You sent him away. Was he related to you?"

He stared at her, unable to answer. He had tried to explain earlier. Yes, he had stepped up Ray's departure, but he had not intended for any harm to come to him.

Billi tried to hold back her tears, but her anger and feeling of betrayal made her shake. She fled up the stairs and disappeared down the hall.

"What have you done, Jack?" his mother asked.

"I don't know." He stood helplessly before the two women who had raised him.

BILLI SAT ON THE SINGLE BED in the small room, crying. She had furiously packed the few things she had, and strands of the hula skirt were sticking out of the bag Duckworth had brought. She wanted to go home. She wanted her mother and Eileen and Danny and to hear her father's soft whistle as he worked. More importantly, she wanted Ray alive.

The door opened a crack. Billi grabbed the bed pillow and heaved it across the room. Lilly sidestepped the flying object.

"Bright Eyes, what on earth is the matter?" she demanded.

"Nothing. Sorry, I thought you were Jack."

Lilly picked up the pillow and carried it to Billi. "Here, I'll send him in and you can take a shot at him. I'm certain he deserves it."

"I didn't mean to disturb you." Billi reached for the pillow.

Lilly looked at her hand, stunned. "Heavens, where in hell did you get that?"

"It seems to be the question of the day." Billi spun the ring on her finger.

"Has Mother seen it yet?"

"Oh, yes."

"And what did she say?"

"Same as you. How did I get such a ring?"

"What did you tell her?"

"That I thought it was ostentatious but it—"

Lilly laughed and lowered onto the bed next to Billi. "You told her that?"

"What is it about this darn ring?"

"It belonged to Mother. She sold it for cash so we could keep the house during the Depression. Well, Jack sold it to a distant relative that no one likes."

"Let me guess, Gladys Richardson."

"Yes, and she lorded it over Mother like you would not believe. Flashing it everywhere in town. So, how do you know dear, dreadful Aunt Gladys?"

"I was engaged to Raymond."

"What? Oh my goodness and he died in the plane…" Lilly moaned with recognition and then burst into tears. "Just like my Todd. They are both gone."

"Yes." Billi's voice softened with the memory.

"And for nothing." Unmistakable anger filled Lilly's voice as the reality sunk in.

"No." Billi put her hand over the frail pregnant woman's. "No. I understand now. There is evil out there and our men tried to stop it. They believed they were doing the best for our country, so we must too."

Lilly looked at her, and Billi recognized the despair in her eyes. "I can't. I don't want to live."

"Do you know how lucky you are? You will always have a part of Todd in your child. I—I have nothing but memories. But you can't touch memories or hear their heartbeat when you hold them." The tears that now began were few as she found some contentment in what the three men in uniform had told her. "Can I hold your baby when it's born?"

The two young women collapsed into each other's arms. "Yes."

"Promise?"

"Yes."

"Good. So we need to stop crying and eat and sleep and live." Billi helped Lilly up off the bed.

"You're right." Lilly wiped her eyes. "I know, we need something to cheer us up. I'll go tell Bella to make us some pies. I could eat a whole pie right now." Lilly floated toward the door. Then paused and turned back. "I think peach sounds good. And ice cream. Lots of ice cream."

THIRTY-EIGHT

Eddy sat on a rock overlooking the ever changing blues of the Pacific Ocean. His afternoons in paradise had been very fruitful. He had managed to find all the best beaches and spent his evenings working on his hula at nightclubs with some of the local girls. But this Saturday morning his attention was glued to the man beside him, who had his radio gear trained out past the blue to faraway places.

"I was driving over the Pali toward base." Eddy pointed up the island. "And I saw something that looked like a sub out past Kane'ohe Bay the other day." He adjusted his Kimmel, fishing for information from his new friend Joe. They had met at one of the local bars in Waikiki and, unlike most of his pals in the navy, Eddy was not beyond talking with someone in the army, if he could elicit information.

"I hope you weren't carrying any pork." The radioman, Joe, moved one ear piece to the side, picked up his thermos, and took a swig.

"You believe that local stuff?" Eddy smiled.

"You bet." Came between gulps. "Never take pork over the Pali, bad luck sailor."

"Well, I'll be sure to spread it around base."

"How do you like being at Kane'ohe?"

"I like it. It's peaceful, not crowded. So what do you think of the subs?"

"Seen 'em. Report 'em. And that's all I can do." Joe watched the water now more intently. "They've been reported recently all over the islands. Usually turn out to be whales."

Eddy took this in and sat in silence, working the situation in his active mind. The Germans would not have their wolf packs in these waters. The subs had to be Japanese. He reviewed the routine the subs would follow. They would surface at night to recharge, then spend their days like sharks gliding along the coast, watching and waiting to strike. It was with some shock that his mind took the next step: The blood, the blood that attracted these sharks would be his and his buddies'.

"Almost time to quit for the day," Joe announced. "You already had breakfast?"

"You guys don't listen at night?" Eddy's voice went up a notch.

"Nah. We have our trucks out at a few places around the island. Top brass doesn't believe in radar. So he has us training before dawn until about 7 a.m. Then we close up. What do you flyboys hear?" He didn't look at Eddy but continued to watch the mesmerizing blue.

"Same. We see subs when on patrol and don't know whose they are. But our patrol bombers will only cover so much shoreline."

"What's it like landing on the water in that thing?"

"I love my PBY. Skimming low over the water and then landing in the chop always gives me a thrill. Makes me hate to have to put her wheels down and land her on the tarmac."

"Got good visibility I bet."

"Those Catalina's are built so we pilots don't even have gauges to distract us. The gears are overhead. Nothing but view. But they have us just focusing on the south shores of the island right now."

"Leaves a pretty big hole up north." Joe's obvious concern matched Eddy's.

"You got radar up that way?"

"Yes, but only in the mornings."

They two men looked straight at each other in the realization of the vulnerable northern approach. The lack of command appeared to invite disaster.

"I'm going to go post a few letters and then I'll catch up with you later." Eddy eased off the rock with dampened spirits.

"Some of us are going to Honey's tonight, a bar on your side of the island. Hear from the locals they have the most beautiful women. I'll be in the bar. Come and join us."

Eddy stood a moment, watching Joe rearrange his headgear and then load his equipment back into the cargo truck the army used to store their equipment. He appreciated that Joe had revealed more than he should have. But he also knew that something had to give at some point, and he wanted his buddies to be alert and ready for battle. They would need to have each other's backs when and if the war took hold.

EDDY PICKED UP THE LETTERS he had written and read them one more time before stuffing them into envelopes. He had been certain to tell everyone to have a wonderful Thanksgiving. Even though November had just set upon them, he wanted to remind his mother that Thanksgiving this year would be celebrated on the third Thursday of the month. The past two years FDR had changed the previously established date and met with fierce resentment. Admitting his mistake of deviating from the day set by Lincoln, Roosevelt planned to sign a bill on November 26, 1941. From this year on the bill will establish the fourth Thursday of November the uncontested official holiday.

He chuckled at himself. As if he had to tell his mother, the great planner of events, which day the feast would fall on. He felt loneliness overtake him. His poor mother. The house would seem so empty. Since he wouldn't be home, he hoped Billi would make it back home to Seattle for their mother's sake.

Ray's memory hung over him heavily. Ray would have loved Hawaii, the look of the Pacific and the shades of green and blue from the air. He would have known whose side those submarines were on. The thought made Eddy shiver. All of the signs were pointing toward a battle, but neither side wanted to make the first strike. And for now, that was okay with him.

THE MIST DRIFTED COLD off the San Francisco Bay, but at least it wasn't raining, David mused, as he took up his lookout across the square watching for Billi's lights to go on. He had some unfinished business with her, and his small reserve of cash dwindled daily. He had won big at a card game in the Shinko Club on Laguna Street and would be joining the table again that night. He needed to double his funds so he could stay out of sight. He knew full well his time was running thin before Jack found him.

After an uneventful hour in the cold, he trudged toward Laguna and the backroom game he had talked his way into. Tonight's game promised to be a different group, a different mix. He hoped his luck held, and that Billi would show her face, or her legs, around town.

He conjured terrible things he planned to do to her as he entered the backroom. Thick cigarette smoke hovered in a heavy cloud over the table. As promised, most of the players were new.

"Scotch," David demanded of the slight waiter who circled outside the haze of smoke. He stood back quietly watching until the game finished. Then the man in charge made room at the table and David willing sat. He stacked the few chips he bought and licked his dry lips as he shifted his focus on the others.

He thought he recognized the young Japanese man who sat across from him. Unable to place the foreigner, David's gazed quickly turned to the pile of money the Asian had accumulated.

The cards were dealt and in no time the Japanese man once again reached for his winnings. David took note of the scar that ran across his stubby-fingered hand.

After only one hour David's pile had been depleted. Yet, he needed to stay in the game. He had to win. "Will you take my credit?" David blew his cigarette smoke from his nostrils like a dragon that had been cornered.

"Credit? What kind?" The man with the scar on his hand squinted at David.

"I have lots of money, just not on me."

"Where is money?" His black eyes studied David, whose hands shook slightly.

"In the bank and elsewhere." David forced a smile on his face. "Just one more game."

"How much you want?"

"Twenty chips. That should do."

"Twenty chips for fifty dollar." He placed his scarred hand on a stack of chips.

"Not a problem." David hated him but smiled again as he stubbed out his cigarette.

He slid a stack of chips in David's direction.

"You know white whores with blue eyes?" He asked the man sitting next to David who had orchestrated the game.

"I know of one who's a real looker," David, oblivious of who the question had been intended for, nodded, salivating at the large stack of winning chips and the cards he had just been dealt.

The Japanese man emitted a sound of acknowledgement, then concentrated on his cards.

As the game dragged on, David tried to bluff, sending his debt to well over one hundred dollars. The table fell silent as they laid down their hands. Once again, the man across from David drew the winnings into his mounting pile of chips.

David scribbled out the address for the Old Federal Reserve Building and promised the man he was now deeply in debt to, he would meet him there at ten the next morning to settle up.

"You no kid me. You be there." His firm voice matched his look.

"Sure," David assured him as he stood to go. "Well, someone will have to take my place and watch out for this guy." He jokingly jabbed a finger toward the winner.

His opponent smiled back, but his eyes were hard and deadly.

David made his way down the street, pulling his coat collar up around his neck to keep the cold mist at bay. What was it about that man he could not place? Where had he seen him before? Without hesitating, David edged down the alley, slipped behind some crates of decomposing vegetables, and waited. No one approached or followed him. He waited several minutes more, and, just as he was about to step out, he saw a shadow stop at the entrance of the alley. The man with the scarred hand approached out of the misty darkness. The way he walked, the bow of his legs, caught David's attention. Startled, he remembered the alley behind the Flower Market and the men who had gathered there. He had been one of them. David held tight, not breathing, not wanting the heat of his breath to mingle with the cool air and signal his whereabouts.

Finally, the shadow turned and moved on.

Sweat poured down David's forehead. Why had he drunk so much? He staggered, weak-kneed, toward the street. Where was he going to get that money? The damn Jap would kill him. An idea floated before him. He headed in the opposite direction than his shadow had taken and burst into a run.

Jack's car bumped down the hill in the midmorning light. Billi sat silently beside him, clutching her pillow. It felt lighter now. She had placed the diamond ring in the top right-hand drawer of Jack's desk without his knowing. She did not want the ring and the unfulfilled promise it held. She wanted only her memories and hoped her mother would forgive her.

"Billi, thank you for helping my sister. I don't know what you told her, but it worked." When she didn't answer, he continued. "We are so close to figuring out Akio's intentions. But your safety is most important."

"I see." She turned toward the side window. "You haven't found David."

"We heard he lost big time last night in a card game. We have some of our people in some of the hot gambling clubs around town."

"Where are we going?" She sat upright, noting they were heading south, not north toward the city.

"I have to ask a few questions and thought it best to have you along."

"Me or Ginger?" She attempted to remain aloof.

"Ginger."

"But I'm not dressed for Ginger."

"Ginger on a good day." He smiled, obviously trying to lighten the mood.

They continued on in silence, and she relaxed watching the oaks and scrub they passed.

Jack once again attempted conversation. "What do you miss most?"

"Climbing my tree," she spoke softly, not really registering her answer.

"I have one to show you that will knock your socks off."

They had pulled down a street that led toward long buildings of yellow stone with scalloping arches under red roofs. The traffic started and stopped, which seemed an unusual back up for a Sunday morning. It could not be churchgoers at this hour. Billi quickly concluded these cars were filled with other worshipers. As they stepped from their cars, the young, energetic crowd carried blankets and some had a thermos.

"What? A football game? We're going to a football game?" She regarded him incredulously.

"No. But I'd love to. We're playing Santa Clara. You know we beat your Huskies last week. And we're hoping to win the Rose Bowl again this season."

He sounded smug with his knowledge. "We?" Her eyebrow arched in his direction.

"Welcome to Stanford, my dear." He pulled into a space reserved for a professor and looked over at her.

She looked around at the sea of moving bodies as they passed stately buildings. Across one of the main buildings, full-figured, white statues stood high above on pedestals against the yellow brick, looking down at those arriving. Billi nodded at the statue holding paper and writing quill. The sculptures set the tone for all students.

As Jack and Billi exited the car, her attention shifted from the trail of sports enthusiasts to the tall tree that rose before them.

"El Palo Alto," Jack announced with true reverence. "This tree is like our mascot. Isn't it grand?"

"If I say yes, does that make me a traitor?"

"Not in my book." Jack had moved closer, and she could feel him behind her as they almost touched. They stood like that for a brief moment before he took her elbow and started her toward the yellow stone arches crowned with red tiles. They headed down dizzying paths of red and white squares that mimicked each other. It became cool beneath the dark, wooded ceiling of the pathways, and Billi tried to take in the many designs and details of the relief that graced the solid pillars and the competing stonework of the curved openings. She unexpectedly felt a bit awkward, realizing the extent of this massive university that sprawled over hundreds of acres.

She looked up at Jack. His step lightened. He seemed comfortable, at ease, at home. She had never asked him any questions about his time on this campus and wanted to start again at the beginning with him. To feel free to do just that—explore each other, not from the side of fear, but that of friends and possibly more. She relaxed her arm into his grip and let him take her where he would.

"Here." He stepped under a large alcove and stood at the base of a set of stone stairs that curved around a tall sandstone wall and disappeared above into the archway of a landing. He took her up a few steps, past a small white-trimmed window that created a peak at the top like those that graced a church. "I'm heading up there, and I want you to go back down and walk past this opening." He pointed to the walkway they had just left.

"Okay." Billi shrugged, hurried back down the stairs, and retraced her steps toward the front of the building. Then she marched past the arch to the stone stairway.

"Can you see me?" he called, his voice echoing from above.

She back tracked into the shaded opening of the archway and looked up. She shifted to the far right, then left. "Are you still there?"

A student walked by, and she turned toward him and smiled innocently. He kept walking past her with a slight nod. When she turned back around, she bumped into Jack's chest.

He caught her in his arms. "Watch it there." He stepped back letting her go.

"What were you doing?"

"Could you see me?'

"No."

"I didn't think so. So who was he waiting for?"

"Who?"

"Akio."

She took a moment to register. "So you knew him when you were a student here?"

Jack took a deep breath before answering. "We were roommates." He let that sink in before continuing. "One night I followed Akio from our room. He had said he was headed for the gym, but then he turned abruptly and started back toward me. I ran up there and hid. When I heard his feet move across the stone again, I looked out, but never knew if he saw me. So if he couldn't see me, especially in the dark, what made him turn back?"

"Where do you think he went?"

Jack was intent on his memories. "He went to the engineering building. I followed him inside, and he spoke with someone in Japanese. But I never found out who."

"Did he make it to the gym?"

"Yes. Later I stood in the shadows watching him practice with his big sword. He was masterful as he worked his routine."

"He was practicing strategy. You can only fight the way you practice."

"Very good. *The Book of Five Rings*. I came to realize that when…" He gazed past her, down the quad toward the distant buildings that seemed to overlap each other.

"Have you read it?" She was taken aback by the turn of events. "I thought you hated the Japanese."

"I respect them as competitors. But I resent them for their brutality."

He looked down at her again, and she felt her throat go dry. There had to be more to the story, but she knew he guarded it, for the memory of the incident had turned him to stone.

In the distance, a clock proclaimed the hour as it chimed twice.

"Was this your dorm then?" She walked back past the many arches that created a covered breezeway and stepped under the main entry of Toyon Hall. It resembled a small Spanish courtyard. He followed her into the enclosed yard where the path circled a pleasing fountain. The arches repeated across three wooden doors with columns on either side. Jack held a heavy door for her, and she stepped onto the highly polished red stone of the foyer. Again, the arch repeated over a solid wooden door at the end of a set of three massive columns. She heard their shoes mark their path as they passed into the high ceiling room where six black wrought-iron chandeliers hung. Soft light reflected across long hardwood tables and floors through the thin, high coved windows. Everything spoke of wealth, tradition, and the importance of camaraderie.

"What kind of fraternity is this?" she whispered.

"I hate to disappoint you, but this hall is for social use only. Toyon is a gentleman's eating club of sorts. I did not want to pledge the big houses. Not my kind of people. But I needed good meals and wanted to meet students from other countries."

Billi moved toward the hearth, set into a wide cream colored wall, the central focus of the room, as she tried to piece together what he had told her.

"Oh, I see. That's how you got to know Akio?"

"At first it was interesting being his roommate. But I came to learn he had many secrets, and I took it upon myself to find out what they were." He rubbed his jaw below his bad eye as he watched her.

She turned back toward him. "How did you do?"

"I'm still working on it. Come on." He led the way back outside and further into the campus. Ahead of them, a burst of loud cheering filled the air.

"Touchdown." Jack snickered.

"Whose side?" She shot back.

That got a laugh from the man beside her, rare, and deep, and full of life. She liked the sound of his laugh and the way it made her feel.

They strode across the campus to the Green Library. The imposing structure looked more like a church, a holy place for books.

She stopped for a moment to look up at the three expansive lead-glass windows over the doors. Above each entrance, life-sized images were carved in bas-relief. She concentrated on the middle figure displaying a gentleman with his long beard and Merlin-style hat reading from an oversized book. Her gazed fell on the two smaller figures below the book. They faced each other. One represented death, the other a young maiden who stood naked with a chalice dangling in her hand. Billi shifted as a chill ran through her. She hoped the figures did not symbolize things to come. She remembered her close experience when her drink had been tampered with.

"Are you okay?" Jack stood staring up at the building, apparently trying to figure out what had caught her attention.

"Do you believe in signs?" she asked in earnest.

"Only the good ones."

"Right, Mr. Sunshine. I'll remember that." She started up the steps without him.

As they entered the building, Jack removed his hat and then led her to a room on the second floor where a group of Japanese students sat at two long tables. There were about twenty-two gathered, all men except for one young woman, her head bent over her book.

Jack bent down toward Billi and spoke softly. "Good. They're still here."

"Who are they?" Billi watched them interact as they spoke quietly amongst themselves, at what appeared to be a study session. She quickly perceived the one who seemed to be in charge.

"The Japanese Students Association." Jack started for them and Billi fell in behind.

"Hello." Jack smiled as if aware his appearance put some ill at ease. "Is Ichio here?"

The one who had stood out to Billi as the leader nodded in their direction.

"I am Ichio." His English held just a slight accent of his homeland. Billi guessed he had practiced his English very hard to accomplish that.

"I'm Jack, class of '37." Jack nodded back and spun his hat in his hand. "And this is Ginger."

"It is a pleasure to meet you." Ichio stood, intently watching the intruders.

"Does anyone here know a former brilliant student named Akio Sumiyoshi?"

The young woman's head snapped up at the name and her eyes blinked with apparent fear.

A handsome young man in glasses spoke softly without emotion in the clip of his Japanese language. "Who is this man? Does he understand us?"

Jack shot a perplexed look toward the man who had just spoken.

Another man smiled from the far end as he sat back in his chair. "I don't think so. But do not say anything just in case."

"Sorry." Jack twirled his hat again. "What did he say?"

"He said we do not know of such a man."

Billi listened, acutely aware Ichio lied in his translation.

"He was my roommate in Toyon Hall and I've been trying to reach him." Jack smiled again.

"Oh, Toyon Hall, yes good food there."

"Yes, Akio never missed a meal. That was for sure. When all this embargo business is over, I want to be the first to expand my business to Japan, and Akio told me if I ever needed help to contact him."

"What business?" The one with the glasses asked in English.

"My father started a bank years ago." Jack's answer came across as strong and convincing. "With lots of investments that are paying heavily. So I'm looking to expand. Besides, I would like to see your country."

"Your father was wise." The one leaning back then changed to Japanese as he continued. "But I do not think his son is so smart."

Billi held her distance observing the young woman hunched over her book. Her hand shook as she turned the page.

"Well, I'll be around for a few days and will check in with you again next Sunday in the event something turns up about my buddy Akio. Thanks." Jack put his hat back on his head and took Billi's elbow and they slowly started for the door.

Behind them the voices were still audible.

"I have not heard of this Akio," another claimed.

"Keep it that way." Came the voice of the man with the spectacles. "Masago, you must not do that again." His spoke harshly.

"She did nothing." Another spoke.

"Let us get back to our studies," Ichio commanded as Billi and Jack crossed to the top of the stairs.

"Wait a minute." Billi looked around. "I'll meet you downstairs."

She headed for the women's room, and she heard Jack's hard soles on the stairs as he descended. Inside the small room, she took out her lipstick and waited by the mirror. Her hunch paid off. A crying Masago pushed the door open and stood frightened looking at Billi.

"Hi, honey. Well, come in and close the door. I never was much for books." She smiled at Masago as she timidly entered. "How ya doin'? Ya sure did look upset when my boyfriend said that Akio name."

"It is not a nice name. It brings back memories that are unpleasant." Her eyes were trained on the floor.

"Oh, so ya knew this guy, huh?" Billi puckered her lips to apply the lipstick she held.

"I cannot speak of him. It is dangerous."

"He can't get ya here. He's in Japan somewhere, ain't he? That's why Jack is trying to find him. Promised to take me there."

"He has tentacles everywhere." Her head came up, and she watched Billi apply her makeup. "Do not look for him. He no longer respects this country."

"How do you know so much?" She smiled with her bright red lips.

"He killed my sister." A single tear slid down her cheek now, taking the same damp path the others had made.

Billi wanted to take her in her arms and hold her. "Why?"

"I cannot speak of this. Warn your boyfriend." She turned to go, but Billi caught her arm.

"Wipe your tears first, darlin'. And if we can help you, find Jack Huntington. He's a good man."

Billi patted Masago's arm as she slipped out the door.

Jack lingered outside in the sunshine and Billi caught up with him. They set out in a different direction as Billi filled Jack in on her exchange with the frightened Masago.

"Okay, so someone in that group knows he's around." Jack kept a swift pace as they headed toward more buildings in the distance.

"Yes, the older one."

"I'll have someone check, but my best guess is he's navy, sent to do reconnaissance."

"At a university?" Billi's voice reflected her disbelief.

"Many have been sent here to learn English."

They walked in silence listening to the occasional announcements over the PA system as the game progressed.

Billi spotted what appeared to be a bathhouse and lifeguard stand. "Is that a lake?"

"You bet. You have Lake Washington, we have Lake Lagunita. But no time for a swim," he put in quickly.

"I hate you, Jack Huntington."

He just smiled in return. "Ah, Ginger. I'm not that bad."

They reached one of the faculty residences, and Jack knocked on the door. A short, white-haired gentleman holding a pipe opened the door.

"We're here to meet Dr. Wilbur." Jack had his hat off and spoke with respect as if he were once again a student seeking a professor's advice, and this made Billi smile.

"Come in. Huntington, isn't it?" The professor looked up at him over the rim of his glasses.

"Yes, Professor Borglund. I didn't think you would remember."

"Do you still like the works of Edgar Guest?"

"'Give me the house whose toys are seen, The house where children romp, And I'll happier be than man has been 'Neath the gilded dome of pomp.'"

"Excellent." The older man adjusted his spectacles further up his nose and glanced at Billi. "I don't believe we've met."

"No." She blushed.

"Hello." This came from a tall man who appeared behind Professor Borglund. "I'm President Wilbur. Please come in."

They hovered in the modest living room with a brick fireplace centered beneath two small white reliefs of medieval figures. Two high-backed armchairs faced each other, while a sofa and table vied for the remaining space against the surrounding bookshelves.

Wilbur waved his long arm toward the chairs. "Have a seat."

"This is my friend…Ginger." Jack cleared his throat.

"How do you do?" Billi lowered demurely into a chair.

"If you will excuse me. I have some reading to catch up on. Good to see you again." Borglund picked up a book and shuffled into the other room.

Jack took a seat across from Wilbur. "Thank you for taking the time to meet with me. You may remember my roommate was Akio Sumiyoshi. I was wondering what you could tell me about him."

"Yes, well, quite the interesting bloke." Wilbur crossed his long legs. "I am certain you are aware that in the beginning, Akio spent a great deal of time with Toshio Miyazaki, who attended Stanford under the name of Mr. Tanni. Rather embarrassing situation to find a Lieutenant Commander of the Imperial Japanese Navy in our midst operating as a spy. Once his true identity was revealed Mr. Tanni or Miyazaki fled back to Japan. That was when we found Akio a new place of residence. You were hand selected as the best candidate as we knew the depth of your moral character and your allegiance to America. We didn't think you would mind."

"No." Jack tried his question again. "Do you know how I can locate him?"

"Is there a reason? I know you had some difficulty with him at the end."

"Just business. I was thinking of expanding some of my investments to Japan, and he had offered to help."

"Not great timing possibly with the rumors of war and all." Wilbur sat, still waiting.

"Maybe, but it might be worth investigating, always looking forward." Jack put his hat over his knee and leaned in toward Wilbur. Billi bit her lip at the blatant tug of war as the two locked gazes in silence.

Wilbur drummed his fingers on the arm of the chair and finally spoke. "Did you ask at the Japanese Student Association?"

"Yes, they don't know of him."

"I see." He did not come across as convincing. "Well, I really don't know where he is or how to reach him. Is there somewhere I can reach you if that changes?"

Jack produced a business card from his pocket and wrote his office number on it before handing it to Wilbur.

"Thank you." Wilbur analyzed Jack's card that claimed he worked for a law firm. "If I hear of anything, I'll call."

"Have you ever heard of a Professor Fujihara? Did he ever visit here?"

"I don't recall that name. Maybe check the yearbooks and the Student Association photos. I'm actually headed to Japan for the holiday."

"What of the rumors you just spoke of?"

"Professors don't listen to drums of war. Besides, I have several old students to visit."

"Well, if you do hear something, just let me know. I think we could both make money, and that equates to more donations for Stanford."

Billi watched Wilbur's eyes light up at the mention of fund raising had hit home.

"Marvelous." He rose, extending his hand toward Jack, signaling the meeting had adjourned.

Outside, Jack put his hand on the small of Billi's back. "One more stop."

"I'm hungry," Billi blurted in revolt.

"Two stops then."

He guided her to another set of houses on Alvarado Row. These craftsman-style double homes were not in keeping with the stately stone structures of the rest of the campus. Each entrance was positioned on opposite ends of the one building under large, covered porches.

Again Jack removed his hat, ever the respectful student, before knocking on the front door. "Professor Niles, please," he said to a man who answered and nodded, then ushered them into the living room.

They sat quietly waiting until a younger professor entered. He wore tortoiseshell glasses and a serious look.

"May I help you?" he asked, extending his hand.

"Thank you for your time." Jack stood and shook his hand.

Jack's request was brief, as was Niles's response. Within minutes he led them out the door and back across the courtyards toward the modest building that housed the engineering department.

Inside, Billi trailed a bit behind, admiring the heavy machinery. She shivered a bit at the cool temperature of the two-story building, before hurrying to catch up.

"Yes, I do remember Akio's scribbling. He was fixated on building a model airplane with interesting wings. Ones that looked like they would disappear," Niles informed them as he led them to a classroom. "I had a hard time getting him to do his required work. But I would find them in here working at odd hours."

"Them?" Jack held the door for Billi as they entered the stark room with chalkboards covered with lines and numbers.

"That other Japanese fellow." The professor had gone directly to his file cabinets and pulled out the middle drawer.

"Toshio Miyazaki?" Jack's voice went flat.

"Yes. I don't know why I kept this. I found it on the floor by pure accident one morning and just thought it interesting. Perhaps I hoped that someday I would further the design."

They leaned in as the professor chose the manila folder labeled "Future Projects, Personal" and lifted it from the file. He selected a piece of paper with flattened creases, indicating it had once of been scrunched into a tight ball, and handed it to Jack.

Jack spread the drawing down on one of the long steel desks. "Could this work?"

"Possibly. I just don't know how you would use such a craft."

"May I keep this and return it to you later?" Without hesitation Jack worked the paper into a neat square.

The professor of engineering gave him a quizzical look, then shrugged. "I suppose so."

THIRTY-NINE

T HE STIMULUS OF WORKING CLOSELY WITH JACK and viewing parts of his past still pumped through Billi. They had grabbed a quick hot dog outside the stadium as the crowd cheered and moaned from time to time. Billi watched Jack's attempt to appear as if he didn't care as they waited for the announcer to call the score. The voice streaming overhead claimed that Stanford Indians were clobbering their Santa Clara rivals.

"I'm pinning my hopes on Santa Clara," Billi spoke between bites. "Revenge for Stanford beating my Huskies last weekend."

"Never happen." Jack squinted at her, cementing the challenge, and bit savagely into his hot dog.

As the announcer's voice broke over the cheering crowd, Billi's shoulders sank.

"Another touchdown for the home team. That makes it twenty-seven for the Indians, and seven for the Broncos. With only five minutes left in the last quarter, it's looking pretty bad for the—"

"Want to hear more?" Jack smiled from ear to ear.

"There's always next time." She tossed her wrapper in the garbage. "Don't stand there and gloat," she threw over her shoulder, heading toward the car. "We have work to do."

And that's why he found himself falling in love with her, Jack reasoned as he watched her walk away. She was feisty, direct, and smart. He eyed the sway of her skirt and thought of her other attributes as well.

WHILE DRIVING BACK TO THE CITY that overlooked the bay, they speculated about what they had unearthed. Her pillow, which had now become a symbol of home and safety for Billi, sat between them on the car seat. Like a beacon of hope and memories of loved ones, it rested there, reminding her of the depth of her deceit toward Eileen and the Japanese culture she loved. How could she face her best friend after all of this? The fan was now the only object in its secret compartment. She lightly touched the pillow and prayed for strength.

Just past ten that evening they drew close to the downtown area, and Billi felt her stomach tighten. There had been no declaration of war from either side. Hope remained.

"Better get down." Jack's voice sounded almost remorseful.

She slid down the seat. Had it only been twenty-four hours since she had left the city as she now returned to it, hidden from sight? She comprehended the extent of her exhaustion. But more than that, she tasted fear. For the first time, she was actually scared. She would be alone soon. She would have to leave Jack, and that made her even more nervous. Especially with a new emotion emerging: She had grown fond of being with him. War had already claimed two innocent men. What if Jack became the next victim?

She saw the darkness and felt the coolness as the car slid down the small delivery garage of the Sir Francis Drake Hotel. They hurried to the elevator and waited in silence. As the large glossy doors closed, Jack inserted his special key into the lock and pressed the mezzanine button. The elevator rose briefly, and the doors slid open to reveal a thick, velvet curtain. When Jack pushed them aside, he opened the glass door and let Billi go first as he switched on the only light—a bare bulb that hung unceremoniously from a long cord in the center of the small room. The walls were all concrete, cold and stark. Empty shelves were the only decoration aside from a mail chute that snaked down the length of one wall, carrying letters to the lobby. Jack pointed to the scribbled names surrounding the light switch, former visitors, he explained, to this hidden room. He crossed to a table and picked up the phone, offering Billi a chair.

"We're here. Any updates?" He leaned against the table and waited.

As the person on the other end of the line spoke, Jack turned his back to Billi. The news, she deduced, could not be good.

"Thanks."

He hung up the receiver and dropped to his knees. He hovered over the small brass peephole and bent close enough for his good eye to look through it. He sat back and motioned for Billi to do the same. She followed suit, kneeling beside him, and crouched over the small observation hole. She found she looked down on the hallway for the elevators off the main lobby. The tops of heads and hats were visible as unsuspecting guests waited for the ride to their floor.

"What is this place?" she whispered.

"Don't worry. You don't have to whisper. No one can hear you in here. During Prohibition, this is where they kept the booze for the customers. The hotel always claimed it had one bottle per guest. They would deliver it in suitcases at the dock we drove into. And guys dressed as bellhops would carry it into this storage room, then deliver it as requested."

"But weren't they raided?"

"As you can see, they always knew when the Feds were around."

"But you're a Fed. How did you find out?"

"My father lent some of the money to build this hotel. However, the crafty architect did not include this space on his drawings."

The elevator sounded a double ring as it arrived and Jack opened the door for Duckworth.

"Be certain she makes it home safe. And stay there until you are positive." Jack's instructions held no doubt of his concern.

She stepped inside the car and looked back at Jack. He cloaked his emotions behind a stern face and merely nodded. To her surprise, the elevator began to climb. Then Duckworth rang the elevator bell twice, and the car stopped. He used a special key to unlock a panel concealed in the woodwork of the elevator; it opened into the other elevator. They stepped into the adjacent compartment, and Duckworth closed and locked the hidden panel. He pressed the lobby button, and the elevator started down. If they were ever followed, she now knew they could escape. For some reason the knowledge did not feel any better and she pulled her pillow closer.

NOVEMBER 14 HAD ARRIVED and nothing had changed. Each day Jack spent hours in the secret room making calls back East, gathering information. America held strong to its isolationist beliefs. Meanwhile,

Roosevelt made more demands of the Japanese to withdraw from Indochina, steadily reinforcing US troops in the Philippines, and assuring the American public there would be no war.

The frightening timeline closed around him. If Akio's men had been telling the truth, the "Christmas presents" supposedly arriving from offshore, were just weeks away. More devastating to his plan remained the fact that there were fewer than four days before Billi got on the train back to Seattle to celebrate Thanksgiving with her mother. He wasn't certain he could convince her to return.

Billi had willingly shared her letter with him, the pure innocent ones from her mother and Eileen and the somewhat disturbing ones from Eddy.

He picked up Eddy's letter again and reread it.

> Hi, Bil,
>
> Crazy times in paradise. I love being stationed at Kane'ohe. It could not be more beautiful. The steep ridge of the Pali rises above us, a sheer sheet of green. I like driving over the ridge and down into Honolulu. And the way back to base is breathtaking.
>
> Too bad you don't see that monster with the one eye anymore. I just know he works for the FBI. I could put a chill in his step with what I am seeing. No one is paying attention to the subs that are out in the waters offshore. No way of knowing whose they are. Furthermore, radar, the baby of Britain, is not being utilized as much as it should be on our shores.
>
> I know you do not understand, but Ray is an even bigger hero to me than you can imagine. What he believed in I have come to realize is the only hope we have if there is a war. I fly for you, Mom, Dahlia, Danny, and for Peace.
>
> And when I am up there, I hear Ray. He keeps me in check, which is a first! So, I hope you can move forward and find someone else to love.
>
> Sorry your job is so boring. Maybe you could visit me here? I've enclosed a travel brochure.
>
> Kiss Mom when you see her.

Jack knew he missed something in what Eddy said. The fact Eddy had figured him for a Fed didn't bother him, but that the kid was correct. Lips remained sealed about the sub sightings. He had questioned as many higher-ups as he could. Something had to change soon.

DARKNESS BEGAN TO SETTLE AROUND DAVID as he stood across the street from The Geary Street Cleaners. He had been waiting for this moment. He watched the man he owed the money with a scar on his hand. He was speaking with another short Japanese man wearing glasses whose storefront claimed "Cleaning, Pressing Repairing." Finally, he bowed slightly to the man he spoke with and then strode toward a dark car up the street.

David pulled his coat collar tighter against his neck and set his plan in motion. He quickly caught up to the stout Asian, but before he could speak, he found himself forced to the ground.

"You lie to me, worthless dog." His scarred hand lifted David and dragged him toward the car.

"Wait, I have something you want." David put his hands up to deflect another blow. He landed in the back seat, blood trickling down his forehead, as the car streaked away.

The car stopped and David recognized the dark alley behind the Flower Market just steps from the room where he had been in hiding for the past month. His attacker pulled him from the car, and David slumped at his feet amid bits of discarded flower heads and petals that trailed to the overflowing garbage cans. He watched as the Japanese man extracted a long sword from the trunk and placed the blade against his cheek.

"What you have for me?" he snarled as he leaned close David.

"The girl." David almost whimpered.

"What girl?"

"The whore with blue eyes."

"Ginger?" The blade shifted slightly.

"Yes, Ginger. In exchange for the money I owe you," David looked up at him now, not certain what name Billi went by, "you can have her for one night."

The black eyes of the other man blinked. David kept his head up, his senses alert for any movement, hoping he had convinced him.

"You lie to me once," he responded gruffly.

"No. She is a good whore."

Emitting something in his guttural language, he pulled his sword away, leaving a small cut on David cheek. "Where?"

David rose. "For one night and then I owe you nothing?"

They stood close. The streetlight reflected off the blade as it slightly shifted in the scarred hand.

"Do we have a deal?" David's voice became stronger in mock bravery.

"You show me Ginger. Then we deal."

"Fair enough. Where should I bring her?" He held his breath, hoping the man would provide him a path to Akio.

"Here. Later tonight. I wait here after."

David did not wait to be told he could leave. He turned on his heel and walked toward the end of the alley where the occasional car passed by.

BILLI SAT AT HER REGULAR STOOL at the nightclub and spun the twist of lemon between her painted red fingernails, dunking it into the amber liquor of her Manhattan. They had changed the program to include a Japanese fan dance number in the hopes of attracting more Japanese men to the show. A few had arrived, but she did not recognize any of them from the growing file of photos Jack had been showing her.

Her thoughts drifted to Jack. She felt torn, pulled in unforeseen directions. Truly she wanted to return to Seattle but she did not want to abandon the quiet bond that had grown between them. She felt a tingle emerge at the thought of his touch. Yes, much had changed since their first meeting.

On the other hand, a deep burning fear tore through her. What would she tell Eileen? Her best friend could always read her mind and sense the unspoken. She created a variety of conversations in her mind and had settled on the most plausible when she spotted the first of the group of five Japanese men hit the top of the stairs and look directly at her. She held Akio's gaze, then looked at the bartender as she regrouped.

With the flair of the consummate host, Charlie Low led the five gentlemen to the side table they had occupied on the other occasions. Akio did not look in her direction but seemed to move with an air of frustration. Billi knew that Shirley Chow, the eccentric Chinese woman, would be placing a call right now to alert Jack that Akio had returned.

The music had not started. She watched the five men lean forward in heated discussion. Time slipped by, she needed to be at that table.

Billi picked up her drink and steered it toward the table with a sway of her hips that drew attention.

"Hey, where've ya been?" She stood across from Akio, lingering above Hatsuro, and smiled.

"Good evening, Ginger." Akio's grin held unabashed lust. "We are just finishing up business and then it will be time for pleasure."

"I can wait."

Charlie approached with a chair for her, and she squeezed in between Hatsuro and Ito. She leaned on the table and winked across at Akio.

"She is a brazen pig," Hatsuro's anger almost slurring his Japanese. "She would be better off headless. Then she would be silent."

The men smiled and nodded as Billi took the lemon twist from her drink and slowly nibbled it between her lush red lips.

Akio drummed his fingers on the table and responded in his dialect. "Ignore her for now. We will deal with the whore later."

"They will only send nine this far, and we are to be spread up and down the coast," Ito continued with the discussion. "I have asked permission to have the area where the oil refinery is."

"I will see to it. Do you have other reports from TO?" Akio turned his attention to Hatsuro.

He gulped before responding, obviously uncomfortable at his superiors glare. "Nothing. The head office seems to be mindless. I do not understand why we have organized such a spy network like TO if it does not keep us informed."

"One would think you would have learned to keep your lips sealed. You are a danger to us. You show no respect for your training. Do not let the Kempei tai hear you speak in such a manner," Ito hissed, his anger apparent at the younger man's inept espionage tactics. "You have lost the professor again?"

"He has disappeared and the drawing with him." Hatsuro's head drooped with his admitted failure.

Billi watched Akio's knuckles turn white as he squeezed his glass. "Yamamoto is showing interest in the drawing. I would hate to see it used against our shores."

In silence, the men waited for Akio to regain his composure and continue.

"Have you heard any more from Tak? Has he sent us the information about the ships I asked him to draw of the naval shipyard up North?"

At the mention of Tak's name, Billi's teeth clamped down on the lemon twist, and she tasted blood. It could not be the same Tak, Tak Nakamura, Eileen's brother, she reasoned as she pressed her tongue against the inside of her cheek where she had punctured the skin.

"His word is of little use. He is the one who lost the professor for us." Hatsuro, demonstrating his disgust, slammed his fist on the table.

Billi jumped and the men looked at her.

With eyes wide, she smiled and nodded toward Hatsuro. "I think he needs another drink."

Hatsuro turned red. "She has a simple mind that thinks only of play."

"I agree." Akio spoke in English as he sat back, his gaze fixed on her low neckline. "Shall we all have another?" He waved at the waiter before continuing in Japanese. "After Tak has supplied us with the information, the Black Dragon will see he pays for losing track of the professor. The drawing cannot fall into the wrong hands. If all goes as planned, we have just over three weeks before we strike. The first stage of attack will destroy our lazy friends while the second will be demoralizing, as our submarines will create fear up and down the coast. Then we secure our position as ruler. Now, let us think of play, like the whore."

The waiter arrived to take the order and Billi rose to excuse herself.

Akio cut her off. "Do not go far, Ginger. You are always disappearing. And that can make a man frustrated."

"Oh, are you stickin' around then tonight?" She placed her hand on her hip and smiled.

"Until we leave together, yes."

She winked. "Sounds good, honey."

Her knees were weak as she attempted to move nonchalantly toward the hall that led to the ladies' room. She had seen the threat in his eyes, the warning. She must keep her wits about her and, more importantly, her head where it belonged—on her shoulders.

She heard a chair scratch the floor behind her and quickly looked back. She instantly recognized the stout figure of the man following her. Hatsuro. She ducked through the door that led backstage and slipped into a dressing room. As she closed the door behind her, she faced four performers dressed in kimonos putting on their makeup. Wigs, not unlike Auntie Katsuko, perched on stands next to them.

The door burst open then closed behind her and in the mirror she saw Shirley Chow wobbling toward her on her crooked legs.

"He want you bad," she announced. "His eyes say so. Evil."

"I need to hide." Billi felt her nerves twist as the older woman acknowledged her fears.

"You dance." Shirley pointed at a kimono.

"What?" Billi looked at her incredulous.

"They do geisha number for Japanese men, simple dance. They say you know dance. You go on stage. Quick."

Her shrieking voice shouted in Chinese, instructing the other girls already in their kimonos and make up. Suddenly, several pairs of hands grabbed at Billi as they tucked her into an intricately designed orange robe. Her hands shook as she applied the white makeup to her face. Taking a long deep breath, she concentrated on the black lines she drew to elongate her oval eyes.

"Her eyes, they are too American." One of the girls stated as Billi turned to them in full attire, replete with a wig adorned with cherry blossoms.

Billi took the offered fan from Shirley's gnarled hand. "I just won't look up. Keep me in the background."

The door opened and Hatsuro stuck his head inside. He brazenly leered at the girls before uttering, "Sorry."

"Out," Shirley screeched and slammed the door on him. With her uneven gait, she moved her twisted legs toward Billi. "Do not fear him, just dance."

They lined up, shortest in front, Billi second to last before a young woman, Ann Lee. She looked down at the fan she carried, and her breath caught in her chest. Her hands. Her nails where flaming red. Shirley noticed it at the same time.

"Go." The older woman commanded, pushing her forward.

To the beat of the drums, the five floated onto the stage. Like the colors of the rainbow, soft shades of petals of delicate flowers, one by one they snapped open their fans. As they started the slow, rhythmic movements, Billi, eyes lowered, tried to mimic the dance. Exhaling long and slow, she let herself relax into the accustomed steps. Repeating the words *don't fear him, just dance*, she let the fan lead the way as she lost herself in the music.

The performance ended to resounding applause as the geishas danced off stage.

Shirley stepped from behind the screen as they all entered the dressing room and shifted her legs to Billi. "They look everywhere for you. But now he want someone new."

Billi sat, relieved. "Thank heaven."

"You too good," the old woman scolded. "I watched him. He now longs for geisha with red fingernails."

Billi stopped breathing. The other dancers looked at each other.

"What does he want?" Ann Lee asked.

"We give him more dance." Shirley clapped her hands.

Billi's lips began to quiver as she tried to catch her breath.

"No problem." Shirley leaned into Billi and grinned, exposing one missing tooth.

As Stanley Toy danced off stage, concluding his Fred Astaire-style performance, Charlie spoke into the microphone. "Well, since you seemed to enjoy our last visit to Japan, we thought we would bring our geisha girls back."

There were a few hoots and applause.

From behind the curtain, Billi saw Hatsuro leave the table and scurry toward the hall that led backstage. The music started and the girls shuffled onstage as the aggressive young man grabbed Charlie Low's arm.

Hatsuro did not lower his voice when he made his demand. "When the dance is over, we would be honored to have the geisha with the red nails join our table. She is most interesting."

Charlie waved toward the dancers on stage. "Which one?"

"The one with the…"

Hatsuro looked on speechless as the dancers opened their decorated umbrellas and held them high, their other hand gracefully moved through the air. Each one had nails painted fiery red.

"…the orange robe."

Billi heard his frantic shout and kept her back toward the wings, as she looked down at the lime green kimono she had traded with Ann Lee.

FORTY

LOUD SCREAMS FROM THE BACK of the audience broke into the music guiding the geishas. A loud thud followed as a chair hit the floor, and two men twisted as one as they fought. A gunshot rang out.

Billi looked up but saw nothing of the commotion through the bright lights. She quickly lowered her head and followed the rest of the girls offstage. She began to shake. Had Akio been watching her or had his eyes been trained on Ann Lee in the orange kimono? If he had seen her blue eyes, would he make the connection?

"Fire!" someone yelled, and the word could be heard repeated through the audience with growing panic.

The smell of smoke drifted from backstage. Staying close on Ann Lee's heels, Billi followed the line of other dancers as they rushed down the hall and pressed into the hysterical crowd. As one, they poured down the stairs like a stream of enraged bulls. In front of Billi, geisha wigs bobbed as the performers descended, distinguishable and eye-catching.

At the base of the steps stood Hatsuro. He grabbed at the geisha dancers as they passed. Billi worked the wig from her head as Hatsuro pawed at the orange kimono of Ann Lee. The sound of material ripping mingled with the voices of the frightened guests.

"You worthless bitch!" Hatsuro shouted. "You rip my jacket."

Billi ducked and, head bent, slipped past him, following the flow of people up Sutter Street. While she hurried along, she untied the obi and took off the kimono, wrapping the wig inside. As she pushed open the side door to the Sir Francis Drake Hotel, she saw a dark car slow across the street. She ran to the elevator and pressed the call button twice, then twice again, waiting for the far right elevator to arrive. She stood close to the shiny bronze doors watching her reflection, the startling contrast of the white paint and matted hair, when she heard footsteps rush up the stairs from the main hotel entrance around the corner. The elevator door slid open and she hurried inside, pushing the button for the nonexistent mezzanine as the doors closed. She gave the signal and prayed that Jack still waited inside the hidden room.

She let out her breath as the elevator stopped on the mezzanine level and the special glass door behind the thick curtain opened. She flew into Jacks arms, smearing her white face paint into his clean shirt.

"I think he saw me." She clung to him, trembling.

Jack gently held her away and examined her. She knew how horrible she looked and a tear rolled down her cheek, smudging her black eyeliner and white face paint. Her hair matted and pinned tight against her head felt damp. Yet, he looked at her as if he found her beautiful.

"Are they down there?" She trembled, pointing to the small lens that allowed them to spy on those waiting below. She fell to her knees and watched. Hatsuro stood at the elevators with an older couple, waiting. The three entered an elevator together.

Jack helped her up. "Don't worry. He can press mezzanine but the car will stop on the first floor."

"I'm sorry."

"Explain." He kept his voice impassive as he guided her to the wooden chair.

Billi sat and tugged at the ball of kimono on her lap as she told him everything she had heard about the submarines and what had led her to escape.

Jack took his clean handkerchief from his pocket and handed it to her. "You're heading home early."

She held his gaze, knowing he sacrificed his dream of discovering Akio's plans to save her.

"And what if I say no?" She felt her breath tighten as she decided she could not bear to leave Jack.

"You have no say."

DUCKWORTH CLOSED THE REAR CAR DOOR for Billi, then rounded to the driver's seat. Although the distance was but a mere two blocks around Union Square to Maiden Lane, they were not taking any chances. After Hatsuro had left the building, Jack had taken her up to his suite. She had washed her face and tried to comb her hair while repeating two more times the conversation she had overhead. Exhausted, she leaned against the backseat and closed her eyes as the car rocked away from the hotel.

She did not realize they had stopped and felt only the coolness of the night air as Duckworth opened her door. She sat up and stretched but then froze as the door slammed shut again. Adrenaline charged through her as she heard the unmistakable sounds of a struggle outside the car. She heard a throaty grunt followed by the thud of someone hitting the ground. Before she could move, a man slipped into the front seat, bringing with him the heavy scent of liquor.

"Hi, doll. Miss me?" David looked back at her, his smug smile making her want to vomit.

As they sped away, Billi looked back in time to see the still figure of Duckworth on the damp pavement.

"Where are you taking me?" She tried to determine the direction he steered the vehicle, but the mist intermittently blocked the view.

"I owe someone a bit a cash, but they'll take you in exchange." He laughed. "It pays to know a good whore."

"David, let me go." She edged toward the door behind him and had her hand on the handle, when he slammed on the breaks. He spun around, pointing a gun at her forehead.

"I wouldn't do that if I were you." He waved the gun. "Move to the middle. We're not far."

When he turned down an alley, Billi lunged for the door. David's shot just missed her, shattering the rear window. She scrambled out of the car.

At the sound of the bullet, the back door to the Flower Market opened slightly, and Billi raced toward the shaft of light. She immediately recognized the tall figure of Akio emerging and turned to run in another direction, but David grabbed her before she could pass.

She screamed and kicked at David. His hand met her face with such force she fell to the ground, landing on the broken stem of a discarded gladiola.

The light in a room down the alley went on as Akio stepped forward, his right hand behind his back.

"Where's that other guy?" David demanded. "She's his for one night. I'll wait here."

Two more men approached from the warehouse's back door. Billi recognized Hatsuro and Ito.

Hatsuro spoke in Japanese to the older man. "I told you the stupid drunk would bring her. Should we kill him now?"

"Patience," Ito commanded.

Billi looked at David in warning.

"Hey." David's words choked out as he seemed to size up the situation. He lifted his gun pointing it at the one with the scar on his hand. "You lied to me."

Those were the last words David spoke. His head separated from his body with the thwacking sound as Akio's sword claimed another. The gun rattled to the pavement as David's headless body swayed, then fell hard and fast just missing Billi.

Car lights bounced around the corner and hurried toward them.

Hatsuro reached for the screaming Billi as she climbed over David's fallen frame for the gun.

A bullet sailed over Billi's head and grazed Hatsuro's arm driving him backward into Akio.

"Drop it," came the deep voice from the far side of the car.

Slowly, Akio let his prized sword clatter to the ground.

"Now back away," the unseen man commanded.

The window with the light on down the block snapped open. "Hey." A man in suspenders leaned out, shouting, "I called police."

It presented enough of a distraction for the three Asian men to run toward the shaft of light from the open door. Shots rang out above their heads as they closed the door behind them.

Jack stepped out from behind the car and knelt next to David's' corpse. He checked his pockets and took the room key and wallet of the man no longer his problem. He picked up Akio's flamboyant weapon, admiring the embossed dragon designs on the blade, guard and pommel. He noted the color of the swords grip. Red, like blood. Testing the weight of the steel he approached the door with the bullet holes.

Duckworth helped Billi to her feet as she vomited on the back of the headless traitor.

Jack and Duckworth sat at the small table in Billi's cramped room, waiting. Finally, she emerged from behind the screen divider in her cotton robe. The hot water had mixed with tears as she had tried to wash away the images of the night.

"Can I have a drink?" She couldn't look up at the man who had saved her.

Jack poured her a stiff bourbon.

She took the drink and looked him in the eye. "You can't kill him, can you?"

"Not yet." He did not blink as he spoke the truth. "We are not to fire the first shot to start the war."

She worded her next question carefully. "How did you find me? Did you know he was there?"

"Thank David for that. We were suspicious after the first beheading, and David led us to the flower market which they were using as a cover."

Duckworth, the side of his face scraped where it had met the pavement, nervously picked at the petals stuck to the side of his shoe, remnants of a golden chrysanthemum.

"The flower of the emperor's seal and the Festival of Happiness," Billi mumbled observing his innocent behavior. "Happiness," her hollow voice repeated. She reached for the comfort of the homemade pillow, where Eileen had embroidered a golden mum, signifying happiness, as one of the four designs.

"Yes, happiness," Jack repeated. "I'm happy you're alive."

"He didn't see you, did he?" Billi watched him concerned.

"No. He hasn't figured that out yet."

"He did tonight. And we both know that." Her voice rose in exasperation. "One of the students at Stanford had to tell him we were there. He's put it together that you know me. He'll kill us both."

"Shhh." He reached for her, holding her close. "Remember, I'm a rich businessman looking for a Japanese investment."

"Who has a whore?"

"A smart, good-looking…" He didn't repeat her word but looked over her head at Duckworth. "Rest."

JACK LEFT DUCKWORTH WITH BILLI once she had fallen to sleep and stepped into the gathering fog, past the plainclothes policeman on guard. When he arrived back at the rear of the Flower Market, he walked inside, only to be stopped by Officer Hennessey.

"We found something that might interest ya, but we want what ya know too." Hennessey stood firm.

An "I'll do what I can" was all Jack offered in response.

"What the hell is going on?" The officer turned and motioned Jack to follow as he stepped toward the far wall.

Jack walked through a hidden opening in the warehouse wall the police had uncovered and followed a trail of blood to Market Street, where it abruptly stopped. Obviously, their car must have been parked at this spot. He would make certain all hospitals were checked for a man with his right arm sporting a gunshot wound. He wished he could have placed that bullet through Akio's heart, but he needed these Japanese men alive, for now.

The fog hampered his vision, but he could feel that Akio and his men were nearby. If this had become their killing grounds, then they would be between here and an escape route. The water, of course. He would have the ships checked and ask if there were any that were in port seeking oil or provisions. Oil, a much need commodity to keep their submarines plying American waters. Ito had mentioned the oil refinery in Los Angeles.

Jack's frustration at his inability to see the obvious drove him back through the Flower Market like a steam ship. The Embarcadero sat a few short blocks away, and then the piers. Fast and convenient. There was no point looking in this soupy fog. Akio had already slithered out of reach.

He took David's room key from his pocket and scrutinized its marking. He walked down the alley to the Bo-Chin Hotel. David's key opened room 217, in the back corner. In the darkness, Jack walked to the window overlooking the very alley he had just left, and for a brief moment wished that David still lived so he could answer the many questions forming in his mind.

He shut the door, flipped on the light switch, and sighed with disgust. Empty booze bottles were stacked up against one wall, while remnants of moldy food filled the garbage can. The sheets were twisted away from the dirty mattress. On the table sat a notepad, which Jack immediately put in his pocket. He opened the closet door and found two shirts and a pair of trousers hanging in the otherwise empty space. Beside a small suitcase he found a second pair of shoes. He turned them over, lifting them closer, and the distinctive scent of diesel fuel filled his nostrils. The docks. David had been spending time on the docks. He moved his hand across the small shelf above the few hanging garments and stopped at the feel of paper. He pulled down an envelope addressed to David at the Seattle office and stuffed it in his pocket with the notepad.

Leaving the room, he closed the door on the sad existence of the man he had grown to hate and asked for forgiveness. Hate only brought destruction. He hoped that David's uncle would forgive him for not taking better care of the wild boy he had placed under his wing. He shook his head considering the call he did not look forward to making.

FORTY-ONE

EDDY STOOD IN THE BRIGHT AFTERNOON SUN and watched the white-tipped waves break over the pearly sand of Kane'ohe Bay. As they skimmed over the glorious waters that morning there had been nothing to report. The south shores of Oahu and beyond held no hints of impending danger. Besides, everyone speculated Japan existed too far from these beautiful islands to be a threat. He thanked his lucky stars he had not been sent to the Philippines, a closer target, much easier to attack.

At the *beep, beep* of a car, he turned to see Sam and Scooter waving. Right on time. He hopped in, and as the three drove toward the winding road that snaked up the Pali, Scooter patted the dashboard of his new prize. The rusted car lunged forward, as if responding.

"My dad would be all tied in knots if he saw this jalopy. He'd say I didn't spend his money well in my investment." The sarcasm in Scooter's voice revealed the spite of his action.

"At least it runs," the youthful Sam pointed out. "An' give me a minute with it and I can fix that stutter in the engine."

The wind seemed to push them up the hill into the glaring sunshine. As they emerged on the other side of the steep terrain, the thick foliage provided coolness with the soothing sea spreading before them.

The radio flickered in and out as Scooter banged on the dash, attempting to sing along.

"Please." Eddy laughed. "Let's wait until we get there and the real entertainers perform for us."

"So, who is this gal's mother, Eddy?" Sam asked for the tenth time, not believing their good luck to be invited to a luau hosted by locals.

"Lani's mother is a well-known singer and dancer here in the islands. And you two can thank me wholeheartedly for getting us invited to this social event. It's Mrs. Daniels's birthday, and everyone who is anyone, that excludes you two, is going to be there."

"Daniels doesn't sound Hawaiian." Scooter navigated a corner as he spoke, heading them up a slope overlooking Pearl Harbor.

"That's her married name. Lani said her mom is Japanese Hawaiian, and her father is Portuguese Hawaiian. Enough to get Lani through Kamehameha School, which is only for those with the real island blood flowing through their veins."

Sam whistled at his newfound knowledge. "Ain't that somethin'."

"What's her father like?" Scooter slowed the car so Eddy could read the signs.

"Very successful with pineapples." He skirted his fear of meeting the man who held the key to his future happiness.

"Geeze, Eddy. How'd ya do it?" Sam, whose sheltered youth seemed to explode in the islands, eagerly leaned forward from the backseat.

"Just stick with me, kid." Eddy checked the number on the invitation Lani had personally handed him. "That one there." He pointed to a house that appeared to be three levels of glass windows tucked into the side of the hill.

The kid whistled again as he leaned out the window. The line of cars parked up the driveway leading to the lush green lawn surrounded by reds, yellows, pinks, and whites of the flowers in bloom displayed an impressive array of wealth.

"Best behavior, boys, and Lani is mine," Eddy warned as they stepped from the rusty vehicle.

"I thought ya had a gal back home," Sam protested.

"When in Rome…" Eddy removed his Kimmel, adjusted his shirt, and shot up the driveway, invitation in hand.

"What does that mean?"

Scooter answered for Eddy. "Just watch us closely and don't drink too fast. Come on."

The trio waited outside the front door with a pattern of pineapples hand-carved across its massive bulk.

As the door opened a hefty man stared down at the three sailors, his dark eyes suspicious.

"Aloha." A light voice sang out from behind the hulk of man, who instantly held the door wide and welcoming.

Lani swayed toward Eddy. Her long, black hair held back over her right ear by a single gardenia, on the right side indicated her single status. The delicate bloom complementing the blue and white Hawaiian print of her holoku dress made Eddy's chest tighten. The fitted garment with the slight train and short sleeves left nothing to the imagination of the glory of her bronze, sculptured figure. Her features were soft with the distinctive dark Asian eyes of her Japanese grandfather.

She draped a lei over his head and kissed him on both cheeks. "Good evening, sailor, and welcome." She added a playful smile.

"I would not have missed this for the world." His sincerity made her blush.

"What about us?" Scooter questioned from behind Eddy, breaking the magic moment.

"Don't mind them, they followed me here." For that comment Eddy received a nudge from Scooter. "Okay. Scooter and Sam, meet Lani Daniels, the pearl of the island."

"Ain't we gettin' leis?" Sam barely spoke aloud.

"Of course." Lani pulled her attention from Eddy and started toward the two anxious sailors.

"But no kisses." Eddy hurried behind to ensure she follow his command.

His two buddies stood sporting their leis in rapt awe as she gently brushed kisses on each of their cheeks.

"Now be gone." Eddy waved his friends toward the expansive lawn where a crowd gathered around a table laden with food. Beyond, seated on a makeshift stage, musicians strummed their guitars and ukuleles, creating the soothing sound born of the islands.

Smiling, Lani extended her hand toward Eddy. He felt his pulse quicken as they touched, and he let her lead him in the opposite direction, toward the outside patio. They stood overlooking the deep green that sloped toward Pearl Harbor, Ford Island, and the sea beyond. The exquisite view of the naval base below, with the ships nestled in their slots and the aircraft carriers at anchor, was a powerful sight. Eddy felt proud.

"Mother wants to meet you." Lani's brown eyes looked up at him from below dark lashes.

"Well, I would like to meet the birthday girl and wish her the best." Eddy, transfixed by the woman beside him, touched her arm.

"Okay." She smiled before turning and he willingly followed the movements of her hips.

Mrs. Daniels's almond eyes were smiling when they approached. Her black hair sat piled high on her head, a red-and-yellow lei draped down her red-and-white patterned gown. Eddy easily recognized the source of Lani's curves.

"A-lo-ha." Dorothy Daniels spoke as if singing, drawing out the three syllables to their fullest.

"It is a pleasure to be here to celebrate your birthday. Thank you." Eddy snapped his feet together and half-bowed.

"I see Lani has not exaggerated your charm. It is my pleasure to meet her friends." She continued watching him closely. "We have people in Seattle."

Eddy blinked, uncertain if her comment held a subtle threat or showed knowledge of the region. "That's what I understand. And hopefully you will visit someday, and my mother and I can have you over for tea." He hoped the offer demonstrated his desire to spend time with her daughter.

"Go." Her hand rose gracefully through the air. "Enjoy some pig and poi. Later we will dance and maybe talk story."

"Sounds wonderful."

Eddy attempted not to sweat as Lani kissed her mother's cheek. She steered him toward the steaming fire pit as she explained the day-long process of preparing the pit. Hours earlier, men had stuffed hot rocks inside the cavities of the pig, placed it on smoldering coals, then covered the sizzling meat with banana stumps and leaves, taro leaves, and moist burlap. The final step, cover the mound with earth. As they watched, the strong cooks, wearing their festive lavalavas, began the ritual of unearthing the succulent pig. The long fronds of green had charred brown and the smoke held the heavy aroma of the cooked pork.

"Who has my daughter?" A deep voice came from behind them and Eddy felt the muscles down his back tighten.

Lani swung around and skipped to the imposing man who stood holding a short cigar between his white teeth. His floral-designed aloha shirt matched the red-and-white pattern of his wife's, complete with a red-and-yellow lei. He loomed tall, robust, and definitely in charge. His dark hair, fruit of his Portuguese and Hawaiian mixture, slightly grayed at the temples. He held a drink that he rattled while he eyed Eddy.

"Hello, sir." Eddy's hand went out immediately. "Thank you for the invitation."

"I had nothing to do with it." He took a sip, broke into a smile, and squeezed Eddy's hand as he shook it. "Where's your drink, sailor?"

"All in due time, sir." Eddy could feel the sweat drip down his back again.

"Well, come with me and I'll make it time." Ben Daniels insisted, then wrapped his arm around Eddy's shoulders and walked him toward the bar.

Eddy accepted the pressure of the large man's weight and knew enough not to try to break free. Obviously, the man that gripped him intended on having a word, and that sat well with Eddy.

"Seattle?" The husky voice spoke again.

"Yes, sir. I hear you have family there."

"University of Washington?"

"Yes, sir. Law school."

"Keep it that way." He smiled at an older couple who were being handed drinks at the make shift tiki bar. "Aloha, Mildred and Robert. I'd like you to meet a friend of Lani's from Seattle. What's your name again, kid?"

"Edward O'Shaughnessy. Better known as Eddy." He extended his hand.

Robert Fisher considered Eddy with interest as he shook his hand. "We have the plantation next door. Seattle? We just met a girl from Seattle in San Francisco—"

"But we are sure she is no relation of yours." A tone in his wife's voice warned him not to pursue the conversation. "What a lovely party. I'm certain Dorothy is very pleased."

"Yes. She is all smiles. Two Scotches," Mr. Daniels announced, and then released Eddy as he handed him a drink. "To your future as a lawyer."

"Thank you, sir. And to your future successes."

Mr. Fisher laughed interrupting the stare-down. "Hell, Ben. You better show this young sailor around the plantation if he can hold your stare that long."

Lani's father nodded. "Tomorrow, here, 7 a.m. Sharp." He turned his back to Eddy and addressed the comment Mrs. Fisher had made earlier about his beautiful wife's party.

Dismissed, Eddy took his Scotch over to the edge of the patio where a lone Japanese man stood with paper and pencil. His handsome face intent as he scribbled notes in his small writing pad. As he quietly approached, Eddy quickly determined that between some of his kanji were American names—Arizona, Maryland, and Gamble.

"Hello." Eddy smiled out past him at the ships below. "Nice view."

"Yes, impressive." The man quickly fumbled his pad into the pocket of his bright Hawaiian-print shirt. The staccato of his voice pegged him as someone straight from Japan.

"There you are," Lani's voice rang out, and Eddy swung in its direction. "How was my father?"

He did not answer her but looked straight into the dark eyes of the man who had been studying him. "Can you introduce us?"

"Certainly." She stepped toward the young man who wore his long hair neatly combed back. "Hello again, Mr. Morimura. This is Eddy O'Shaughnessy."

"Nice to meet you." Fully aware that the Japanese did not shake hands in greeting, Eddy thrust his forward.

"Herro." Mr. Morimura bleakly shook Eddy's hand as he attempted the American greeting.

Eddy memorized his face and height, then broke out his winning smile and led Lani back into the crowd.

"Who is he?" Eddy attempted to sound casual.

"Mr. Tadashi Morimura is vice-consul with the Japanese Consulate on Nuuana Avenue. He's new to the islands, so mother invited him," she explained in response to the serious look on Eddy's face.

"Yes, good for business."

Eddy became aware of Lani's every move as the evening sped by. While the other guests roamed the grounds and enjoyed the grand offering of the feast, Lani and Eddy remained side by side.

The unique sound of a conch shell beckoned the guests to the torch-lighting ceremony as the sun disappeared from the brilliant red sky. When the final torch blazed, the streaks of red hews evaporated into darkness and the party moved to chairs now covering the lawn before the stage. Eddy sat close to the stage as mother and daughter readied for their anticipated performance.

"Aloha, e-komo mai, welcome," Ben Daniels began over the public address system. "We have a special treat. Alex Anderson is here to sing his new hit song. And even though he went to Punahou, he is still welcome in our house."

This statement brought laughter and shouts from graduates of the opposing schools on the island.

Ben waited for the audience to quiet down before beginning again. "Alex claims he wrote this song about my wife. And he is still welcome in this house."

Whistles went up toward the night sky, sparkling with clusters of stars.

"Okay, okay. I know you don't want to see me." He shifted his cigar to the hand that held the mike and gestured broadly. "My beautiful wife and my LeiLani, under the starlit heavens to entertain you."

Anderson nodded at his host and began strumming his ukulele. Mother and daughter glided onto the stage as he began his song.

"'Lovely hula hands, graceful as the birds in motion, gliding like the gulls over the ocean, lovely hula hands, kou lima nani e.'"

The lyrics fit the name sake. Mrs. Daniels's hands caressed the night like a lover. And when Eddy shifted his gaze to Lani, his heartbeat quickened in contrast to the soft flow of the gentle tune. The two were exquisite as they swayed as one in the amber light of the flames; and in the Hawaiian tradition, their expressive hands that told the story.

Eddy began to breathe again when the song ended. No words could express the emotion the quiet, sensual song had on his spirit or his longing. He started for the bar again for fortification and stood beside Mr. Fisher.

"Excuse me, Mr. Fisher. Do you remember the name of this young woman from Seattle you met in San Francisco?" Eddy waited for his drink to be refilled and the answer.

"Well, son. She was with a friend of mine. Didn't catch her real name." Fisher scooped up a handful of macadamia nuts from the monkeypod wood bowl designed like a pineapple. "Called herself Bright Eyes. Boy, she was a spitfire."

"I'll bet." Eddy tried not to show his shock. "That's the way we breed them in my hometown." He waited a moment, trying to prepare the question. "I met a fellow from San Francisco. Quite distinguishable with his eye patch and all—"

"Jack? You know Jack Huntington?"

"Sure. He helped my sister find a job in San Francisco." Eddy fished for more hints.

"Well, not the job this gal has. She's a companion of sorts, if you catch my drift. Too bad. She was a cute, skinny thing, with those big blue eyes."

"Do you mean a lady of the night?" Eddy choked out, turning red.

"Listen, kid…Eddy isn't it? Jack is one hell of a fine man, but he has his needs too. Great lawyer." Mr. Fisher regarded Eddy again. "You okay?"

"Sure. Just the surprise that we both know that scoundrel Jack." Eddy took a long drink. "Say, you don't know how I can reach him, do you? I didn't bring any numbers with me. But I have some free time while I'm here, and I sure would like to talk with Jack."

"Have Lani bring you over for a visit. We're just up the road a bit, and I'll get his number for you. That is, if you live through tomorrow morning with Ben." He laughed and patted Eddy on the shoulder before leaving.

As the drums began, Eddy hurried back toward the side lawn and the stage. He sat down in a stupor next to Scooter and Sam. What the hell was going on? Billi was parading as a whore?

But his mind quickly shifted to the male dancers who entered with their nifo' oti—fire knives—twirling in the air, leaving trails of light against the dark night, as their legs moved to the beat of the drums. The athletic abilities of the performers held Eddy's rapt attention, with its primeval allure of man and fire. When the last performer left the stage, the crowd quickly applauded in appreciation for the dance that spoke to the core of man.

"Ain't this somethin'?" Sam shouted. He stood when a line of girl dancers rocketed onto the stage, hips undulating to the sound of the Tahitian drums, their white, grass skirts a shimmering vision of motion. Above the ring of decorative shells at the top of each skirt, their bare bellies led to red tops and multicolored leis that matched the band of flowers around their foreheads and ankles. In their hands, tufts of white grass accentuated the rhythm with an occasional swish.

Eddy pulled Sam back down with a thud but kept his eyes on the girl in the center. Lani shifted upstage with the others, her long hair trailing to her waist, gently swinging in comparison with her hips that seemed to be detached and gyrated with an unparalleled swiftness. How did she do that? If the hands told the story in hula, the hips spoke loudly in the Tahitian dance. And the story she told him right now made it hard to think.

Sam, listing from liquor, tried to find his footing. "I'm gonna get me one of those." Luckily, his announcement, one of pure rapture, brought laughter from those within earshot.

The dancers left the stage to thunderous applause, and Eddy stepped back to the top patio, just off the house, for air. Below, on the second-tier patio, children played while a gray-haired woman sang softly, rocking a baby to sleep in the folds of her muumuu. The night's soft breeze wafted over his face, cooling him, and he breathed deeply of the taste of the great Pacific Ocean that rolled ashore below.

Movement on the lowest level patio caught his eye. Mr. Morimura stood there, alone again, looking out at the ships whose mooring lights created angular patterns against the dark waters.

Eddy shifted, frustrated he could not place what bothered him about those names the man had written. They did not make any sense?

"Arizona, Maryland, and Gamble," Eddy mumbled to help his brain focus. They were not all states. And then it hit him in the gut. They were names of the ships that rested undisturbed below.

As if the Japanese man had sensed Eddy's recognition, he turned from below and looked up. In answer, Eddy lifted his glass to the man, then stepped back onto the grass to follow his heart.

He found Lani among a group of young men and watched her face light up as she spotted him. He returned her smile and it felt right. Encouraged, he moved through the others and whispered into her ear. She giggled, blushed, and took his hand just as Mrs. Daniels approached the group.

"Come." Her command came soft. "We all dance. Especially you, haole." She nodded at Eddy.

As they followed her mother, Eddy bent into Lani. "What did she just call me?"

"White. Don't take it as an insult. Just dance with me." Her eyes slanted up toward him.

Eddy took up the challenge and swayed with Lani under the watchful eye of her mother as her voice rose and fell with the Hawaiian lyrics.

Soon the lure of the dance swept over the guests like a gentle wind. Eddy and Lani watched from the shadows. He wrapped his arms around her, pulling her back into his chest and they stood entwined, their bodies moving as one, gently swaying to the rhythm.

A hoot sounded above the lyrics, and Eddy spotted Sam, wearing a hula skirt and lei, gyrating with the alcohol-induced moves that he knew the kid would feel tomorrow.

"Sorry," Eddy apologized, but Lani just laughed as some of the other female dancers joined the young exuberant sailor in his floor show.

"No problem." She turned to Eddy and kissed him, and the fire between them ignited.

The music stopped, and Eddy straightened. "I'd better get those two back to base before they totally embarrass me and I'm never allowed back here again."

"That will never happen." Her eyes were gentle and ravishing in the soft light.

"Well then, before I embarrass myself. Besides, I have a 7 a.m. meeting with the man of the house. Can't be late for that one."

"If we don't answer, check our chapel around back. We will just be finishing mass." She took her hands from his and slowly drifted toward the main house.

FORTY-TWO

At 6:55 a.m. Eddy stood on the doorstep of the Daniels's home. He had risen early and gone for a long swim before borrowing Scooter's car for the drive. And, he hoped, all of his efforts would pay off.

His finger pressed the doorbell, and he heard Lani sing out from behind the large, wooden barrier. "Dad, your guest is here."

And then he saw her as the door swung wide. She wore a yellow summer dress that made her skin shimmer, golden and smooth. He wanted to touch her, but Mr. Daniels, briskly stepped right behind her, observing the two young lovers' powerful, silent interchange.

"Let's go then." Ben kissed his daughter's cheek and closed the door on her beaming face.

They drove Ben's old truck along Kamehameha Highway inland as he grilled Eddy with needling questions. Eddy held his own with the image of Lani in the morning light as his goal. The red earth greeted them as they approached Wahiawa on the Leilehua Plateau. Ben pulled down the dusty road toward a small, green building with white trim and an overhanging red roof.

A middle-aged man, red dust on his tan trousers, smiled as he walked down the short gangplank from an entry way to what Eddy concluded must be the office. The three men exchanged pleasantries, and then Ben led Eddy down a path beneath tall foliage that created a little shade from the hot sun.

Eddy smelled the horses before they entered the small corral and tried not to look uncertain as Ben handed him the reins to an old mare standing at about fourteen hands. She flicked her tail and stomped her foot, eyeing her prey.

Another older man, missing three of his front teeth, appeared from inside the small barn. He walked Eddy to the mare's left side, offering his hand to help the young sailor up. As he mounted, Eddy pulled too hard on the left rein, and the horse started to turn in circles. Once in the saddle, he wiped the sweat from his brow and looked over at Ben. The look in Lani's father's eyes told the story: Eddy was failing the test.

"Just need a bit of a brush up." Eddy loosened the reins so they dropped down on either side of the horse's mane as he grabbed the pommel of the saddle for security. "What's his name?"

"Her name is Lolly Pop," Ben smiled, challenging. "Are you ready then?"

"Sure." Eddy tried not to show the fear that crept up from the pit of his gut and secured the reins in both hands.

"Just give her a little kick." Ben sat back in his saddle, both reins neatly tucked between the fingers of his left hand, while his young, black gelding snorted in anticipation.

Eddy smiled back, leaned forward, shifted the reins to his left hand, and imitated the same grip as Mr. Daniels. He gently nudged Lolly Pop with the heels of his shoes, and she took off like lightning. At first, he jerked back with the jolt, but quickly recovered, reined her in, and then bounced mercilessly with her trot.

Ben caught up with him, nodded, then took the lead and slowed both horses to a walk as they entered the fields. The pineapples grew on short stems in the middle of pointed foliage, some all green, some with a reddish tone. The rows seemed to go on forever.

The large man swept his arm toward his crops. "I started as a child in the sugar cane fields but got hired on in these fields when I turned fifteen. The owner had no children and took a liking to me. He made certain I went to school and then helped me become manager. I was lucky but I worked hard. Very hard."

"It's beautiful." Impressed, Eddy nodded.

"I've added acres over the years, but I don't need any more. You don't need more if you are not able to use it with an open heart."

Eddy already felt the impact of the saddle when Ben crossed a small road and started to ride farther away from the office. They came to Kaukonahua Stream, and the horses bridles rattled with delight as they drank. Eddy watched Mr. Daniels dismount and splash the refreshing water over his dusty face. He smiled at Lani's father, but refused to budge, fearful he would never get back in the saddle.

The sweet smell of the ripening fruit greeted them as they started back. The hot sun working through his shirt left a long streak of sweat down his back covered in the rich red dust of the fields.

Just before they reached the stable, Lolly Pop's head went up and she gave a quick shake to the reins, which had grown slack in Eddy's hand. Before he knew what had happened, she worked the bit into her teeth and took off, brushing past Ben's mount in a cloud of red tinged dust. The smell of the stable enticed her forward, and the old racehorse set her pace as if she were once again going for the finish line.

"If Father gives you Lolly Pop, don't let her get the bit between her teeth," Lani had warned him the night before. "If she does, just grab her mane and hold on."

Eddy thought Lani had been kidding when she began to rattle off the accomplishments of his mount. The original owner had named the candy sucker he created after the horse! Lolly Pop had a long list of notorious winnings across the country, but that morning, when Eddy first glimpsed the mare, he didn't think the old plug could still move.

But now, Lolly Pop flew into her winning stride. He clung to her mane as he listened to the pounding of her feet. As the stable and corral come into view, Eddy ducked, hugging her neck, while low branches swept across his back. He became convinced this devil horse collaborated with Mr. Daniels.

The older, toothless worker hustled to swiftly open the gate as Eddy whizzed by; and then, without warning, Lolly Pop stopped, her hooves sliding briefly in the dust. Eddy went flying over her head and somehow managed to land on his feet, twirling toward the slats of the corral. He grabbed onto the railing and managed to stand upright when Ben trotted into view. The old man smiled up at Ben, picked up Lolly Pop's reins, and led her steaming and snorting into the shade of the stable.

Eddy felt every bump of Ben's old truck as they wound down the hills, but smiled over at Lani's father as if his backside—and other parts—were not on fire. He could not wait to get back to base and plunge in the cool water of the soothing ocean.

"You ever notice any subs out in the waters?" Eddy couldn't restrain from asking the question as the Pacific Ocean now spread before them.

"Yep," Ben assured him, keeping his eyes on the road.

"Do you think we're headed for war?" Eddy pressed on.

"I wouldn't be itching to fight." Ben looked over at him. "But there is no calmness with the wind lately. A volcano can hold only so much steam before the hot fires of lava spread wild and furious across the lands, consuming all. If we do go to war, Lani stays here with her family."

"What do you know of the different consul officers around here? Especially the ones from Japan."

"Usually they are mere faces, collecting information. But this new one from Japan is very curious and busy. He spends time in taxis, exploring."

"Do you find that odd?" Eddy felt his stomach tighten.

"Pa'a ka waha is all we can do for now."

"Pa'a ka waha?"

"If words are exiting your mouth, wisdom cannot come in. Be silent, learn." He looked straight at Eddy, man to man. "And if war touches our shores, pray to your Ke Akua, your God, and be prepared."

They pulled up his driveway and under the carport.

Eddy spotted a newer truck now parked next to Scooter's rusted auto. "You have company?"

"No." His grin had a mischievous quality. "Lunch?"

Eddy surmised even the bouncing of the old truck had been part of the test. "Sure." He tried to move his wobbly legs in a straight line and not wince with each step.

THE LEFTOVERS FROM THE LUAU were delicious, and Eddy wolfed down two plates before leaning back in the rattan chair to let the magic of the food appease his nerves. Lani watched him in silence, as did her mother, while her father gave his morning report on the fields.

When her parents left them alone, Eddy sighed in pain.

"You did well," she whispered. "He would not have asked you to lunch if he wasn't impressed."

"Thanks, but I'm not certain I'm going to live." He bleakly smiled.

"Yes, you will. And I will meet you tomorrow for a swim." Lani's eyes were twinkling with passion.

"I'm off at one." His offer sounded breathless with promise.

"I'm through with classes by then, so I will come to you at Kailua Bay. On Kaumana Road there is an old house at the very end. Meet me there at two o'clock."

By the time Eddy returned to base and folded his sore frame onto his bed, sleep came quickly. He did not notice until early morning, when rising for duty, that he had slept on two letters, one from his mother and the other from Dahlia. With mounting guilt, he pushed both under his mattress and dressed.

EDDY SKIPPED ACROSS THE SURF on the shimmering waters of Kane'ohe Bay, avoiding the sand bar, then lowered his wheels. He steered his PBY patrol craft out of the water and felt the wheels of his Catalina bump onto the pavement that led up the small incline and out of the bay. Again, his report remained empty of detail except for the sighting of the shadow of another sub. He had passed over the long, dark image of undeterminable origin until it blurred farther below the surface, about six miles off the southeastern shore. But there were no large vessels on the horizon, threatening war today, at least.

By the time one o'clock rolled around, his mind felt ready to explode. Mr. Daniels had all but admitted he knew enemy submarines were in the area and that the new man at the Japanese Consulate presented a problem. He still had not addressed the situation with Dahlia, and even more worrisome the connection that might lead to Billi. Eddy would have to prioritize. His head began to spin, and most of it had to do with Lani.

"Be prepared," her father had warned.

He hurried the short distance to Kailua Bay and turned down a bumpy road toward the old house on Kaumana. The one-level structure sat alone, sheltered from the road by the pink blooms of a thick hibiscus plant. The white house resembled the other building he had seen in the pineapple grove, with a big covered porch and the distinctive, red roof peak of the local architecture. It sat perched in the thick grass, resting just above the peaceful beach with giant palms at the edge of the light-colored sand. He stepped up onto the covered porch and looked in the windows. A small table and chairs filled one corner, and a couch covered in island-floral print sat in the other. Modest, yet promising all of the essentials. While it appeared deserted, it remained well kept.

He walked to the edge of the pearly, smooth sand, stripped down to his swim trunks, and plopped down, regarding the tranquil U-shaped beach. Farther down, to the north, he could see the small strip of land that led to his base, with the lump of Pu'u Hawai'i Loa hillside that shielded the air strip, hangars, and the bay. At Kane'ohe Bay, some of the PBYs sat on their pontoons just offshore, while others were on the tarmac with the fighter planes, resting peacefully under the stormy skies. He had viewed this stretch of land so often on his scouting duty, as he flew in search of the enemy that he hoped would never breach these shores.

By two-thirty he began to think he had dreamed up the meeting. A good long swim would help his thoughts and put them in order. He started into the water, marveling at its warmth, as the sand worked around his toes. The clouds out on the ocean were dark and heavy with rain, the ocean moody with the dense light.

He dove into the small surf and came up refreshed, the heat in his head dissipating. He set his course straight out and then back again, watchful of the shore. Finally exhausted, he emerged from the saltwater and lay back on the white sand, watching the ominous clouds work their way toward him. A tension swirled in the air that set his nerves on edge. Where was she?

By three-thirty the storm hung overhead and the warm rain hit his bare chest, arms, and legs. He let it fall on him without stirring. The storm had swept across the water with a wind that now cooled the moisture that covered him. Lightning dazzled over the waves while the crack of the thunder rolled up the hillside behind him in an echo. In the next blaze of light, she stood before him, the heavy drops from the heavens soaking her sarong so that it clung to every curve. Lani smiled, and that was the only invitation Eddy needed. He pulled her down onto the sand beside him, and as she lay back, the bits of white shell clung to her damp hair like a veil. They did not speak as they caressed each other beneath the storm overhead, the rain like silk covering their actions with its intense deluge, the monsoon rains shielding their passion.

The sand stuck to her naked body as Lani stood and waded into the water. The exotic creature who had captured Eddy's heart disappeared into the turbulent ocean, and he hurried right behind her. Their heads bobbed in the green-blue water as their laughter chimed in with the thunder around them.

"Time to head in," Lani abruptly announced.

"Why?" He enjoyed the feel of her naked body pressed against his in the sensual water.

"Visitors." She pointed and then took off toward shore.

Eddy turned and saw two tips of fins, about five feet apart, coursing fifty feet offshore. His adrenaline spurred him forward, and he swam just behind Lani, protecting her. They rode the last wave to shore as the fins turned toward them. They sat in the surf and watched the tips of the wings of a spotted eagle ray dip into the water then breach, exposing its white underbelly and long dark tail.

"It's the storm," she spoke softly into his ear. "And a good sign."

Eddy stood transfixed, watching the water in hopes the elegant creature would sail through the air again like a bird. As if on command, a second ray imitated the first, soaring above the turbulent waves, following the path of the first ray.

"He's looking for his mate." Lani stood beside him.

Eddy took her in his arms, "Not me. I've found mine."

"'Ae. And so have I."

They kissed tender and long, the seal of their love and future life together.

"Let's head inside." She shook the sand from her sarong, enticing him toward the house.

"Whose home is it?"

"My grandparents'. Their spirits are strong on this beach. That is why I brought you here."

Eddy only nodded and went willingly to the home of her ancestors.

The sun set quickly on the young lovers as they strolled the now mellow beach one last time before heading in their separate directions. The waves hitting the shore in the moon's light held a silver glow, with twinkling sparks of light ebbing across their feet as they splashed back toward Lani's grandparents' home.

She scooped up a small bead of phosphorescence and used it to draw a heart on Eddy's chest.

"Now you wear my heart." She pondered the glowing image in the soft light from the water's edge.

Following suit, he drew a matching heart on her bare skin above her left breast. "And you mine."

Soon they had smeared the magical offerings from the ocean playfully across each other's cheeks, the war paint of lovers.

In the distance, the lights from Kane'ohe drifted toward the sky, and reluctantly Eddy remembered his duty as a gentleman.

"If you don't head back soon, your father will—"

"Shhh." Her finger pressed against his lips. "But we will meet here again and soon."

"I'll run, bike, swim. Whatever it takes to get here."

She cautioned, "Well, be careful of the swimming, especially at night off your base."

He waited.

"It is another mating ground," she explained. She cocked her head and the light of the moon made the designs on her face glow.

"That's not so bad. Remember? Good spirits."

"Only if you're a hammer head shark."

Eddy felt a tremor of fear at the reminder of what lurked in dark waters. He scanned the ripples of the moonlit surface of the vast horizon for any enemy submarines that had to surface to recharge their batteries, so that their days could be spent just below the surface, secretly observing life on the island.

An urgency came over him, not of the playful kind, but of duty.

"Time to go." He commanded.

After watching Lani's father's truck disappear into the night, he rounded the house toward the beach. His lover's war paint still glowed on his cheeks as he sat on the sand in the shadow of a tall palm tree and watched the horizon.

"Where are you, you bastards?" he asked the night.

FORTY-THREE

THE TRAIN RATTLED AS THE RAILS CLICKED in their soothing promise of home. Billi faced the faithful Duckworth, whose watchful eyes had never closed.

Taking pity on him, she stood. "Look. I'm heading off to my berth and will lock the door. You get some sleep too."

He stood and followed her to her compartment. Billi heard his footsteps start down the train once she had locked the door.

It had been harder than she had expected to leave Jack. His insistence that she leave San Francisco as early as possible had been coupled with his gentle touch and a look of concern that spoke of the growing attraction between them. She had straightened her small room and left behind a treasure so that she would be compelled to return after the holidays. For some reason, she now felt naked without that silly pillow. She gave a short laugh as she crawled between the white sheets of her berth. Jack had looked so ridiculous standing there, holding the decorative object of Eileen's making. But he had taken it willingly, accepting it as she had intended, a symbol of her return. She hated herself for her impulsive behavior and hoped Jack saw her as a woman not a child.

How on earth would she explain her last few months to her mother or Eileen? She began to straighten the lies in her head, and her confusion made her sleep come in fits and starts. By the time she reached Seattle, exhaustion left her weak. As she hit the bottom step, she fell into her mother's arms and cried, the musky rose perfume her mother always wore filling her senses with relief.

Eileen stood to the side while Danny attempted to control Pepper on his leash. The small dog barked in protest and pulled at his collar, trying to reach Billi. She hugged Eileen next, then scooped up Pepper and planted a kiss on Danny's cheek. Home. She had made it safe and felt like she could sleep for days.

Her father ambled in their direction. "Parked the car," he announced in his lilting brogue. "Come here, darlin'."

He smelled of saltwater and hard labor as he held her.

They made their way back to 30th South, all talking at once in the joy of the reunion. By the time Billi made it inside the door, a list of events claimed her entire week.

JACK PRESSED THE PHONE RECEIVER TIGHTLY against his ear and listened as Duckworth gave his report

"She's safe with her family. Should I head back?"

Duckworth's words were a relief, and he tried not to let his voice show emotion as he answered. "Don't let her see you, but don't let her out of your sight. For now."

Jack hung up and looked over at the pillow Billi had stuffed in his arms before mounting the steps to the train. She had gotten to him. He had broken rule number one: Don't get involved. The phone rang, and he snapped it up.

He barely had time to say hello before the voice on the other end let fly with some very creative expletives wrapped into a threat.

"Why, hello, Eddy, and how are you?" He let the young man rant, buying time. "And back at you. Now how the hell did you get my number? I see." He shook his head at the coincidence of Eddy meeting the Fishers. "All right, you have my attention. Wait, repeat that."

He put the phone down on the desk and picked up pencil and paper, as Eddy's voice boomed into the small concrete room.

"Last night, just after sunset, I saw a submarine just off shore. It was Japanese and so were the people loading onto it."

"What people?"

"I don't know, but there were men and women and they had suitcases. They rowed out and met the sub and got aboard."

"Did they see you?" Jack wrote down the date, Monday, November 17.

"I don't think so. I was, ah, on the beach."

"Where?"

"Kailua Bay, south side." Eddy sounded oddly defiant and protective.

"How many people?"

"Hard to tell, they were in the distance. But you can't miss a sub."

"Who else have you told?"

"No one." Eddy hesitated. "I thought of you first."

"Why did you think of me?"

"Cut the crap, Jack. You're FBI."

"And your superiors won't listen or are you afraid to tell them?"

Eddy hesitated again. "I'm not certain they're paying attention. There are subs out there, not just whales, and this guy with the Japanese Consulate is snooping around a lot."

Jack paused a moment. "What do you want, Eddy?"

"Billi. I want you to leave Billi alone. I'll get you more information if you promise."

"She's home with your mother."

"Leave her there. And what the hell is she doing being a prostitute?"

"My, you are good," Jack snorted. "Perhaps you should be working for me."

"Do we have a deal? You leave Billi alone, and I get you information so you can be a hero?"

Jack leaned back and looked over at the emblem that Billi had explained claimed "peace" on her pillow. "You have your deal. Who is this guy in the consulate?"

"The new young one, Morimura. I'll get as much as possible." And then the phone went dead.

That damn kid, Jack mused, as he put his phone back in its cradle. He appeared to be as full of surprises as his sister. His thoughts turned to his friends the Fishers, and he placed another call.

BILLI ALMOST SKIPPED DOWN SOUTH JACKSON STREET in anticipation of spending the day with Eileen, forcing the events of the past few months aside as surreal and impossible. She lightly swung her purse in keeping with her stride, then stopped in front of the Nakamura Grocery store. She watched Mr. Nakamura precisely arrange his vegetables, the oranges and yellows of the squashes next to the green chives, a testament to his artistry. She lingered a moment and let the soothing manner of his actions wipe away her fears. When he picked up a bunch of chrysanthemums, she felt her heart race and her breathing tighten as the image of the dark alley and the broken stem of a mum protruding from under David's headless body rocketed before her.

"Are you all right?" Mr. Nakamura stood beside her.

"Oh…yes." Billi blushed, and then forced a smile for her old friend who innocently held the offending flowers.

"Eileen is pleased you are home. As am I." He nodded, and his eyes shone brightly.

"Thank you. It feels wonderful to be here."

"Later, you will make me tea." The statement a sign of welcome.

"I can't wait." She nodded then continued toward the door to the upstairs apartment.

Time had not changed her memories. The smells, the sounds from the shop below, and the kanji claiming peace remained pillars of her childhood. She rapped on the door, and it flew open to an exuberant Eileen. She put her shoes in the line next to her friend's and observed another pair. Tak was home.

Billi stood still, uncertain, as Tak rounded the corner. She began to tremble. Could Eileen's brother be the same Tak that Akio had referred to as being part of the spy net? He greeted her with a sickening smile.

"How was your trip? And new job in San Francisco?"

He had never been interested before and this only heightened Billi's fears.

"Fine." She fumbled with her purse.

"When are you heading back?" he pried.

"Tak, behave. She just got here," Eileen scolded and grabbed her friend's arm, leading her down the hall.

Once inside Eileen's room, Billi sat hard on the bed.

"Don't mind him." Eileen waved toward the closed door. "I am surprised he is even here. He has been so busy lately. Very secretive. I think he has a girlfriend."

"Really?" Billi smiled at the concept.

"He doesn't come home until late, way past when the restaurant where he works closes. Anyway, you are going to come to the football game with us, aren't you?"

"Oh, yes. Mother is serving Thanksgiving dinner much later so I can be at the championship game. Broadway High School doesn't stand a chance against Danny and Kenny. Garfield will win again this year."

"Yes. Those two are amazing together. Now tell me all about your new job." Eileen sat on the small bench that went with her dressing table, the one where they had sat side by side applying makeup so many times. A picture of the two of them, heads touching, sat in a frame next to the jar of white cream. The photo had been taken just before Billi left for her new job. The Kodak color print brightly reflecting their smiles and shining eyes seemed like a snapshot of a lifetime ago.

"Oh, it's boring. Filing and things." Billi twisted the leather strap of her handbag.

"You're not telling me everything." Eileen leaned toward her friend and waited.

When Billi didn't speak, Eileen did. "Are you in love?"

Billi's shoulders raised and lowered with the release of the tension. "Maybe."

"Tell me everything."

"Can we talk over some tea?" She could not tell if Tak remained in the house, but she did not want to be anywhere near him in the event he decided to listen to their conversation. She squeezed her purse, what if she mixed up her stories.

"You're buying." Eileen's black eyes were almost lost in the folds of her cheeks as she smiled broadly.

The walk through Japantown felt uncomfortable. She had not been around so many Japanese in a long time and sensed shadows everywhere. When she saw the long, thin sign announcing the NP Hotel, she remembered the photos Jack had shown her that first afternoon. They entered the small restaurant and sat at a table to the side, Billi positioning herself so she could watch the windows and the front door. The impact of her experience overshadowing what would have been a time to treasure with Eileen.

The two friends lingered enjoying their tea when the door opened and a tall Japanese man entered. Billi went clammy and gripped her cup. His back remained to her as he took off his hat and turned to cross the room. The gait of his stride told her it was not Akio, but she began to shake in the environment that once brought joy.

"What is it? What is the matter?" Eileen did not turn to see what had startled her friend.

"I just miss being here so much." Billi appeared too quick with her answer, so she added a smile.

"I think something has happened." Eileen did not look up at her friend but concentrated on her teacup. "Did someone try to harm you?"

"Don't be silly." And then Billi concluded she could not lie to her best friend. "Living alone is so different. You have to be on guard all the time in a new city, and I didn't realize how tired I am."

Eileen looked into Billi's eyes, holding her stare for quite some time. "How can I help you?"

Billi reached across and touched her friend's hand. "I'm fine. I just need to be home for a while and be with you and Mom and Dad."

"You must miss Eddy terribly. Are you afraid for him?"

"Eddy can take care of himself. He's already gotten in and out of so many shenanigans. When he was at boot camp, he got sick and they sent him to the infirmary. He talked them into an easy job, working the steam iron while he recuperated. In no time he had rigged up the room and sold steam baths to his buddies. Well, as he tells it, these buddies got a bit miffed when they figured out how much money he was making. So once, when Eddy went in to take his own steam bath, some of the guys stole his clothes. He had to walk past the nurse on duty at the ward naked as a jaybird."

The outburst of laughter brought stares from the other occupants.

Eileen leaned forward in conspiracy. "Maybe we should visit Hawaii over Christmas. Will you have time off? I have money saved and want to travel."

"Does your father still want you to return to Japan?" Billi could not imagine allowing her friend to return to the country of her heritage. She felt dizzy at the thought.

"He speaks of it now and then, but he will be sending Kenny after he graduates this summer. So I may have to go with him."

The two sat with their own thoughts until the door opened again, and Billi once more tensed. She turned her head as the man who had entered took off his hat—dark with the light band—and surveyed the room. She had seen him before, but where?

"You are so jumpy."

"Do you recognize the man who just entered?"

Eileen carefully looked around. "No. He is new. There are so many new men coming into the store. Father is trying to find one for me, he teases."

"Do they ask for Tak?" She held her breath and waited.

"I don't know. Like I mentioned, Tak is gone most nights. And if it is not a girlfriend then I think he is gambling." Eileen changed the subject. "Father found one of the new arrivals a job at the restaurant downtown. He thought this new fellow very smart, very precise. I'm waiting to meet him. Can you imagine arriving with only one trunk? When we go to Hawaii, we will have two trunks each."

Billi understood her friend attempted to cheer her. And at the same moment it hit her that she should not be sitting in a Japanese restaurant with her Japanese friend, speaking her language. For a white woman with blue eyes stood out in Japantown.

FORTY-FOUR

A NAME HAD ALREADY BEEN ATTACHED to the decoded message sent from Tokyo to the Japanese embassy in Washington, D.C. The "winds code" sat before Jack in black and white, sent November 19, 1941. *Higashi no kaze ame.* He did not need Billi to translate. The Japanese planned to insert the phrase *East wind rain* in their radio weather report, and if repeated twice, it would mean war with America. It seemed all talks and hopes of any conciliation between these two major powers were at a standstill. Jack knew that while America still slept soundly with its isolationist dreams, Japan had been methodically orchestrating its attack. As far back as January 1, 1941, when the first hints of such an event made it through the various channels to the commander in chief, President Roosevelt had openly seemed to invite such behavior by cutting off oil and much-needed war supplies to the country hell-bent on invading all of Asia. And now, it appeared, the United States.

East wind rain, Jack circled the three words. It sounded so nonchalant. He thought of Seattle and the days he had spent listening to the patter of rain against his windshield or watching the drops splash against his window while waiting for Billi to agree to his plan. For all of her efforts, he still had nothing substantial except for his growing fear of the reality of war. Where? Where were the Japanese forces going to strike their first blow?

More American pilots had just been sent to the Philippines, but when they arrived, they had no planes, little fuel, less ammunition. The list of needed supplies and men for preparation seemed endless. And time was not on their side. If Akio relayed accurate information to his men, an attack at Christmas loomed just around the corner. Furthermore, what had he meant by a second attack?

He picked up the phone and called Seattle, hoping he could keep himself from asking too many questions about Billi. "Hello, Duckworth." He smiled at his assistant's voice, someone he viewed as a friend. "Any news from Fort Ward?"

"I just checked again, sir. Station S has been humming away. They won't tell me much over the phone. Do you want me to head to Bainbridge Island and check in?"

"Yes. How is the other situation?" He couldn't help himself.

"There's been quite a bit of activity, lots of coming and going from the Japanese Consulate. Tak has been spending time at the Star Pool Hall, the Golden Donut Café, and the Stacy Street Tavern. There is a new guy in town too, and they seem to be spending time together." As if he could hear the unasked question in his boss's silence, he added, "Billi has been spending time with Eileen. They were together yesterday in a Japanese restaurant."

Jack felt relief Duckworth sat watch over eight hundred miles away and could not see the concern on his face. "East wind rain," he mumbled into the phone.

"What, sir?"

"East wind rain. The winds code. It's to come over the Japanese radio to alert the consulates that war with America has arrived."

"Damn. When?"

"Anytime."

IT TURNED INTO A REMARKABLE THANKSGIVING DAY. From the torrential rain Seattle is known for, the football field at West Seattle Stadium had transformed into a thick mud playfield with the white lines smeared in places. The audience huddled together for warmth in the crowded stands. While the rain had subsided, a chill hovered in the air that brought puffs of gray mist as people breathed, spoke, or laughed.

The enthusiasm that swept over the crowds came in waves of thunder as the arch rivals slushed their way up and down the field. The unstoppable team of Danny's wiry frame catching the football launched by Kenny's golden arm kept stunning the opposing team. Billi and

Eileen jumped in unison when the defensive players scrambled to catch the young redhead's twisting and twirling body as he ran for yet another touchdown. The score turned unmercifully lopsided in Garfield High's favor over Broadway High, with the purple and gold side of the stands constantly erupting in joy.

The crowd appeared a mixture of races on the Garfield side, like a global conference of the world's species. This made Billi proud and comfortable as the many different cultures worked together toward one simple goal, to win. Why did the outside world remain at odds with each other?

Tak entered the stands but did not join them. He sat below, next to a man in a dark colored hat with a light gray band. Billi fixed her attention on the two as they seemed to be talking to each other. She doubted their intent discussion riveted on the game.

The Garfield band encouraged the onlookers, raising the noise level, as the fans screamed into the last few minutes of the game. Eyes were glued on the time clock. As it ticked down on the scoreboard, the Garfield students and parents shouted each second until the excited crowd hit "one," and the field exploded.

His teammates hoisted Kenny up on their shoulders and paraded toward the sidelines as the spectators bellowed the rousing chorus of the school song from the stands. Mr. Nakamura, in an untypical fashion, let a tear roll down his cheek over his smile. An obvious tear mixed with joy and sadness that Mrs. Nakamura had not been sitting next to him to watch her son's victory.

Tak had hardly clapped but remained stooped in conversation with the handsome, young man in the dark hat. Then he turned and looked up the stands at Billi. Or did he eye his father and sister? Billi stared back, when unexpectedly the man beside him turned and looked in her direction. The afternoon light shone on the strangers face. She recognized him instantly as the man from the restaurant where she and Eileen had tea two days ago. The same man she thought she had encountered before but could not place. A chill ran through her, and she leaned into her friend.

"I'd better get back. Mom will be wanting to know what she should be putting on the cake she baked for Danny. No pies this Thanksgiving. Just the winner's cake."

"Give your mother our love." Eileen hugged her still smiling at her younger brother's success. "We are having a celebration party for Kenny tomorrow. Would you like to join us?"

"Yes. Thank you." Billi had not hesitated to accept but knew she could not attend. "I have to write a letter to Eddy tomorrow and tell him about Danny."

"Brothers." Eileen sighed and then started off, following her father's trail.

"Yes, brothers." Billi's smile held little joy.

Only one true exit from the stadium parking lot allowed the cars onto 35th Avenue South West, and Billi sat in her mother's new car within sight of the trail of cars leaving and waited in the onset of dusk. Conspicuous in the shiny new car, it had been her only choice when she decided to try to follow Tak. Possibly she should be following the man in the dark hat in the hopes she might remember where she had first encountered him.

The two men exited together, and Dark Hat led Tak to a car parked behind her. She slid down in her seat and waited until she heard the other car cough to life and its headlights swept above her.

She followed as far back as possible. Certain the car headed to Japantown, she could give it some room as they wound down Avalon Avenue, over the Duwamish Bridge, and down 4th Avenue toward the city. But the car turned west toward the docks just a short ways ahead. She hesitated but kept driving straight. The docks at night were no place for anyone.

This Thanksgiving had already been a mixed bag of emotions with the exciting Garfield win. But now Billi sat at the subdued table laden with the special meal. The two shining stars that had always provided endless entertainment were missing, and the stark reality of the situation hung over them like a heavy shawl. She longed for Ray's touch and Eddy's banter.

In an unexpected turn of events, her father had been invited to join them. He and Pepper were quite the pair as they attempted to cheer up the two ladies. Her father would sing and Pepper would howl, which brought giggles as the antics grew with encouragement.

"It was a wonderful turkey, Dad. And we have much to be thankful for. I'm so glad you have found steady work."

"'Tis honest work. Nothin' to be ashamed of." He patted her hand.

"Yes, and the beef you bought is good and fresh, just like the turkey." Mrs. O took another sip of her sweet Riesling wine.

"I picked it myself. I know it to be the best."

The scene warmed Billi's heart. She watched her father's bright smile, pleased at being the provider once again for his fractured family. The irony that her maternal grandfather had been a butcher and now her father delivered for the biggest meat packaging farm in Bremerton did not escape her. A tranquility existed between her parents' this Thanksgiving, a quiet resolution to live life and not pick it apart.

The rattle of the door sent Pepper flying, as Dahlia and Danny, with Susie by his side, streamed into the dining room.

"Happy Thanksgiving. Did you save me some of your stuffing?" Danny plopped in a chair and held out his plate before Susie had a chance to sit.

Mrs. O beamed at the praise. Billi shook her head as her mother turned to Susie and began as if she were preparing the young girl to be the cook of Danny's dreams. "It's the Italian chestnuts that gives it a sweet flavor. Bake and peel them, then add them after you have sautéed your onions, celery, and mushrooms in butter and fresh sage. Then add your bread."

"Excuse me. Manners, young man," Dahlia slapped her brother's hand. "Ladies first. We need Eddy here to teach you a thing or two."

Mrs. O nodded approvingly at her future daughter-in-law.

Billi sipped her Manhattan and let the warm liquor do its magic. She shook away the dread of the last few months. The dinner table had grown and shrunk, and now expanded again as new extended family members joined them. This emerged as life for now, with change served up daily.

The phone rang. She jumped and then settled back, toying with her lemon twist, letting her mother answer it. She had not heard anything from Jack since she had been home. She struggled with her feelings. Maybe he had feigned his attraction for her just to seduce her into this vile work. She had done her job and been dismissed.

Her mother's announcement brought everyone to their feet. "It's Eddy. How is my one and only baby boy?" she cooed into the receiver.

All stood around the phone waiting to speak with the one they missed wholeheartedly.

When Billi took the receiver, Eddy's voice sounded strained. "Hey, Bil. I miss my little sis. How are things? Have you heard from the one-eyed bandit lately?"

She thought his question odd and tried to hold the resentment out of her voice as she replied an honest no.

"Good. I have a favor to ask. I have to talk to Dahlia soon and I'm afraid it isn't going to be to her liking. But I'm in love."

Billi sat with a thump on the arm of the chair, trying not to look at the blonde woman across from her, eagerly waiting her turn on the phone with Eddy. "But," she began, and then looked up into the various sets of eyes that were now trained on her and forced a laugh. "Oh, sure. How silly. Of course. But you'll owe me."

"Thanks. I knew you'd have my back. Ah, Bil, I can't wait for you to meet her. But don't tell Mom yet. I need to settle with Dahlia first."

"I get it." And she did. She got that Dahlia would be in more pain than ever before in her short life. That Eddy held her dream as the only man she had cast her eyes on and now he had charged off exploring manhood without her. "When?"

"Saturday morning. I had no idea how it felt to really be in love."

She heard the intoxication of pure love in his voice and knew he spoke the truth. They had all grown up in the same neighborhood, walking the same streets, and envisioning the same dreams. But nothing had braced them for the real world or the frightening dark cloud that approached. She wanted to talk to him for hours, to step back in time and laugh like life was meant to be —simple, without complications.

After the fine dishes had been dried, restacked with protective paper between them, and tucked safely back into the sideboard, Billi poured herself another drink and carried it up to her room. She pushed aside the devastating news that lie ahead for Dahlia as it reminded her of Jack.

She had not visited Eileen's home again since that day they had gone to the restaurant for tea and she had returned home a nervous wreck. How frustrating to realize she needed to be cautious in her own hometown, but her world had developed dark edges. It frightened her how she now searched every face of every man in Japantown for Akio and his men. Jack had been quite clear that Akio's contacts "up North" reached all the way to Canada.

She sat on her bed and looked at the birds in their cages spread across her wallpaper. Was her life to be nothing but rooms with walls that closed in on her mockingly as she hid from the unknown? And how long would this continue? Thanksgiving had come early this year, November 20. If the Imperial Fleet indeed promised a Christmas delivery to the American shores of an unimaginable scale, the crisis lurked just over a month away.

The image of Tak's sneer came back to her, and she held up her drink to his apparition. She had nothing to lose at this point. Not even Jack.

ACCORDING TO EILEEN, the celebration party for Kenny would begin at six that evening and Tak planned to help with the food. In the early darkness of Seattle's late autumn, Billi decided to cruise the streets of Chinatown before turning into Japantown. She parked the car up the hill from the Nakamuras' home. This position provided her with an unobstructed view down the street as she watched several of Eileen's family members and friends walk to the door and be swallowed up into the entrance.

She waited over two hours, until she nodded off, and scolded herself for not bringing something to eat or drink. Clearly spying required more preparation. She left her headlights off while she backed up the street to turn down South Main, but stopped. A figure hurry through the shadows, his breath leaving a trail of white puffs behind him. As he crossed the street below the light, she noticed he carried a book and wore the same dark hat with the lighter-colored band as the gentleman who sat beside Tak at the stadium. He disappeared down the street behind her.

Billi quietly backed up and then pointed her car down the street in the same direction as the stranger had headed. No one appeared in sight. She proceeded to the corner and saw a couple heading in her direction. Now in the open, she hurried back up Jackson toward her home, turning her headlights on only after she had traveled a few blocks. She would return tomorrow and note the doorways along that block.

Pepper lay on Billi's white bedspread, his eyes moving between his mistress and Dahlia who sat inches from him.

"I guess I knew something like this would happen." Dahlia blew her nose again, and her blonde curls fell over her face. "I mean, Eddy was so good to me. But I guess I just wasn't the right woman for him."

"We can never know what the next day will bring," Billi mumbled. She hated herself for being there and hated her brother for putting her in this position.

"I'm doing well in nursing school and that will keep me busy. I guess." Her acknowledgement of her situation seemed far off and lonely.

"Forget my brother, he is an idiot. He doesn't deserve you."

"Who is she?"

"I have no idea. But let's go out, see a movie or something. Will you still be my friend?" Billi could not lose Dahlia too. Her world seemed to grow smaller and more complex.

"Of course." A shy smile played across her pretty face. "Forget men."

"Oh, sweetie, I don't think men will forget you. My brother is just plain stupid. Real stupid," she added, thinking the word would help erase the hurt.

The two women sat side by side, broken dreams clattering around them.

"A comedy would probably do us good?" Billi's suggested listlessly.

"Well, I'm not going to go see *The Bride Came C.O.D.*," Dahlia scoffed.

"If Bette Davis and James Cagney can get hitched, there's hope for us." Billi took Dahlia's hand.

"The only good thing about Seattle right now is that it's swarming with handsome young servicemen who are shipping out. I say we go make some of them laugh." Dahlia pulled Billi to her feet. "With me?"

"I feel it is our duty."

Pepper, feeling the tension change to eagerness, wagged his tail and dashed through the door.

FORTY-FIVE

Eddy sat at Honolulu Harbor near the Aloha Tower. Kulolia, as the locals referred to the principal seaport of Oahu, bustled with merchants and tourists. The big white Matson Line boats loomed at the docks, beside two other large vessels. Eddy focused on the passengers, not the ships. Lines of Japanese families boarded the boats. Two ships were filling with the unexplainable exodus. What was going on?

He checked his watch and calculated he would be late to meet up with Lani. They were having Sunday dinner with her parents after a quick swim. He noted the names of the ships— *Tatsuta Maru* and *Hikawa Maru*—then started toward Ewa Beach and Mamala Bay. He would report his finding to Jack later.

As he drove toward their planned meeting spot, he passed the small Ewa grocery store and stopped to grab two sodas. He noticed the large black consulate car parked outside and quietly proceeded through the open front door. He recognized Morimura instantly, his brightly colored shirt and long hair, as he stood talking with the older Asian couple who ran the store. At the sound of pinging, Eddy turned to see another Japanese man concentrating on the pinball game tucked into a corner.

Eddy stepped down an aisle when he saw the flamboyant member of the Japanese Consulate pick up a piece of yellow paper off the counter, fold it neatly, and put it in his shirt pocket. Signaling to the man at the pinball machine, the two exited. Through the open door, Eddy watched the black car pull onto the road and head back toward the city.

He rounded the corner, smiling, with the two sodas and said hello to the elderly owners who were watching him closely. As he paid for his drinks he asked how long they had been at this spot.

"Long time. Before you born." The white-haired man had let his wife answer.

"Business must be good," he replied. His tongue moved over his lips as he surveyed the contents of the small store, only to note that most of the shelves were bare. "Have any Crows?" Eddy mentally took stock.

The old man's eyes hardened. "Coming on next boat."

"My gal loves licorice. Do you know when exactly?"

Neither answered his question; they only shrugged.

He stepped out into the heat of the afternoon and stood next to Scooter's miserable excuse for a truck. Before him lay Pearl Harbor with all of the ships lined up neatly. His chest puffed a bit with pride as he admired the fleet resting in all of its glory. A magnificent show of strength. Whatever might be out there across the waters presented no match for these gray-hulled beauties.

Eddy landed in the sand next to Lani. She accepted the drink and his apology for being tardy with her gracious smile. "I was reading some of the students' papers." She tucked a stack of work back inside her large woven bag. As an afterthought, she pulled one back out and showed it to Eddy.

"Look at this drawing and the title."

Scrawled across the paper, with no apparent concern for the rules of forming a straight line, appeared a child's attempt at a sentence.

"'God is all thinks and make me lub.'" Lani read over Eddy's shoulder where a rainbow arched over the tangle of letters.

"And Eddy thinks he lubs Lani."

"He only thinks?" Her hand traced his spine.

"Knows. And so does God. Marry me, Lani."

They kissed, and the paper flew from his hand in the breeze off the ocean. He ran to chase it, his progress difficult with the thick sand, and grabbed it just before it twirled into the water. As he stood he saw a large dark shadow below the green of the water a ways off the shore.

He took note of the time and then returned to Lani with the child's handiwork. She stuffed it back inside her bag.

He knelt next to her. "Well?"

She looked at him and bit her lip. "Yes. But you must convince my father."

"Done." The confidence in his voice did not match his twisting apprehension. "Now, swim with me."

THE TWO YOUNG LOVERS ARRIVED at the three-tiered home and parked up the driveway. Eddy lingered, drawn in by the expansive view, breathing deeply of the warm fragrant air that swept across the gardens and rows of blossoms.

Lani twisted her hair back into a knot, bits of white sand dripping to the ground with her movements. The salt from the ocean had left a trail across her back that dripped down her dress, making Eddy want to trace the line and touch her forbidden soft skin.

Mr. Daniels stood at the window and lifted his drink in their direction. As they entered Lani's father swiftly corralled Eddy into his office.

Eddy felt his heart stop when he saw Mr. Fisher sitting next to Jack.

"Take a seat, Eddy," Mr. Daniels instructed as he closed the door.

He sat slowly, watching Jack as if the one-eyed man were going to spring in his direction.

"Give the kid a drink," Fisher advised.

The rattle of the ice and the sound of slushing Scotch filled the room as the tension mounted. Lani's father handed Eddy a drink and took up his post behind his desk.

"Thank you, sir." Eddy did not want to forget his manners, even in this dark situation.

"How was the water?" Jack started the conversation gently.

"Refreshing and interesting." Eddy returned his stare. "Aren't you a long ways from… Where is it you live anyway, Jack? You seem to pop up everywhere."

Out of the corner his eye, Eddy saw Fisher's eyebrows raise as Lani's father sat behind his desk.

Jack put his drink on the coffee table in front of him. "I've kept up my end of the promise."

Eddy looked at Mr. Daniels. "Sir, this has nothing to do with your daughter."

"If the way you look at each other tells me much, it has everything to do with her." His eyes narrowed, his face concrete, uncracking, and hard.

"I broke off my relationship back home and have only honorable intentions toward Lani."

The man who held the key to his happiness with Lani looked at Jack, who gave no indication of his knowledge of Eddy's activities.

"Can I speak with him?" Jack said, then added in a menacing tone, "Alone."

"Come on." Fisher pushed up from the couch. "Let's let them at it. This looks like old business and I smell the coals. I don't like my ono overcooked. Who caught it anyway?"

Eddy liked the kind, older man who attempted to defuse the situation as he led his host out of his office.

"How is my sister?" Eddy started the attack once the door closed.

"Like I said, I've kept my promise and have not contacted her since she went home to Seattle weeks ago."

"So why are you here?"

"Some things need to be said in person."

"I have more for you, but this time you need to do more for me."

"I will speak to Lani's father on your behalf." When Eddy had nothing to say, Jack added, "Favorably."

The next twenty minutes were spent exchanging information that left both men irritated and more concerned. Eddy would continue to report directly to Jack, who would in turn send the information on in a concise report to the highest chain of command.

"One more thing." Eddy enjoyed his newly formed position. "I need my own car."

"Keep it clean," Jack warned.

Eddy realized the "clean" was not in reference to washing the vehicle regularly and gave Jack one of his sly smiles.

JACK WATCHED EDDY AND LANI over dinner, and his thoughts went to Billi. The siblings were much alike: bright, stubborn, and their infectious love of life intoxicating. As the meal ended, he stepped out onto the top terrace and noticed the lights below, the warm tropical breeze inviting his emotions toward passion. He thought of their swim in Lake Washington that night after Eileen's mother had died, how Billi's long arms broke the surface with such strength and determination. He wondered how she would look in the azure waters of the islands. He let out his breath with a sigh that spoke of the hunger she had roused in him. He brushed his mounting desire aside. For now he must make amends for his appearance, which could drive a wedge between Eddy's intentions and future father-in-law.

FORTY-SIX

ILEEN SAT ON BILLI'S BED with her head down. "I don't know what could have happened to the picture. I thought maybe you had borrowed it." She slowly raised her head, her dark eyes fixed on her friend. "But I've looked everywhere for it for the last two days."

"We'll have another one made." Billi tried not to show her concern that the Kodak photo of the two of them had gone missing off of Eileen's dressing table. She attempted to remember every aspect of the photos. Eileen had worn a floral print dress while she had chosen her new blue blouse and brown skirt. "When did you notice it gone?"

"The morning after the party for Kenny. Oh, you should have seen my little brother. He was bouncing all over the apartment, all smiles. We are so proud of him."

"Were there any strangers there? Any of the new men?" She spoke quietly realizing the slippery slope these questions posed, but waited for the answers without explanation.

"No, I don't remember seeing anyone I didn't recognize. Just mostly family."

Billi smiled. She had known most of the guests, since she had been watching from the dark of her car as they entered. "How nice. Maybe it got knocked over and the glass broke and whoever did it is going to have it fixed and hope they could put it back before you had noticed it missing."

This explanation seemed to appease them both.

"If not, like you said, we'll make another copy," Eileen assured her friend.

Their discussion turned away from the missing photo as the friends discussed their plans for Christmas. After some time, Billi brought the conversation back around to Eileen's family.

"What will Kenny do over Christmas break?"

"He is going to work with Tak at the restaurant. They are always so busy, and Tak has still been working very late."

"Do you still think he has a girlfriend?" Billi leaned back on her pillow.

"No, it's strange. He never speaks about where he goes or what he's up to, but he has been easier to be around lately."

"And are any of those new men he is hanging out with interested in his little sister?"

"No," Eileen blushed. "But there is one who little sister has noticed. Sanzo is his name. He is handsome and always reading. He carries books with him everywhere he goes."

"Have I met him?" Billi remained motionless.

"No, but he said he would like to meet you." Eileen blushed again.

Billi sat up, her nerves tightening. "How does he know about me?"

"He saw us one day having tea and asked who you were. And, I think, at the football game."

"How did you meet him?" The words traveled over dry lips.

"Tak brought him home the other day and introduced us."

"Who else was there?"

"Father worked in his store below, so we were alone. Well, Tak stayed in the kitchen, of course, when we spoke." Eileen's smile disappeared. "Have I done something wrong?"

"What color is his hat?"

"His hat? Dark, with a light gray band. Sanzo is very stylish. Why?"

"Yes." Billi spoke slowly. "I think I remember him. And what all has he asked about me?"

"We didn't speak for long, he had to get back to work, but I told him you should have won the competition and gone to Japan. Tak must have told him you were away working, because he asked. Are you all right?"

Billi felt faint but pressed forward. "What did he ask?"

"Where you had gone for your job. But I told him I really didn't know exactly."

"Do you still have the letters I sent you?" Billi's turned as white as her bedspread.

"Yes."

"Will you burn them? No, let's go and get them. Will you give them back to me?" Billi began to tremble, trying to remember if she had in the least referred to any part of her job. "I just... It's personal. Please don't ask. Just let's go and get them."

"Now?"

"Yes, I'll drive you and you can run in and then we'll come right back. I want to explain something in one of the letters."

"You have been so strange since you got back. Okay, let's go." Eileen stood and started for the door.

"Wait." Billi jumped up. "Where did you say Sanzo works?"

"The Taisho-Do Bookstore."

"The bookstore." Billi had a sudden recollection of where she had seen the handsome face beneath the dark hat. The Gosha-Do Bookstore in San Francisco's Japantown. She had been reading about the emperor's gardens, and he had spoken to her in Japanese.

Her possible exposure pushed her into action. She raced out the door with Eileen on her heels and drove hell-bent down Jackson. She pulled the car to the curb in front of the door leading up to the apartments. Eileen hopped out while Billi pulled up the hill to turn around. On a thought, she rounded the corner and drove down the hill to where the man in the dark hat, carrying a book under the streetlight, had mysteriously disappeared. She had forgotten to come back in daylight to look at the many doors that faced the street. Most led to restaurants or upper apartments; only two were unmarked.

She hurried back and waited for Eileen, who soon appeared with a cloth-covered box tucked under her arm. She slid into the seat next to Billi.

"Here they are. All of them." Eileen put the box on her knees and looked down at it as if for the first time. "This better be good."

"Oh, it will be. I promise you that."

The shiny blue car pulled out of Japantown and headed up the hill toward 30th South.

Pepper followed them back up the stairs, and Eileen sat next to Billi as she opened the box. Neatly arranged in order by dates received, the letters were tied with a beautiful red ribbon.

"Have I done something wrong? Are you mad at me?" Eileen sat still as Billi counted the letters.

"No." Billi leaned over and hugged her. "You will always be my best friend. I love you like a sister."

"That is because we are sisters." The words were softly spoken in Japanese.

Jack sat in his secret office in the Sir Francis Drake Hotel and cleaned the barrel of his gun, something he did daily in preparation. He stood and patted his pocket knife for reassurance. Ready, he stepped outside, adjusted his hat, and pulled up the collar on his coat. San Francisco, draped in lights for the holidays, felt chilly and damp, vastly different from his five days in Hawaii. Akio had not been seen in the Bay Area lately, and Jack did not expect him to show up, as the second headless body had created quite the stir in the community. He knew Akio felt empowered by his high standing in the Japanese military with his many years of condoned murders and had not been able to contain his unchecked violence. He never could. But now his killings had brought him unwanted attention, much to Jack's dismay. However, he knew his old roommate would feel trapped, and his arrogance would lead him to make another mistake. And Jack counted on that mistake.

He had put the pillow he had promised to keep for Billi in a bag and headed for her apartment. The note he had spent hours constructing had been whittled of all emotion or promises of a future to merely "Stay well, Merry Christmas." He perceived himself to be more the coward than he thought and hoped someday he could write to her of his deepest desires. He would leave the bag in her room and have someone pack up all her things to be shipped home. Her time working for him was over, and the pillow brought back the memory of her smile. A smile he would give up his life for. But she needed to stay away. Since Akio had gone underground her involvement became too dangerous. Besides, he had promised that hound dog Eddy he would stay away from his sister.

The red, green, and gold lights of Christmas were distorted in the fog, their shapes outlining the various buildings, giving him his bearings as he crossed Union Square. The lights, like beacons, drew the danger closer as time escaped without any more clues. The information from Eddy had been an incredible stroke of luck. But where and when this attack would take place became the commanders of the White House main concern. Magic, the machine of pure genius, daily translated bits and pieces of the puzzle that foretold of disaster.

Japan sat too far away for an air strike on American soil. Things were not lining up. It must be the submarines that Akio, the engineer, continued to develop.

The exhaustion from the uncertainty dragged his shoulders down, and even the bag holding the pillow felt heavy as he passed through the street-level door off Maiden Lane. He trudged up the stairs, working the circle of problems over and over. When he reached the fourth floor and turned toward Billi's apartment door, he slipped back into the shadows. The door stood ajar. He drew his gun and set the bag down farther in the darkness. He listened but heard nothing. Gingerly, he stepped forward and slowly pushed the door open.

The smell from cigarettes filled his nostrils, and he crouched in preparation to attack. Nothing moved. Stealthily, he inched forward and crossed the room to the window. Outside, the fog drifted in layers below, concealing all movement. He crossed to the sink and found the stub of a cigarette, cold to the touch, the lingering smoke meant whoever had been in the room had been there recently. He flipped the light switch on and felt his gut heave. He stepped over some of Billi's things as he hurried to the bathroom and searched it. Empty, except that all of her make-up and belongings were strewn about. He picked his way through the upturned dresser and discarded clothing and came back to stand over her single bed. Her dress, Ginger's dress, the one with the orchid print that Akio liked so much, was laid out neatly, as if in repose, with a slit running from the top ruffle to the hem. The sword had left a precise, even cut. On the pillow rested a

Kodak picture. Eileen smiled at the camera, holding hands with a woman in a brown skirt and blue blouse.

Jack instantly recognized the long legs of Billi as the headless women standing in the picture next to Eileen.

FORTY-SEVEN

BILLI SLAMMED DOWN THE PHONE for the third time. No one answered at the office number Jack had given her to call. Where the hell was he? Why had there been no message or call since she had left San Francisco?

December 2 had arrived, and she helped her mother get out the Christmas decorations. This included the three sets of life-sized nativities that Mrs. O had commissioned an artist to render on large pieces of cut-out plywood. Each stand-alone figure had a sturdy kickstand to prop it upright on the various sites prearranged to handle such images. The three kings and their large camels were placed behind Mary, Baby Jesus in his crib, and Joseph at the intersection of Jackson and Boren Avenue. The two other nativities were scattered around the city, her mother's one-woman homage to her favorite season and day of giving. Then there was also the Christmas party to consider and organize at the Blue Banjo for the less fortunate who roamed the city streets in the Pioneer Square neighborhood.

Billi's lists of duties grew daily, and she feared Jack would call and need her, and she would unexpectedly have to abandon her mother. She planned far in advance and got as much done as possible in her attempt to push all thought of Jack and the impending danger aside. But being overwhelmed with work did not provide enough of a distraction. Her mind wandered to the large home in Hillsborough and Lilly. She would love to send her a Christmas card and see how the pregnancy progressed. And Jack, that irascible, stubborn… She could go no further, because the image of him made her heart beat faster, and she prayed he was safe.

The anticipation of the upcoming attack at Christmas kept her up nights; and her nightmares became more vivid and violent. She spent hours reworking the words Akio and his men had uttered. "Expect a Christmas present…spy network along the coast…the drawings." In her attempt to piece the words together, she kept focusing on Tak and the professor.

While she had spoken with Eileen daily, she had avoided Japantown and entertained her friend at her home instead. She had gone over her letters to Eileen thoroughly, and with great relief found she had been very careful in her lies about her new job. Her friend had seemed satisfied when Billi explained she wanted to reread the letters and would get them back to her.

But avoiding her friend's neighborhood would have to change. If Jack was not going to contact her with updates of his findings, she simply would have to ferret out as much as possible on her own.

She put on her raincoat and took her umbrella from the stand by the door. Pepper looked up at her in the hopes of a walk, but she shooed him away from the door.

"Not this time, my little guard dog. When I get back, we'll go for a nice long walk."

He barked up at her and cocked his head in the adorable plea of one used to getting his way.

"Stay here and watch the house. I won't be long." She petted his head.

Her mother had left early for a meeting at Gai's Bakery to determine how many loaves of French bread they would donate for the Christmas party. And Mrs. O had pledged she would not leave until Phil Gai had offered two full trucks. Billi knew her mother meant to have her way if it took all day and hoped the generous Italian would give in early.

The rain hit her umbrella with the hard plops of a heavy winter storm. No one would be out much in this deluge and the umbrella provided a great shield against the weather and being recognized.

Billi left Jackson and splashed up the hill, with small rivulets of water chasing themselves down the sidewalk as she passed. At Main Street, she turned and headed past Kumamoto Fish, with its fragrant reminder of life, the sea. Then on a hunch, she entered Miyoshiya Restaurant and positioned herself as close as possible to the window to view those coming and going, not really knowing what she looked for. But, she reasoned, this cold and wet day would draw more seekers of warmth to the Japanese baths next door than a normal day. Her tense frame huddled over her tea, and she tried not to look around. She thought of the hot, relaxing waters of the baths and became jealous of those who could find such a reprieve from this cruel weather.

The clientele had changed twice and newly arrived patrons, dripping wet, waited for her table. With a resignation of failure, she collected her still damp coat and made her way down the stairs to the glass doors and the wet street. As she stood putting on her coat she caught sight of a passing umbrella with two sets of men's legs beneath it, scurrying through the rain. She hurried into the rain, opening her umbrella, and followed the dark-blue, oil-paper umbrella with the soft design swirling around the top in typical Japanese fashion. She focused beneath the dripping wagasa cover where one pair of legs, in Western clothing, stepped lightly, while the other feet, below a traditional yukata robe with a worn hem, shuffled with age.

A black car pulled to the curb, and the elderly gentleman climbed in the backseat while the young man hurried to the front. As they passed, Billi lowered her umbrella, shielding her face. Professor Fujihara hid in plain sight, and the young man with him appeared to be the one Eileen had set her hopes on. She knew she could not involve Eileen, but Tak was already in this mess, and she would just have to ask him some questions.

As she raised her umbrella, Billi saw another man across the street stomping out his cigarette, his head bent forward, tilting his hat so the rain poured from the brim. She quickly lowered her umbrella again and sped in the opposite direction. When she reached the corner she peered back, but he had disappeared. Once again only the thick rain filled the streets.

EDDY SPENT HIS AFTERNOON UP ABOVE the Ewa grocery store, about one block from where he had concealed the car Jack had arranged for him—a green-and-yellow Bantam with a faded convertible top—in an abandoned driveway. Some days paid off more than others. He took detailed notes of the number of visits and time of day Tadashi Morimura had a driver bring him to Pearl City; and afterward, Eddy rewarded himself spending time with Lani.

Her mother, now resigned to their betrothal, taught Eddy the phrase in Hawaiian "I pledge my love to you alone." But he stumbled over the pronunciation.

"Ka`u Ia E Lei A`e Nei La." He practiced to the wind as he watched the roads below.

His back straightened when he saw the car and driver bringing the bold spy from the consulate. He glanced at his watch marked the time Morimura stayed inside with the older couple. After five minutes, the big car turned and headed out of sight.

Putting his notepad away, he climbed in his new prize and headed for the Waikiki Elementary School, where Lani rehearsed with some of the young girls for a Christmas presentation. He slipped into the back of the small stage area and watched as the children shook their feathered gourds, the red and yellow uli ulis, keeping rhythm with the music.

"Wonderful." Lani clapped as the young children finished with heads bowed, gourds held out before them touching, and right legs extended in pau, all done. When they began to giggle, she turned to see Eddy sitting with a puili in each hand. He hit the slit sticks made from bamboo together to applause and even more laughter.

"Do you want to show us the dance?" Lani raised an eyebrow with her question.

He came toward her and whispered, "I might hurt myself."

"Girls." She looked down at the bright faces. "Let's show the sailor how to use these properly."

The mischief in their faces was magic. One of the tiniest stomped toward Eddy and shook her finger at him.

"Maika`i`ole," she scolded and took the puilis from him.

"Bad," Lani explained, then bit her lip, stifling a laugh.

Eddy half-bowed to the fearless child, who then turned on her heels and with a swish of her hula skirt joined the others, each of whom held the long sticks above their heads and waited for the music.

Lani stood behind them, and as the music began she stepped into the dance with her eyes fixed on Eddy.

When the rehearsal finished, Eddy stood in the late sun, thankful for the breeze that cooled the heat his body felt when near his beloved. As they walked together in silence through Kapiolani Park, below the shade of the large banyan trees and toward the rolling surf, his mind wandered back to his report he would give to Jack.

"Do not worry so." She squeezed his hand. "Father is coming around, and he said he would like to talk with you about us this Sunday."

"Is he going to make me ride Lolly Pop again?" Eddy's throat went dry at the thought.

"Would you for me?"

"Of course, but I might not be able to walk for a few days. Would you be my nurse?"

Her head went back with her laughter, and the sun's light caught the movement of her hair.

"Sunday. I'll be there. He has got to say yes. I'm almost through with this round of training and I have no idea if they are going to send me—"

"He will. We will marry soon." The confidence of her statement did not convince Eddy. "The children told me the Duke is swimming at the Natatorium. Shall we go there?"

"Heck, no. I want you all to myself." He wrapped his arms around her. "I don't trust any duke around you, even if he is Hawaiian."

"Duke Paoa Kahinu Mokoe Hulikohola Kahanamoku." The words slipped beautifully from her mouth.

"What did you just say?"

"His name."

"What? Do our children have to have such long names? I won't be able to call all of my sons to dinner in time."

Her smile lit his heart. "I will give you many sons."

He kissed the lips that claimed the promise.

"Say, there's a football game on Saturday night. University of Hawaii versus Willamette Bearcats, and a friend of mine is playing. I'd love it if you would come with me."

"Where is Willamette?"

"Sorry. Salem, Oregon, just below Washington State."

"I know my states." She removed her sarong revealing her floral bathing suit hugging her curves and started for the water.

Eddy gulped and stripped to his swimming trunks. As they swam out past the coral, he caught up with her.

"Was that a yes?" He could feel the saltwater dripping into his eyes as he watched her closely.

"I would like to meet a friend of yours." She dove into the slapping of the waves and disappeared.

Eddy took a deep breath and followed.

LIGHTHEARTED, EDDY PROPELLED his convertible back to base, his mind full of the feel of Lani's body pressed against his in the warm waters. Their marriage would have to be soon. They had planned to meet again in Kailua on Sunday at the small house with the beautiful deserted beach that had once belonged to her grandparents. Lani had assured him it would be a celebration of her father's acceptance of their marriage.

Eddy rummaged through his footlocker when Sam appeared and bounced down on his bunk next to him.

"We've had some new orders." The youth's eyes reflected his concern as he looked around the room.

"Well?" Eddy's chest tightened. Were they being confined to barracks?

"All our submarines have been told to stay within a small radius that's been designated just for them offshore." He took a deep breath before he delivered the next news. "And our pilots are on alert. We're to shoot at any sub outside that radius. Are we at war?"

"Not yet." Eddy put his hand on the seventeen-year-old's shoulder. "You'll know when we are."

"Ain't that somethin'?" Sam shook slightly.

"Listen. Just stay attentive. What did I tell you to do if bombs start to drop?"

"Stay in a push-up position on the ground."

"Remember that, because the Brits have been through this for years, and that's what their manual says to do. Get out of sight and stay in a push-up position so the blasts don't make your body hit the ground. How many push-ups can you do anyway?"

"About a hundred and fifty." His chin, with its few scraggly hairs—not enough to shave—shot out in pride.

"Well you'll only need one to stay alive. I'm going to a football game Saturday with Lani. Want to join us?"

"You bet. Scooter too?" The youth clung to his buddies that formed his new family.

"Of course." He ruffled Sam's blonde hair playfully, and the kid smiled back. "Remember, push-ups."

"Yeah, well, ain't nothin' gonna get me." He pretended to box a shadow.

"Good, I'm counting on it. Now I have to go make a phone call. But thanks for the tip, and keep your nose close to the ground for more."

"Sure thing, Eddy." He stood and continued to shadow box as he worked his thin frame out the door.

FORTY-EIGHT

"WHY ARE YOU LEAVING US AGAIN?" Lilly sat with her feet up, the small bump of her belly beginning to show on her slight frame. Next to her bare feet on the coffee table a ball of yarn coiled up to the hook she held in her hand. Jack marveled that she had found a pastime. The blanket she crocheted gained in length, the pale blue a sign in her confidence that the child she carried was of the male gender.

"Not for long." He bent to kiss her forehead, then approached his mother to do the same.

She tilted her head to accept his peck on her cheek. "Well, if you are heading back to Hawaii, work on your tan this time. You are so pale. And, of course, more macadamia nuts please."

Jack felt encouraged that her spirits were high with the coming grandchild, and she accepted her role with newfound strength.

He crossed the hardwood floor and started up the steps into the foyer, as Bella came at him with a large bag in hand.

"Yous don't look likes yous eaten'. Here." She held out the sack, and Jack could smell the food from where he stood.

"Fried chicken?"

"Mm-hmm." She thrust out her cheek and waited.

His women. How could he explain to them the fear that carried him to far-off places? He brushed a quick kiss on the cheek that still smelled of frying oil and took the bag.

"Keep an eye on things." He looked into her deep brown eyes.

"Hear from dat Ginger lately?" Bella had a knack at seeing through him.

"No."

"Hmmph." She folded her arms across her bosom and stood back so he could pass.

With building anxiety he drove the short distance to the airport, but he had to wait for the fog to lift so the private, four-prop plane could take off. He had put everything in order, forwarding Eddy's latest updates to his boss, Hoover, and replying to Duckworth. Apparently, Billi had started to spend more time in Japantown, possibly due to the fact that the professor had been spotted. He picked up a long, thin case to carry onto the plane when the pilot nodded in his direction.

Jack had been practicing his skills using Akio's sword with the flamboyant red grip and dragon guard below the blade which he had concealed in the case. Like his days at Stanford, he spent hours on balance, stance, and strategy. However, his one eye created a new challenge. If he removed his patch, his blurred vision in that eye upset his balance and perception. Practice meant everything. The weight of the bag reminded him of how he first met Akio.

"We have found you a wonderful roommate," the housemaster of Toyon had announced in early September of their junior year. "As you both like fencing, or swords, we thought it the perfect fit."

Perfect, Jack mused as his hand grasped the handle to the leather case tighter, the case that held his rivals prized long sword. He had watched Akio's movement when the blow removed David's head from his body. Right to left, simple, clean, the way of strategy as taught by Musashi in *The Book of Five Rings*. But the emotion he saw on Akio's face at the moment of impact was against the rules of the warrior. Emotion; the trained killer's downfall. And Jack planned to incite that emotion. If it came to a battle between them again, he would be ready this time.

But more importantly, he remembered how Akio cheated. He fought without honor. One spring night of their senior year, they were fencing alone in the gym. Jack had bettered his Japanese roommate with three on-target hits to his protective jacket. Exhausted and sweating, Jack had removed his face mask, and that was when he struck. Akio had attacked him out of rage, wielding a small sword. Using the hilt of his sword, Jack had knocked the smaller blade aside, but not before the tip of the blade had sliced his eye, leaving the scar he would carry forever.

He had hoped his old roommate would lead him to his plans, the plans that would expose the machine of destruction the enemy would use against America. And Jack hoped that somehow he could still accomplish what he had set out to do months ago. But for now, if he could not stop the war from happening, hopefully he could save Billi.

He leaned his head back against the seat as the plane took off and prayed he was not too late.

"Tak is elusive these days. He spends most of his time in the Golden Donut Café or the Star Pool Hall." Eileen looked at her friend as they worked their way down the aisles of the Higo Store. "Should I tell him you are looking for him?"

"No. No, that's fine." Billi smiled. "I hear the kendo competition is going to be exciting." She nodded toward the poster that announced the event Thursday night at the Nippon Kan Theatre.

"Maybe Tak's friend Sanzo will be there," Eileen smiled back.

"Has he been around lately?" Her questions repeated themselves, and she attempted to not sound interested.

"Not since the first time Tak brought him home. He is so nice." From the sound in her voice, Eileen's longing for the handsome young man became more like a dream.

"Yes." Billi fingered some beautiful imported material. "Does he have family here?"

"I do not know. But I can not wait for the two of you to meet so you can give me your opinion. He certainly seemed like he wanted to meet you."

"I take it you want me to go to the competition with you?"

Billi watched her friend's eyes light up at the suggestion.

"Will you?"

"Yes. I'll be at your house at 6:30 and then we can head over together. Will Kenny or your father be going?"

"Father does not go out anymore. He only comes home after he has checked his cherry trees for frost. Then he inspects the orchid that sits by the shrine and is silent. He misses Mother so, and the little orchid is her soul. So he talks to the flower daily."

"We'll ask him. That might lift his spirits." Billi tried to hide her concern, not yet convinced that Sanzo was as nice as Eileen willed him to be, as she inspected a scarf. Red-and-white arches covered one side, like fans stacked on each other, while the other side showed blue-and-white waves. Both traditional Japanese patterns, yet offered different uses in one garment.

DANNY BEAT HIS FINGERS to the rhythm of Mrs. O's singing as she examined her lists: Two truckloads of bread from Gai's, free shaves from the barber on Cherry Street, candy and popcorn to stuff the red-and-white-striped bags, and someone to play the piano as everyone sang the lyrics of Christmas songs. And, of course, Father Peretti would be there to give his blessing.

"Danny, are all three nativities up?"

"Yes, Mrs. O. And I'm picking up the candy next Wednesday. Want it to be fresh, not the old stuff." He smiled with pride. Taking over the jobs that Ray and Eddy used to perform at this time each year kept him busy. It was going to be lonely this Christmas without those two to hang around with. And Billi seemed in another world lately.

"Wonderful," she sang. "I've started baking my Weihnachtsplätzche early. There are Pfeffernusse, angel eyes, and Zimtsterne cookies on the counter I haven't packaged up yet. I need to keep my elf happy. You are looking far too thin these days."

Mrs. O had been doting over Danny of late, and he relished the transference and the sense of duty. Her motherly love became almost overwhelming at times, but he knew she had also spent a bit of time with his sister Dahlia, to soften the blow her son had inflicted on the young blonde when he jilted her for this Lani girl. Mrs. O would have much to say to Edward when he returned home, and Danny did not envy him that lecture.

Pepper followed Danny into the kitchen and lingered at his feet as he stood eyeing the array of Christmas cookies. Without warning, the small dachshund ran to the back door and growled. Danny walked to the window and looked out as the limbs of the large cedar tree moved with someone's weight. It felt too cold for Billi to be heading up the tree, but then Billi climbed to her spot in all kinds of weather.

He carefully selected his favorites and took a stack of fragrant cookies back into the dining room. He lowered into a chair across from Mrs. O as she worked at the table, and she nodded approvingly at the size of his helping, not breaking her humming to speak.

As Danny devoured the last bite, the front door opened, and Pepper scurried off to greet his mistress.

"How is my little guard dog doing?" Billi bent to pick him up and carried him into the dining room as he struggled against her damp coat.

"He sure is your guard dog." Danny stood and headed toward the kitchen. "He knew you were just up in your tree."

Billi clutched Pepper closer, thankful Danny had his back to her. He hadn't noticed that her skirt and coat were clean, with no telltale signs of a recent foray into the limbs of their special cedar tree. She quickly let Pepper loose and headed up the stairs.

She hurried down to the end of the hall and into the back bedroom, which would put her about eye level with some of the cedar tree's tall branches. Nothing but the wind moved through the sweeping limbs. From her perspective all seemed well, and she headed back to her bedroom and flopped onto her bed.

How to get to Sanzo without involving Eileen proved very difficult. While there appeared to be no harm in attending the sword competition, there was great risk if she could not speak to Sanzo alone. What could he be doing with the professor?

She took her notes from under her bed and checked them again. Christmas was three weeks away, and with no word from Jack, she would just keep her search in high gear. Tomorrow, before she met with Eileen, she would return to the Taisho-Do Bookstore.

She hid her lists, picking the box Eileen had given to her that contained the letters she had penned to her friend. Her fingers rested on the hand-decorated box. Inside represented two lives: one with her best friend and the other of the treachery that led toward destruction, and she set her mind to unearth the source of the destruction. Both centered on the two worlds of Japan—those who had come to love American and the others from the country that desired to conquer the East and would soon focus on the West.

Reverently, she hid the box beneath her bed.

With pen in hand, she scribbled a letter to Eddy in his distant paradise of sun, saltwater, and love. She envied him and his simple lifestyle. She wanted to tell him everything she had uncovered. She knew his quick mind would pick out the piece she had overlooked. She missed him dearly and told him so. Signing with a "Stay safe," she sealed her letter and fell fast asleep.

BY 1:15 ON THE NEXT AFTERNOON, Eddy headed into Honolulu to the docks to see if the luxury liner carrying the Willamette football team had arrived. His old classmate, Carrel Deiner, better known as Truck, was one of the twenty-eight team members expected to set foot on Hawaiian soil.

The drive over the Pali turned windy, and he had a hard time keeping his Bantam on the right side of the highway. As the road continued down toward the docks, he contemplated the steamers underway. Remembering the ships filled with Japanese departing en masse the previous week, he convinced himself he was actually doing a bit of reconnaissance by going to the docks today. He turned down toward the Matson Line Aloha Tower with the Hawaiian gothic clock and parked so he could walk to the port. It appeared quiet. One large ship already steamed through the blue-green waters leaving a wide white tipped wake. It was hard to tell the ethnicity of its passengers. From a distance, the figures could have been any nationality.

He drove back toward the Ewa grocery store run by the older couple. It appeared deserted. He walked up to a sign that hung lopsided on the door.

"On vacation. Mele Kalikimaka," he read aloud.

Eddy went around the back of the small store and discovered overflowing bags of garbage with flies buzzing around some papaya that had been left to rot in the sun. Stacks of empty Coca-Cola bottles sat against the wall in crates. Next to them rested a crate with some unopened drinks. He reached for his pocket knife and popped the top. Smelling it first, he took a sip, and then a long drink. Never missing an opportunity, he took the crate of unopened Coca-Cola and put it in the trunk of his car.

He turned his jalopy around and headed up the hill to where he usually sat to watch, but he saw no sign of the black consulate car traverse any of the roads. The air hung humid, and Eddy dripped with sweat as he drove down Kalakaua Avenue to the Moana Seaside Hotel and parked. The football players from Willamette and San Jose State who were to compete against the Hawaii Rainbow Warriors in the Shrine Bowl were living in luxury. He passed between the tall art-deco columns of the recently renovated hotel owned by the Matson Navigation Company and strode across the open lobby toward the sea. He stood in the sunshine of the steps, searching the tables that dotted the patio beneath a sprawling banyan tree. He easily spotted his football player friend Truck.

Truck stood as Eddy approached, looking exhausted and excited at the same time.

"Man, this is some heat. How do you do it?" were the first words Truck spoke as they caught each other in a big, welcoming hug.

"I stay on the windward side. You'll have to come and visit me there."

"Coach Keene won't let us out unless we're swimming or practicing." He sat down and gulped his soft drink again.

"Old Spec is pretty notorious." Eddy knew of the coach's tight-fisted approach. "How was the trip?"

"Man, oh man, it was somethin'. That *Lurline* ship is incredible. What a beaut, and nothing but luxury all the way. We had one hell of a great trip. But boats and I don't really match," he finally admitted. "My stomach was upset most of the time. And some of the others are still in the rack trying to get their feet back under them."

"It takes time, but you'll be fine." Eddy signaled the waiter for a glass of Coca-Cola. "Say, you'd better win. I have a bet going with my fiancée and I'm riding on the Bearcats."

"Did I hear you right? Did you finally ask Dahlia to marry you?" Truck's broad smile matched his broad shoulders.

"Well, no. I've met a girl here that is…well…the most amazing woman I've ever met."

Truck rocked back in his chair. "And what does your mother have to say?"

"Damn you, Truck. Mom will adjust to her being part Hawaiian."

"Wow, I want to see that one. You'd better invite me." The large football player raised his glass and eyebrows to accentuate his statement.

"Only if you win." The challenge had begun.

"Not a problem."

Their glasses touched in high hopes.

Abruptly, Truck jumped up and held onto the table. "I have to go. Sorry, but I keep getting a bit…"

"I know. Watch those wobbly legs. Take a long swim. Believe me, the water will help. And I'll see you after the game Saturday so you can meet Lani before the wedding."

The afternoon spent at the bookstore proved to be a waste. Sanzo never showed, nor had anyone seen the professor in quite some time. Frustrated, Billi retied the new scarf she had purchased while shopping with Eileen over her head, pulling the material with the blue-and-white waves forward so it hid some of her face. As the sound of her steps clattered up the stairs toward the Nakamura apartment, she heard Tak's voice, loud and demanding. She hurried to listen at the door, but the argument had gone silent. She waited a minute and then knocked gently on the door.

Kenny opened the door slightly, "Oh, hi. Eileen is ill and will not be able to go with you tonight." His eyes were big with his lie.

"I see." Billi felt her stomach twist. "Please tell her to get well fast. I will phone her tomorrow."

"Thank you." The young boy seemed relieved that the conversation had ended.

Just as Billi turned to leave, she looked back. "I bought two tickets. Would you like the other?" She grabbed Kenny's hand and put the ticket against his palm. She felt him tremble slightly.

He nodded and then quickly closed the door.

Billi made certain to step loudly as she marched down the stairs so her friend would not be exposed to Tak's wrath. As she walked up the hill, it began to lightly snow. The flakes caught the streetlights and glistened in mesmerizing beauty. There was something so peaceful, clean, and calm about the first snow of the season. The children would be happy if this continued and school closed for a three-day weekend.

As she had suspected, Mr. Nakamura stood below the bare and gnarled branches of his cherry trees, his face turned upward toward the heavens where his wife now watched over all, with the silence of the snow falling around him. She quietly stepped beside him, imitating his stance, letting the soft flakes hit against her cheeks, cold and wet.

"Is my daughter not going with you?" His voice came as a low brush against her ears.

"She is afraid she is getting ill and prefers to stay at home tonight."

"Yes. It would be best. There are fearsome doings in the dark these days. You must be careful."

They both watched the dancing flakes settle around them.

"The professor asks for you."

As Billi's drew her breath in sharply, she felt the burning cold catch in her throat.

"You are to bring him gifts that were given once for the winter." He mumbled as if not speaking the words himself but those that had been channeled through him.

"Where do I find him?"

"That I do not know. Do not look to Tak for advice." He did not look at her as his gaze moved down the hill toward his store and apartment. "Good night. I am an old man and tired."

He left her then, standing alone as the puffs of his breath trailed behind, his shuffling feet leaving a pattern in the new blanket of sparkling, white snow. His words had been in English, heavy with accent and the uncertainty of tomorrow.

FORTY-NINE

BILLI HURRIED TOWARD SOUTH WASHINGTON STREET and the theater. Her gloved fingers held the scarf even farther forward, shielding her face from the growing force of the drifts of snow that swirled around her, collecting on her head and shoulders. Hopefully, Kenny would be able to join her later. Her mind reworked the words spoken by Mr. Nakamura in his unaccustomed English—"gifts that were given once for the winter"—and could not extract their meaning. She hoped that if the professor sought to speak with her, she simply needed to stay in the open and he would approach.

She snapped the wet scarf free of snow and then tied it once again on her head, attempting to hide her face as she entered the brick building. It pleased her to be alone and not have to worry about exposing Eileen to any further danger. She sat toward the back on the far aisle. Seeing the match had never been her objective.

The rounds of kendo competitions were staggered by age and ability. Family members, old and young, watched hypnotized as the masked men strutted in their traditional attire and bare feet, flaunting their precise training with the long swords. Kendo, the way of the sword, was alive and well in the Nippon Kan tonight.

From where Billi sat, she grasped how hard it became to distinguish who wore the meshed hoods, and fear crawled from her stomach to her fingertips. The sound of the blades hitting made her tremble, not with enjoyment for the match but with the memory of David, the dark alley, and his brutal death. Her head began to spin while the figures lunged and grunted in their own style of strategy—masterful, swift, deadly.

She had been beyond foolish to attend this event, and her tight ball of nerves propelled her outside for fresh air. She stood outside sweating with the snow melting on her hot face.

"Come."

The command came from behind her. She turned to see a man dressed for the competition, long sword at his side, slip back into the shadows.

She followed him around back to the stairs that led to a small room off the stage area. The oddity of her situation brought back memories of hiding from Akio, hiding in plain sight, as a geisha dancer.

In a half-dark room sat another competitor, smaller in stature. She entered, while the man she had followed stood guard outside the door.

"Come, my butterfly." The seated man waved her forward. "You, my best student, in so much danger. I never meant that to be."

Billi did not know why the tears started down her cheeks, but they did. Relief trickled through her at the sound of the quieting voice of the professor.

"I am glad you are well." Her head bowed in the respect she had always felt for him.

"We do not have long. Forgive me. I gave you something because I thought you would be the one—"

A loud crash startled them as something hit the other side of the door.

"Go." He stood. "Bring it to me. Give it to Sanzo. Ask no more questions."

His hand felt tight on her arm as he pushed her through a second door behind him. Billi stood in the dark of a second room and stumbled toward the light under the door. When she opened it, she found herself on the far side of the stage behind a group of men who were waiting their turn.

Still in the shadows, she flipped her scarf to the red-and-white side with the arches like fans, hunched her back, and imitated the bow-legged sway of Shirley Chow, the old Chinese lady from San Francisco. Stooped, she crab-walked through the lobby and out into the storm of twirling whiteness.

As she hurried down the block, a plug of a man, hat pulled down tight, took her arm and led her toward the dark car she knew only too well. He smelled of cedar pitch, and Billi almost laughed. As he slid in beside her, she relaxed into the front seat.

"How long were you up in my tree, Duckworth?"

"Nice view up there." He eased the car away from the curb and started down South Washington toward the water.

"See anything?"

"Only the other guy who's been tailing you."

"What? Hey, where are we going?" She sat up and watched the wipers clear the snow with a swoosh as the roads became steeper.

"Don't argue. Just do as I say and trust me." His hands gripped the wheel.

She watched in silence as he maneuvered down South Washington to Alaskan Way and then turned left into the gusts of snow.

"Where are we going?" Billi attempted to keep the panic out of her voice. "I need to get home. There's something I need to do."

Duckworth did not say a word, but continued driving past Coleman Dock and the Black Ball Ferry terminal. Billi let out a sigh of relief. For a moment she thought he headed away from the city.

He pulled the car into Pier 39, where the Coast Guard kept some of their large vessels and those on loan. At the dock, he spoke with the petty officer who approached the car as Billi stepped out into the snow, pulling her coat closer. She tightened her scarf with the red-and-white designs against the wind as she approached the long Coast Guard cutter, *Haida*, in port for repairs. The size of the ship made her feel small as she looked down the massive pier.

"This way, ma'am." The young seaman's twang drifted back at her.

She turned and followed him, head bent into the chilling breeze. When she reached a gangplank, she paused and looked up at the lights on the *Haida.*

"We're over here," he called from down the dock.

She continued past the cutter to the *Vagabond,* a smaller, streamlined pleasure boat built by Seattle's master, Norm Blanchard.

"Watch your step," he instructed as she climbed aboard. He led her down the few steps into the galley and closed the hatch behind them.

She smelled diesel mixed with coffee as she sat. Removing her damp scarf, she folded it before placing it on the table as her guide put a hot cup of brew before her.

"I'm Morgan, ma'am." He smiled and pushed some cream in her direction. "You need anything, you let me know."

"Where are you from, Morgan?"

"Baton Rouge." He puffed up at the name of his home town. "I love bein' a Coastie. You get sent some interestin' places."

The engines started and Billi jumped to her feet.

"Wait." She pushed past Morgan. "I can't go anywhere. I need to get back home."

"Sorry, ma'am. We have our orders."

Morgan followed her to the porthole. They watched the last of the lines being tossed aboard as the *Vagabond* slid forward past the other docked tall ship.

"Where are we headed?" Billi's voice was low, threatening.

"You'll have to ask the bosun that one."

"Where is he?"

"On the bridge. He figured you'd have questions and said he would be down as soon as we were clear of port and on course."

Billi stomped back to the seat. "Where's Duckworth?" she demanded.

"Who?"

"The man who brought me here." She plopped down.

"Back on shore. He didn't board, ma'am." His even tone held a bit of pity.

"He what?"

The young man gulped in obvious discomfort. "Are you hungry?"

"No. But this is kidnapping. I want to go back."

"Just relax, ma'am. I'm making you a sandwich. They always calm me down."

Billi crossed her arms and squinted at the poor seaman whose job appeared to be keeping her entertained and at ease.

"Is there anyone else on this ship?"

"Just the engineer."

"No other noncrew members?" She changed her tone in an attempt to get more information out of the young man.

"Just us Coasties."

"My brother is in the navy." She turned on her charm, not realizing the inbred rivalry between the two factions of the service.

"Jolly for him, ma'am." Morgan slammed some meat onto the bread he had set out.

Billi squirmed in her seat and watched the snow cross the porthole at an angle as the ship moved through the storm. She began to hum, then tap her fingers, then she pushed herself up.

"Where is this bosun anyway?" her word tense.

"Right here."

The growling voice came from behind her and she jumped.

"Oh, yes." She turned and smiled sweetly. "Well excuse me, but can you please tell me where you are taking me?"

"Orders say Bremerton." He eyed her up and down.

"And whose orders?" She lifted her chin.

"Not sure where they originated." He kept his gaze fixed on her. "Everything okay, Morgan?"

"Tip-top, sir," Morgan placed the sandwich next to Billi's scarf.

The man in charge looked at the Japanese scarf, folded so that both sides with their different designs were showing. His eyes flicked back at her, his lips tightened, and then he left.

"What was that about?" She addressed Morgan as if they were conspirators.

"Got me. But he sure didn't like that scarf of yours."

Billi lowered back down before her food and took a big bite.

BREMERTON SPORTED A THICK BLANKET of snow that left a white veil over the hillsides and large ships moored dockside. The *Vagabond* motored into port, and the bosun came below. As he started in her direction, Billi slipped her scarf below the table and stuffed it in her pocket.

"I am to see you ashore. Personally." He stood over her, waiting. "Let's go."

"Thank you. I think." She mumbled then threw a quick look in Morgan's direction. "Thank you for the sandwich. I needed it."

"Good luck." The young man shook his head.

The air outside was bracing, yet Billi left her scarf stuffed in her pocket and stood bareheaded in the falling flakes. As the bosun led her down the dock, a tall figure emerged out of the falling snow, hat forward shielding his face and the patch over his right eye. Billi could tell his walk a mile away and she felt a surge of both lust and concern at seeing Jack. Her heart raced and she wanted to kiss him, but her anger reacted first.

She put her hands on her hip in frustration. "What have I done now?"

"I'll take her from here." Jack had his hand on the small of her back. "Thank you. And you know how to reach me in the event there is movement."

"Not a problem." The coast guardsman nodded.

"Oh, yes she is." Jack smiled as he guided Billi through the snow.

THE CAR PULLED OFF ERLANDS POINT ROAD to Tanda Avenue and up her father's driveway, past the tall trees, to the ramshackle house overlooking the water. They had not spoken during the short ride, and Billi's stomach twisted in knots.

"Why are you bringing me here?" Her confusion led her questioning.

"Hopefully it will be safe." Jack looked over at her. "I'm not going to lie. There has been a disturbing development. I needed you out of Seattle but close."

"Does my father know about this?"

"Some of it, but not all."

He parked behind the woodshed but did not attempt to leave the car. The snow began to fill up the windshield with the wipers stopped.

"I saw the professor."

"Yes. I heard. What did he want?"

"Something he gave me. I was going home to try to find it when Duckworth kidnapped me."

Jack chuckled. "He didn't kidnap you, Billi. I did."

"Is this how you get all of your girls?" She folded her arms over her heart to try and keep it from beating so fast.

"Just the ones I want to keep alive." He reached over, pulled her to him, and kissed her. The heat of their exchange fogged the windows, making the snow slide down the windshield in slow motion.

When they broke away, Billi was breathless, her chest heaving, her lips wanting to touch his again as her body pulsed with desire.

"Oh." Her throaty sigh escaped into the darkness of the car.

The cabin door opened, and the amber lights glowed through the steamy windows.

"Come on, let's get you inside." Jack's voice was deep and sounded dry.

"Yes." She hesitated, not wanting to go.

The young couple passed Mr. O'Shaughnessy as they entered. He grunted before closing the door tight against the chill of winter.

His mock joy at seeing her became evident in his tone. "Well, darlin'. Now isn't this a pleasant surprise?"

Jack took off his hat and put it on the table next to an unopened bottle of Jameson Irish Whiskey. He removed his gun and slid it under his Stetson.

Catching the swiftness of his movement Billi whispered, "Expecting someone?"

His shrugged, noncommittal, but he twisted the black onyx ring on his finger and Billi felt the chill run down her back. She felt her knees go weak. The two men she loved were beneath the same roof where danger could strike at any moment.

"Dad, I'm thirsty. Any hot chocolate?" She kept her focus on Jack.

Her father moved toward the stove. "Do you want a nip in it, Bright Eyes?"

"No thanks."

"Yer boyfriend here brought us a bottle." His distaste for Jack and all he stood for lingered like a heavy cloud in the room.

"Yes, that was nice." She wanted to lighten the conversation.

She sneezed and headed to the hearth were a roaring fire crackled and popped with the intensity of the blaze. She stood for a moment with her hands extended toward the welcoming heat. Aware Jack watched her silhouette dancing on the wall, she removed her wet shoes and put them on the warm stones that blended into the hardwood floor, but could not face him.

She heard Jack move across the room, the rattle of the curtains being drawn tight, and the squeak of the chair as he sat.

She turned, her back muscles relaxing with the heat, and pondered the situation in silence.

"Here, darlin'." Her father carried an old mug toward her.

She accepted it and then handed it to Jack. His half smile spoke volumes as he took the hot cup from her hands.

Mr. O mumbled as he headed back to his stove to prepare another cup.

Billi sat in the other chair facing the fire, mesmerized by the leaping blue-and-red flames. Her father pulled up a straight-backed wooden chair from the table and placed it between them with a snort. Retrieving the hot chocolate for Billi, he plopped down onto the hard, wooden seat.

"I have to drive in the mornin', but Billi can have my bedroom fur tonight."

"Not unless I'm in there with her." Jack's voice remained unflappable but stern.

Father and daughter both sat up straight and looked at each other.

Billi gulped. "Thanks, Dad, but you sleep in your bed. I'll take the upper bunk in the back room and Jack can sleep out here on the floor."

Jack leveled his gaze on Mr. O. "No dice. Billi gets the lower bunk and I'm in the upper."

"Now just a—"

"Dad. It will be all right. We'll leave the doors open to both rooms."

Mr. O stood and opened the bottle of whiskey, then poured a shot into his warm cocoa. "But I'm warnin' you." He fixed an evil eye on Jack as he sat. "You lay one finger on my girl and you'll marry her."

"I'll take that chance."

Billi snuck a quick look at Jack's stern face as the words rocketed through her, and her eyes misted. Something had changed between them. His determination she found startling and comforting. She wanted him alone, not in the hopes that he would touch her again, but to know what he insinuated by "disturbing development."

FIFTY

DARKNESS FILLED IN BEHIND the white drifts that had fallen all day on the street below the bay window on Boylston. Duckworth steadied his nerves and hoped he had not drawn any attention to the O'Shaughnessy home. Last night his tire tracks in the deep, icy snow had been easy to follow from Japantown. And when he had turned his car around at the dock, a dark Buick lingered just beyond the streetlight.

He had circled until the Buick retreated and then made his way to 30th South. He sat with Mrs. O long enough to explain that Billi had been put on a boat headed to Dyes Inlet because her newly acquired special skills were needed at the Bremerton Naval Base. Being the gracious hostess at any hour, Mrs. O had merely smiled and offered him a piece of cake and coffee. He sat a while longer enjoying her cooking then bid her goodnight and returned to the makeshift office on Boylston.

More radio transmissions were coming in from Station S at Fort Ward on Bainbridge Island. Magic, the wondrous machine, hurriedly decrypted messages that, according to the Japanese Purple code, would be sent in fourteen different parts. So far nothing stood out, except for the Seattle consulate mentioning Erlands. The translators wanted to send that much out immediately as the name might help identify movement.

He tried the line again, but no one answered at the cabin on Dyes Inlet where Jack watched over Billi. He walked to the map that sprawled across the office wall, where a few straight pins designated important hot spots of interest. Erlands Point sat not that far from Bainbridge Island. The roads would prove a challenge in the snow, but approaching Dyes

Inlet by boat presented a completely different story. And that shook Duckworth to the bone.

Why hadn't Jack returned his call? Was something the matter at Dye's Inlet or was Jack preoccupied with his torn interests? Love. Yes, somehow Duckworth believed they belonged together, he had watched the longing build between them. He sat back down at his desk, put his feet up and head back to wait. Jack would call.

THE MORNING SUN BEGAN ITS ARC over the southeast corner of the island. Eddy sat on the rocks at Koko Head next to Joe's makeshift radio station. Below the tuft of rock, Hanauma Bay, with all of its various colors from green to blue, spread before him toward Molokai.

The Coca-Colas he had confiscated from behind the closed store had come in handy, as he'd offered a cool drink in the hopes of some information. He had made the rounds with his offerings to four of the six radar locations on the island manned by the Army Signal Corps. Today he planned to try his luck with his friend Joe at the KoKo Head hilltop.

"Yes," Joe answered Eddy's question as he stepped from the radio shack. "I was sitting on the hill above the truck having a snack, and this big black car pulls up over there." He pointed to a spot down the road with an excellent view out over the water. "The Japanese man wore a bright aloha shirt and had a camera around his neck. He didn't take pictures. I waited to make sure, would have called it in. But he just got back in the car and they drove off."

"They?"

"Yes. He rode in the backseat and I couldn't see the driver."

"That in your report?"

"No. They only want what's coming in over the radio for now, they still don't trust radar. We're training new fellows because there are so few of us who have experience with radar. We're still under orders to only run the radar from 0400 to 0700."

"You're kidding? Holy shit, what if someone doesn't attack on our schedule? Is there a lot going on out there?"

At that, Joe clamped his mouth shut, rolled his eyes toward the heavens, and shrugged his shoulders.

"Got it." Eddy exhaled loudly.

"What do you think, Navy? We headed for a war soon?" His deep-blue eyes held Eddy's gaze, seeking the same thing: knowledge and reassurance.

"Keep watching closely. There's something out there. And let me know if you see that Japanese guy in his aloha shirt again." He stood and brushed off his pants, leaving a bit of dust on the breeze that lifted past them off the water.

"Are we supposed to be talking?" Joe's brown army uniform symbolized the long-standing conflict between the forces, especially with the white of the navy.

"Hell, yes." Eddy watched the horizon. "No one else is."

"You've heard about the war warning, right?" Joe could barely contain his anger.

"Yep, they stacked all of the planes, wings almost touching, on the tarmacs and took out the guns at Hickam. Afraid of sabotage." The anger in Eddy's voice echoed his frustration. "Let's just hope if anything is coming, those guys have the thirty minutes they need to reinstall their guns before they take off."

EDDY PICKED UP LANI for their evening swim and sat next to her in silence, moody. The war warning had arrived on November 27, they were to be on alert and to expect an aggressive move by Japan within the next few days. But the days had passed with nothing but anticipation, and it made Eddy sweat with panic. Radar working on limited hours, sabotage expected instead of an attack, submarines seen in the area, and the order to fire on anything outside of the established area for US submarines. He kicked at the sand.

"Come and join me," Lani cooed as she stood and moved her luscious hips toward the water. He watched her long black hair, thick and shining, an attribute of her Japanese blood, sway with her movement. It flowed softly like her mother's and unlike most of the Hawaiians, whose coarse hair soared wild on the wind. He thought of Eileen and Kenny. What would happen to all of them if America went to war with the Empire of the Rising Sun?

But then he remembered his German heritage and the impact of what being at war with Hitler would mean. He brushed aside his worries for the peace and beauty that awaited him under palm trees and the pink clouds of sunset. Tomorrow remained far away.

Catching up to Lani, he wrapped his arm around her waist, and they walked into the warm water as one.

PEPPER STARTED TO BARK at the back door, his furious growl drawing the attention of Mrs. O'Shaughnessy.

"Danny? Is that you?" She shuffled her slippers to the door.

Beneath the light of the moon, the snow sparkled with an ice-blue hue. There were several imprints up and down the stairs where Danny had diligently brought her wood and kindling before he had gone home, a piece of strudel for his work tucked into a sack for a late-night snack.

"Come on, Pepper. It was nothing."

He barked once more before following her through the kitchen and into the living room. She drew the large wooden pocket doors to keep the fire's warmth from escaping and sat in her chair. As she sipped a bit of her hot chocolate, with just a nip of the spirit added, she settled back with her lists as Pepper nestled in her lap.

Before she heard the knock, Pepper flew across the room toward the front door. Mrs. O, tightened the sash on her bathrobe and peeked around the corner into the foyer. Seeing someone standing outside, she reached around to flip on the porch light.

A slight man, covered in heavy clothing and snowflakes, stood looking back at the street.

"Who is it?" She shouted over the dog's bark.

"Eileen's brother, Tak." He turned toward her, but did not smile. "She left something here and I was wondering if Billi could get it for me. Eileen sent me because she is sick."

"Eileen's sick?" Mrs. O ventured into the hallway, toward the door.

"Yes. Is Billi here?"

"She's out sledding. Loves the snow." Mrs. O took her cue from Pepper, who had not stopped barking and growling at the man outside. "Can I have her call you when she gets in?"

He looked at her through the glass pane of the door, then at Pepper, and his eyes narrowed. He nodded once and clomped back down the stairs.

She watched as he disappeared into the darkness beyond the glistening, snow-covered street.

"Good boy." She kissed the puppy. "Now let's give your mother a call and see what this is all about."

She shuffled back to the phone and began to dial when she discovered the line was dead.

"Do you think it will ever stop?" Jack looked out the window at the snow piling up against the woodshed out back.

"Do you want it to? I love the snow. It's beautiful and peaceful." Billi poked the fire, and a spark flew onto the hearth. She kicked it back with her shoe.

"Do you think your father is stuck somewhere?" He twisted the ring on his little finger as he paced to the other side of the small cabin and looked out at the flakes falling into the water and disappearing.

"He's used to driving in this, and his truck has weight and chains. He'll be here soon." She sat in the chair to watch the piece of wood she added as it shifted with the flames. "I will admit it seemed a bit unusual for him to head out this morning. But when you are delivering food supplies, like meat, you are needed. And my father likes to be needed."

"Have I told you that you are needed?" He looked back at her, his eye patch in his hand.

"Yes, I know my country needs me."

Jack moved to the other chair by the warmth of the blaze and sat, his eye patch over his knee. "Look, if anything happens to me, I want you to hide somewhere. Where would that be?"

"I would head up a tree." She laughed at her immediate response.

"Okay." He smiled. "I should have figured that one. How would I know you were okay?"

"I would leave you a sign." She giggled, enjoying the game. "A spoon. A silver spoon. Small, for desserts."

Jack did not miss the implication of how they met. "You know, my father always had the table set with six spoons."

"My mother would have approved." She leaned toward him. "Can you name what they are for?"

"Soup is the large one, the teaspoon is, well a teaspoon, the grapefruit spoon has those jagged edges, the small salt spoon. How am I doing?"

"That's four, keep going."

"Okay, your dessert spoon and the ice cream scoop."

"Ice cream scoop? Not formal enough. What about the demitasse?"

"Oh, I can see where this is going. No, I want the ice cream scoop, thank you."

They laughed, and the tension dwindled as they envisioned a gentle, elegant life of old.

"Seriously, Billi, I won't always be here to protect you. I wish I could. But at some point I am going to have to leave and I don't want to have to be worried about you."

"I'll be fine." She sank back against the chair with a look of pure determination.

"And I'll be back. Would that be all right with you?" He watched her closely.

"When?" The word had an endless feeling to it.

"As fast as I can." His hand reached out and covered hers.

The sound of Mr. O's truck came from the driveway as his headlights swept the cabin.

Jack had his patch on, along with his gun, coat, and hat in one swift movement. He positioned himself on the far side of the door and felt for his pocket knife.

The engine stopped, and Billi stood. Jack signaled her away from the window, and she slowly moved across the small room. Bile rose in his throat as he watched her soak in her new reality: Every car, every person now became a suspect in Akio's search to find her.

As her father entered alone, Jack slid out the door and went around the front of the cabin. He checked the back of the truck, then worked his way past the woodshed to the far side of the driveway and walked through the woods toward the road. Once he could see the tracks of Mr. O's truck on the roadway, he hid behind a low boxwood plant and waited. The silence of the snow lingered undisturbed by car or man. But still he waited.

MRS. O STOOD ON HER PORCH and watched the children from across the street file back into the warm glow of their house. Night had fallen quickly and the youngsters were laughing and looked wet to the bone. Pepper, having left his yellow mark on the white crystals, jumped out of the wet mess and left a trail with his low belly that looked like a long sled had been dragged through the white fluff.

"Victor," she yelled at the oldest boy who bent to take off his boots. "Can you ask your mother if her phone is working?"

"Sure." He leaned inside and then shouted back at his neighbor. "Yes. Do you need to use it?"

Mrs. O pulled her coat tighter over her red long underwear and hiked up her hem, exposing large boots. "I'll be right there. Come, Pepper."

As she started down the stairs, the dachshund ran back and forth, attempting to find a path that did not include being buried past his midsection.

"Come." Her voice rang out again, and the small pup leaped into the deep snow and surfaced with puffs of white stuck to his black nose.

The two marched across the street to the scrunching sound of her boots, while Victor waited to hold the door.

Once inside, Mrs. O scooped up the dog as the pink-faced children gathered around to pet him. He wiggled free, and commotion ensued with little chilled figures chasing the wagging tail.

"Sorry to barge in on you like this, Nancy." Mrs. O began to apologize as her neighbor came from the kitchen with a hot drink in each hand.

"I put a little touch in there for you, Gertrude." Nancy winked as she extended the steaming mug toward Mrs. O.

"How thoughtful." She sat on the only spot on the couch that did not have wet mittens and hats.

"Oh, here, let me get those." Nancy bustled the items of snow gear into the hallway. "What is the matter with your phone?"

"I don't know, but I would like to make a call."

"Of course. But finish your drink first. It's just so nice to have someone to talk to after children in and out all day long."

"Yes, isn't the snow grand?"

The two chatted over a second cup, and their giggling brought the flock of children back with the puppy in their arms. They had dressed Pepper for the journey home. The youngest had wrapped a yellow blanket around his belly, and her sister had added her doll's pink hat and tied it under his chin.

He glanced up at his owner in absolute embarrassment, his brown eyes sorrowful for his appearance.

"Aren't you darling?" She blew kisses to the distraught dog. "Wonderful job, young ladies." The two women burst into laughter again. "Well, I suppose I should head home and see if his new outfit works."

"What about your call?" Nancy pushed herself up from her chair.

"Oh, good heavens. I forgot."

She tried the cabin on Dyes Inlet, but there was no answer.

"Lines must be down over there." She shrugged her shoulders. "Oh, well. May I return if I need to try again?" She handed her empty cup to her hostess.

"Of course."

"Thank you. I'll bring a little something back with me." She winked. "Now how about a Christmas carol before I go?"

"'Jungle Bells,'" the youngest demanded.

Victor scoffed, "He means 'Jingle Bells'—"

"Dashing through the snow," Nancy began singing before her visitor could object.

Victor held the door open as he shouted the joyful words of the song and Pepper was released to try out his snow outfit. Mrs. O stepped onto the porch then stopped mid-verse and watched in disbelief as a flashlight went off in the upper bedroom of her home across the street.

Pepper flew into action and shot off the steps. The small yellow blanket got caught in the snow and trailed behind as he dashed toward his home and fortress, barking at the top of his lungs. Miraculously, the small pink hat stayed on as he bounded up to the front porch and barked at the front door. Following a sound from inside, he ran around to the back.

Mrs. O fished a card from her pocket and ran back inside Nancy's home. Her hand shook as she dialed the number. The phone rang only twice before a voice came through on the other end.

"Duckworth here. That you boss?"

"No. Call the police. Someone's in my house. Upstairs. There's a light." Her high-pitched voice squeaked.

"Mrs. O? Where are you?"

"Across the street."

His "Stay there—on my way" were the last words she heard before the phone went dead.

FIFTY-ONE

JACK'S HANDS WERE BLUE with cold. There had been only one other old truck on the road for over twenty minutes. That vehicle had chugged by with its tire chains clicking at the same rhythm and disappeared. He had recognized the truck as a neighbor's. That meant that anyone following the snow-filled tire ruts would be confused as to what direction Mr. O's truck had gone. He shook the snow from his legs and started back to the warm fire.

He didn't want to leave, but the phone not working was creating a dark pit in his stomach. Maybe it was best to move Billi tonight. However, the roads posed a problem, and he felt the cabin was safe. One more night, he convinced himself.

Billi was already at the door when he opened it and brushed the snow from his heavy coat.

"What were you doing out there?" Her tone of voice like a mother hen's.

He didn't answer and knew she wasn't expecting one. Exposing her father as little as possible to the possible danger was their concerted effort.

"Give the man some space, Bright Eyes. He just needed out for a bit." Mr. O clucked into his mug of hot cider. "Get him somethin' hot."

Jack stamped his feet and put his gun back beneath his hat on the table. "That sounds about right." He confirmed the older man's wisdom.

"Now, don't you two go ganging up on me," Billi warned as she stepped up to the stove to retrieve the hot drink.

Jack barked a laugh as she started for the fire with his drink in hand. "Don't worry. We both know who would come out on top."

"Well put." Her father's eyes never left Jack as he lit his pipe. "I brought us some dandy steaks fur dinner. Need beef in the cold."

"Thanks." Jack accepted the offered drink.

"I bet you're a well-done man."

Jack returned Mr. O's gaze with a blank stare.

"Oh, no, Dad. He's rare," Billi quipped as she headed back to the stove.

"Well, ain't that somethin'. I took him for well-done." The older man tapped his pipe against his one ashtray.

"He's full of surprises."

Jack shifted. The heat he was feeling was not coming only from the fire.

"Lord help me," Mr. O mumbled and pulled the table chair in between the two others to take up his guard position, then pointed to the chair to his left. "Sit before you fall."

Jack, eyebrows raised, did as he was told.

Duckworth maneuvered his car up the hills toward 30th South. He had slid backward into a tree, but then had dug himself out and gained on the slopes. He had been a fool to wait at the office for Jack to call. As the day passed, the snow created the arctic streets he now faced.

He rounded the corner wide and heard a siren coming up from behind. Damn. He needed to get there first. His car drifted to the side of the road, and he was out the door and racing up the steps to the house. The front door was unlocked.

"I'm over here," he heard Mrs. O'Shaughnessy holler from across the street.

"Stay there."

"I can't find Pepper." Her shriek was pitiful.

He drew his gun and went inside. With relief, he heard the barking of the dog. Mrs. O had said upstairs. He started up, hugging the wall of the spiral stairs. As he reached the fifth step, it creaked with his weight, and he hurried on.

As he had expected, whoever had broken in was long gone. In the back bedroom a window was open, and the curtains flapped. The wet prints of the intruder on the carpet were filled with melting snow.

He closed the window and took up his search. All looked fine until he reached Billi's room.

The drawers to her tall chest were pulled open, with a few articles hanging over the edges and more clothes scattered on the floor. The closet was also in disarray. Her nightstand had been gone through. The only good thing about the situation was there was no dress lying on her bed with a knife stuck through it. Maybe the intruder had not made the connection between Billi and Ginger. A threat of imminent death was not the message.

Duckworth wracked his brain. What had Billi said she needed to go home and get? What did the professor have to do with this?

A yelp from the dog drew him back down the stairs and toward the kitchen. Huddled in the corner, his paw over his pink hat, Pepper lay on his side.

"Come on, boy." Duckworth knelt beside the shaking animal. "Let me see you." He gently felt the dog as he whimpered. "You're okay."

A toenail was missing from his front right paw, and a bit of blood was pooled on the floor.

"Let's see if you can stand." He coaxed the pup onto his feet, and the little creature gingerly walked in a circle, then plopped back down with a woof.

"Okay, you're going to be fine. I'll go and get Mrs. O."

He had no sooner said her name when he heard her bustling through the front door.

"Where's Pepper?" she demanded.

"In here." He stood and held the door for the charging woman as the pup's tail began to wag. "He's fine."

"Who said?" As she gathered up the dog, his silly hat remained on the floor next to the spot of blood. Mrs. O marched him back to the living room, where the fire had died down.

Duckworth met a police officer at the front door and gave instructions for no one to go upstairs until Mrs. O had time to identify what was missing. The two men began to work on the fire as the older woman nestled into her chair and held her dog close. The little guy was licking the tears running down her face.

"Oh, my little soldier," she hummed to him. "Who was it? Who hurt my baby?"

"I don't know. But I'm not leaving," Duckworth assured her. "Can I use your phone?"

"Line's dead."

At her announcement, the two men bristled with concern.

JACK SLUMPED IN HIS WOODEN CHAIR, lightly snoring. His long legs were stretched out in front of him as Billi tiptoed around the kitchen, cleaning up after their big meal. The steaks and potatoes had brought drowsiness to all three of them as they sat before the fire. Keeping busy was her way of keeping sane. She was drying the steak knives and lining them up on the table when her father rose from his chair.

"He looks like he could use the nap," Mr. O whispered as he stretched his cramped frame.

"Shhh. Yes, he didn't sleep at all last night." Billi set the last clean knife in the lineup.

"And how would you know that?" His one eyebrow rose with the question.

"He never slept in his bunk. He sat up all night."

"Huh." He shuffled to the table. "It's still comin' down like heaven's little angels are havin' the biggest pillow fight ever."

Billi reached for her coat.

"An' where is it you think you're goin'?"

"Firewood. Shhh." She held her finger to her lips.

"I'll go." He took her coat from her and waited until she had gone to sit in the other chair facing the fire. He picked up Jack's Stetson, exposing his gun. Mr. O perched the hat on his head and, as an afterthought, slid the gun into his belt.

When the cool breeze from the door opening passed through the room, Jack shifted. Seeing Billi, he closed his eyes again.

She stood and approached his chair. Kissing his forehead, she began to remove his patch.

"Get away from my damn wood!" The shout was followed by the gun exploding into the silence.

Jack knocked Billi's hand aside and was on his feet. When he noticed his gun was missing, he pulled out the leather case from behind the door. Motioning for Billi to get in the backroom, he drew Akio's long sword with the red grip and flung the door open as a second shot was heard.

He rounded the corner to see Mr. O face down in the snow, blood pooling around him. Jack flipped the older man over, and his eyes rolled back in his head. He was breathing, but the gun was gone. Jack picked up his hat from the snow and followed the fresh set of footprints out of the woodshed. He went a few more steps before realizing the trail circled around the other side, to the front of the house. Jack quickly backtracked to the front door, but no telltale footprints had rounded the far corner. He stood perfectly still, and then he saw a puff of breath drift into the half-light from the far side of the house. He crept past the front door. Billi, ashen, was standing with her back to the table.

Jack flung his hat in the direction of the steaming breath, and a sword swept through the air, slicing the brim.

Akio stepped from his hiding place, sword held in both hands, ready, Jack's gun tucked in his belt.

"I will kill your girlfriend slowly, with pleasure." His fierce words steamed from his mouth.

"You will fail, as usual."

When the tall Asian stepped closer, Jack recognized the anger in his dark, squinting eyes and knew his taunt hit its target.

"It is you who will fail. And pay for the insults you continue to bring upon me."

Jack's menacing laugh was laced with hatred. "You only bring these things upon yourself. I have the drawing and you will never see it again. How will it feel to die by your own sword?"

Akio's cold eyes blinked, and Jack's smile broadened.

"You have been clever this time, Jack." His eyes were glazing over and Jack recognized Akio's lust for blood.

"Yes, we know your plan and have passed on every word you foolishly spoke. You are the insult to your country."

As hoped, Akio began his charge. Jack waited, ready for the blow. Akio struck right to left, his preferred pattern, and his blade slipped down Jack's, not making contact with flesh.

If you wish to control others, you must first control yourself. Jack repeated the steadying words from *The Book of Five Rings* in his mind, easing his breath.

"Does Ginger like Japanese men?" Akio shook off his averted parry and found his footing. "How many of my men should I share her with?"

"Your drawings will make the Americans stronger against such a weak country that breeds such incompetent creatures as yourself."

With the fury of a wild animal, Akio attacked again. Jack momentarily lost his footing in the snow, and they slid together to the ground, blades landing beneath them. Blood dripped onto the white snow from the gash in Jack's leg.

He reached for his gun in his opponent's belt, but Akio rolled, pulling Jack with him. They slid partway down the snow-covered hill toward the water. The gun fired and the muscular body of his attacker shook with the impact, as a spout of red sprang from a hole in Akio's shoe. Jack scrambled back up the hill and swayed as his good eye blurred. A shot just missed his head. He dove for his sword as another bullet hissed overhead. Gripping his long sword in his right hand, he felt for Akio's blade in the deep snow, but it was gone.

Jack stood and turned around to find Akio on his belly, his own gun pointed at him.

"I will cut her slowly, the face first." The gun remained on Jack as Akio struggled to his feet and limped up the hill.

"Once again you dishonor your samurai blood. The gun is not a tool of strategy." Jack's breath was labored but his words precise.

"I will save the sword for her head." His laugh was vicious, his eyes greedy with intent, as he placed himself between Jack and the door to the cabin.

There was movement behind Akio. His arm holding the gun jerked skyward, and the bullet fired into the heavens. He spun around, his right shoulder dropping with a steak knife protruding from his back. The gun slid into the snow.

Billi spoke in Japanese to the weaponless man before her. "Not if the woman holds your sword." With both hands gripping the weapon, she lifted the point of his blade toward his throat.

Jack sprang forward, catching his prey, tumbling with him down the hill, driving the steak knife farther into Akio's back until it protruded out the other side. Jack's fist smashed into his old roommate's jaw with the fury born of many years of hatred.

His assailant's left hand reached for the eye patch and ripped it from his face.

Jack flinched and squeezed his bad eye closed to keep his vision clear and stable. Then he pushed Akio's face deep into the snow, holding it there as the man struggled for breath.

"Jack!" he heard Billi's shriek from above.

He rolled off the limp body and struggled up the hill, slipping in the compact path of icy snow they had created when they had slid down. He moved to the deeper snow to find his footing. His legs throbbed, and the cut in his leg had lost feeling with the cold. He shook his hands for circulation, then stopped as he rounded the side of the house.

The man who restrained Billi held her in front of him as a shield. The hand over her mouth had a scar across it.

"Trade," the stout Japanese man offered.

"Let her go first." Jack closed his right eye and quickly focused on the butt of his gun, barely visible in the disturbed snow, to his right. "You take your boss and I keep the worthless girl."

There was a moan from below and coughing as Akio spat blood and snow from his mouth.

Hatsuro pushed Billi to the ground, and she fell inches from where she had dropped Akio's sword, its weight sinking it below the white crust of snow. Their puffs of breath mingled as she felt for it, but the hand with the scar across it was swifter as he searched the snow. He growled as he withdrew his hand, blood spewing from the deep cut that left his index finger dangling. He slapped her face, and blood sailed across the pure white crystals covering the earth.

Jack pressed the pocket knife against Hatsuro's neck, and felt him bristled momentarily. Then, like a cat, the smaller man sprang into the air and rolled down the snow bank.

"Get in the cabin." Jack didn't look at her but kept the two men in his sight as he dug in the snow for his gun.

"My father. I—"

"My jacket. Get me bullets."

Billi was by his side in seconds, his jacket in hand. He reached inside his pocket for the small box containing more rounds. With his right eye still closed, he didn't look away from the two men who were staggering toward the water as his cold, shaking hand filled all six chambers of his gun.

The snow had begun in earnest again, swirling up the hill on gusts of wind. The two figures disappeared behind the blanket of white as they splashed into the cold saltwater. Jack slid back down the hill as the sound of a boat engine sparked to life. He fired in the direction of the motor, which was quickly picking up speed. Intent on not missing this time, he emptied his gun into the drifts of falling snow.

FIFTY-TWO

"No." Lani giggled at Eddy and his two friends. "When you do the hula, your hands go the same way as your feet. Elbows up."

She worked her way between the four men, adjusting their stance.

"Bend your knees and stick your okole out." She patted Eddy's derriere to demonstrate her vocabulary. "Okole."

"Woo-wee." Sam's young voice screeched, filled with zest. "Won't this be somethin'? Those gals won't know what hit 'em."

"I'm not certain we're going to get the response we're hoping for." Joe sounded doubtful.

"Ah, come on, Army, live a little." Eddy watched Lani's every move. "We're building morale."

"I'm not so sure about this." Joe squatted and stuck his rump out.

"Just see it as part of your duty. A cultural experience." Eddy's contagious smile did not convince his friend.

"Who are we doing this for again?" Scooter shook his hips.

The question did not get answered, for Lani began the music and stepped in front of the four men, who breathlessly waited for her hips to move.

"One, two, three, key." She sang to the tune of "My Little Grass Shack." As she moved through the song, her sway held the men's undivided attention.

"Are you following me?"

"Yes, ma'am." Sam squatted, his skinny arms shot up into the correct position, and he sidestepped with his big feet, first right, then left. He looked more like a crab stiffly moving from side to side than a dancer.

"Not like that," Joe corrected him and took his turn at the movements. His hula demonstrated a vast improvement over the young sailor's.

"Why, Joe, I do believe you will impress the ladies with those hips." Eddy ducked as Joe swung at him.

"Boys." Lani had her hands on her now stationary hips. "Shall we? Let the hands tell the story."

They practiced the one song for twenty minutes before Joe shook his head. "I need a beer. This is hard work."

"I'm with you." Scooter untied the hula skirt that wrapped only around the front of his body and led the others toward the door.

Lani chuckled, putting her record back into its paper shield. "See you tonight gentlemen."

Eddy pushed her hair back behind her ear. "Meet me at the beach for a swim."

"Eddy." She turned toward him, her black eyes intense. "Mother has said Father has agreed."

He picked her up and twirled her around. "I knew he would."

"Shhh." She put her hands over his mouth. "But we must pretend we don't know. He is my father and we must respect his ways. The wedding will be here, soon."

"Yes. Yes, anything you want." He thought his heart would explode. He kissed her long and softly, their passion sparking as his hands traveled down her body, past her firm breasts, to her hips.

"Now go. And practice. Remember okole out." She teased as she gently pushed him away.

He kissed her once more before rushing out into the sunlight and those cold beers with his buddies.

"I DON'T KNOW IF ANYTHING IS MISSING." Mrs. O stood with her hands on her hips in Billi's bedroom. She had put Pepper on the white bedspread, his right front paw carefully wrapped in a clean handkerchief.

"Do you remember any gifts she received from any of her Japanese friends?" Duckworth tried to frame his questions without raising concern.

"She and Eileen were always exchanging gifts. They liked to make things for each other as little girls and surprise each other. Knowing Billi, the gifts are probably in a box somewhere."

"Would they be in any other room beside this one?" He picked up the corner of the bedspread and looked under the bed, but saw nothing.

"I can't imagine why. How many rooms does one girl need?"

"You said Eileen's brother came by earlier tonight?" Duckworth watched Mrs. O.

"Yes, Eileen is sick and Tak, her brother, said Billi had something of—oh, you don't think he had something to do with this do you?" Clearly, she became startled by the concept.

"Don't worry, we'll find out who it was."

"But I saw him leave and head down the block. They are such a nice family." She sat on the bed next to Pepper. "In fact, they are family to us."

"Okay." Duckworth attempted to mollify her. "Why don't we head back down to the warm fire? I'll be staying here with you until Billi returns."

"Well...okay, you can stay in Eddy's room." She sighed. "Come on, Pepper, let's go and warm up."

The little dog whimpered as she picked him up, cradling him to her large bosom, and headed for the door.

Duckworth remained in the room and once more checked for any signs of what the intruder had been searching for.

BILLI KNELT IN THE SNOW next to her father. His breathing relaxed, and he emitted only an occasional moan.

"Can we move him?" She looked at Jack as he slumped against the frame of the cabin.

"The snow has stopped his bleeding. Let's try to get him by the fire."

Together they worked Mr. O inside. Billi pulled the chairs away, and they laid him in front of the fire.

"I'll get his wet clothes off and you get a blanket." Jack lowered himself next to the Irishman and started to undo his shirt buttons. "And bring me that bottle of Jameson."

The gash on Mr. O's head would need stitches, and Jack hoped they still had enough whiskey to keep the man down. The probability of a concussion seemed high.

Billi ran back and forth with the needed items, ripped a sheet for bandages, and helped Jack tie a strip of cloth over his bad eye to help with his vision. She sat next to her father and held his arms down as Jack began with the sterilized needle. She felt her father jerk before he passed out again.

"You make a good nurse." Jack's voice sounded hushed as he tied off the thread, sweat dripping down his forehead.

"You're next." Billi released her father's arms and pulled the blanket up closer around his shoulders.

"Mine's just a scratch." He attempted to avoid her level stare.

"No."

"Then hand me my pocket knife."

She frowned at him, not understanding the request.

He pushed himself up into a chair and held out his hand.

Billi went to the table that looked like an armory. The two long swords, Hatsuro's small blade, Jack's pocket knife and the two remaining steak knives were haphazardly covering the bare oak.

"Off with your wet clothes," she demanded, handing him his knife. "Now."

She tossed him another blanket and stepped into the back bedroom. "Let me know when I can return."

Jack watched her go and smiled. He slid the blade down his damp pant leg, slicing his slacks past his gash, the material pulling the already-forming scab loose. Blood began to run down his leg as he removed the rest of his wet clothes and pulled the blanket up over him.

"Ready."

Billi entered and stopped short, her breath caught in her throat at the sight of his blood. "Get on your back and get that leg up. You're losing too much blood." She barked her orders and set into action at the same time.

Jack lie motionless on his back next to her father. She knelt beside him and held up his leg to inspect the gash.

"It's clean." Tears were forming, blurring her vision.

"Pour whiskey on it then cauterize it. Burn it shut." His words were tense with pain.

"I can't...I..."

"Use the knife. You can."

"Jack." She hovered over him as his head slumped to one side. "Jack, you bastard, don't you dare."

She calculated the long sword would not work and hurried for a steak knife, putting the blade in the fire until she could feel the heat streaming up toward the handle. It hissed as she put it on the blanket next to Jack and knelt beside him. Picking up the amber liquor, she took a swig and then poured some on Jack's open wound, where it mixed with the streaming blood. His leg jerked.

She sat on his thigh, steadied her hands, and pressed the hot blade against the wound. The smell of his burning flesh filled her nostrils as his spine arched and his voice rose in a growl. She struggled to hold the hot object against his skin until the blood stopped, then rolled off him and lay panting between the two men she loved the most.

She woke with a shiver, uncertain how long she had dozed there between them. A few burning embers remained in the hearth. She pushed herself up, trembling with cold, picked up his loaded gun, and headed out the door for more firewood.

The moon, almost full, shone on the glittering white of her surroundings as she picked through the stacks of wood. Funny how just a few hours before life had been a snowy dream, ideal. She paused under the clear sky with the stars twinkling against the deep blue and listened to the gentle sound of the waves as they reached the wet stones of the shore. The new blanket of pristine snow formed a wonderland of shimmering blues and white, covering the blood of their struggles.

After rousing the fire to its full force, she nestled between the two men again, fully aware of her father's breathing and her proximity to the man she had fallen in love with.

As if in response, Jack wrapped the blanket around her, drawing her against his bare chest. She could feel his breathing down her back as his hand slid down her side and then across her belly, up to her breasts. She let him touch her, her breathing matching his in deep desire. She felt his gentle kiss on the back of her neck as his hand inched back down across her belly.

Her father emitted a loud snore, and they both jumped a bit. Gently, she reached down, took his exploring hand in hers, and held it tight.

THE BAR AT HONEY'S NIGHTCLUB was packed. Lani had just finished her dancing and that always made Eddy thirsty. He needed a cool drink before he faced her in person.

"Ain't this somethin'?"

The accustomed statement of the young sailor brought a smile to Eddy's face. "Behave yourself, now. I don't want to have to carry you home tonight. So does anyone besides Sam need a beer?" He looked around the table at his friends before standing.

Scooter raised his hand for another brew.

"I'll take one." Joe followed Eddy to the bar.

"Seen anything?" Eddy asked quietly.

Joe shook his head no.

"You heard we were told to fire if we see any subs outside of our established area?"

"Damn. What if we fire first?"

"Then we start the war." Eddy's harsh statement echoed their new reality.

Joe's blue eyes filled with the fear Eddy already felt as he spoke. "I really need that drink."

Sam's young voice almost squeaked as they returned to the table. "What if they don't like our dance?"

"That's why I'm having another." Scooter grabbed at the offered drink and chugged.

"What has Eddy gotten us into?" Sam's concern made his voice go up a notch.

"Aloha." The proprietor, Honey, had her arms in the air, her skirt swishing as she glided onto the stage.

"Aloha," the audience called back in response.

"Oh, kanes and wahines, we have special treat. Especially you soldiers."

The whistles from the crowd designated the tables of servicemen who had come to be entertained.

"Oh, oh." She wagged her long finger at the crowd. "Maybe not what you tink."

Joe quickly swigged his remaining beer, sweat pouring down his forehead.

"We have my son, Don Ho." She waited while her eleven-year-old son sauntered up next to her, carrying his ukulele to loud applause. "And we have the Aloha Wahines." Grass skirts shimmered in the lights, as the young women swayed onto the stage with the encouragement of whistles and hoots.

Her hand went up again, and the crowd quieted down. "And special." She pointed at Eddy's table as Lani and three other dancers worked their way through the crowd and pulled the men to their feet.

"You practice, no?" Honey asked Eddy when they reached the stage.

He leaned into the mic. "As envoys of the navy—"

"And army." Joe defended his branch of service as a grass skirt was tied around his hips.

"…we would like to demonstrate our appreciation for the islands of paradise."

"Aw, bring on the goils." The Jersey accent reverberated from the back of the club.

Don strummed his ukulele, and his young melodic voice echoed over the crowd as the hula-skirted men stepped into the dance they had practiced. The outbursts of laughter only heightened the festivities as the evening melted into a blur.

THE WINDWARD SIDE OF OAHU, with its dense clouds that swept across the sea, was known to be unpredictable. Tonight, the rain outside the club carried a bit of a chill. But tomorrow's football game brightened their spirits and the weather forecast promised blue skies.

"So, I'll meet you at the game tomorrow?" Eddy's lips brushed against Lani's again.

"Only if I get to meet this friend of yours, Truck, as promised." She kissed him lightly back.

Scooter hit the horn on the old beast again. "Come on, lovebirds. I have to get back to base."

"Me too." Sam's arm barely raised then swiftly went to his stomach where his beer and whiskey were raising havoc.

"Aloha." Lani kissed Eddy one last time and turned back toward the club.

FIFTY-THREE

H ER FATHER'S MOAN pulled Billi from her sleep, and she felt Jack's grip tighten around her waist, holding her close a few moments more, the heat of his body pressing against her.

She sat up as her father's blues eyes struggled to gain recognition of his surroundings.

"What the hell is—" Mr. O stopped as he looked across the floor at Jack. "Is he dead?"

"Hardly." Billi flipped the blankets off her legs and stood.

As she put on her heavy coat, she watched her father's hand gingerly feel the large lump and stitches on his head. She pressed her finger to her lips, alerting her father to remain quiet, and slipped out the door. She returned with a blast of cold air, Jack's eye patch, and a bucket of snow. She gently pressed the frozen ice on her father's wound.

"Jesus, Mary, and Joseph," he grumbled. "That's cold."

She ignored him and went to the fire, adding wood and blowing the flames to life.

"Is anyone dead?" Her father's question hung in the air with its reality.

"No. Everything is fine, Dad. But you stay down a bit longer."

Jack twisted his blanket around him and pulled himself into a chair. His wound, fiery red, looked as angry as the man. Billi grabbed her bucket and knelt before him fingering a small scoop of icy snow over the burn.

He tried not to show the pain. "We all need to head back to the city. They will not be back here. But I need to get to a phone now." His frustration not meant for anyone in the room.

"You're not goin' anywhere with my daughter without trousers on, man." The feisty Irishman's raised voice filled the room.

THE SUN DIPPED BEHIND THE WHITE TIPPED MOUNTAINS as Pepper stood on the porch, tail wagging in welcome as Mrs. O raced down the stairs to help her estranged husband. Danny emerged right behind her and placed Mr. O's other arm around his shoulders.

"'Tis okay, Gertie," his voice weak. "I slipped."

Duckworth nodded at his boss, quietly watching Jack limp through the door. Each step exposed the angry scar on his leg through his ripped trousers. Jack nodded back. The journey home had been long and exhausting, but he knew they had work to do.

"Are you hungry? Do you need something to drink?" Mrs. O, the eternal hostess, offered.

"I'm going to check my room first." Billi stood at the bottom of the steps looking up to the landing above.

"I'm coming with you."

Jack had his hand on the small of her back as they slowly proceeded up the flight of steps.

They stood together at her bedroom door and Jack heard her gasp at the condition of her room. She stood momentarily, taking it in.

With cautious steps, she circled the room as Jack watched from the doorway.

"What's the first thing you notice?"

"All of my small objects that the professor and Eileen gave me are gone. The dolls and the—" She lowered next to her bed and lifted the bedspread. "The letters I sent her."

"The ones you said had nothing in them?"

"Yes. They were right here in a box she had made."

She felt below her mattress and blushed.

"What is it?"

"Nothing." She sat on the bed.

He walked to her and put his hand under the mattress and extracted the erotic book, the shunga, that Eileen had given her.

"It was a wedding gift of sorts." She fumbled the fringe on her white bedspread. "For when I married Raymond. So I could…" She gulped.

Jack opened then closed the book immediately. "I see." He gently slid it back in its hiding place for safekeeping.

She stood and walked the room again, picking up articles of clothing as she passed them. "Eileen has nothing to do with this. I know her."

"What about Tak?"

"I don't know if Eileen's brother is the Tak they mentioned." Her defense sounded weak.

"I want you to sit down and tell me everything the professor has given to you."

She sat and looked at her wallpaper. "There was a small box, black lacquer, with a flower painted on top, very small. Nothing actually fit in it. I had a pair of tiny shoes, getas, very small. Then there was the fan that he gave me right before the competition."

"The one in the purple silk case you had that day?"

"Yes, the one you picked up. The fan. Eileen's pillow." She bounced from the bed, hysterical. "Where is my pillow?"

"That's what I thought. It's safe."

THE SUN BEAT HOT on their heads as Eddy guided Lani toward their seats in the stadium.

"Aloha and welcome to the Territory of Hawaii," the announcer's voice crackled over the microphone. "Today is the first game in the Shrine Bowl, where our Rainbow Warriors will show the Willamette Bearcats how to play football."

The far side of the stadium, where most of the University of Hawaii fans were seated, hooted loudly in response.

"They are sending you a little aloha." Lani sat on the warm bench, adjusting her sunglasses and hat. "I feel like a traitor. But we will win."

"You have that wrong," Eddy assured her. "We will knock their socks off."

He lowered next to her and looked at the others around him. The San Jose team sat above them, watching and waiting, along with a few others who had made the journey on the great ocean liner the S.S. *Lurline* from San Francisco to watch the games. He squinted into the sun in an attempt to see the other side of the stadium where the Rainbow Warrior fans sat, but the reflection hurt his eyes and made him blink.

"Where are your sunglasses?" Lani sounded concerned.

"I forgot them." He shaded his eyes with his hand. "But that's okay, I don't need to watch. The Bearcats will make mincemeat of your team."

"What was our bet?" Her suggestive tease stirred Eddy's desire.

"You will owe me many things by the end of this day."

"I do not think so."

Sam, guided by Scooter, came down the aisle on wobbly legs and sat on the other side of Lani.

"So whose team am I rootin' for?" Sam licked his dry lips.

"Mine," the lovers chimed in unison.

"Well, that makes it easy," Scooter quipped.

"How is your head this morning?" Lani spoke softly.

"Don't know how long I'll be able to stay with all that shoutin' noise. But we did okay last night with our hula dance, didn't we?" The youth glanced over at his idol's girlfriend and smiled weakly.

"You were most impressive. I am certain the other girls will never forget how well you can hula."

"Oh," he groaned. "That bad."

"We were great." Eddy looked across Lani at the pale face of the young sailor. "Have a Coca-Cola. You'll feel better."

The football soared high into the air as the game got underway, and Eddy lost the arc of its travel in the glaring sun.

Joe joined them after halftime and squeezed in between Eddy and Scooter in the blazing afternoon heat. "Looks pretty bad for our fellas out there."

"Ain't this somethin'?" The disgusted tone of Sam's voice carried the emotions of all of those around him except, of course, Lani. He pulled his Kimmel back over his face and returned to his napping.

"Hello, Joe." Lani leaned forward, looking across at the new arrival. "You got here just in time to witness Eddy lose his bet."

"There's still time." Eddy forced a smile in Joe's direction.

"A snowball's chance in hell." Joe covered his blue eyes with his sunglasses, leaned back, and crossed his arms.

"Twenty to six. Sure there's still time?" Lani jumped to her feet to clap again as her team made a first down twenty yards from another goal.

"Any news?" Eddy's eyes blinked as he looked at Joe.

"Had a request to leave KGMB AM radio station on tonight."

"They're running off hours? Why?"

"Must be expecting some bombers from the West Coast. They follow the signal for navigation."

Eddy leaned into Joe to exchange the latest news. "They're burning papers at the Japanese Consulate."

"Good God. What do you think?" Joe gulped.

"It's not good. And I hope God is on our side."

Lani dropped back into her seat when the Bearcats stopped the University of Hawaii from scoring again.

By the fourth quarter, Eddy had his head lowered between his hands, sweat dripping down his back from the balmy weather. "My head is splitting."

"It was the sun. You have burned your eyes." Lani's concern grew as she continued. "You need to get some cold compresses with aloe on those eyes. I will ride home with my friends. You need to get out of the sun." She stood.

"What, and not see the final decimation of the Oregon team?" Joe kidded.

"How about if you three tell Truck and the guys I'll try to swing by later. But I think Lani's right. It was stupid to forget my sunglasses." He lifted off the bench. "Man, my head hurts."

He hesitated as he watched the movement of young sailor's hat as his snore vibrated his kimmel.

"He okay?" Joe asked.

"I suppose he'll be ready to go at it again when he wakes up." Scooter shook the kid.

Sam popped up, sweat dripping down his face, his hat landing in his lap. "What'd I miss? We win?"

"Looks like Eddy owes Lani." Joe stood as the opposite side of the stadium exploded with the final cheer of the game.

"Ain't that somethin'?" Sam blinked.

"Hey, Army, you joining us?" Scooter adjusted his sunglasses as he stretched his legs.

"For a bit. I'm training a guy up at Opana at 0400. Come on, kid, grab your hula skirt. Time to party."

Eddy followed the smiling Lani and led the dejected procession out of the bleachers.

JACK AND BILLI WERE ONE OF THE ONLY CARS on Capitol Hill venturing down Broadway. The winter sun was making an appearance, casting a startling brightness over the cold white that covered the ground. The slanted roofs of Jack's Tudor apartment were the picture of serenity as the afternoon light outlined the building.

Jack held the door for Billi, his one torn pant leg flapping like a train behind him as he limped in behind her.

"What made you think to leave it here?" She started up the stairs.

"Duckworth."

She stopped before the arched wooden door with its small stained glass window design of the knight in armor and waited. Jack swung the door open to the cold room. An icicle hung outside the bay windows.

Billi pushed past him toward the fireplace. "I'll get the fire. You change." Funny how the dynamics had morphed since the first time she had entered this room.

Jack headed down the hallway and then returned, carrying a bag. "Here." He handed her the light package before disappearing.

She peeked in the bag and felt a sense of relief. She put the pillow on the chair and set to work on the fire.

"That feels better," Jack announced as he rounded the corner, his wound now covered by his clean trousers.

The kindling crackled with bursts of flames as he sat watching her methodically feed the fire.

"You never camped, did you?" She watched him ease into the chair, putting the pillow on the floor beside him.

"But I've built a few fires in my day."

"Comes in handy." She stood, slapping the bits of wood from her slacks and hands.

He reached for her and pulled her onto his lap. "I don't think I've thanked you properly."

"There's plenty of time for that. We have work to do."

She blushed and struggled against his grip, but his arms were around her and his kiss felt warm and tender. She melted into him and let his free hand rest on her knee. A spark exploded from the fire and went unnoticed.

The phone rang, and they both jumped. Billi stood while Jack shuffled his bad leg toward the desk.

"Hello." He quickly turned his back to Billi, and she held her breath until he spoke. "Yes, sir. I do think we should take the war warning seriously. Have the islands been warned at this point for high alert?" He listened, but his anger reached full throttle when he replied. "Yes, sir, 'east wind rain' was heard twice on December 4th. It is only a matter of time before they strike, according to our intelligence. Japan would not have sent the messages out if—"

His back arched with frustration as the voice on the phone bellowed unintelligently.

"Yes, the code 'east, wind, rain' is vital. Magic has been deciphering for hours. Please remember last January our own ambassador in Japan warned us that if there were trouble with the US, they would attack Pearl Harbor. How has Hawaii prepared? Have they found the Japanese fleet yet?"

Billi gripped the arms of the chair and lowered into it, listening in disbelief as Jack paced, his face red with anger.

"But the last time you knew the location of the fleet was over ten days ago. Doesn't that alone raise questions?" From his look of exasperation, she could tell he was losing his argument. "Yes, sir. Expect a call very soon. A new-style submarine is what he is building. You have to warn the general, speak to the admiral, warn the islands and make them listen this time."

The conversation ended. Jack slammed the phone down, then ran his hands over his face and through his hair. "The bastards. The goddamn stupid bastards."

"What do you mean, we have been warned?"

"Earlier today, the president again asked Emperor Hirohito for peace, but there has been no reply." He stood above her now. "Billi, you heard the men at Charlie Low's. They sat at that table with you and said America was to expect a Christmas present. Well, the Japanese are on the move. Six carriers, with planes and escort ships, have somehow been lost by American intelligence. We have just intercepted and are decoding thirteen messages sent in the last few days from Japan to their consulate. We are to expect fourteen in all, according to intelligence. When the last one is in, it will tell the entire story."

"Where will they strike? Eddy is in—"

"I know. But we think Southeast Asia, the Philippines. Not Hawaii. Too far for planes."

He wasn't telling her everything, and she felt her pulse quicken with the impact of the coming of the war. The waiting game was ending and death would replace speculation.

"The drawing." She reached for her pillow. "The fan is…" Tears were spilling down her cheek as she extracted Professor Fujihara's gift from the hidden compartment in Eileen's sewn treasure. Her hand shook as she held it toward him.

He bent and kissed her wet cheek. "Thank you."

Outside, the snow glowed pink in the setting sun as the mantel clock chimed four times. Jack snapped on the desk light and slowly opened the fan, holding it in the brightness. Billi moved her chair closer and scanned the design of the three dragons that grew in size, swirling across the paper. The face of the largest mythical creature snarled fiercely as he drifted above the cresting waves.

"Is there a compartment?" Jack held the fan out to her.

"Yes. I found it by accident." She flipped the concealed opening on the lacquered base of the fan and shook the small piece of rice paper from its hiding place. Uncurling it, she read the words again. "Spare her."

"You were to take this to his family, correct?"

"No. He planned to give me other presents to take to his family."

"But you were to take this along as well?"

"He had said I would need it for the heat in his homeland, I think. Something like that."

"Not to give it to anyone?"

"No." She looked straight at him. "He did not mention that to me."

"Did you think it odd that he would give you a fan with dragons on it?"

"Of course. Watatsumi." Billi barely breathed. "The dragon god, ruler of the sea."

"Watatsumi," Jack repeated.

He put the fan down on the desk, and, as if for guidance, began to spin his father's ring on his little finger. Nervously, Billi picked up the fan and instinctively began to twirl it through the air. She worked the fan high and low as Jack sat mesmerized by her movements.

"Stop." He jerked forward. "Do that again."

She moved the fan again by twisting her wrists exposing both sides to the light.

"Again." Jack took the lamp shade off the desk light and nodded. Without questioning, she repeated her movements.

"There. Stop." He took the fan, his breathing fast. He held the fan up to the light, and the outline of a second image appeared barely visible in the forms of the dragons. "Do you see it? Does that remind you of something?"

She shook her head no then, with startling realization, she leaned closer. "His scribblings. Akio's line drawings at Stanford. I mean, it's a stretch but maybe…"

"That's what I see. What did the professor at Stanford say? Akio scribbled wings that—"

"Where are the drawings? Do they match?"

Jack pulled the once-crumpled piece of paper from his desk and set it next to the fan.

"Wings that disappear."

FIFTY-FOUR

"THE ROADS ARE TOO SLUSHY AND DANGEROUS," Billi repeated into the phone. "We tried to get up the hill, but we slid back down. This rain will melt the snow by morning." Billi looked briefly at Jack as she listened to her mother. "Yes. Okay. See you tomorrow, bright and early. I love you too, Mother."

Jack had his bad leg raised on the wooden chair. He watched her turn back toward him where he sat by the fire. "What did she really say?"

"To watch you closely. And that she would not tell Dad. He's resting nicely and eating everything in sight." Her laugh did not cover her nerves.

"Oh. I don't have much in the way of food here." He shifted and began to lower his leg.

She sprang into action before his leg reached the floor, anxious energy propelling her toward the small kitchen around the corner.

"Two cans of Campbell's chicken noodle soup, two pork and beans with tomato. One bottle of Scotch, one of bourbon, and something green in the icebox, but it's not lettuce anymore."

She rounded the corner with a can of each soup in her hands and stood before him. "What will it be, mister?" She used her Ginger voice.

"Will you marry me?"

"I…I beg your pardon?" she stammered, lowering the cans she had held out.

"I can't have you staying here with me and not be engaged."

"Why?"

"I don't trust myself."

"What would Bella say?"

He did his best imitation of the big woman's "Hmmph."

She bit her lip, speechless. He reached for her and pulled her down on his good knee. "You haven't said yes yet."

"Haven't I?" She gulped, the heavy cans awkward in her hands.

"Billi, I'm going to have to leave tomorrow."

Uncontrollable tears started down her cheeks as his soft words echoed through her foggy mind.

He brushed away a tear before continuing. "And I can't take you with me. But I don't want anyone else touching you in any way again. I will be able to get more done if I know you are here waiting for me."

"I can't wait again. You might not come back too." She trembled with the horrible truth of loss.

"Marry me in the morning, before I leave."

"Oh...oh...okay." She wiped her tears with the back of her hand that held the Campbell's soup. "Can Mother come?"

"And your father." His throaty chuckle reflected his thoughts. "I wouldn't want to face him without a ring on your finger." He slipped his father's ring from his finger and slid the black onyx stone with the diamond cut into the center down her ring finger. Their kiss was soft, a mere brushing of the lips, but the desire that brief touch stirred ran deep.

Billi's breath caught in her throat, suddenly aware of what he expected, and she jumped from his lap.

"Okay, we'll skip the soup. How about a drink? I mean, I don't know how. I mean, I've never been with a man before." Her words tumbled into each other as she took a precautious step backward, twitching with unease.

"Let me guess." Jack ran his hand through his hair, then began again. "Your mother never told you she offered the use of your picture to the Home of the Good Shepherd for their advertisement, the home for unwed mothers?"

"Of course she didn't. Do you think I wanted everyone to think I... Did you think I—"

"No. You wouldn't have needed that Japanese book on lovemaking if—"

The can of soup just missed his head, and he caught it as it bounced off the wall.

"Make mine Scotch." He smiled devilishly, then removed his eye patch and placed it over the can of soup on the floor. "Double."

She stomped into the kitchen, then leaned against the counter in laughter.

"Next time I won't miss," she insisted. The ice rattled as it hit the glass.

"I know you won't, Mrs. Huntington."

She reappeared with two stiff drinks. "Not yet I'm not. I have a few hours to change my mind."

"By then it will be too late." The look he gave her and the slant of his smile made Billi tremble as he drew her onto his lap.

EDDY RESTED HIS FOOT ON HIS BUNK, tying his shoelaces. He watched Sam, passed out cold in his bunk, smacking his dry, liquored lips. No reason to wake the kid for breakfast. Eddy put his sunglasses on and stepped out into the morning breeze. Radio KGMB had just announced clear skies and good visibility, and that proclamation proved to be what the heavens offered, clear and blue. The faint white of the setting full moon still hung over jagged-tipped Pali. It made him think of how he would have loved to be with Lani last night beneath such brilliant moonlight illuminating the dark heavens and waters around them. He headed for the mess hall. The cool air morning tasted salty, as it swept in from the green-tinged ocean. Paradise shimmered, something to behold today, for tonight would be dinner with Lani and her parents. The glorious surroundings indicated he fathers favorable decision.

Inside the mess hall, Eddy sat next to the sandy-haired captain and those who had just returned from their scouting mission. The new patrol had left, they already soared up in the heavens, and those who had returned were huddled over their coffee, discussing their mission.

"What are you doing here so early, Seattle?" The captain considered Eddy as he checked his watch. "It's only 7:50. I thought you said you were going out with the team last night." He took a long drag on his cigarette, letting the smoke out with his words. "Not much to celebrate, I guess."

Eddy smiled from behind his sunglasses, not wanting to admit his mistake of hurting his eyes at yesterday's game. Protecting your eyesight was a cardinal rule of pilots. "Couldn't sleep." He filled his mouth with egg so that he didn't have to continue the conversation.

McNees, a pilot returning from patrol, rushed up to their table. "Hey, Captain, I just landed. But when I was flying, I saw a sub close to shore. I fired on it." The sweat poured from his young face. "I followed orders. We were told to fire on any sub not within our established holding area for our subs, and this one was close to shore. Do you think we're being attacked?"

The response came from outside as bullets strafed the building. Eddy dashed to the door and stepped out. Bullets buzzed over his head and bore into the metal behind him. Blasts of gunfire peppered the control tower.

"Holy shit." He jumped back as he recognized the red, round insignia under the wings of the nine low-lying planes and yelled back to the captain. "Japanese bombers."

"What the hell?" The captain threw his cigarette aside, barking orders as he ran to the window. "Call Chief Finn and get him here. We need the guns."

Eddy raced for the tarmac where the aircraft were easy prey. The Zeros circled back. He watched horrified as the wing commander's Kingfisher on the flight line burst into flames. At the whistling sound of a bomb descending, Eddy dropped to the push-up stance as the ground buckled and rolled like a wave. Hangar #3 had been hit, and clouds of smoke billowed black against the blue sky. Eddy snaked through the shield of black haze and shell-shattered tarmac toward the planes neatly lined up on the apron. He helped three other sailors remove the fifty-caliber, mounted machine guns from the burning carcasses of the bullet-riddled aircraft. Hangar #1 exploded in flames as another round of blasts hit the base.

A bomb whizzed and ripped the earth, knocking the men off their feet. Eddy hit the ground and pushed himself up again into the position the British manual said would save his life. His arms ached as men around him were bouncing on the hard landing strip with the violent explosions.

"Hell no, don't lie flat!" he yelled as the man next to him hit his head and went limp. Like a rag doll, his body flopped against the solid surface with each blast.

The undulating earth subsided, and Eddy said a silent prayer for the dead as he went back to work carrying machine guns through the smoke.

"Over here." Chief Finn's voice coming from the haze. "Where's the fire truck?"

"They got it, sir." Eddy became the bearer of the worsening news.

"Get moving. We have a war to fight." Finn's command resounded clear and strong. "There." He pointed to an instruction platform that seemed to be near the heart of the battle. "Mount the machine gun there."

Another round of well-orchestrated planes swooped down just above the runways. The Zeros soared low, spitting their death at planes and people. Eddy ran through the bursts of enemy rounds that ricocheted off the tarmac to the bullet-scarred remains of Patrol Squadron VP-11's incapacitated PBY's in search of more ammunition. Dashing past the spray of water from the hoses attempting to douse the flames, he slipped where the water mixed with the oil. Blood dripped from his forehead and the salty taste dripped on his lips. He could not think of anything, he could just do. He delivered another machine gun to Finn's gun pit.

"Yes!" He heard Finn's angry voice in the mist rise above the rat-a-tat-tat of his machine gun as he raked the plane above him. "Got one. Goddamn Japs."

The sound of the whining Zero was followed by the blast as it hit the peak of Pu'u Hawai'i Loa. A roar of cheers went up from the battered sailors who scurried with newfound hope to complete their overwhelming task. Like the games yesterday, scorekeeping had begun, and so far, the US Navy had a hell of a way to go to catch up.

Eddy kept his focus. If the enemy were attacking their naval air station and patrol squadrons, their bigger prizes were just over the lush green hill that rose above Kane'ohe's base. He had seen a group of fighters with their Japanese markings wing up toward the top of the Pali. They were headed for Pearl Harbor.

Eddy wiped the blood from over his eye and fought his nausea as he stepped over a young man's limp body, the boy's childlike face looked like he slept peacefully. Thankful it was not Sam, Eddy brushed the sight of the dead boy away and kept going. He had to stay alive to reach Lani.

The smoke trailed on the wind and a clamor now rose from the shouting men as the attack from overhead subsided.

"They'll be back," Finn announced. "Let's get ready."

Eddy's movements became mechanical as the sailors worked in teams to put out the fires, remove debris, and prepare in the event of another attack. There were no planes on the ground that could be flown, and the hope rose that the three airborne on patrol had not been hit too.

"Hey, Eddy, wasn't that somethin'?"

The kid's voice sounded like heavenly music to Eddy's ears as he watched Sam sway toward him out of the black smoke, dragging a rifle.

"I shot one. And I did it. I did like you said. I had my arms out and counted like I was doing push-ups." He smiled, and the whites of his teeth showed through the black soot that streaked his face. Then he coughed, and blood spewed from his mouth.

"What's that, Eddy?" The seventeen-year-old sounded cool-headed and innocent as he looked at his blood that had dripped down his shirt.

"Get to sick bay, now." Instantly, Eddy had his arm around Sam's light frame, and they hurried toward the hangar as the sound of Sam's rifle rattled onto the dirt. A medic saw them approach and pointed at a space on the ground in the line of other wounded soldiers. Those not so lucky already had their faces covered with cloths, the simple telltale sign of the passing of their souls.

Eddy lowered the kid next to an unconscious sailor whose blood oozed through the bandages that covered his chest.

"Hey Sam, I'll be right back. You stay here and get better. Where's your hula skirt?" Eddy attempted to ease his young friend's mind. "You're going to need it to celebrate when we destroy the Japs."

Eddy took a deep breath. It was the first time he had referred to the bloodline that ran through his beloved's veins with the slang word that reverberated over the battlefield this horrific morning.

"Okay, Eddy. Now go and kill Japs." Sam held his side where a new trickle of blood seeped through his uniform.

"I'll be back. You just get better."

Sam grabbed Eddy's arm. "I did good, didn't I, Eddy?" His young eyes showed fear as death, like an uncontrollable machine, marched his way.

"Kid, you were somethin'."

Eddy found a nearby medic and pushed him in Sam's direction. "Keep him alive."

THE ENGRAVED DOOR OF THE SACRISTY had been closed tight for over thirty minutes. Billi stood in the reception room of Saint Mary's Church with her ear pressed against the thick wood, listening. Inside, at this early hour, others were determining her fate.

"Father Peretti, I understand this is sudden." Jack's muffled voice again took up the plea.

"Sudden? Lord have mercy. Her first fiancé, he is barely in da grave." His rolling Italian accent rose with his words.

"Father," Mrs. O implored, "it would be such a…a…"

"A relief," Mr. O'Shaughnessy finished for her. "She needs a husband."

At that, Billi jerked the door open. "I don't need a husband. I love Jack and I want to marry him. And Father, if you won't perform the marriage, someone else will." She stood fearless before them.

Jack rose, smiling, and crossed the room to stand by her side. "Well, Father. I don't think you can argue with her. I know I can't."

Father Peretti pushed himself up. "After mass. And, I expecta to see you in da front pew. Praying." He took the time to point his gnarled finger at each of them. "Now, avanti, I must attend vestments."

Billi kissed Jack, and the memories of their long night together rushed through her.

"*Avanti*," Mr. O growled from behind them. "You heard Father. To the front pew, and I'm sitting between you." He grabbed Billi's arm and dragged her into the nave of the church.

The four sat on the hard, oak, front pew at the end of the mass. During the liturgy of the Eucharist they had all prayed their silent ways, each with their own hopes and dreams for the young couple's future. Duckworth had joined them, along with Danny and Dahlia, and the nervous anticipation was palpable.

Billi shifted in her light blue-chiffon dress, the one she had been wearing that fateful night when Jack took her to his office for questioning. The same dress that Raymond had sent the money for her to purchase. She knew Ray would want her to wear it. She smoothed the fabric and waited to become Mrs. Jack Huntington.

Finally, Father Peretti stepped to the altar. Shaking his head he made the sign of the cross, his Latin words like music filling the air.

Billi and Jack stepped forward. She carried a dried hydrangea that had still maintained a bit of its blue hues into the snow-covered winter month. Their vows were exchanged with the dignity of true love—deep, rich, and full of promise.

As the newly married couple led the way of the small gathering into the sanctuary, movement caught Billi's eye. Eileen and Mr. Nakamura emerged from the shadows.

"We are sorry we arrived late. Thank you for honoring us with your invitation," Mr. Nakamura began to apologize.

"Nonsense." Mrs. O stepped forward. "Will you join us at the house?"

Eileen and Billi were wrapped in an embrace of sisterly love. As the large doors leading out onto the rain-soaked street swung wide, a ray of sunlight broke through the dark clouds.

FIFTY-FIVE

The sun streamed brightly through the smoke of the numerous fires. Machine gun pits were being established, and as much ammunition as could be gathered was being piled near the sites.

As the men rushed into the hangars for more ammunition, Eddy dashed toward the water. A few of the PBY Catalina seaplanes were damaged beyond use. He could see through the small flames on her wing that his baby still floated, barely. He stripped off his shirt and dove in. The salt of the ocean stung the gash over his eye. Grabbing the rope attached to the burning seaplane, he pulled the line to those standing on shore. They leaned into their work and the tail of the craft drifted closer to shore. They pushed and pulled, positioning the burning wing so that the fire could be extinguished. As the blast from the hose smothered the flames, a black-and-white dog stood on the sandy shore, barking encouragement.

Eddy stepped from the sea, the wind bringing coolness over his tense muscles, when the sound of plane engines in the distance momentarily halted all progress.

"They're back." Finn's snarl rose toward the sky. "Give 'em hell."

It was just over one hour when the second attack of the Imperial Japanese Fleet swept down upon them, raining more destruction. Eddy sprinted for cover, a palm tree. He lay half-exposed, looking back as flames devoured one of the seaplanes he had trained on and grown to love. The craft slowly sank, resting half in water at the shore. A sailor's body floated face down nearby. Eddy braced himself as the reverberating thunderclap announced another hit on Hangar #3. Some of the men who had just entered to get more ammo staggered out of the haze; the others were not so lucky. Hell was back.

Around 10 a.m., the strafing and eruption from the air receded a second time, and the grim, devastating work of collecting the deceased and removing the mangled and burnt debris in preparation for battle continued. The demoralizing war, with all its brutality, death, and destruction, had found them first in paradise.

Eddy stood and breathed deeply of the salty sea air, tinged with smoky death. Then slowly, with great determination, he strode past the debris, the charred wreckage, and his fallen brothers. The Japs would pay. They had mistakenly enraged a country that would seek revenge and defend its shores for liberty. Freedom was not free, and the cost that day in lives and twisted metal would ring across the country, sounding the alarm of war.

He looked up at the Pali, its razor-sharp peaks the cutting divider, obstructing his view of what lay beyond at the other bases and Japan's main target, Pearl Harbor. More importantly, the green, jagged hillside hid the woman who held his heart. He knew she was still alive. He could her heart beating with his. He would go to her, and together, hand in hand, they would face the enemy and live.

A MAKESHIFT BRUNCH WITH CHILLED CHAMPAGNE hosted at the O'Shaughnessy home turned into the celebration of their marriage. The night before, Mrs. O had baked two batches of schnecken, her extra-sticky cinnamon buns covered in walnuts, and the makings for apple pancakes, but she had not expected a crowd. So she added scrambled eggs and sausage to round out the meal.

"We'll have a proper party soon," the hostess explained as she bustled around the table, Pepper at her heels.

"This is perfect." Jack raised his glass. "To my mother-in-law." They all sipped and then he raised his glass again. "And my father-in-law, the bravest man I know."

Mr. O grumbled, then toasted back. "May your troubles be less, And your blessing be more. And nothing but happiness come through your door."

"Here, here," Duckworth added.

"May God bless them," Father Peretti chimed in.

"You can now use that book of Mother's," Eileen whispered into her friend's ear.

Billi straightened and winked. "I already have."

"Yancha!" Eileen shrieked, her eyes growing large as she looked over at Jack.

Mrs. O's eyes misted. "To my beautiful daughter and her husban--"

At the shrill ringing of the phone everyone stopped and Billi saw Jack's jaw flinch.

Danny jumped up, Pepper trailing behind him, and scooped up the receiver. "It's for you, Jack."

Billi watched her husband cross the room and saw his back tighten as he listened to the voice on the other end of the line. Finally he spoke, "I'm on my way."

She rose. When Jack turned to face her, she instantly knew their life had changed.

"The Japanese have bombed Pearl Harbor. Turn on the radio. I have to go."

The small gathering at the table sat in the shocked silence of their new reality. Danny moved hesitantly to the radio and turned it on.

"...attacked this morning." The newscaster's voice crackled over the airwaves. "Alerts have been posted..."

"Eddy." Mrs. O's hand went to her heart.

"Eddy will be fine. He's not at Pearl Harbor." Mr. O picked up her hand, and she squeezed his back. They looked at each other to hush their fear.

Tears rolled down Dahlia's stricken face.

"I'll get your coat." Billi found herself saying as she hurried past her husband of two hours. When she returned to the silent gathering, she noticed her mother sat staring across the table at Mr. Nakamura as if she did not recognize him.

"What just happened?" Mrs. O whispered.

"My worst fears have been realized and my country has greatly dishonored us. We are Americans. We are not the Japanese who attacked the United States. We are Americans." He repeated to the stunned group.

"Your mother?" Billi's tears spilled onto the folds of her blue wedding dress as she looked up at Jack's strained face.

"Write her. I'll call her too." He kissed her long and hard. "And introduce yourself to her as Mrs. Huntington. I'm certain she will be pleased."

"What will happen?"

"I don't know. You will hear from me, but I need you to be level-headed and fearless. If you hear anything, send me a message through Duckworth. Stay here, you will be safe, and I will know where to find you."

Duckworth waited outside, rocking onto his toes in agitation, his fists clenched. The fourteenth message had been deciphered that morning at Station S on Bainbridge Island and quickly sent to Washington. Yet, from the sound of the shocked voice coming across the radio, the men in Hawaii had been the last to receive the warning and the first to be under fire.

The sun streamed through the clouds as Jack stepped over the threshold of 304 30th South, the house that needed paint, the home of his new wife.

He paused a minute in the warm light from above and prayed. A mixture of failure and relief ripped at his soul. War had found them; the waiting now over. His goal had shifted, gloves now removed. He could not let Akio's dragon of death rule the sea. He would find Akio, the purpose behind his Watatsumi drawing, and then, with great pleasure, Jack planned to kill Akio.

Silently the two men headed for the black sedan. A new day dawned for America and their mission had finally been unleashed, their target, Akio and revenge.

Billi quickly wiped her tears and went back to the dining room table where now warring cultures sat with half glasses of champagne.

"To peace." She held up her glass. "That our two countries may find a way to stop what has started before...before..."

"Before our worlds are destroyed," Mr. Nakamura finished for her.

"Yes," they all mumbled, unable to look each other in the eye.

"We must go." Mr. Nakamura stood.

Eileen followed her father's lead and started for the door, her head bowed in disgrace, when Billi reached for her.

"We are still sisters. Nothing can break that." Billi took her hand.

"I hope it can be so." Eileen's dark eyes filled with uncertainty as her grip tightened around her friend's hand. The colors of their skin now in contrast in their newly shattered world.

As Father Peretti led a prayer over the bowed heads listening to the turmoil spewing from the radio, Billi closed the door on her Japanese friends. They were the Americans she had grown up with in this land of the free.

The buzz of the radio vibrated through her as she took her place across from her mother and listened to the anguished words of the sketchy details from the reporter.

There was much to do to stop this war, and with that realization, her back straightened, ready to serve. As the product of the best list-maker on the face of the earth, she would start tomorrow—organizing, planning, and praying for the safe return of her brother and her new husband.

She shivered. In just a few hours' time, lives had collided and split wide open, emitting the wrenching drums of war. Her thoughts turned to the words Akio had spoken regarding a second attack before Christmas.

And for the first time in her life, Billi's plea to the heavens took on a different hue. Her vision was not the white of celestial light, like the orchid Mr. Nakamura tended diligently, but the color red, like the hand grip of Akio's sword. She bent her head and prayed for the spilled blood of one particular Japanese man.

Glossary

Bon Odori A traditional Japanese Buddhist custom in honor of the spirit of one's ancestors.

Chakin A small usually white cloth used during the tea ceremony to wipe the tea bowl.

Getas Traditional Japanese footwear, like a sandal.

Hachimake A stylized Japanese headband with a representative symbol.

Heiwa Peace or harmony.

Hishaku A water scoop used for tea ceremony.

Issei A term in the Japanese language that means the first generation to immigrate to North America. Issei were born in Japan. Their children born in America are Nisei.

Kama A kettle or metal pot used in the tea ceremony.

Kempei Tai The Military Police of the Imperial Japanese Army, like the Nazi Gestapo.

Kendo Translates as "sword way." A marital art form.

Kibei Literally "go home to America," used during the 1940's to describe Japanese American's, Nisei, those born in the United States, who returned to Japan for schooling and require military service.

Mon Emblems used to decorate or identify specific Japanese families.

Natsume Used in the tea ceremony it is a vessel that has a slightly convex top and narrows at the bottom.

Netsuke Miniature sculptures used as a button or toggle attached to a cord that hung a purse or basket from the obi.

Nisei Japanese children born on American soil, considered the second generation.

Obi A sash for traditional Japanese dress.

Raku furo Raku is a type of pottery used to make the (furo) portable brazier for the tea ceremony.

Sensu Japanese folding fan.

Shunga Japanese term for erotic art, usually woodblock printing, meaning "picture of spring." "Spring" being a euphemism for sex.

Taiko Japanese drums shaped like a barrel.

The Tale of Genji Is a classic work of Japanese literature written in the 11th Century.

TO The name given to the Japanese spy network in the United States during World War II operating through Spanish embassies and consulates in America, Britain and Australia.

Ukiyo-e A style of art, woodblock prints, that flourish in Japan during the 17th and 19th centuries.

Wagasa Japanese umbrellas made from paper and bamboo, some are coated with oil for use in rain.

Wagashi Traditional Japanese sweets or confections generally served with tea.

Watatsumi Japanese dragon and water god, deity of the sea.

Yukata A Japanese garment, a style of kimono, generally made of cotton.

Questions for Book Club

1. What was your impression of the significance of the title before and after you read the book?

2. Before you read the book were you aware there was a Japanese spy ring in existence in the US preparing for World War II?

3. How did this story alter you perception of WWII espionage?

4. Were you aware of "Magic," the machine developed by the US Army's Signal Intelligence Section, that allowed the US to read the Japanese "Purple" code before reading this book?

5. Had you ever heard about the "Winds Code" or the terminology "East, Wind, Rain" and the part this code played in forewarning the outbreak of war between America and Japan?

6. Did you have a relative who served in this war and if so in what arena; Pacific, European, or on American soil? Did they share any stories of their time in service?

7. Do you think that all countries had spies before WWII?

8. When Americans heard the broadcast over the radio about the attack on Pearl Harbor, do you think most people knew where Pearl Harbor was?

9. Do you think that many of the people living in the central region of the United States had ever seen a Japanese person before WWII?

10. What is the importance of honor in the Japanese culture compared to other cultures?

11. What was your favorite scene in the book? Why?

12. Who did you identify with the most in the story? Why?

13. Did you think the bits of humor helped with the flow of the book? Did you have a favorite character who brought comic relief?

14. Have you traveled to any of the cities mentioned in this book?

15. Have you visited any of the naval or army bases mentioned in the book?

16. Have you ever worn a kimono or yukata or attended a Japanese tea ceremony or Bon Odori?

17. Was there anything new that you learned about the year leading up to the Second World War?

18. Kendo is "the way of the sword." Have you ever been to a demonstration or participated in kendo martial arts? What was it like to work with the sword?

19. Have you visited any museums of flight or any other museums that might have air planes used during WWII?

20. What do your foresee happening in the next book, *STORMS FROM A CLEAR SKY?*

Please go to Denise's webpage for a list of the books and interviews she used in her extensive research.

www.denisefrisino.com

About the Author

Denise has taken to writing novels late in life. Her first, *Whiskey Cove*, was nominated for the Pacific Northwest Bookseller Award.

The majority of Denise's career has been centered in the arts. She began performing at the age of five and has worked as an actress, playwright, producer, director for theater and in similar capacities for film and TV. One of her passions is teaching theater and a course she developed for writers, Creating Memorable Characters. She has won various awards as an actress, writer, and teacher.

Her mother, Harriette, born in Seattle in 1920, was a great inspiration for many of the scenes in this book. Denise enjoys traveling with her husband, playing in the snow and being on the water.

For blogs and videos of the men and women she interviewed for *Orchids of War* and some of the books she used for research, please go to her author's web page: www.denisefrisino.com.